THE
PENGUIN
BOOK
OF
CONTEMPORARY
CANADIAN
WOMEN'S
SHORT
STORIES

Also by Lisa Moore

Degrees of Nakedness

Open

Alligator

THE
PENGUIN
BOOK
OF
CONTEMPORARY
CANADIAN
WOMEN'S
SHORT
STORIES

SELECTED
AND
INTRODUCED
BY

LISA MOORE

PENGUIN
CANADA

PENGUIN CANADA

Published by the Penguin Group

Penguin Group (Canada), 90 Eglinton Avenue East, Suite 700, Toronto, Ontario, Canada
M4P 2Y3 (a division of Pearson Canada Inc.)

Penguin Group (USA) Inc., 375 Hudson Street, New York, New York 10014, U.S.A.
Penguin Books Ltd, 80 Strand, London WC2R 0RL, England
Penguin Ireland, 25 St Stephen's Green, Dublin 2, Ireland (a division of Penguin Books Ltd)
Penguin Group (Australia), 250 Camberwell Road, Camberwell, Victoria 3124, Australia
(a division of Pearson Australia Group Pty Ltd)
Penguin Books India Pvt Ltd, 11 Community Centre, Panchsheel Park, New Delhi – 110 017,
India
Penguin Group (NZ), cnr Airborne and Rosedale Roads, Albany, Auckland 1310, New Zealand
(a division of Pearson New Zealand Ltd)
Penguin Books (South Africa) (Pty) Ltd, 24 Sturdee Avenue, Rosebank, Johannesburg 2196,
South Africa

Penguin Books Ltd, Registered Offices: 80 Strand, London WC2R 0RL, England

First published 2006

1 2 3 4 5 6 7 8 9 10   (RRD)

Introduction, author biographies, and selection copyright © Lisa Moore, 2006

The credits on pages 365–366 constitute an extension of this copyright page.

LIBRARY AND ARCHIVES CANADA CATALOGUING IN PUBLICATION

The Penguin book of contemporary Canadian women's short stories / edited by Lisa Moore.

ISBN-13: 978-0-670-06552-3
ISBN-10: 0-670-06552-8

1. Canadian fiction (English)—Women authors. 2. Short stories, Canadian (English)
3. Canadian fiction (English)—20th century. I. Moore, Lisa Lynne, 1964–

PS8235.W7P45   2006   C813'.01089287   C2006-902584-3

Visit the Penguin Group (Canada) website at **www.penguin.ca**

Special and corporate bulk purchase rates available; please see
www.penguin.ca/corporatesales or call 1-800-399-6858, ext. 477 or 474

For Eva

CONTENTS

LISA MOORE

Getting Away with It

First there must be a mechanism that allows entry: an invisible zipper, a wave of heat shimmer that ripples the landscape, an incantation, a click. But once you're in, you're in. The beginning of the short story is the hardest part to write. Casual, intimate, grandly sweeping, austere, arresting, or delicately simple, it must have an iron grip. It convinces you. It seduces and provokes infidelity. You will be untrue to the four walls of your room, the weather outside, the city or field, supper bubbling on the stove. You will give up everything—the armchair, your lover, your children—and step through, briefly but absolutely gone.

I began writing stories and sending them to Canadian literary magazines about twenty years ago. I read *Prism International, Descant, The New Quarterly, The Fiddlehead, TickleAce, Canadian Fiction Magazine, Quarry, The Malahat Review, Grain,* and others. I had subscriptions to some of these magazines, and I roamed the library stacks to dig the others out. Reading these literary journals was a kind of apprenticeship. I grew familiar with contemporary short story writers across the country. And I collected my rejections and paid attention to the editorial advice, however scanty.

At first these rejections were only form letters with an illegible signature. Nevertheless, I studied them for clues, turned them over, sniffed the paper. They were authentic artifacts from the world of literature.

Sometimes a single line would be scrawled on the bottom of a form letter that had the power to torque my expectations beyond endurance: "Try us again." I kept trying.

I wanted to know all the things the short story could do. I decided it could do everything a novel could, only faster. In some ways, short fiction has more scope than the novel—a collection of stories contains several worlds, each whole and detailed, compressed into comparatively few pages. Whether the content of the short story covers centuries or days, the experience of reading it takes no longer than an afternoon and is undiluted; it packs a walloping punch.

The writers who excited me the most were those whose language was exacting and unexpected, on the level of the paragraph, the sentence, the verb, and the adjective. Every word had to be canny and strange. I was particularly interested in writers who experimented with the shape of the story. As John Metcalf, the editor of Porcupine's Quill, a great promoter of Canadian short stories and emerging writers, has said, "New shapes allow us to see and feel in new ways; they also allow us to feel old problems and old situations with new intensity."

I wrote those early stories on an electric typewriter. I wrote them in a downtown house overlooking St. John's harbour, and then in an attic bedroom in Toronto. My husband was a student at York University and I had followed him to the big city. We each had a desk in a small bedroom where every square inch of floor was covered by a futon, books, and clothes. We were not tidy. We were absorbed. We each faced an opposite wall, and the backs of our wooden chairs touched while we wrote.

When my first story was published by *Canadian Fiction Magazine,* we went out looking for it in the middle of a rainstorm. The sky had gotten very dark in the early afternoon; the rain lashed the street and bounced back up. We were soaking wet and water squished noisily out of my sneakers onto the floor of the bookstore. I dripped all the way to the magazine racks, my teeth chattering from the cold. I found my story and I was ecstatic.

I was twenty-three and I'd managed to get a few waitressing shifts at a restaurant on Bay Street. They kept me on, even after I sloshed an entire bowl of cod chowder down the back of an expensive silk blouse. I was such a pathetic waitress the customer ended up apologizing to me for choosing to sit in the trajectory of the soup. She wanted me to stop crying. "Oh come on," she said. "You must be good at something."

I was spending as much time writing and reading short stories as I could. I never once questioned the sanity of this enterprise. I didn't wonder if it was such a good idea for a young wife to be isolated in a room while her husband was out making his way in the world. I didn't think about financial security, nor did I imagine I was learning to write novels by studying a less ambitious, less complex form. I didn't even ask myself if I was any good at it. It certainly wasn't a career. It was an obsession. The possibilities of the short story form seemed infinite to me, and I wanted to see what it could do.

I blame Alice Munro. Like every other young woman in the country who thought she could get away with spending all her time writing stories, I could always argue, "But Alice Munro does it!" Instead of worrying, I got on the subway and cracked open a new collection of stories and the world whipped past in a grey blur with a big roar. It was a bodily absorption, an addiction, a kind of lust. I had no choice.

I started collecting the stories in this anthology with the idea of representing all the geographic regions of Canada. I thought that having writers from regions as far apart as British Columbia and Newfoundland would ensure a diversity of voice. I also wanted a good mix of emerging and established writers. I wanted an anthology that would reflect Canadian experience and innovation in form, the way the prism that hangs in my kitchen window refracts light, sending shimmers of unexpected rainbows over the cupboards, walls, and appliances.

I gathered together the best short story collections and literary magazines I'd read over the last twenty years. I thought of the writers I'd heard read at literary festivals across the country, and writers who had come to Newfoundland to read through the Canada Council.

I was looking for the short fiction that had moved swiftly through me, over those twenty years, whipping me up into an altered state, changing me for good. I wanted the new stuff too, the stories that reflected the twenty-first century, the buzzing paranoia of post-9/11, and the white noise of the information age. I sought dislocation, bomb scares, sexual freedom, aberration, fractured identities, nakedness, awakenings of every sort, redemption, and love.

Sometimes I found myself reading the stories here for a second, third, or fifth time, determined to discover how they worked, but at the very last minute, I always fell in. The stories were like swimming pools, and just when I leaned in close enough, I'd lose my balance, be fully submerged.

In my search for these stories, I fell in, again and again. I quickly lost track of who was emerging and who was established, or if I had covered all the geographical ground. I lost interest in borders of any kind. The term "emerging" applies only to the time when an author's work begins to get published and noticed. In terms of skill, writers seem to be born fully formed. Early stories dazzle with the same wattage as an author's later work. Perhaps the stories employ more elaborate card tricks and different sleights-of-hand later on, but talent is talent, raw or polished.

I was obsessed by form, and my guiding rule was that the writers be as obsessed as I was. I wanted to be shocked by a plot turn I hadn't seen coming. I wanted images that made me see the world new. I wanted characters I empathized with wholly and felt I knew inside out, and who were about to make an awful, life-altering mistake. I wanted suspense, innovation, and language as sharp and necessary as a scalpel for a heart transplant.

In every great story, the reader is left with the impression that the author has gotten away with something, pulled off a big heist; the story is what you, the reader, have always known, always thought, always felt on the tip of your tongue. You have the illusion that the story is familiar because, as the reader, you have imagined the story into existence. It is essentially yours.

What is left unsaid is all-important. The writer leaves big empty swathes for the reader to create. Just as a visual artist can capture a quick likeness with a few strong, telling lines of charcoal, so a few well-placed details in a story allow the reader to experience a scene full of texture, sound, smell, and light.

A clean, declarative story such as Jacqueline Baker's "Bloodwood," full of insight and bold honesty from the very first paragraph, might have a character standing by the garden gate in a yellow hat. The hat is yellow, but each reader decides if it is straw or felt or of some finer fabric. There is immeasurable pleasure in conjuring this hat; this is the unique pleasure of reading fiction. The reader's imagination engages fully, revs up, just as a car engine engages when the key is turned.

We are familiar with Baker's world in the way we recognize the alien landscapes of our dreams. We know this story even if we have never been to the Prairies; we know the adhesive love between brothers and sisters, parents and children. We know what it means to grow old in isolation. We recognize the young woman in the yellow hat under the shade of the tree. We will be haunted by these characters for the rest of the day.

There are many stories by Mavis Gallant that I've read and re-read with a set of tweezers in one hand and a powerful magnifying glass in the other. I've tried to stand back from these stories, to understand why I was so deeply affected. But these are stories with riptides and under-tows, and there is no stepping back. Often the whole half-century after the Second World War sweeps through. Here are the displaced immi-grants of Europe after the war, trying to get a footing, some kind of hold. Here are women cutting out on their own, men as lost and vulnerable as women. Humour, history, piercing emotion.

Gallant's protagonist in "The Concert Party" is Steve Burnet, a young academic with a new wife, living in Europe. Burnet decides at the onset of the story to imagine himself in the shoes of a despised acquaintance, Harry Lapwing. The idea is to allow him to empathize with Lapwing, to come to an understanding about him—which also happens to be what we do whenever we read fiction. But Burnet imme-diately imagines—and this is Mavis Gallant's prodigious wit at work—Lapwing coming to terms with the fact that he is a Prairie socialist and a William Morris scholar. "All your life this will make you appear boring and dull. When you went to England in the late forties and said you were Canadian, and Socialist, and working on aspects of William Morris, people got a stiff, trapped look, as if you were about to read them a poem."

Gallant adroitly sums up a complex political and academic social milieu in a few brief sentences. Here is one sort of Canadian abroad: stuffy, self-satisfied, parochial, and faintly ridiculous—not to mention the humorous jab at those eager to share bad poetry, tossed in for good measure. As the story progresses, Lapwing becomes more pompous and insufferable, until we eventually understand why we have been given this deliciously scathing portrait—because Lapwing is not so different from our protagonist. Gallant affects a shift here that is revelatory and moving. The reader, who has been looking on with delight, realizes she or he has, in turn, been walking around in Steve Burnet's shoes and is also not so different from Lapwing.

Gallant is that rare writer who can inhabit the skin of male and female protagonists with equal comfort. But the skill with which she portrays her female characters through the eyes of a male protagonist in "The Concert Party" made me wonder about the notion of a gendered voice. How does writing by women differ from writing by men?

As this was going to be a collection of stories by Canadian women, I often had to remind myself that certain men—Michael Winter, Michael Crummey, Lee Henderson, Michael Redhill, David Bezmogis, Lawrence Mathews, and Norman Levine—were not women. I was grateful they were not women. A great many stories that I had fallen for had to be left out of this collection simply because a book has only so many pages. It was good to have an arbitrary reason to cut the pile in half.

It was only after I had selected the stories that I began to consider the implications of gender. Are these stories particularly feminine? Are they feminist? Is the subject matter more intimate, quieter, or more polite? Is it more brazen, raunchy, or desperate? Are these stories less political than stories written by men? More political? Are they more concerned with domestic spaces or themes such as sexual awakening, subjugation, the family? What about sex, money, food, trust, courage, love, fashion, and war? What about power? Language? Form? An anthology of writing by women is subversive because it asks these questions: How are we different? How are we the same?

And how are these stories different from each other?

Some voices here will be immediately recognizable. Margaret Atwood, Alice Munro, Carol Shields, Jane Urquhart—here is innovation, surety, and self-possession. Here is laconic social commentary, feminism, and strong, narrative voice. By voice I mean the sound vocal chords make, somehow trapped on the page.

I have never heard Zsuzsi Gartner, Emma Richler, and Eden Robinson speak, but I am certain that if they were behind me in a supermarket line I would recognize their voices. Their stories are audible, full of texture and cadence uniquely their own. These are writers whose stories you hear as well as see.

Madeleine Thien's transparent language is full of tenderness. "Four Days from Oregon" is a story about mothers and daughters and obdurate loss. The ocean and wind, all of childhood, violence and peace, co-mingled. Thien's story is straightforward yet lush; she shows the quaking vulnerability of childhood, and the desperation of mothers trying to make it right for their children.

Jessica Grant's "My Husband's Jump" is funny, quick, daring, irreverent—a satire and a celebration of spirituality, brief and buoyant.

Lynn Coady's "Play the Monster Blind" is overflowing with East Coast candour and understated wit. Authentic, taut, busting open with familial love and discord, and alcoholism. Coady's female characters are refreshingly ungirly. The male protagonists are full of brute strength—there are headlocks, tipped over lamps, and tickling.

Ramona Dearing's "An Apology" is a harrowing story about the tragedy of the sexual abuse of boys in the Newfoundland orphanage Mount Cashel. Dearing is both compassionate and clear-eyed in providing this staggering exploration of the moral consequences of the abuse of authority.

In "Chemistry," Carol Shields portrays a music class studying the recorder at a Montreal YMCA during the seventies. This story is a lyrical and unsentimental flash of light and racing emotional currents in the mode of Virginia Woolf. Shields captures the ephemeral, meaningful cohesion between strangers brought together through music.

The cast of characters is caught with succinct, vivid strokes. Mr. Mooney has "stubby blackened fingers and alien appetites, also built-up shoes to give himself height, brutal hair oil, gold slashes in his back teeth." Pierre, with his neglected teeth, has "something amiss with his scalp, a large roundness resembling, under the strands of his lank Jesus hair, a wreath of pink plastic."

Here is Shields on the transformative power of music: "Something else happens. It affects us all, even Mr. Mooney with his criminal lips and eyes, even Lonnie H., who boils and struts with dangerous female smells. We don't just play the music, we find it." Shields's story does something similar—we don't just read it, it rushes through us.

Alice Munro is subversive. There is often, in her stories, a furious unravelling of security, a giving way to the disorder that occurs when fate creeps in. Everything is upturned—the escape afforded by a good education, the safety of a marriage, smart clothing, hard-won social standing—when unruly passion sets upon her narrators.

In Munro's story "Wenlock Edge," the narrator, a young, ambitious college girl, tells us, "I meant no harm. Or hardly any harm." The harm here is the stripping away of a girlish faith in culture as a social stepladder out of the squalor of ignorance or appetite. Munro's narrator is gently, thoroughly, ingeniously humiliated. The tension in this story mounts with calibrated precision, causing the reader's skin to prickle.

Frances Itani's "Clayton" has an image that will stick with me for a long time. Itani's protagonist, Clayton, is tortured by the cries of a beached whale near his house. He also is not sleeping with his wife, and the tension between them is the subject of this story. The story is told from Clayton's point of view, but we recognize it as his wife's story in the following scene:

He had slept in the attic again, but not restfully. There was something wrong and he did not know what it was. He drove down to the old barn, climbed the ladder and again lifted the binoculars towards the house. He was shocked when Zeta stepped suddenly into focus, pointing a pistol at his face. She aimed, but did not pull the trigger. Instead, she turned towards the poplar and aimed at it. Then, at the stoop from which she hung the clothes. Then, at the birdhouse. Smiling, she turned quickly and went back into the house.

Feeling weak and perspiring, Clayton realized that she could not have seen him.

Itani shifts the point of view, skewing the angle dramatically and without warning, creating a weird distortion. In the innocent aiming of the gun—Clayton's wife doesn't know she is being watched—the discord between the husband and wife flares up. Itani intimates a quiet violence, inexplicable and eerily accurate—the inevitable emotional damage lovers cause without ever meaning to hurt each other. Later, Clayton's efforts to bring the whale relief are impotent and sorrowful.

The stories in this anthology are the stories that I found most haunting. They are the stories that *worked*, but I could not say how. I'd look up, while reading, and see that the oranges in the bowl on the kitchen table were more orange. They were fiercely orange. The chrome on the stove was more chrome. The cracks in my leather shoes had meaning, character. A shift in weather was full of mood. A single gesture—the hesitant, lost way a woman on the bus touched the back of her neck—suddenly had the shimmer of significance. The bluish cast of aquarium light inside the bus was atmospheric and foreboding. Nothing was recognizable, nothing was simply itself. Everything felt foreign, altered, and new.

MARGARET ATWOOD

Spring Song of the Frogs

Women's lips are paler again. They wax and wane, from season to season. They haven't been this pale for years; not for fifteen or twenty years at least. Will can't remember when it was, when he last saw those shades of rich vanilla, of melting orange sherbet, of faded pink satin, on women's mouths. Some time before he started really noticing. All this past winter the lips were dark instead, mulberry, maroon, so that the mouths looked like the mouths of old-fashioned dolls, sharply defined against the china white of the skin. Now the skins are creamier, except on the ones who have ignored whatever wordless decree has gone out and have begun to tan.

This woman, whose name is Robyn, has a mouth the colour of a fingernail, the wan half-moon at the base. Her own fingernails are painted to match: someone has decided that they should no longer look as if they've been dipped in blood. She has on a loose cool dress, cotton in a pink so faint it's like something that's run in the wash, with buttons down the front, the top three undone. By the way she's glanced down once or twice, she's wondering if she's gone too far.

Will smiles at her, looking into her eyes, which are possibly blue; he can't tell in this light. She smiles back. She won't be able to keep staring him in the eye for long. After she blinks and shifts, she'll have three choices. The menu, on grey paper with offset handwriting, French style, which she's already studied; the view off to the side, towards the door, but it's too early for that; or the wall behind him. Will knows what's on it: a framed poster advertising a surrealist art show of several years back, with a drawing on it, fleshy pink with pinky-grey shadows, which suggests a part of the body, though it's difficult to say which part. Something about to grow hair, become sexual in a disagreeable way. Either she'll react to it or she won't see it all. Instead she'll glance at her own reflection in the glass, checking herself out as if she's a stranger she might consider picking up: a deep look, brief but sincere.

The waitress arrives, a thin girl in a red brushcut, with a purple feather earring dangling from one ear. She stands as though her head is fixed on a hook and the rest of her body is drooping down from it, with no tendons. She's wearing what could be tuxedo pants. The restaurant is in a district of second-hand clothing stores, where foreign-looking women with stumpy legs and black hair pulled back into buns come to shuffle through the racks, and also where girls like this one get their outlandish costumes. The belt is wide red plastic, and could be either twenty-five years old or brand new; the shirt is a man's dress shirt, with pleats, the sleeves rolled to the elbow. The girl's arms, bone-skinny and white, come out of the puffs of cloth like the stems of peonies that have been grown in darkness.

Her thighs will be much the same. Will can remember the thighs in the ancient men's magazines, the ones that were passed around when he was at school, black-and-white photos on cheap paper, with no air-brushing, the plump women posed in motel rooms, the way the garters would sink into the flesh of thighs and rump. Now there's no flesh, the thighs have shrivelled up, they're all muscle and bone. Even the *Playboy* centrefolds look as if they're made of solid gristle. It's supposed to be sexy to show them in leg warmers.

Will asks Robyn if she'd like something to drink.

"A Perrier with a twist," says Robyn, looking up, giving the waitress the same smile she's just given Will.

Will orders a Bloody Mary and wonders if he's made a mistake. Possibly this waitress is a man. He's been here several times before, never without a slight but enjoyable sense of entering forbidden territory. Any place with checked tablecloths gives him this feeling, which is left over from when he was a student and thought he would end up being something other than what he has become. In those days he drew illustrations for the campus newspaper, and designed sets. For a while he kept up the drawing, as a hobby, or that's what his ex-wife called it. Maybe later he'll go back to it, when he has the time. Some days he wanders into the galleries down here, to see what the young kids are up to. The owners approach him with cynical deference, as if all he has to offer, to them or anyone else, is his money. He never buys anything.

The waitress returns with the drinks, and Will, in view of the two slight bumps visible on her ribcage, decides that she really is a woman after all.

"I thought for a minute she was a man," he says to Robyn.

"Really?" Robyn says. She glances at the waitress, now at the next table. "Oh no," she says, as if it's a mistake she herself would never have made. "No. Definitely a woman."

"Some bread?" Will says. The bread here is placed in tiny baskets, suspended over the tables by a sort of rope-and-pulley arrangement. To get to the bread you have to either stand up or lower the basket by unhitching the rope from where it's fastened on the wall; which is awkward, but Will enjoys doing it. Maybe the theory is that your food will appeal to you more if you're allowed to participate in it, or maybe the baskets are just some designer's fiasco. He always has bread here.

"Pardon?" says Robyn, as if *bread* is a word she's never heard before. "Oh. No thanks." She gives a little shudder, as if the thought of it is slightly repulsive. Will is annoyed, but determined to have bread anyway. It's good bread, thick, brown, and warm. He turns to the wall, undoes the rope, and the basket creaks downwards.

"Oh, that's very cute," says Robyn. He catches it then, the look she's giving herself in the glass behind him. Now they are going to have to make their way through the rest of the lunch somehow. Why does he keep on, what's he looking for that's so hard to find? She has generous breasts, that's what impelled him: the hope of generosity.

The waitress comes back and Robyn, pursing her pastel-coloured lips, orders a spinach salad without the dressing. Will is beginning to sweat; he's feeling claustrophobic and is anxious to be gone. He tries to think about running his hand up her leg and around her thigh, which might be full and soft, but it's no good. She wouldn't enjoy it.

CYNTHIA IS WHITE ON WHITE. Her hair is nearly blonde, helped out, Will suspects: her eyebrows and eyelashes are darker. Her skin is so pale it looks powdered. She's not wearing the hospital gown but a white nightgown with ruffles, childish, Victorian, reminiscent of lacey drawers and Kate Greenaway greeting cards. Under the cloth, Will thinks, she must be translucent; you would be able to see her veins and intestines, like a guppy's. She draws the sheet up to her chest, backing away from him, against the headboard of the bed, a position that reminds him of a sickly Rosetti madonna, cringing against the wall while the angel of the Annunciation threatens her with fullness.

Will smiles with what he hopes is affability. "How are you doing, Cynthia?" he says. There's a basket on the night table, with oranges and an apple; also some flowers.

"Okay," she says. She smiles, a limp smile that denies the message. Her eyes are anxious and cunning. She wants him to believe her and go away.

"Your mum and dad asked me to drop by," Will says. Cynthia is his niece.

"I figured," says Cynthia. Maybe she means that he wouldn't have come otherwise, or maybe she means that they have sent him as a substitute for themselves. She is probably right on both counts. It's a family myth that Will is Cynthia's favourite uncle. Like many myths, it had some basis in truth, once, when—just after his own marriage broke up—he was reaching for a sense of family, and would read Cynthia stories and tickle her under the arms. But that was years ago.

Last night, over the phone, his sister used this past as leverage. "You're the only one who can talk to her. She's cut us off." Her voice was angry rather than despairing.

"Well, I don't know," Will said dubiously. He has no great faith in his powers as a mediator, a confidant, even a strong shoulder. He used to have Cynthia up to the farm, when his own sons were younger and Cynthia was twelve or so. She was tanned then, a tomboy; she liked to wander over the property by herself, picking wild apples. At night she would wolf down the dinners Will would cook for the four of them, five if he had a woman up—plates of noodles Alfredo, roast beef with Yorkshire pudding, fried chicken, steaks, sometimes a goose which he'd bought from the people across the way.

There was nothing wrong with Cynthia then; she wore her hair loose, her skin was golden, and Will felt a disturbing sexual pull towards her which he certainly doesn't feel now. The boys felt it too, and would tease and provoke her, but she stood up to them. She said there was nothing they could do she couldn't do too, and she was almost right. Then they got into their motorcycle-and-car phase, and Cynthia changed. All of a sudden she didn't like getting grease on her hands; she began painting her nails. Will sees this now as the beginning of the end.

"It's an epidemic," his sister said over the phone. "It's some kind of a fad. You know what she actually said? She actually said a lot of the girls at school were doing it. She's so goddamned competitive."

"I'll go in," Will said. "Is there anything I should take? Some cheese maybe?" His sister is married to a man whose eyebrows are so faint they're invisible. Will, who doesn't like him, thinks of him as an albino.

"How about a good slap on the backside," said his sister. "Not that she's got one left."

Then she began to cry, and Will said she shouldn't worry, he was sure it would all turn out fine in the end.

At the moment he doesn't believe it. He looks around the room, searching for a chair. There is one, but Cynthia's sky-blue dressing gown is across it. Just as well: if he sits down, he'll have to stay longer.

"Just okay?" he says.

"I gained a pound," she says. This is intended to placate him. He'll have to check with the doctor, as his sister wants a full report, and Cynthia, she claims, is not accurate on the subject of her weight.

"That's wonderful," he says. Maybe it's true, since she's so unhappy about it.

"I hardly ate anything," she says, plaintively but also boasting.

"You're trying though," says Will. "That's good." Now that he's here, he wishes to be helpful. "Maybe tomorrow you'll eat more."

"But if I hardly ate anything and I gained a pound," she says, "what's going to happen? I'll get fat."

Will doesn't know what to say. Reason, he knows, doesn't work; it's been tried. It would do no good to tell her she's a wraith, that if she doesn't eat she'll digest herself, that her heart is a muscle like any other muscle and if it isn't fed it will atrophy.

Suddenly Will is hungry. He's conscious of the oranges and the apple, right beside him on the night table, round and brightly coloured and filled with sweet juice. He wants to take something, but would that be depriving her?

"Those look good," he says.

Cynthia is scornful, as if this is some crude ploy of his to coax her to eat. "Have some," she says. "Have it all. As long as I don't have to watch. You can put it in your pocket." She speaks of the fruit as if it were an undifferentiated mass, like cold porridge.

"That's all right," says Will. "I'll leave it here for you."

"Have the flowers then," says Cynthia. This gesture too is contemptuous: he has needs, she doesn't. She is beyond needs.

Will casts around for anything: some hook, some handhold. "You should get better," he says, "so you can come up to the farm. You like it there." To himself he sounds falsely genial, wheedling.

"I'd be in the way," Cynthia says, looking away from him, out the window. Will looks too. There's nothing out there but the windows of another hospital building. "Sometimes I can see them doing operations," she says.

"I'd enjoy it," Will says, not knowing whether he's lying. "I get lonely up there on the weekends." This is true enough, but as soon as he's said it it sounds like whining.

Cynthia looks at him briefly. "You," she says, as if she has a monopoly, and who is he to talk? "Anyway, you don't have to go there if you don't want to. Nobody's making you."

Will feels shabby, like an out-of-work man begging for handouts on the street. He has seen such men and turned away from them, thinking about how embarrassed he would be if he were in their place, shuffling like that. Now he sees that what counts for them is not his feeling of embarrassment but the money. He stands foolishly beside Cynthia's bed, his offering rejected.

Cynthia has a short attention span. She's looking at her hands, spread out on the sheet now. The nails are peach-coloured, newly polished. "I used to be pretty, when I was younger," she says.

Will wants to shake her. She's barely eighteen, she doesn't know a thing about age or time. He could say, "You're pretty now," or he could say, "You'd be pretty if you'd put on some weight," but either one of these would be playing by her rules, so he says neither. Instead he says good-bye, pecks her on the cheek, and leaves, feeling as defeated as she wants him to feel. He hasn't made any difference.

WILL PARKS HIS SILVER BMW in the parking space, takes the key out of the ignition, puts it carefully into his pocket. Then he remembers that he should keep the key handy to lock the car from the outside. This is one of the advantages of the BMW: you can never lock yourself out. He drove a Porsche for a while, after his marriage broke up. It made him feel single and ready for anything, but he doesn't feel like that any more. His moustache went about the same time as that car.

The parking space is off to the left of the farmhouse, demarcated by railroad ties and covered with white crushed gravel. It was like that when he bought the place, but that's what he probably would have done anyway. He keeps meaning to plant some flowers, zinnias perhaps, behind the railroad ties, but so far he hasn't got around to it.

He gets out, goes to the trunk for the groceries. Halfway to the house he realizes he's forgotten to lock the car, and goes back to do it. It's not as safe around here as it used to be. Last year he had a break-in, some kids from the town, out joy-riding. They broke plates and spread peanut butter on the walls, drank his liquor and smashed the bottles, and, as far as he could tell, screwed in all the beds. They were caught because they pinched the television set and tried to sell it. Everything was insured, but Will felt humiliated. Now he has bolt locks, and bars on the cellar windows, but anyone could break in if they really wanted to. He's thinking of getting a dog.

The air inside the house smells dead, as if it has heated and then cooled, absorbing the smells of furniture, old wood, paint, dust. He hasn't been here for several weeks. He sets the bags down on the kitchen table, opens a few windows. In the living room there's a vase with wizened daffodils, the water stagnant and foul. He sets the vase out on the patio; he'll empty it later.

Will bought this place after his marriage broke up, so he and the boys would have somewhere they could spend time together in a regular way. Also, his wife made it clear that she'd like some weekends off. The house was renovated by the people who lived here before; just as well, since Will never would have had the time to supervise, though he frequently sketches out plans for his ideal house. Not everything here is the way he would have done it, but he likes the board-and-batten exterior and the big opened-up kitchen. Despite some jumpiness lingering from the break-in, he feels good here, better than he does in his apartment in the city.

His former house is his wife's now; he doesn't like going there. Sometimes there are younger men, referred to by their first names only. Now that the boys are almost grown up, this doesn't bother him as much as it used to: she might as well be having a good time, though the turnover rate is high. When they were married she didn't enjoy anything much, including him, including sex. She never told him what was expected of him, and he never asked.

Will unpacks the groceries, stows away the food. He likes doing this, slotting the eggs into their egg-shaped holes in the refrigerator, filing the spinach in the crisper, stashing the butter in the compartment marked BUTTER, pouring the coffee beans into the jar labelled coffee. It makes him feel that some things at least are in their right places. He leaves the steaks on the counter, uncorks the wine, hunts for some candles. Of the pair he finds, one has been chewed by mice. Hardened droppings are scattered about the drawer. Mice are a new development. There must be a hole somewhere. Will is standing with the chewed candle in his hand, pondering remedies, when he hears a car outside.

He looks out the kitchen window. Since the break-in, he's less willing to open the door without knowing who's outside. But it's Diane, in a car he hasn't seen before, a cream-coloured Subaru. She always keeps her cars very clean. For some reason she's chosen to back up the driveway, in memory, perhaps, of the time she got stuck in the snow and he told her it would have been easier to get out if she'd been pointing down.

He puts the candle on the counter and goes into the downstairs bathroom. He smiles at himself, checking to see if there's anything caught between his teeth. He doesn't look bad. Then he goes out to welcome Diane. He realizes he hasn't been sure until now that she would really turn up. It could be he doesn't deserve it.

She slides out of the car, stands up, gives him a hug and a peck on the cheek. She has big sunglasses on, with silly palm trees over the eyebrows. This is the kind of extravagance Will has always liked about her. He hugs her back, but she doesn't want to be held too long. "I brought you something," she says, and searches inside the car.

Will watches her while she's bending over. She has a wide cotton skirt on, pulled tight around the waist; she's lost a lot of weight. He used to think of her as a hefty woman, well-fleshed and athletic, but now she's almost spindly. In his arms she felt frail, diminished.

She straightens and turns, thrusting a bottle of wine at him, and a round of Greek bread, fresh and spongy. Will is reassured. He puts his arm around her waist and hugs her again, trying to make it companionable so she won't feel pressured. "I'm glad to see you," he says.

Diane sits at the kitchen table and they drink wine; Will fools with the steaks, rubbing them with garlic, massaging them with pepper and a pinch or two of dried mustard. She used to help him with the cooking, she knows where everything's kept. But tonight she's acting more like a guest.

"Heard any good jokes lately?" she says. This in itself is a joke, since it was Diane who told the jokes, not Will. Diane was the one Will was with when his marriage stopped creaking and groaning and finally just fell apart. She wasn't the reason though, as he made a point of telling her. He said it could have been anyone; he didn't want her to feel responsible. He's not sure what happened after that, why they stopped seeing one another. It wasn't the sex: with her he was a good lover. He knows she liked him, and she got on well with the boys. But one day she said, "Well, I guess that's that," and Will didn't have the presence of mind to ask her what she meant.

"That's your department," Will says.

"Only because you were so sad then," says Diane. "I was trying to cheer you up. You were dragging around like you had a thyroid deficiency or something." She fiddles with her sunglasses, which are on the table. "Now it's your turn."

"You know I'm no good at it," Will says.

Diane nods. "Bad timing," she says. She stands up, reaches past Will to the counter. "What's this?" she says, picking up the chewed candle. "Something fall off?"

THEY EAT AT THE ROUND OAK TABLE they bought together at a country auction, one of the local farmers closing up and selling out. Diane has dug out the white linen table napkins she gave him one year, and has lit both candles, the chewed and the unchewed. "I believe in festivity," she said.

Now there are silences, which they both attempt to fill. Diane says she wants to talk about money. It's the right time in her life for her to become interested in money, and isn't Will an authority? She makes quite a lot, but it's hard for her to save. She wants Will to explain inflation.

Will doesn't want to talk about money, but he does it anyway, to please her. Pleasing her is what he would like to do, but she doesn't seem too pleased. Her face is thinner and more lined, which makes her look more elegant but less accessible. She's less talkative than she used to be, as well. He remembers her voice as louder, more insistent; she would tease him, pull him up short. He found it amusing and it took his mind off himself. He thinks women in general are becoming more silent: it goes with their new pale lips. They're turning back to secrecy, concealment. It's as if they're afraid of something, but Will can't imagine what.

Half of Diane's steak lies on her plate, untouched. "So tell me about gold," she says.

"You're not hungry?" Will asks her.

"I was ravenous," she says. "But I'm full." Her hair has changed too. It's longer, with light streaks. Altogether she is more artful.

"I like being with you," Will says. "I always did."

"But not quite enough," Diane says, and then, to make it light, "you should put an ad in the paper, Will. The personals, *NOW* magazine. 'Nice man, executive, with good income, no encumbrances, desires to meet …'"

"I guess I'm not very good at relationships," Will says. In his head, he's trying to complete Diane's ad. Desires to meet what? A woman who would not look at herself in the glass of the picture behind him. A woman who would like what he cooks.

"Bullshit," Diane says, with a return to her old belligerence. "What makes you think you're that much worse at it than anyone else?"

Will looks at her throat, where it's visible at the V-neck of her blouse. He hasn't seen an overnight case, but maybe it's in the car. He said no strings attached.

"There's a full moon," he says. "We should go out onto the patio."

"Not quite," says Diane, squinting up through the glass. "And it's freezing out there, I bet."

Will goes upstairs for a plaid blanket from the boys' room to wrap around her. What he has in mind is a couple of brandies on the patio, and then they will see. As he's coming back down the stairs, he hears her in the bathroom: it sound as if she's throwing up. Will pours the brandies, carries them outside. He wonders if he should go in, knock on the bathroom door. What if it's food poisoning? He knows he should feel compassion; instead he feels betrayed by her.

But when she comes out to stand beside him, she seems all right, and Will decides not to ask her about it. He wraps the blanket around her and keeps his arm there, and Diane leans against him.

"We could sit down," he says, in case she doesn't like the position.

"Hey," she says, "you got me flowers." She's spotted the withered daffodils. "Always so thoughtful. I bet they smell nice, too."

"I wanted you to hear the frogs," Will says. "We're just at the end of the frog season." The frogs live in the pond, down beyond the slope of the lawn. Or maybe they're toads, he's never been sure. For Will they've come to mean spring and the beginning of summer: possibilities, newness. Their silvery voices are filling the air around them now, like crickets but more prolonged, sweeter.

"What a man," Diane says. "For some it's nightingales, for some it's frogs. Next I get a box of chocolate-covered slugs, right?"

Will would like to kiss her, but the timing is wrong. She's shivering a little; against his arm she feels angular, awkward, as if she's withholding her body from him, though not quite. They stand there looking at the moon, which is cold and lopsided, and listening to the trilling of the frogs. This doesn't have the effect on Will he has hoped it would. The voices coming from the darkness below the curve of the hill sound thin and ill. There aren't as many frogs as there used to be, either.

JACQUELINE BAKER

Bloodwood

At age seventy-one, Perpetua Resch could honestly say she had loved only four people: her mother, her father, her brother Martin and her sister Magda. At one time she had hoped to include Joe, but she had long since recognized this idea as the romantic illusion of a teenaged bride and the expectation attached to a young and promising marriage. This was not to say she felt no affection for her husband. On the contrary, she was very fond of him. Over the years, there had been almost nothing to complain of about Joe. The worst she could think to say was that he tended toward complacency. But even this characteristic was a minor flaw given his easy nature, his generosity and, of course, his patient and seemingly unwavering capacity for love. But to speak in terms of loving him in return … no, she had none of that fierce blood-rush of feeling that could thrum music from the rib cage and swell one's throat to bursting, as though it contained some beautiful, terrible balloon. Though she knew she would rather not do without Joe, she suspected that she could certainly make the adjustment with little emotional strain. Once, long ago, in a tender moment (there was a moon, she remembers), Joe had said to her, "Don't you ever die on me first. I don't know what I'd do without you." And she'd looked into his shining eyes, so pleasantly dark, and thought, *Well, all right,* even though she knew her heart should have wrenched at the thought of living without him. Oddly, she had not felt dismayed to discover, early on in marriage, the truth about her feelings for Joe. After all, it was not particularly rare in those days to be married to someone you did not love. Not unusual at all. So she had waited, instead, for the arrival of children to kindle the sort of love she knew she could expect with some degree of certainty from motherhood. When it became clear that the long-awaited arrival was not to come, Perpetua suspected that the number of those she could say she had truly loved would remain limited to four. And she briefly grieved.

Perpetua's inability to love Joe (or anyone else she had met—there had certainly been opportunities) was the result of a too-happy childhood; this she knew. Looking back, she recalled none of the petty tensions and jealousies, none of the potentially grave, deep-rooted resentments that she knew sprouted in other families. There had been quarrels and sometimes tears, even the occasional fit of temper (Martin, once, after an argument with their father—Perpetua could not now remember over what—had broken his knuckle taking a swing at the barn wall), but these had been rare and short-lived and, once past, entirely forgotten. What made possible these easy family relations, she could not suppose. But the lack of conflict and strife neither amazed nor puzzled her—after all, her own marriage had rolled along easily for fifty-five years. Rather, it was the absolute, unshakeably deep love that Magda and Martin and Perpetua and their mother and father had all seemed to feel for one another, and only for one another. Even now, when she conjured up an image of Martin, sickly always, with his too-skinny legs, walking to school through ditches bloated yellow with buffalo beans, or the unbeautiful Magda coaxing a kitten to take milk from a saucer in the little sunless back porch, she felt that huge swelling of her heart, at once so agonizing and so tender. And she was keenly aware, yet again, that she had never once had this feeling for Joe.

She liked to believe Joe had never known. She had certainly always done her best to conceal it from him. She had cooked his meals and washed his clothes and once, before they were married, when all things still seemed possible, she had danced with him under the stars on a summer night choked with the scent of hot sand and wolf willow and

sage. She had held his hand and changed his sour sheets when he lay
delirious with rheumatic fever, she had worked beside him in the field
and in the corrals, and they had prayed every Sunday shoulder to
shoulder in the little church at Johnsborough. She had lain next to him
each night, peaceful or tired, sometimes angry. She had stayed, after all.
And been happy, more or less. Back then, she had still had Magda and
Martin and, for a few years after her mother's death, her father. And
that had been enough.

Perpetua supposed her parents were to blame. Somehow, they had
produced a tight iron band of love that could not be expanded or
reshaped or broken. They were good people, unexceptional people.
Perpetua's father was a quiet man, a German, from Odessa, given to
long absences, days sometimes, out in the hills, from which he would
return peaceful and oddly rested—younger-looking, as though the
sandy blasts of wind across the land had polished him smooth, like a
stone. He could read and write German fluently—an unusual ability,
she learned later, for a man of his background and means. He took the
German papers and read each one carefully all the way through,
puzzling his forehead in the light from the coal stove as though solving
some unpleasant mystery. And on Sunday mornings without fail, until
the children were too old for him to do so, he would take each of them
in turn on his knee—Magda and then Martin and then Perpetua—and
he would tell them in German, *You are the light of my heart.* And then,
while the children stood grinning expectantly, he would rise and wrap
their mother's thickened waist in his big hands and whisper something
in her ear—they never knew what, but they could tell by the look on
her face it had to be the same thing each time. And she would smile
and put the palm of her hand just so across his lips, as if she had placed
a kiss there. She seemed to do this secretly, as she seemed to do all
things, almost as though she worked some sort of magic in the everyday
acts of living—in coaxing hot brown loaves of bread from the oven; or
conjuring from that terrible gritty earth string beans fat and green as
elves' stockings; or polishing the scuffed pine-board floor to a shine that
made Martin giddy with sliding in his stocking feet, and Perpetua and

Magda foolish with imagined dancing shoes and shimmering satin gowns the colour of birds' eggs. She was a large woman, broad-shouldered and wide through the hips, but she moved quickly and lightly, with the grace of love upon her limbs. No one outside the family would have called her beautiful. But there she was, nevertheless, soft and sudden and full-blown for them all like the wild roses by the gate in summer. And love, love, it was as if someone had dreamed them.

Only later, much later, did Perpetua realize her loving family had not taught love, but only collected it and stored it selfishly, like the bushel baskets of potatoes and mealy apples in the root cellar. No, they did not teach love. What they taught was this: everything for the family. And just the family. No friends to go visiting on a Saturday afternoon in December, no skating parties, no fall suppers; no group picnics at the river with baskets of other women's roast chicken and pickles and chokecherry strudels; no brandings, as they did not graze their cattle in the community pasture at the Sand Hills. Not even church, for they prayed at home, led by their father in German from the great black Bible brought from the old country. Always just the five of them. Yes, her parents were certainly to blame. When Perpetua thought this, she always paused uncomfortably over the word *blame*. But when she considered the effect of their love, it seemed that a little blame was necessary.

For many years, Perpetua had thought this failure to love was some-thing wrong only in her. Then she had received a letter from Magda, poor Magda, alone in Saskatoon with a child, on the edge of her first divorce, who had written, *Tell me how it feels to go to bed each night and wake up each morning beside the man you love* (she had underlined *love*). *I feel sickened and empty. And my child, who is flesh and blood, asleep in the next room, her I can't even speak of, can't even look at some days without shame.* And Perpetua had read the letter twice over and wept terribly, big wrenching sobs, her apron up over her face and her shoul-ders shaking as though her body would break itself apart—wept, not for her husband, whom she did not love, nor for the children she had never had, whom she could not love either, but for poor Magda, whom she did love. She had wept that way until it was time for Joe's supper, and then, seeing him step heavily across the yard, she had slipped the letter into the breadbox, washed her face and greeted him, as she did each day, with a smile and a kiss.

And that letter had made everything clear. This is how it would always be. Magda, ending her marriage because she was waiting for love; Martin, never married, alone for years on their parents' farm; and Perpetua, married to a man she did not love. It was tragic. And terribly unfair. But, nevertheless, it was. Now, past seventy, with her parents and Magda long since buried in the little Catholic cemetery on the outskirts of town, and Martin rarely able to know her anymore, and only Joe to fill her days, it seemed a thing beyond worrying about, this love.

So when she looked out the window that Wednesday morning to see a woman in a yellow hat talking to Joe by his woodworking shop, she was taken aback by the great swelling that expanded her old ribs. The feeling came so suddenly and so powerfully that she stepped away from the back door and sank into a kitchen chair, her head swimming with the impossible emotion that trembled her fingers and sheathed her body in a fine layer of sweat. Her knees threatened to give way beneath her, not for Joe, but for the woman in the yellow hat. It took her a few moments to reassure herself that it was not Magda who stood awkwardly among Joe's larkspur, but Magda's daughter, Myra, who had written weeks ago that she might be passing through. Perpetua had not seen Myra since before Magda's divorce, not since Myra had gone off to live with her father in Manitoba. But that had been almost thirty years ago. The woman standing in the garden was not that rather homely, rather unhappy little girl she had known, but a woman approaching middle age, a woman who, for all Perpetua's rationalizing, *was* Magda, was Magda's blood, as she once said, Magda's body—with the same swelling thighs and narrow shoulders, the same straight yellow hair, the same uneasy stance, the stance of someone slightly cowed by the acceptance of her own graceless appearance. Perpetua had consumed all this detail in a flash as she'd looked briefly out the back door, seeing first Joe standing and nodding, clearly pleased with this visitor (so rare now), and then the woman in the yellow hat, wearing a white skirt and a striped blouse, holding a big straw shopping bag over one shoulder (did she mean to stay?).

Perpetua rose slowly and went back to the window, but both Joe and the woman (she could not, no matter how she tried, think of her as Myra) had disappeared. Perpetua felt a small quiver of panic before she realized that Joe had no doubt invited her into his workshop. They were probably standing right now beneath all those neat rows of jars he'd glued by their lids to the low ceiling, to hold nails and screws and bolts; she was probably smelling wood shavings and pretending to admire (or genuinely admiring) his carvings: tiny cowboy boots and miniature horses, trains and racing cars and semi trucks (these latter mostly for children around town, and now their children). She would ask politely if he'd done the enormous, elaborately carved slab of varnished cedar out front that announced *Dunworkin,* and below that, in smaller letters, *Joseph and Perpetua Resch.* He could keep her there for hours, pointing out the intricacies of detail in a boot or a wheel or a horse's mane, the character of each different wood—the soft, cheap convenience of knotty pine or the hard, red richness of cherry (blood-wood, he called it), so rare and expensive out west—the grain, the weight, the variations in colour and texture, the shine that could be brought to any piece through sanding. How one could make even the softest wood gleam like marble. He could keep her there all night. But just as Perpetua was deciding whether or not to go out to them (she rarely left the house now, not much at all since the surgery), they both appeared at the doorway to the workshop. Joe pointed toward the kitchen, and the woman looked up, shading her eyes. Perpetua stepped back from the window, even though they probably could not see her. She knew what Joe had said as he pointed: "Your Auntie Pet's up at the house there. Go on up. She'll be real glad you're here."

So Perpetua busied herself around the kitchen, wiping the already spotless counters, moving canisters a fraction of an inch into alignment, her hands shaking, and all the time thinking, Magda, Magda.

And then the doorbell.

"Come in," she called pleasantly, as if half-surprised.

When the woman opened the screen door and stepped into the air-conditioned kitchen on a wave of hot, dry heat, with all that sunlight still streaming in ribbons from her yellow hat, Perpetua came slowly toward her, trying as much as possible to hide the limp from the surgery, trying to swallow that terrible lump in her throat. She took a breath and tried to smile, holding her hands out. "Well, well, look at this," she began to say, but before she had finished, the woman turned away and covered her face with her big red hands. Magda's hands.

Perpetua took her in an awkward embrace. The woman held the tips of her fingers pressed to her eyes. "What is it, dear?" Perpetua asked (she could not say Myra). "Tell me. What's wrong?"

The woman shook her head, still half-turned away, returned Perpetua's embrace with one fumbling, fleshy arm that smelled faintly of geraniums. The woman shook her head, lifted her crumpled face as though in a tremendous effort to stop her tears. She shook her head again and said something that Perpetua could not hear, and in spite of the fact that she hated to do it, Perpetua said, "What? What's that?" and the woman repeated herself. Perpetua thought it was either "Glad to come back" or "Sad to come back." Impossible to ask again.

The woman was embarrassed, Perpetua could see, so she said, "Come in," and walked her slow, rolling walk to the table, knowing it would give the woman a moment to pull herself together before she followed. Perpetua sat down first, folding her hands in her lap to still the trembling, then looked across the table as the woman pulled out a chair for herself, planted the heavy straw bag with great care at her feet and adjusted the waistband of her skirt. She removed her hat, lifting it too daintily for her hands, with two fingers at each side of the brim, and finally raised her face, gave that same crumpled smile. And it was Magda's face, streaky red and swollen from the tears and the heat—Magda, who had never been beautiful but who could look at you with a kind of light in her eyes that would set your very bones gently humming. Perpetua stared at the woman, so hungry for that feeling, just one small glimmer, that she almost reached across the table and grasped her by the shoulders to bring her closer. Perpetua looked, and she saw no light there. And then the woman was not Magda, but only Myra, with the red and swollen and lightless eyes. Perpetua felt her heart spill over again, not for Magda now, but finally, after all this time, for Myra. This woman. How could it be?

"So," Myra was saying, her voice soft and trembling, "it's been a long time."

Perpetua could barely catch the words. These last years, her hearing had been growing gradually worse, was so bad now that all conversation had a strange, dreamy quality. She leaned forward a little, working her hands in her lap, forcing the awful clenching of her heart to subside.

"How are you?" Myra asked. "What's going on with you these days?"

And before Perpetua could stop herself, she said, surprised at the sudden feebleness of her voice, "Nothing good. Joe had a heart attack last summer"—she thought Myra said, "I'm sorry, I didn't know"—"and I had surgery on my leg, and they put a pin in that's giving me a lot of trouble, it's painful, I don't sleep much anymore." And then she thought, Why did I say that? I didn't mean to say that. How terrible I must sound to her.

Myra said, "I'm sorry," again, and then, "Uncle Joe looks good. How is he?"

"What?" Perpetua said. "Joe?"

Myra raised her voice a little, leaned forward also. "Yes, how is he? He looks good."

"Yes." Perpetua nodded. "He's good. He's the same."

"He keeps busy out there, I guess."

"Yes," Perpetua said, "he keeps busy."

She thought of Joe in his workshop, every day now since he'd retired, puttering around, sawing and sanding and patiently scraping. He wouldn't admit it, but his eyes were going. He wasn't as good anymore with the fine detail.

"He didn't know me," Myra said, pushing out a little laugh. "I guess he wouldn't. He thought I was selling something."

Perpetua smiled and nodded. "Yes, they come around sometimes. Always selling something." She shrugged. "We never buy. Just from the Hutterites."

The woman nodded, leaned her elbows on the table, took them off again. "And how," she said, "how is Joe's family? He has a sister, doesn't he?"

"Yes," Perpetua said, thinking how strange it was that Myra should remember that. "In Medicine Hat. We don't see her much now. She's busy. With the grandchildren."

"Oh," Myra said, "she has grandchildren?"

"What?"

"She has grandchildren?"

"Yes. Great-grandchildren now. Two of them. Joe has pictures up," she said, rising slowly and leading Myra into the living room. Her hands had stopped trembling, but she was so conscious of the nearness of Myra's breath and her arms behind her that she still felt a little flutter of her heart. She wanted to touch her again, but it would seem strange. Myra would wonder. So instead, she pointed to where the pictures stood on a little shelf, all of them, in their brassy frames.

"There's more," she said, "out in the shop, all their school pictures. Joe probably showed you. Don't ask me their names. There's too many now."

Myra looked at the pictures, each in turn, making polite comments Perpetua did not always hear. She wished Myra would remember to speak up. She didn't like to keep asking her to repeat. Myra paused over a big black and white one in a wooden frame.

"That one," Perpetua said, "is me. And Joe. Our wedding picture." Stupid. Of course it was their wedding, Myra could see that.

Myra picked it up. "You were lovely."

"Oh," Perpetua said, shrugging. She knew she was not.

Myra placed the photograph gently on its doily, then picked up a small blurry snapshot of Magda and Martin sitting on one of their father's horses—Shotgun, Perpetua thought, though she couldn't really remember.

"This is Mother, isn't it," Myra said, pausing.

Perpetua wondered if she saw herself in that face. Surely she must, she must have pictures of her own. Wouldn't she?

"And Uncle Martin," Myra said. "How is he?"

Perpetua was about to say, Not good, but instead she said, "The same," and wiped a bit of dust away from the frame with her thumb.

"I'd like to see him," Myra said. "Is he still on the farm?"

Perpetua looked up in surprise. "No," she said, "he's in the home. For years now."

"Oh," Myra said, and put the picture down on the shelf.

She is ashamed, Perpetua thought, she thinks she should know these things. How could she know? She had been lost to them all for years, to Magda even. To Magda most of all.

"Your father," Perpetua asked then, because she felt she should, "how is he?"

"Fine. In Brandon still. With Lois. They're fine."

The stepmother, Perpetua remembered. The one who'd sent Magda Christmas cards faithfully, each year, with a brief letter and a picture of Myra standing posed in front of their upright piano, always the same pose, to show how much she'd grown. Lois, a stranger, who knew more about Magda's daughter than Magda herself did. It was too sad. Perpetua would not let herself think about it any longer.

"Where do you live now? Brandon?"

"Nipawin."

"Where?"

Myra raised her voice. "Nipawin. I teach there. Two and three."

Perpetua nodded. She watched Myra pick up pictures, set them back down, the same ones she'd already looked at.

"What, are you on a holiday?"

"Yes. Sort of. It's summer vacation." She smiled a little. "I guess that's my holiday."

"Out here?"

Myra turned away.

Perpetua straightened a couple of the frames. "You picked the worst time, July. You have air conditioning in your car?"

"Yes," Myra said without turning back. "It's hot, all right."

"I was never one for the heat," Perpetua said. "Everyone complains about winter. Not me. Joe neither. Nothing bothers him."

Then, finally, she asked, "Are you married?"

"Yes," Myra said, replacing the photograph she was looking at. "Robert Russell. We met at the university. His family is from around Kindersley. The Malcolm Russells. His grandparents are Aida and Clemens Russell …?"

She trailed off.

Perpetua frowned. "Where is he? Working?"

"Yes," she said, "he had to work."

"You have children?"

"No."

Perpetua gave Myra's wrist a little squeeze and, though she was reluctant to let go, went slowly to sit in the armchair by the window. She made a motion for Myra to take a seat on the chesterfield.

"You want coffee?" she asked.

"No. Thank you."

"Juice? Water?"

"No, I'm good, thanks."

Perpetua folded her hands in her lap. The clock ticked out from the mantel, softly. Beyond the yellowed blinds, a car rolled past on the gravel road. She tried not to stare at Myra, though she felt as if she could swallow her whole with her eyes. That face. When she thought of it, her throat ached, and so she thought instead about Joe, working steadily out in the shop, listened for the sound of his radio or the high whine of the saw. But all was quiet.

"I guess," Myra said finally, fiddling with the hem of her white skirt, her eyes glistening in the yellow light, "I guess you and mother were pretty close."

Oh, Perpetua thought, oh, my dear child. And she wanted more than anything to pull that sad body to her, hold her close against her chest. Poor unlovely child. Child of my heart. My sister's child. Perpetua hid her hands beneath her apron.

"Yes," she said slowly, "there was just the three of us. We had no close neighbours. Just us."

Myra nodded. She wiped the tip of her awkward nose, stared up at a basket of silk flowers, then a brass cat, then a framed sampler Perpetua had been given years ago, decades, as a gift: *Act and suffer in silence.* She couldn't remember now who had given it to her, only that she had hated it always. She watched as Myra looked about the room. Finally, she could stand it no longer.

"You want to know about your mother?" she asked. "What do you want to know?"

Myra stared back at her.

"She was a good singer," Perpetua began. "She liked all animals. On the farm, she liked to be with the animals. Except mice, which she was afraid of. I don't know why; she wasn't afraid of anything else. She liked the horses, her and Martin both. I was always too scared. She liked the garden. She worked hard. We all did. She wasn't much of a one for housework." She smiled. "She got in trouble with Mum all the time for not doing this right, not doing that right. She baked an apple pie once, Mum left all the directions, but Magda used salt instead of sugar. Martin tried to feed it to the dogs so Mum wouldn't find out, but they wouldn't eat it. She got in trouble for that. She liked to sing." She lifted her hands. "I don't know. My memory is getting worse. If you ask questions, maybe I'll remember."

But Perpetua felt like a fraud, looking across at that unhappy face. This was not what Myra wanted to know. Not really. She leaned forward over her knees, as close as she could get without rising, and said slowly, clearly, "She was my sister. And I loved her. Just as I loved Martin. And my mother and my father. It was all we had. Do you understand? We didn't know anything but each other." She stopped here, hoping Myra *would* understand. "Our family, it was everything. More than that, I can't tell you."

Myra stared at the carpet, unblinking.

Perpetua rose and seated herself on the chesterfield next to her. She put one arm around her shoulders and thought, This is what we've all come to, then, all that love. How could she explain it?

"The truth is …" she began.

She looked up then to see Joe standing in the doorway, holding a small carved horse, a red one, gleaming with all the light of new marble. She could tell by the way he turned the figure slowly in his hands that he'd been standing there for some time. The horse, she knew, was for Myra. Though his carvings fetched quite a price in the city, he'd always given away far more than he'd sold. It was his way. He lifted the horse slightly, as if he would say something. But he did not. She stared back at him, with Myra between them, her face in her hands. They listened to the clock tick. And then, still looking at Joe, Perpetua said, "That's enough now." And she smoothed a hand across the back of Myra's hair. "That's enough."

BONNIE BURNARD

Jiggle Flicks

The sailboat Heather had been tracking across the bay was small in the distance now, almost gone, so she gave her attention over to the other boats. She counted five moving back in to the shoreline, homing gracefully to the squat, brightly painted boathouses which lined the bay like suburban garages.

She didn't try to imagine the people who sailed the water, their faces given over to laughter or hesitancy or plain brute effort. She didn't wonder what elaborate skills were needed to control the direction and speed of a sailboat, or what kind of nerve it took to sail on a bright western afternoon out of Vancouver Harbour into the Strait of Georgia. Sitting there, holding her seven-dollar glass of Scotch, trying to put to memory the surprising colour of the sun on the water, she thought the most compelling argument for sailing is that it gives people on the shore something magnificent to watch.

She was tired. She'd come down to the lounge from the conference rooms with all the others hoping to unwind, hoping for pleasure or, at the very least, distraction. They'd taken the available tables in a fluid five-table rush and ordered their drinks anxiously, as if thirsty, and as they settled they took care of the first order of business, which was to dismiss the last panel discussion they'd heard as not especially useful or incisive. They always did this. And then the stories began.

Complaints and accomplishments were brought out like baby pictures and passed from one to the other around the tables, the interest expressed sometimes sincere, sometimes not quite. Although they had been together once or twice a year for some time, there was some backtracking to do; people tended to forget what they were supposed to remember. A few pas de deux were under way: a coy or steady glance, devout attention proffered like a gift certificate, a hand on a back, felt, and known to be felt. Married, not married, troubled, trustworthy, pitiful, wild, careless, smart, just about everyone had something to offer. Those who had performed together before were discreet, tolerant of new couplings, ignoring the signs they'd received or sent themselves another time. Insurance people did this, she thought, museum people. Plumbers?

After she'd got her Glenlivet, Heather had turned a deaf ear to the conversation and swivelled her chair an inoffensive half turn to face the windows. There was a full bank of them, from floor to ceiling, overlooking the wide blue bay. Her sightline across the lounge was interrupted only intermittently by the heads and shoulders of the other drinkers and occasionally by deferential waiters in tight rose jackets bending to deliver drinks. She supposed the drinkers seated closest to the windows were regulars, or real tourists who knew enough to flash a bit of money.

Tom was already in up to his ears. Heather had talked to him briefly at the first conference breakfast; he'd told her she looked beautiful, he'd asked about the kids. When they came into the lounge she had stalled and watched to see where he was going to sit and had pulled out a chair at another table, but then he'd moved, following in the wake of a happy young woman who smoked, much to everyone's annoyance. Six feet away, he leaned eagerly forward into the smoke, taking care to catch the young woman's words, prompting her. Tom listened well in the beginning, although what he remembered later, at least in her case, had been a little distorted, the names of cities and towns got wrong, significant people thoughtlessly dismissed. She had tried once or twice to correct him, but she'd waited too long. Things had set in his mind.

The happy young woman who smoked had several spectacular bangles on each arm and she was playing with them, pushing them up to her wrists and letting them slide down her forearms again, explaining their origins, the words Africa and New Mexico carrying through the air more forcefully than some of her other words. Tom reached over and slid one of her bangles off and, laughing, attempted to push it down over his own hand. Heather knew it wouldn't go past his knuckles, and it didn't. She wanted to call over, Take note, sweetie, of those large hands.

Someone had ordered her another Scotch. The waiter was smiling down at her, lifting her empty glass from her hand. She heard talk about dinner. Vietnamese, someone said. She thought she might skip out, an aunt to call, an old friend. But then again. She looked out once more over the water. The formation of the sailboats had changed. The one she'd been tracking was lost entirely and three new ones, recently set sail, drifted close to the shoreline, anxious for the wind. The colours over the bay had deepened, almost imperceptibly.

She turned back to her companions and threw herself wholeheartedly into the middle of a discussion about municipal bylaws. There were seven people around the table. She gave her attention to a quiet, balding man she'd sometimes seen but never talked to, who had never, as far as she knew, shown much interest in her or in any of the others. His name was Jim. She thought perhaps he was deliriously happy with someone none of them had ever heard about. She thought perhaps he was loyal to someone. She wondered if this loyalty signified moral stature or if he'd just had himself some blind luck. It certainly made him worth talking to.

One of the other women at the table, Sheila, from New Brunswick, had begun to talk earnestly about being hungry and so it was arranged that the drinks would soon stop and they would meet in the lobby in half an hour and get cabs to a restaurant on East Hastings. As she was digging in her briefcase for her share of the bill, Heather noticed that the happy young woman who smoked had stood up and was moving to another table to talk to a colleague from Calgary, a too-young corporate lawyer who looked a bit like Donald Sutherland had looked when he was young. When the young woman approached him he wrapped his arm around her waist as if all along he had been simply waiting for her to finish up with the other guy, as if he had waited before for other women and didn't mind at all. Tom looked a tad dejected, but then who wouldn't?

HEATHER HAD MET TOM three years earlier at a subcommittee meeting in Thunder Bay, when she was still subject to a childlike shame at being so obviously on her own in the world. After an initial, fairly aggressive session in his room, they'd had another, quieter go in hers. Near the end he'd casually wrapped his arms around her and held her with a steady, easy, perfect pressure, and he'd said the word beautiful. And then they'd rented a car and taken off, to Kakabeka Falls. They got a cabin and he hurried away to talk to the management about renting a canoe, he was very excited about getting a canoe. He soon returned with one, carrying it like a woodsman over his shoulders, grinning. She stood on the dock watching as he lowered it to the shore, pushed it into the water and walked it out along the dock with a paddle. Then he stepped down into it and held it steady for her, his free hand extended. She shook her head. "Thanks anyway," she said.

"I thought you liked the water," he said. "Why don't you like the water?"

"For the same reason fish don't like land," she said.

"You told me your family always went to a lake," he said. "There must have been boats."

"Motorboats," she said. "My brothers skied."

"Ah," he said. "Motorboats. And sunglasses and bikinis and cases of beer and very loud music."

"And convertibles," she said.

"Ontario," he said, chuckling, pushing off. He paddled with some expertise out into the cold northern lake.

She sat at the end of the dock, her legs dangling over the edge, and when she looked down through the water she could see that good-sized rocks had been piled around support posts to hold the dock in place. She could see small dark fish hovering near the rocks, moving as if chased from one crevice to another. A few tangled plants appeared to be rooted to the rocks' smooth surfaces and they drifted with the water's movement, untangling. There was no wind that she could feel and she wondered what made the water move like that, below the surface.

She heard, intermittently, the quick plop of fish, pike, she supposed, coming to the surface for food, and one other sound, surrounding her, composed like orchestral music from dozens of smaller sounds. Some of the insects were in the air above the water, some hovered on the surface, snacks for the pike, but most of them were behind her, tight to the earth or in it. Although she couldn't hear any animal sounds, she assumed there would be several species not very far away, which, if she didn't disturb, she could comfortably ignore.

Tom had moved directly to the centre of the lake and some tension on the surface of the water kept him there. He'd lifted the paddles and was lying back in the canoe, stretched out. On the surrounding shoreline, boulders which had been deposited in half-submerged clusters held the lake in place, reflected the wet light. Substantial trees, mostly spruce and pine, pulled back from the shore and grew dark and thicker in the distance, which was clear enough under the stars. She waved to him, in case he was watching, but he didn't respond. She guessed he was looking at the sky.

From the dock, it appeared perfectly safe out there and she thought she'd likely made a mistake, refusing. She thought perhaps it would be smarter to welcome something new, something never tried, never trusted. There was lots to be replaced, many things she had once done well, often with panache and some grace, that were out of the question now: the long jump, the jive, giving birth, falling in love.

Although she couldn't have put an exact time on it, before her divorce or during or after it, before one miserable, middle-aged cancer death or during or after another, somewhere along the line she'd come to believe that beauty was nothing more than a man-made distraction, an anxious imperative, that much of what was called beautiful was only cruel and raw, barbaric: rocks, for instance, and rivers, the wind-tempered growth of a tree, the black sky and the secluded stars that sometimes seemed to fill it, certainly mountains. Once, shortly after her divorce was finalized, she was sitting alone in her backyard with her face turned up to the sun and a Monarch butterfly took rest on her bare shoulder. She was breathless, amazed, thankful. But it stayed too long, longer than seemed possible, and when she turned her head to look she saw that it had been partially dismembered. It couldn't leave. Through those years she'd never stopped hearing the word *beautiful*, it's a word people frequently say, but she'd come to understand the word the same way she understood the sound of a whip used on a circus lion, as the sound needed to enforce distance, to create an illusion of calm.

Sitting on the dock, watching Tom float at the centre of the lake, surrounded on all sides by the shadows and the sheen, the haphazard, moving patterns, the oblivious confidence of even the mindless pike, she understood the word differently. It bounced off the water like light, like crystal. It was absorbed by the dense growth of trees along the shoreline and re-emerged to hover softly over the drifting canoe. It pushed across the lake toward the dock, toward her, not a trick word at all, just a word like any other, used to describe things which could not be otherwise known.

Later in bed, with her face comfortably tucked into Tom's fleshy shoulder, she could smell the lake still on his skin, she could see with her eyes shut tight the trees and the boulders and the light. When his casual arms enclosed her, with their perfect pressure, as if some dreamed of perfect coupling had been achieved, she tried to tell him how things had looked from the dock.

SHEILA STOOD UP and was asking was she coming for dinner, so she finished the last of her drink and followed her through the lobby past the fake statuary to the elevators, resisting the urge to run a hand through her dishevelled hair as they passed the inevitable mirrors. They were joined in the elevator by a young bellman in a grey and rose uniform who carried, at shoulder height, a silver tray of drinks and cocktail food covered by a white cloth. As the elevator rose he slipped his hand under the linen to get a cracker spread with smoked salmon pâté, and when Heather laughed out loud he got one for her too.

At her room, she walked out of her shoes before the door closed behind her and made for the bed, thinking about fresh sheets and room service and the recommended book of stories she'd bought written by a guy named Hodgins, set on Vancouver Island. She dropped onto the bed and curled up on her side, closed her eyes. She wondered briefly if this more than occasional preference for solitude, for the absence of sound, this choosing sometimes only the dimmest of lights, was some kind of gradual backhanded practice for the hereafter, and then she thought she could likely have done without the last Scotch.

Her third conference outfit hung on the closet door. Two down, two to go. It was a floral print dress, long and loose and bright. Stockings the exact shade of the chrysanthemums were in the pocket. Stockings to match the mums, she thought, no one could say you aren't trying. She'd bought the dress in a brief fit of post-divorce confidence, the same week she'd bought an expensive new mattress and decided to have the sofa recovered in chintz. She'd read in the *New Yorker* that divorced women should avoid chintz furniture like the plague and she'd thought, Chintz would be nice. The dress was still good four years later; she was still sure of the dress.

In the shower she remembered home, the kids. When she was away from them they came to her more concretely than when they were in her arms. Some kids they'd made. Worth every fight, every humiliating session with the divorce lawyers and the judges, all the regretful separation tears. Once she had gathered the kids together in the chintz living room and tried to tell them how they filled her. It was a stupid idea. The language she'd needed to use was too rich for them, they resisted mightily, shrugging, saying that they only wanted her to be happy, that they were fine. I know that, she said, that's the whole point, how very fine you are. And then she'd backed off and one of them cracked wise and it was over.

In the dress, in the stockings, she stood at the mirror lifting her hair up and letting it down again. It should be up, she thought and I should be young, and there should be a saucy hat to match the dress, but there isn't, so there you are.

The cab ride to East Hastings was long, detoured through Stanley Park, because everyone wanted to see it again. Sheila rolled her window all the way down and the wet air moved through the cab, lifted hearts. It was dark and the smell of the bay in the air and the lights from the city and the bridge and the moving stream of cars sent Heather into the inevitable Vancouver spin. I'll move here, she thought, I'll live here and drive through this park every night, drive over that bridge, up and down those streets. She never would, she knew, but she let herself play with the details: call a realtor in the morning, find out about high schools, ask a couple of colleagues about possible openings, discreetly.

At the restaurant, there was one long table already set up for them, it filled half the room, and they moved around it and began to find places. Just as she found a seat there was sudden loud laughter from the other end of the table, and when she looked down she saw the bangled young woman who smoked standing in her own floral print dress, mums and all, waving and grinning, what a coincidence, what a funny thing. The others clearly wanted to enjoy this so she gave it to them, graciously. What the hell, she thought, and then Tom was at her arm, pulling her chair out. She thanked him and they sat down.

She picked up the menu immediately but Tom pushed it down to the table and took her hand, introducing her to another young woman, who sat across from them. Andrea something was her name, Andy, she wanted to be called. She was shy and reticent at first but Tom drew her out and then she had lots to say, and no one stopped her. Those at the table who were older, which was most of them, looked suddenly tired, the meetings, the talking, the wine, but they listened and smiled occasionally, and she wasn't half bad, this one, pretty bright as it turned out. Heather watched Tom wonder if his luck, after all, had held.

The last time she'd been with Tom, in Ottawa, in winter, sitting in an East Indian restaurant eating tandoori chicken, he had steered the conversation deliberately, which was unusual for him, coming finally to his point by inviting her to open up about her ex-husband and any other past loves. She wouldn't do it. That was then, she'd said. This is now. As it turned out his curiosity had been only a courtesy, a chance for reciprocity; he had something he wanted to tell her.

Later, in bed, he began the real telling by saying that he'd turned fifty-five since they'd last been together. Happy Birthday, she said. What should I get you? What do you want? He told her that he'd had a new will drawn up and that he'd lost fifteen pounds, jogging, and she said, Oh, yes you have, of course you have. He told her he'd decided there was enough deterioration in middle age without extra weight to compound the problem and she laughed and said, Don't I know, although weight had never been that much of a problem for her. She did say, I used to have a chicken pox scar as big as a dime on my fore-head, and now it's in my eyebrow. She did say, Where do you think it's heading? And when he told her he'd culled his wardrobe and his personal files, filled three bags for the Sally Ann and as many again for the dump, she said, I should do that.

Then he asked did she believe in one true and perfect love. Not any more, she said, but he didn't hear. This was to be a telling, not a talk. She laughed at him, already afraid, and then a fog settled in around her, as thick as the fog in a field of icebergs.

"When I was forty-seven," he said, "there was one perfect woman."

"More than one," she said. "Surely."

"No," he said. "Just one."

She got up to turn on the late news, hoping for war, famine, earthquake, anything, but there was only insipid weather, and it didn't stop him.

"Her hair," he said, "was the colour of coal."

She got back into bed, keeping to her own side, but he rolled over, wrapped his arms around her, held her with his perfect pressure.

"She had a really magnificent back," he said. "Long. And long legs. Although she wasn't very tall standing up."

He threw his leg over hers, the way a twin would in the uterus.

"Could we finish this another time?" she asked.

"She had buttocks like a boy's," he said. "And perfect high breasts, as white as clouds." He traced his palm over her own. "Her waist came in from her hips really sharply, like this." He put his hands in the air just above her face, formed a shape. "And all of it held in the most impeccable skin I've ever seen. Even the soles of her feet were flawless."

"Did you get a chance to look in her mouth?" she asked.

"She had no flaws," he said.

"I'd have to call that bullshit," she said.

"I'm trying to tell you," he said.

Heather knew what her moves were. She should ease herself out of the bed, whisper something that would hold a cutting edge for years, then dress, pack and leave. But she stayed where she was, pissed off at the sheer inconvenience of such a course of action, apparently too dulled in middle age for even a little bit of half-decent theatre.

"There is no one else to tell this to," he said. Soon he dozed off, deeply saddened and apparently exhausted from his telling. She watched the dark hair on his chest rise and fall peacefully beside her.

She propped her pillow up behind her back and looked toward the television, and when she could see again she saw Tina Turner madly gunning an armoured jeep through some kind of desert war zone, sitting at the wheel in a suit of chain mail. Her glossy white hair was high in the wind and wild, but the set of her jaw implied the calm that comes from wit, from skill, and her eyes were clear and focused. She was as beautiful as any woman could hope to be and she was having a fine time gunning the jeep through that desert, hanging on hard, hell-bent. Watching from the bed, Heather wanted, as much as anything she'd ever wanted in her life, to be Tina Turner in that jeep, courageously outrunning a monstrous enemy. Or was she burning up all that energy to save someone else? Not likely.

She threw Tom's leg off and lifted her own leg high into the air above the bed, contemplating the length, the shape, the bulky knee, the tough casing of skin over muscle and fat and blood and bone.

When she let it drop down onto the bed, heavily, his large hand reached for her forearm and squeezed.

In the morning, they had breakfast together before she arranged for the cab and left him. When their coffee had been refilled, she said, "Do you know about your hands?"

"What about my hands?" he asked.

"They're too large for the rest of your body," she said. "It's the first thing I noticed about you. As if some chromosome was out of whack when you were just a wee embryo. As if a madman cut them from someone else's arms and attached them to yours." She reached across the table. "I've never looked at your wrists really closely," she said. "There might be marks. Let me check." She tried to take one of his hands in her own but he yanked it away, tucked it under the table.

"This is simpleminded retaliation," he said. He bit the skin from his lower lip as he talked, a habit she'd noticed only once or twice before. "I didn't say you aren't beautiful. Although you're not, not this morning."

He wrote to her later that he didn't think her leaving solved anything, and that he didn't think she was being particularly fair to him. He didn't think her leaving was very original either, or profound. He said he was only trying to understand love and its relationship to beauty, and that he didn't see this as a necessarily despicable undertaking. He said he did love her, he couldn't imagine not loving her.

WHEN THE VIETNAMESE DINNER was cleared, and it had been delicious, the best she'd ever had except for the one time in London with her ex-husband, the waiters brought fortune cookies, which were passed around to everyone and opened. Her fortune read, "Your future success will depend on your kindness." Good news, she thought, rolling it up like a spitball and dropping it into the onions she'd left in her bowl. Someone decided the fortunes should be read aloud and beginning with Jim on her left, moving around the table away from her, each person shared his fate. "Much success in words and music," they began, "Avert misunderstanding by calm, poise and balance," "A merry heart maketh a cheerful countenance."

When it got back around to their end of the table, Heather unrolled her soggy bit of paper and licked the sauce from her fingers. She could hear the smile in Tom's voice as he read, with all the effect he could summon, "You will live long and well, beloved by many." This brought hearty laughter, he'd known it would.

Then it was her turn and she read aloud, "Your future success will depend on your kindness." More laughter, first from Tom and then from the others. In Tom's laughter she could hear just an edge of the vicious, as if he'd been waiting with his laughter, not impatient but ready, for a while. And all this time she'd thought at least that part was over.

When she looked up, people were involved again in whatever conversations they'd left, they were waving pieces of fortune cookie around in the air, breaking and eating them. Tom was leaning across the table talking in a low voice to Andy. Jim nudged her arm and said he didn't think she had anything to worry about, she looked pretty kind to him.

Cabs were called again, and when Tom followed her and climbed in after her with Andy in tow, she took his hand in the dark back seat and drove her thumbnail as deeply as she could into the thick flesh just below his knuckles. He shook her off, his face a quick and honest mask of shock. She checked her nail for blood, disappointed.

"I'm only trying to understand love," she said quietly. "And its relationship to bruises."

"What did you say?" Andy leaned forward, smiling.

They rode back through the park again, Jim and Sheila in the front seat chatting up the cab driver, who gave them all the touristy facts and all the oblique mockery anyone could be expected to absorb. Jim didn't much like the mockery, and after the cab driver said he didn't think they'd like living in Vancouver, Jim slugged him playfully on the shoulder, laughing only slightly.

When they were out of the park approaching the bridge, to include her in a vision of the city lights reflected off the water, Tom put his hand on her knee and shook it, as if to waken her.

In the hotel lobby she walked to the front desk with a question about check-out time to which she already knew the answer, waiting until Tom and Andy had excused themselves before she rejoined the others. Jim and Sheila had decided to go for more drinks. She said she thought she'd pass, and yes, she'd meet them for breakfast at eight-thirty, that sounded fine. Jim shrugged his shoulders and smiled, happy that a decision had been made for him.

The elevator doors were just about closed when a fist, and then a bangled arm, blocked them, forcing them to open again on the lobby. The young woman in the floral dress giggled her way in, followed by the lawyer from Calgary. They were holding hands. "Hello," he said, grinning. "Done for the night?"

He hit a button and then moved to stand unnecessarily close to her and, with no warning, slipped his free hand into the pocket of her dress. He said he loved the dresses. He said it was good to see women wearing clothes that belonged on women again. He said good for her, what the hell, she could still get away with a dress like that, so why not? She pulled his hand out of the pocket and placed it on the delicate shoulder of the happy bangled young woman, who was now enclosed in his other arm. "How very kind," she said. She read the neon indicator, hit a button and got out three floors early.

In her room she took off the dress and hung it in the closet. She thought when she got home she'd offer it to her neighbour, an energetic young woman with four kids and an artist husband. Maybe she could get some use out of it. In the bathroom she brushed her teeth and pulled her pyjamas on, pitched the stockings into the garbage. She walked out to the television set and sat down on the carpet in front of it, pulled the off/on switch. She turned the channels knowing there would be no news, it was too late, but hoping for a movie. She got lucky. She found *Russia House,* with Sean Connery, who had earned, since he'd allowed himself to age and let his hair go, a very secure spot on her shortlist. The kids had deduced this small lust through her video preferences at home and they had teased her without mercy the first time they'd seen an old James Bond film.

And Bette Midler was on, in something obscure that she'd once half thought of seeing but missed. The other movies were restricted and she was offered only samplings. Jiggle flicks, Tom called them. She tried one of the samples. On the screen, just a few inches from her hand, a thin young woman panted loudly into the ear of a man whose dark hair was either very greasy or wet. He was going at her attentively, with discipline and control and his eyes wide open, as if she were some kind of machine with a seized motor. It looked like it would go on for quite a while, and then it stopped and the screen faded. A message came on telling her that she should push seven on the control panel on top of the set if she wished to watch the movie in full, that the cost would be billed automatically to her room. She found Sean Connery again. He was playing a reprobate, a drunk who'd known better times, but he was nonetheless enticing and Michelle Pfeiffer, who was fated to fall in love with him, was wasting her time resisting. Heather thought it would have been much nicer if Connery had turned up in the jiggle flick. Michelle Pfeiffer could have the guy with the greasy hair.

She went back to the bathroom and brushed her teeth again, and her tongue, trying to get rid of a taste from dinner that had been better the first time around. Standing at the window, she wished she'd agreed to pay the extra for a room overlooking the bay. Below her there were only cars, rows and rows of them, dull and similar.

Suddenly tired, she pulled back the covers of the bed and climbed in, taking the heaviest of the pillows and placing it over her feet, as was her habit. Perhaps because she already knew the plot of *Russia House*, she was nearly out when she heard his knock.

She got up and turned the movie off and walked to the door, peering through the glass in the small security hole. The glass worked like the side mirror on a car, it made his face look more distant than it actually was, and slightly malformed. She opened the door.

"She's heard I'm a bit shallow," he said. He walked past her into the room, but not too far. "She says she's been burned before." She let the door close. "Imagine that," he said. "Burned." He moved tentatively to the chair beside the television and sat down. He put one of his massive hands on the channel changer and turned it all the way around, clunk, clunk, clunk, although the set was dead.

"She was quite lively," Heather said. "Doesn't she believe in quick involvement?" She was parroting the phrase from telephone conversations overheard at home.

"Is there any other kind?" he asked.

She climbed back into the bed. She turned from him and shifted around to find the place she'd made for her body just a little while before. "Did you come to tell me how much it hurts?" she asked.

"She was just good company for the night," he said. "I wasn't really trying." He was taking off his shoes. She heard them drop, one after the other, to the floor. He hated shoes. He would be rubbing his feet now, working his toes. "She's too young to be expected to ..."

She interrupted him. "Tell me how much it hurts," she said. "And put your shoes on."

"You want me to agonize?" he asked. "You want me to agonize over one sweet young thing who won't have me? Because I'm not cock-of-the-walk any more? Because I no longer have quite enough of whatever it is it takes? That's nothing," he said. "That's life."

She lifted her head from the pillow. "You're so brave," she said.

He extended his hand toward her. "I've got your bruise," he said. "It's small but it's going to be a good deep purple." He smiled.

She smiled back.

"You lie there," he said, "grieving for yourself and for me because you won't accept the way things are. Everyone else has to. You waste all this damned energy resisting what can't be resisted. And for what?" He went on, more gently. "We'll be a long time dead. But we're alive now, and we could have ..."

"This isn't grief," she said. She turned again, this time onto her stomach. The sheets were still cool and they smelled slightly of something she couldn't name, something close to lemon.

"So it's not grief," he said. "Whatever you want to call it, it's not worth ..."

She decided if she wasn't asleep before he finished his rant she would pretend to be, she would pretend to be in some other place entirely, beyond avoidance, safe. She willed herself to dream peacefully, conjuring the images that worked: each kid, separately; a dock in a dark Northern Ontario night; the desert. She hoped against hope that in the morning when she woke up he would be gone, gone and grateful for her kindness.

She did fall asleep. Oblivion came and was eventually overtaken by a dream. She stood in the middle of a luxuriant vegetable garden, a neighbour's, which she was supposed to tend during some absence. She surprised herself with knowledge she'd assumed she was without; she was able to recognize and identify each buried vegetable by its tough surface growth, she was able to trap the various bugs which were hidden under the leaves and pinch them off, flick them from her finger. She danced along the vegetables, stepped from row to row, a good neighbour.

Tom watched her sleep. It wasn't what he'd come for. He tried not to think about crawling into the warmth he knew she made, in any bed, or about offering up, just one more time, the conviction of his need. He tried not to think about her arms around him, or her legs. He muttered the word "bitch," once, hardly meaning it. If she heard, she didn't respond.

He settled into the chair and waited, unwitnessed, cold and sharply awake, wondering what earthly goddamned good it did, this celibate watching through the night. Toward daybreak he heard her speak several disjointed words from a very deep sleep. One of the words sounded impossibly like turnip.

LYNN COADY

Play the Monster Blind

Drinking

The father was drinking again, in celebration. John said it bothered him. He remembered being three, tooling around town in the green station wagon with fake wood on the sides, watching his father drink. He would drink and visit his friends, at their homes or at the boxing club. He would pull into the driveway, pause to smile at John, take a quick couple of swallows before reaching over to unbuckle the boy. And he would hoist his young son inside to show him off, both of them pink-cheeked. He showed her a picture of himself then, his little hands tied inside of a pair of enormous boxing gloves, his father perched behind him, holding them up to take aim at a smiling, sweaty man in trunks.

John was strapping then, and he was strapping now. One of the first things the father told her was that they used to have to pin John into three layers of diapers, he was such a big eater. It was obvious the old man and he were close. The second evening after she and John arrived, she stayed inside doing dishes with the mother, and saw the two of them sitting out in plastic chairs on the lawn, facing the shed with rums in hand. The mother said, "That should keep him happy for a while," and the plastic chairs sagged and quivered from the weight of men. The father was built all of hard, stubborn fat, but John was just big. They sat quietly torturing their lawn chairs together.

He told her he used to be fat. He was very sensitive about it. He told her he had never told that to anyone. In high school he stopped eating and started taking handfuls of vitamins, which made him thin and absent-minded, but his mother stopped buying them and he had no choice but to go back to eating. In university he just gave in to everything and ate and drank until he ballooned. Now he was approximately in the middle, a big man with a thick beard. When he was fourteen, his father had him collecting UI for all the dishwashing he had done at the family restaurant, because the workers didn't know any better from the size of him. She had thought, when she met John, that he looked like a lumberjack. He wore plaid shirts and work boots whenever she saw him in class, not because it was fashionable, and not fashionably, but because it was what he wore. She learned where he was from and imagined they all must dress like that, that it must be a very welcoming place, rustic and simple and safe, like John himself.

When his sister showed up, pasty and in leather pants despite the August swelter, the first thing she said to him was, "Hey, you fat shit." Bethany knew that they had not seen each other in a couple of years. He reached over and grabbed one of the sister's wrists. Her knees buckled at once and effortlessly he turned her around, already sinking. Then he grabbed the other wrist and held them together in one large paw while guiding her face-first to the kitchen floor, using her wrists as a sort of steering apparatus. Then he sat on her.

"Pardon?" he kept saying.

"You fat bastard."

The father sat nearby, laughing. The mother saying, "Johnny, Johnny, Johnny," now, as she tried to move around them to the stove. Bethany and the sister were exactly the same age. She felt she should have something to say to her.

When the brother arrived, he at once began to beat and contort the sister in the same way, as if this were some sort of family ritual. She railed at him as he pulled her feet up behind her to meet her shoulders. Whereas John just used the sheer force of his bulk and his size, Hugh, smaller and wiry, was a dabbler in the martial arts. He said he used to box, like his father, but got bored with all the rules. Now he was interested in something called "shoot fighting," which scarcely had any rules at all. He knew all sorts of different holds and manoeuvres, some of which he demonstrated on the sister for them. When he was finished—Ann yanking herself away, red-faced and hair awry and staggering towards the kitchen for a beer—he darted at John, head down and fists up. John responded in the way she had seen him do at bars whenever drunken men, maddened by his size, ran at him. The strategy was to reach out his big hands and simply hold the opponents at bay until they got tired and embarrassed.

Bethany thought of herself as an easygoing person and tried not to be nervous, but she and John were going to get married, and she knew that the family was striving to be civil in a way they were not used to. John kept cuffing his sister in the head whenever she said "goddamn" or "cocksucker," and quietly stating, "Dad," when the father did the same. Bethany and the sister tried and tried to talk to each other, bringing up woman-things like belts and shampoo. She knew that the sister worked in theatre in Halifax and lived with a man who was thirty-five, and everyone was disappointed in her, but hoped she would soon turn her life around. It was touching the way the family spoke of Ann when she was out of the room. The father, overwhelming his armchair, ponderously clinking his ice cubes and turning to John.

"What do you think, me boy?"

"Well, who knows, boy."

"She's getting by," the mother would say.

"But for how long?"

"We'll talk to her at some point," John promised, this being what the father was waiting to hear. The father was always turning to John and waiting to hear the right thing, and John always seemed to know what it was.

The father didn't ask the other son to talk to the sister, and Hugh didn't seem interested in doing it anyway. Hugh and Ann presented themselves as allies, of sorts, against John's authority, even though they fought with one another more furiously than they did with him. They

rolled around the living room, knocking over lamps and bothering the
mother's nerves, as she complained from the kitchen, and John would
come in and bark at them to smarten up. They would call him a big
fat fruit and he would sit on them both, the sister on the very bottom
of the pile. At one point she looked up at Bethany, blood vessels
throbbing to burst in her face, and squeaked, "Can't you control
him?" Which Bethany lightly laughed at.

When the parents went to bed, the four of them sat around the table
drinking rum. She had never had so much rum in her life. She
normally liked spritzers, which John said were for pussies. John tried to
talk to his brother and sister seriously about the father. How the drinking bothered him.

"It keeps him in good cheer," said Ann.

"You two don't remember how he used to get. I remember how he
used to get."

"Maybe he's too old to get that way now."

"It bothers Mum's nerves."

"I think he's been dandy," said Ann.

"Just because he's not yelling at you all the time doesn't necessarily
make it fine and dandy."

"I disagree," said Ann.

Hugh said nothing, waiting for the conversation to turn to sports or
parties. Bethany noticed how jolly Ann looked when she said she
disagreed with John. She thought, once or twice, that John might grab
his sister's head and slam it into the table a couple of times. Ann looked
capable of disagreeing with John in her sleep.

Hugh never seemed to bother getting into a conversation with his
brother. He merely lurked in corners, behind chairs, waiting for an
opportunity to get him in a paralyser hold, but John would always
shrug him off like a summer jacket. Hugh showed some of his holds to
Ann, who in turn tried them out on her mother, but the mother
complained loudly about her arthritis whenever this occurred.

"Hugh said they're not supposed to hurt—they just immobilize,"
the sister protested, chin digging into the mother's head.

"Well, they do. Get away before I clout you."

Ann released her mother with much reluctance, sorry to lose the fleeting power. The mother had just stood there politely the whole time. She probably could have broken out of it if she wanted to. Like everyone else in the family, the mother was bigger than Ann.

Ann wore combat boots with her sundress. The father made fun of them, and the mother wanted to know if her feet didn't get overheated. Bethany felt sorry for Ann, because when they all were sitting around the picnic table eating lobster, Ann couldn't open hers but she wouldn't ask any of them for help. Bethany finally passed her a cracking utensil under the table.

"I never used to eat lobster until last year," Ann explained. "It grossed me out. Then I decided I want to be the kind of person who'll eat anything she's given."

"She won't eat the pickled alewives," said the father through a mouthful of roe.

"Don't count as food," said Ann, sullen. Hugh was sneaking up behind her with a lobster that had not yet been boiled alive.

Boxing

They would pick up the uncle and the bunch of them, some in the father's car and some in John's, were going to tour around the trail, staying in cabins and eating in restaurants and swimming at beaches. This was the father's gift. John told her that doing it was important to him and she would have to have fun. She was surprised he would put it this way, because she was looking forward to seeing the island. She was worried about being in the car with the father, however. At the airport after they arrived, he made them stop at the duty-free liquor store and purchased an armload of tiny bottles of Crown Royal. Once they were in the car, he handed one to each of them and said, "Slug 'er back, you two. The vacation has officially begun." Bethany had never drunk straight whisky in her life and had no idea how to properly respond. She looked at John for help and he took it from her and dropped it into her purse.

"Can't be into this on the road, boy," he said, smiling and blinking ahead of him.

"Ach, I'd need fifty or so of these before anything good started happenin."

"Let me drive, boy."

"No, we can't have you drinkin and drivin."

"I don't need to drink."

After scant argument, the father declared, "Betty, it's just you and me!" turning around in his seat to beam at her. "My God," he added, "did you down yours already? Well, good boy, yourself."

So the father sat in the back seat with her the whole way, making jokes that John was their chauffeur and kicking his seat and telling him to step on it while Bethany watched the innumerable veins road-mapping his nose and cheeks begin to glow as if filling up with lava. She was terrified of everything. They were on a stretch of road where one sign after another read things like: JESUS IS COMING! PREPARE THYSELF! REPENT! SAITH THE LORD.

All the way to the house, he told her about boxing. He rhymed off one boxer after another, not famous boxers like Muhammad Ali but ones from, as he said, "nearby." Men with names like Sailor Dave and Fisher MacPhee and Ronnie the Dago. He said he had met more than a few of these fellows in the ring, and could tell her something about the style of each if she was interested. The Dago, for example, was a smart fighter, a thinking fighter. Always went in with some kind of strategy. Archie the Rigger, however, had nothing going for him but a hard head and had the record to prove it. Fisher was the prettiest of fighters, floated on air. Sailor Dave was like a goddamned bull, just an ox. The father went on and on in this vein. He handed one little bottle after another to her so that when they finally got out of the car her purse clinked and sloshed.

"Johnny," the old man pronounced, holding the kitchen door open for her, "this is a goddamned good girl right here." He went to bed almost at once, and so they sat up and had cornflakes with the mother.

THE SISTER very much admired Bethany's luggage as they loaded up the car. She marvelled at it, it was so nice, so much that Bethany was embarrassed. John intuited this and kept making jokes that some people had moved beyond Glad bags and cardboard.

"It would never even *occur* to me to have bags like that," the sister persisted, and finally John told her to shut the hell up and she told him to kiss her rosy red arse and he strode over to her and picked her up and placed her, barely able to squirm, in the trunk of the car and then held the hood down, not completely closed, until Bethany told him, for Pete's sake, to let her out of there, and Ann, who throughout the performance had not made a sound, flung one bare leg out and then the other and hopped away like a crow. Hugh stood by looking pensive, as if he wished he had thought of it first.

Hugh himself was a strange one, because, although he had gone to university, he spoke with an insanely nuanced accent that was nothing like the rest of the family's, and every second thing he said had something or another to do with his hole, and he wore an Expos cap just perched on the top of his head, but when she asked him what he did for a living, he replied that when he was not "partying his hole out," he worked with computers. Bethany asked John about it later on and he said, "Oh, yah. He's the brain. Straight A's. Could have done anything he wanted." What he chose to do was teach courses at the vocational school and help people around town with their systems. He didn't go anywhere after university because, he said, all his friends were here. "Friends're pack a retards," John once remarked. And after a few days Bethany began to realize that Hugh didn't own any shirts except T-shirts with sayings on them. He sat around in T-shirts that said things like: I'D RATHER PUSH A FORD THAN DRIVE A CHEVY and IT'S NOT HOW DEEP YOU FISH, IT'S HOW YOU WIGGLE YOUR WORM!

After the mother, the uncle was the one she felt most comfortable with. They picked him up at a group home where he stayed in Port Hastings the night before the trip. Bethany knew in advance that he was Mentally Handicapped, and having this foreknowledge made her calm about meeting him, far less nervous than she had been about the rest. It was good to have a label, something her mind could scrutinize. It was good to have an idea what to expect.

Lachie was his name, and she found him delightful. He reached out one hand and wished her Merry Christmas as she shook it, and then he extended the other to wish her Happy Easter. He puttered away, then, announcing, "There now! He knows Betty!" to all present. For the rest of the evening he sat in a chair in the corner of the living room and raised his eyes every once in a while to ask if it was time for corn-flakes. Bethany felt at home in the chair beside him. Now and again he would show her the fingers of his right hand to let her know that he'd been nibbling at the nails. Apparently this was a great pastime of his, much frowned upon by the rest of the family, and he seemed to enjoy the disapproval it provoked.

"Breaks his nails," he remarked more than once.

"Tch. Isn't that terrible," Bethany answered.

Lachie would smile back and reach over quickly to poke her in the cheek with a ragged fingertip before reclining again.

"You kick his arse if you catch him at that!" the sister yelled from across the room, the uncle plunging both hands into the tucks of his armchair and closing his eyes.

The uncle was the fattest. John said that his grandmother had spoiled him from birth, heaping his plate and feeding him entire pies, and Lachie had never done anything but follow a few cows around on the farm for exercise. Now he had arthritis in his knees, and he could hardly walk around any more. The fat hung off Lachie in an unpleas-ant sort of way, like it wasn't quite a part of him, something that had to be strapped on in the morning. John said that was how *he* would be if he let himself go, how would she like that? He said it was in the genes. He constantly had to be working against it.

"Your sister's a bone rack," Bethany pointed out, "and she looks more like your uncle than you do."

"She had the anorexia all through high school," John explained, dismissive and also somewhat grudging. "Sees the nutritionist once a week."

"All she talks about is eating," Bethany said.

"I know."

"What about Hugh?"

"Works out every day," John said with a bit of contempt, because anyone could see this with one look at the chest beneath the T-shirt slogans.

AT THE DINNER TABLE the father congratulated Bethany for her fine appetite, unaware that she was only eating so much because he kept insisting more be offered to her and she was afraid of offending him.

"Get Betty some more potatoes, Annie. Jesus Christ, she's wasting before our eyes."

"Do you want more potatoes, Betsy?"

"Ummm ... sure."

"She doesn't want any more, Dad."

"She just said she did, for the love of God!"

"Quit forcing food down the woman's throat."

"Well, Jesus Christ, I'll get her the potatoes if you're not up to the challenge," said the father, practically spreading himself across the table.

"No, no, no! I can get them for myself!" Bethany exclaimed, horror-struck.

"There now," the father said, emptying a greyish, steaming mound out of a Corningware dish and onto her plate. "Some of us know how to be civil to a guest."

"You're making her sick," said Ann.

Bethany was a big eater most of the time, however, and only went to bed in slight discomfort, having eschewed the evening's cornflake ritual. She asked John if he thought she needed to lose weight and he said who gave a shit one way or another. He would not have asked her to marry him if he thought she was a tub of lard. It was being around Ann and the mother that made her feel that way. The mother said having her "nerves on the go" all the time was what kept her skinny, and Ann, meal-obsessed, hopped about the kitchen a pale crow, swallowing the occasional fastidiously selected morsel. John had said that he and Hugh had teased her about being fat all throughout their childhood but had to stop once she decided to forgo eating altogether, and felt guilty for the rest of their lives. Now John would wrap a hand around one of her thighs whenever she passed by and squeeze, feeling for meat. "Get in the kitchen and eat a tub of ice cream or something, ya stick," he'd say, thinking he was being kind. And the sister Ann would smile at her brother as if she were thinking it too.

Swimming

Lachie couldn't get his clothes off fast enough. Scarcely had she put the picnic cooler down than his shirt was in a heap on the sand and rolls of white flesh sprouting the coarsest of black hairs gave salute to the sun and the ocean. The effect of the sight of so much exposed skin caused her to reach instinctively for a bottle of sunscreen. She tried to hand it to him, but the uncle was busy unbuckling his pants and muttered, "No, you put it on me. He can't get his pants, can't get them." She waited a moment to see if any of the family would come down the path before finally squirting a little onto her fingertips and trying to apply some to Uncle Lachie's shoulders, but he had the pants around his ankles and staggered out of her reach a second later. Then he regained himself, muttering about the ocean, and, in his haste, yanked off his swimming trunks on top of everything else. Bethany was not so embarrassed as to be unable to imagine her embarrassment if someone other than John came down the path at that moment, so she said calmly to the uncle, "Put on your trunks, Uncle Lachie. You need to put your trunks back on."

Lachie was irritated at anything keeping him from the sea at that point and protested vigorously for a good minute or so as Bethany stood there beside him, trying to come up with a persuasive argument. She thought it strange that he would argue so much and yet not actually defy her outright, trundling away, a white blur against the blue sky like a walking snowman. Finally she just said, "You can't go *swimming* without your *swim* trunks, Uncle Lachie," like it was the most logical thing in the world, and he gazed meditatively down at the shorts for a bit before hauling them back up about his hips and plunging towards the Atlantic. Bethany thought this a profound triumph and almost wished there had been someone around to witness the crisis, and her unexpected competence. At that moment, Ann appeared. Struggling with a cooler and in a polka-dot bathing suit with moulded bra-cups that must have belonged to the mother in 1968. She lingered beside Bethany for the briefest of moments before taking in the sight of Lachie. White like a plump cloud had fallen directly out of the sky and now bobbing free and independent with the waves.

"Lord lifting Antichrist, he'll fry like a pork rind!" she hollered, seizing the sunscreen out of Bethany's hand and giving chase. Bethany could see that he was seated up to his belly now, and seemed to be looking down at the point where the water divided him up.

Eating

The father drank too much at dinner and made the waitress cry. She wouldn't come back to the table and John had to get up and walk across the restaurant and talk to her and talk to the manager. She watched him standing there with them, grinning under his beard, gesturing in an open and accepting sort of way with his enormous hands. The girl was being charmed by him and the manager was being charmed by him in a different manner. She knew how he was charming the waitress, because she had been charmed like that too. How a big man like that could grin so open-handed and vulnerable. He could take your head between those two hands and pop it like a zit, but he was decent enough not to do that, not to even remind you that he could. He smiled, instead, and cajoled. He had no interest in bullying you—the easiest thing in the world for him to do. Everything about his demeanour said: *I am just a great big guy with a drunk dad and a new fiancée and nobody wants to feel like this, so let's not.* It was brave of him. It was exactly what made him so good.

Pretty soon the girl was laughing with tears still in her eyes and John was laughing and picking her up from the ground with a bear hug which made her shriek and laugh even harder. She could not have been more than seventeen, and was in love now. He sauntered back to the table, his mouth pursed in a comical sort of way.

"A little thing out there called PR," he said to his pink, smirking father.

"A little fucking thing called incompetence in the work force," the dad shot back. "If one of my girls had ever pulled any of that kind of shit back when I was running the Bluenoser ..."

"Boy, boy," said John. "Jeez, eh?" He went on making inarticulate noises of comfort and reprimand. The father made noises of declining outrage and increasing shame, as his awareness of the situation grew. But she could see that he wasn't going to acknowledge it, blustering about incompetence all throughout dessert and, while waiting for the bill, about teenager girls with earrings in their noses instead of their ears where God intended them. Blustering all the while but now drinking out of his water glass instead of the other one that was poised beside the wreckage of his meal. Bethany could tell he hoped to bluster until he was blustering on a different topic, one that made everyone more comfortable and jovial. Blustering wittily and cheerfully, no longer blustering at all—a benevolent father regaling the family with priceless and innumerable anecdotes from a rich and varied life.

THE SISTER PUKED for what seemed like hours. Bethany in an agony because she thought she should go and see if she was sick, but on the other hand, John had said she used to be anorexic, and she knew that this was what anorexics sometimes did after big meals. It was an impossible situation. It was almost dawn, and she and John and the sister had made a deal—that Bethany would sleep with John for a little before slipping through the bathroom that joined their rooms and crawling into Ann's bed. This being the arrangement the parents would be expecting when they arrived from the other cabin to make breakfast.

But now it was getting light and Ann was still in there, puking away, and Bethany was in an impossible situation. John snored.

Lying there angry, it took her a couple of seconds to realize that the retching echoes from the bathroom had ceased. The bedroom was now almost fully illuminated, and she flung the blankets away, fully awake, deciding she didn't care if Ann knew she had heard her puking or not. When Bethany didn't get a good night's sleep, it did terrible things to her body. It gave her indigestion, made her cranky and intolerant, red-eyed and snippy. She had to catch a good couple of hours in Ann's bed before the parents stormed in wanting to take pictures and see them splashing around in canoes.

"Ugh," said Ann as Bethany crawled in beside her.

"Are you okay?"

"The *dreams* I was having!"

Bethany licked her lips. She wasn't going to pretend she was stupid. "But you were throwing up, Ann."

"Before I was throwing up," she said. "Sick dreams. It has to have been the scallops. Sometimes my stomach doesn't welcome the shellfish."

"Hm," said Bethany, in a way she hoped sounded as if the explanation had been accepted and the incident forgotten about in almost the same moment.

"Ohg," moaned Ann some moments later. "Did you ever dream that you were *where you were?*"

"I don't know what you mean," Bethany said around a yawn.

"You're not supposed to dream about being where you are. It's not natural. I'm not supposed to be dreaming about being in this cabin with all of you. In my grandmother's house. Or in school, or in Halifax or something, or somewhere I've never even been. Nobody dreams literally, for Christ's sake."

"What were we doing?"

"Oh God, it was horrible. We were just doing all the things we've been doing all along."

She was snoring not five seconds later.

Driving

They drove another few miles, on their way to still more rented cottages. The father made a point of repeating all through breakfast he hoped these would be more amenable than the ones they had spent the previous night in.

"No TV, no radio," he kept saying. "Nothing but four walls and a goddamn bed. I can haul a cot into the closet at home, if that's what I want. Charge people fifty bucks a night to use it."

"It's a *cabin,* boy," John said. "You're supposed to sit on the porch and watch the sunset. What do you need a TV for?"

"It's the principle of the thing. What if it rains? What if there's a ball game? Beds not fit to piss on—I can see plain as day that poor Betty didn't get a moment's sleep. I should have complained. I should have complained at that goddamn restaurant, and I should've complained the moment we showed up here. Reservations two jeezly months in advance and this is the best they can give us."

"You *did* complain at the restaurant," Ann reminded him, looking around to confirm that no one else was going to do it. "Don't you remember?"

"To the manager, not to that young one. Poor girl didn't know what I was talking about."

"You might have thought about that before you called her a useless twat."

"Well, goddamnit, I was mad!"

"Leave it now, Ann," said John. Bethany was beginning to see that this was the way they commenced most mornings. John saw her understanding this.

"All I wanted," rumbled the father, "was a good dry chip. That's all I wanted. What do they bring me? *Potato wedges!* What the Jesus? Greasy old potato wedges with some kind of crap sprinkled all over them. That's not chips. I asked for chips. I just wanted a *good dry chip!* Not that gourmet crap swimming in Christ knows what."

"Well, it's done with now."

"Well, I'm not letting them get away with that shit."

"Good, then, boy."

"You have to let them know, Johnny. You can't just let them keep on with that kind of shoddy service."

"All right."

"You have to remind them—I'm the customer. I'm payin' your salary. You need me. I don't need you." The father seemed to whisper to himself for an instant as if imagining some outlandish response, and then turned to Bethany and smiled suddenly. "You just ignore me, Betty," he said. "John here's the family dip-lo-mat. We'd get kicked outta where-all we went if the dip-lo-mat wasn't around."

"I guess to God," said John.

"I'm just an old boxer," said the father, manoeuvring his bulk from the confines of their picnic table. "I hit people. Don't take mucha the dip-lo-mat for that," he chuckled, moving off to examine the work-manship of the cabin's front step. Intermittently they heard quiet excla-mations of disgust from his direction as they cleared away the breakfast things.

He wanted John and Bethany to ride with him to Dingwall because he felt as if he wasn't spending enough time with them. He told the mother to take the car with the other two. The mother announced that she would have to drive, then, because Hugh was a maniac and Ann had always been too stubborn to learn, and they couldn't expect her to go for very long because her nerves were bad. The three of them chewed at each other for a bit, but Bethany got the feeling that they were pleased to have been thrown together—a day off from the father's gruff bullying and the more genuine authority of John. Lachie was content to ride with herself and John and the father, however, because he didn't care either way. They were taking John's Escort, and that was the one he had climbed into immediately after breakfast, and so that was the car he was going in.

"Come on, come on, come on," he kept saying, watching them load the baggage. "Ding-Dong. Going Ding-Dong now."

They stopped at a lookout point, and Bethany climbed out of the car before the rest. In every direction she turned, she could see nothing but dark, fuzzy mountains. The ever-present ocean was nowhere in sight, and it disoriented her. She didn't know if this was beautiful or not. The green mounds sloped upward uninsistently, and then came together in dark, obscene valleys that reminded her of the creases in a woman's flesh—her own. Reminded her of sitting naked and looking down at the spot where her stomach protruded slightly over her thighs. She didn't like how these low mountains were everywhere, their dark rolling motion completely uninterrupted by a view of water, or patches of field. John suddenly moved past her and jumped up onto the wooden railing, framing himself against them.

"Get down. John, get down. Get down now," she said.

"What? Take my picture!"

"Get down," she hissed, queasy at the sight of him poised there, ready to disappear into one of the dark creases. Meanwhile, Lachie refused to get out of the car to look. She could hear the father's persistent cursing as he tried to yank him by the hand, then coming around to the other side of the car and trying to shove him out the opposite door. Lachie remained where he was, however, unmoved and only a little irritated with the father's proddings. All he wanted to do was go, to drive in the car. "Come on, come on, come on," he said, and, "No, no, no." With their arms around each other, Bethany and John watched him easily resist the father. Bethany was thinking that John could probably go over there and lift him out, but she hoped that he wouldn't. By this time the father was laughing with frustration. He said that they were going to stay there and see the view and Lachie could drive the friggin' car to Ding-Dong all by himself, if he wanted to go so badly.

The rest of the trip, the father told her the story of Archie "Fisher" Dale, a fine boxer he knew out of the Miramichi, "who some people called Tiny because he was such a little fella, in fact his manager had wanted to bill him as Tiny Dale, but Archie would have none of it. In actual fact, he wasn't all that small—five-six—but smaller than what you'd usually see hanging out at the boxing clubs and whathaveyou. Well this one—you wouldn't find yourself taking him too-too seriously to look at him, I mean, some of the fellas you'd see at those places were like Johnny here, great big bastards, and a lot of them figured they could fight simply by virtue of the fact that they were bigger than anybody else. But that's not always the case, you know, and there's nothing more pathetic than seeing some big lumbering bastard getting all tangled up in his own legs trying to keep up with some little lightning rod like Fisher himself who lands you a good right cross before you even see him in front of you."

Because, besides height and mass, this little fella had it all. John's father had never seen a fighter so well equipped for greatness. He fought single-mindedly. He often appeared vicious, but he never actually got angry—to get angry at your opponent was just foolishness, the quickest way to spot an amateur. He was fast, he was graceful, he had arms like steel cords lashed together, but for all that grace he was *tough*. You could just *hit* him. He didn't care. John's father and Fisher Dale would go drinking downtown in Halifax, and after downing a few, the little prick would just grin at him with his gap-filled mouth and say, "Hit me, John Neil. Hit me a good one, now." Well, John's father was never one to oblige in this respect, but there would always be one or two fellas nearby just chompin' at the bit to take a poke at Fisher Dale. You couldn't drop him. You just could not drop him. He'd weave and teeter, blood pouring out of his mouth, and, by Jesus, that grin would never leave his face. "Hit me again, why don'tcha?" was all he'd say.

"What would he do that for?" Bethany asked, genuinely mystified.

"Because," John's father told her with very precise enunciation to give the statement weight, "Fisher was crazy as mine and your arse put together. Everywhere except the ring. He was Albert Jesus Jesus Einstein in the ring. The drinking, you know. What it does to some people. Archie Dale was such a one."

"This is the saddest story I know," the father reflected, after having paused for some time. "Now that I think of it. What that boy couldn't have done. And he was one of the hardest working in them days too.

The stamina. Fight in Halifax one night, under one name, hop on the train right after for one in Yarmouth or somewhere, callin' himself Wildman Dale or some such thing. You could only fight a certain number of matches in them days if you wanted to keep your licence, but the more ambitious and greedy of the bunch—Dale was both— would just hop from town to town, fighting under different names. Sometimes he'd go ten, fifteen fights a week. Outlandish, if you knew anything about the circuit. I could never go more than five.

"You know, the only time he had the boozin' under control was when he was fighting that way—hopping from town to town, some- times going two a night. Kept him busy, kept him focused. See, he wasn't the type a fella could just fight a couple times a week, and then head down to the tavern for a couple of beers with his buddies, waiting for his manager to call about the next one. It was all or nothing with Dale. That was his problem right there. If he stopped fighting, he started drinking, it had to be one or the other. Manager shoulda just kept putting him up against one guy after another till he dropped dead of a brain clot—least he wouldn't've ended up a drunken failure."

"What happened?"

"What happened was that he got caught, they found out he was fighting illegally like that, and he got his licence suspended. And howls just went up all across the country, you know, with the gamblers and everything, because the boy was on a streak—he was winning every match he fought. He'd pounded me long ago, I don't mind telling you, not to mention pretty near every other fella on the circuit, and his manager was talking about taking him over to the States. "But that was that—suspension for a month."

"That's not so bad."

"Ach, no. Most boys'd take their winnings and go off on a tear. Well, that's what he meant to do at first, but, like I said, with Dale it was all or nothing. I went downtown with him the one night, we drank ourselves stupid, and the last I seen of him"—John's father began to heave and shake at this memory—"he was chasin' a cop down Gottingen Street at four in the morning. He was chasing the cop!

Somehow he got his nightstick away from him, and he was chasing him down the street, waving it around his head like a lasso! Cop hollerin to beat hell."

"So what happened to him?"

"*That* happened to him. Like I said, it was the last of him I seen. Never fought again, I can guarantee you that much. Disappeared into the night."

"You saw him again, Dad," John's voice came from the driver's seat. It was as if he were repeating something by rote.

"Oh, yes, wait now, I did see him again. Eight or so years later, in Inverness, of all places, walking home from a square dance. This little frigger in a trench coat shuffling towards me with great deliberation, you know. I didn't know who it was, some queer or something, I was getting ready to pop him. Well, isn't it Fisher Dale. 'John Neil!' he shouts. 'Whad'llya have?' Then he yanks something from the pocket of his trench coat"—the father began to act out the role of Fisher Dale, now. "'A little *puck* a whisky? Or'"—reaching into his other pocket with the opposite hand—"'a little *puck* a rum?'" The father shook and heaved and gasped. He repeated the gesture a couple of times for effect, the yanking of one bottle out of the right-hand pocket upon the word "puck," and then another from out of the left. It was like Lachie wishing her Merry Christmas and Happy Easter in succession.

"This is all he has to tell me after eight years," John's father finished, jovial and refreshed from the story's telling. "Ah—Jesus, though. Lord save us if it wasn't a shameful waste of a beautiful fighter. Just a beautiful little fighter."

John told her later that he told that story to everyone. It was his favourite story. She would hear it a hundred more times in the upcoming years, he said. In the meantime, the road rose and sunk like a sea serpent's tail. Every so often they would come around a craggy bend, after miles of nothing but the low, fuzzy mountains, and all of a sudden it would seem as if the whole of the Atlantic Ocean was glittering before them, so big it eclipsed even the sky. And then the road would sink lower and lower imperceptibly, until they were trundling through some infinitesimal community and she'd see grey, half-demolished barns with black letters spelling CLAMS painted across the roofs and little stores with Pepsi-Cola signs from the early seventies in the windows, the red in the logo faded to pink and the blue now a sick green. She went into one of them to get lemonade and ice-cream bars for everybody, and the woman behind the counter was not nearly as friendly as Bethany had been expecting. The woman had a little girl sitting with her back there, and every time the little girl did something other than just sit there the woman would bark, "Whad I tell ya? Whad I tell ya?" at her—oblivious to Bethany's presence—so the little girl would place her hands at her sides and arrange her legs and sit chewing on her lips until the fact of being a child got the better of her and she would once again reach for something with absent-minded curiosity. Then the woman would bark again.

"You've got a lovely place here," said Bethany, and the woman regarded her with terror. She thought Bethany was talking about the store, and not the island, and therefore must be insane. She added, "This is my first visit," to make it more clear. The woman looked down at the little girl, as if hoping to find her trespassing again so that she could yell at her and ignore Bethany. But the girl was being good, so the woman ignored Bethany anyway, a confused and queasy look taking over her ruddy, mean face. "Six sevenny-five, wha?" she said. Bethany gave her a five and a two, hoping she had understood correctly. She gathered up her ice-cream bars without asking for a bag and staggered out the door and into the sunshine, cowbells clunking rude music behind her.

Fighting

She ate barbecued bologna for the first time in her life. John was trying to convince her it was a delicacy of the area as he slathered Kraft sauce onto it, splattering the coals. She kept telling him in a low voice not to lie to her, to quit lying to her. She made her voice low because if he was telling the truth, she didn't want the rest of the family to know she hadn't believed it.

"Listen here," he kept saying. "You haven't *lived* until you've scarfed a good feed of barbecued bologna."

"Shut up," she said, giggling and looking around. "Liar." She saw that Ann was nearby, sprawled in a sun-chair and drinking a beer. She had probably heard everything, and so Bethany took a chance and looked seriously at her for confirmation. Ann smiled and raised her eyes to heaven. She turned back to John.

"I knew you were lying!"

"What?"

"Ann says you're lying."

"Ann's not gonna get her share of barbecued bologna."

"Quit teasing the woman," said Ann. "You're always teasing her. How long do you think she'll put up with it before she kicks your arse?"

Bethany smiled at Ann. They were getting somewhere. Most of the time the sister had seemed too high-strung to even talk to, but Ann had started taking long, slow draughts of beer early in the afternoon, and now her movements were easy and fluid—nothing of the crow remained. She had been in the sun-chair most of the afternoon, letting the sun burn it out of her, while the rest of them played badminton and lawn darts. Her smiles became slow and amused instead of fleeting and anguished. Bethany sat on the grass beside her every once in a while to drink a beer of her own and together they would holler insults at John about whatever he happened to be doing at that moment. Hugh came over and capsized the chair at one point, but Ann simply rolled away from it and fell asleep a few feet away in the grass.

They must have eaten the red, charred flesh of every beast imaginable that evening, and the lot of them sat exhausted in chairs they had each pulled up around Ann's chair as if she had become some sort of axis during the afternoon. The father's face was the same colour as the meat they'd consumed, and bloated, and he blinked constantly as if a breeze was blowing directly into his eyes. While Ann had relaxed herself with long, slow, sunny draughts of beer, the father had done the exact opposite—disappearing without a word at steady intervals throughout the day in order to shoot rum in the kitchenette, the imperative of it seeming to make him more and more anxious. She knew he was doing that, because she had stupidly kept asking, "Where's your father gotten to? Isn't it your father's turn? Where's your father?" until John finally had to tell her. He said this was the only way the father had ever learned to drink—like a teenager sneaking swigs at a dance. He'd never sipped a cocktail in his life, much less enjoyed a beer during a fishing trip or something. John said that his father had never understood the purpose of beer. He didn't see the *point* of an alcoholic beverage with so little alcohol in it. Why something should take so long to do what it was intended to do.

"He's an alcoholic," said Bethany, epiphanic. They were walking along the beach when he told her this.

"Oh Christ," John said, then, letting go of her hand. "You don't know much." It hurt her feelings but she didn't tell him.

On the path back to the cabin, they saw the father coming towards them. The sun had set moments before and their eyes were used to the dark, but the father's weren't. They saw him first, walking with great clomps, his arms stretched out in front of him like Boris Karloff in *Frankenstein*. Bethany remembered hearing that, in *Frankenstein*, Boris Karloff had stretched out his arms before him like that because the film-maker had at first wanted to have the monster be blind. They never followed up that aspect of the story, but they kept the footage of Lugosi playing the monster blind anyway, and that was why the enduring image of Frankenstein ended up being this clomping creature with his arms stuck out in front of him. The problem was that this was what John's father looked like, coming towards them—a frightened, blind monstrosity. John made a sound beside her, before speaking to him in a loud, fatherly voice. She almost thought she'd imagined that sound. It could have been mistaken for a brief intake of air which would have been necessary before speaking so loud to the father. But it hadn't been that.

"Jesus, Jesus, Jesus, boy!" was what John said. "You stumbling around looking for some place to take a piss or wha?" Bethany jumped at the "wha." High-strung like the lady at the store.

The father tittered, focused in on their dark outlines, and came forward, blustering jokes about getting lost in the raspberry bushes and their having to send in a search party for him in the morning. He had just wanted to walk with them on the beach, he said. Was he too late? Were they on their way back?

"We'll have another walk," said John.

"No, no. Betty's tired. Are you tired, Betty?"

"No, no." So they headed back to the beach.

She couldn't remember what he said. All she could think about was Boris Karloff clomping around confused and horrified, chucking a little girl into a pond. She pretended to be enthralled with the moon on the water. The truth was, the old man was incoherent. She could hear John mm-hmming in response to him. It seemed as if he had something very important to say, a zillion different things, none of which he could keep straight. He said that they were blessed. He said that they were lucky. He said that he would help them. He said that family was the only important thing. He kept saying that he was old, and that life could be difficult. He said wouldn't it be nice if people sometimes understood each other. Nobody had ever come close to understanding him in his godforsaken life. But at some point he'd decided that being understood wasn't as important as being good. So just because nobody gave a shit about him and had no respect for him and thought him a foolish old bastard—he'd decided that wasn't what was important.

"Boy, boy," John kept saying. "You need to get to bed."

At the cabin they shared with the brother and sister, they found the same two locked in violent combat, the worst Bethany had seen so far. The two of them laughed hysterically throughout, Hugh with a giddy and unrelenting "Huhn! Huhn! Huhn!" and Ann with an ongoing, high-pitched shriek. John was not in the mood for it. There was a broken glass on the floor and a lamp on its side. Hugh was trying to manoeuvre Ann into one of his paralyser holds, but Ann was resisting heroically. Bethany had never seen her quite so nimble—just as he managed to position his arm about her throat, or somewhere equally critical, she would slither away as though greased. "I've uncovered the secret!" she kept shrieking when she could speak. "I've uncovered the secret!" And Hugh would gasp, "Shut up! No you haven't! Shut up! No you haven't!"—so that for an instant Bethany thought there must be some hideous secret about Hugh that Ann was threatening to reveal. But Hugh was laughing too hard for it to be that. He seemed to be hysterical with disbelief that Ann was suddenly able to wrench herself out of his every grip.

"Settle the fuck down!" John was shouting.

"You just move …" Ann sputtered, near to the point of being too winded to speak, "where *he* moves …" She dove around her brother and jabbed a fist into his solar plexus, Hugh howling pain and laughter. "You just move"—she threw her hands into the air and brought them down onto his ears—"*with* the hold! You move *with* the hold!"

"Shut up!" Hugh roared, holding his ears as if he couldn't stand to hear it. Giggling and panting, she scrambled for a phone book to defend herself from his next onslaught. John stepped forward and wrenched it out of her hands and hit his stampeding brother with it himself, which stopped both his laughter and his forward momentum at exactly the same time. Ann flew across the room, but might have caught her balance if not for staggering against an end table, which propelled her, arms like windmills, into Bethany, who caught an elbow in the mouth.

All night she lay wriggling the tooth with her tongue, tasting for blood. Everyone was deeply upset with Ann, but Bethany didn't care. She could hear them in the next room yelling at each other. She could hear Ann crying like one betrayed and broken-hearted. Tomorrow, Bethany thought, she would have to go up to her and assure her that she was all right, that it wasn't her fault and all that. But she didn't feel like doing it at the moment. Hugh had given her a 222 that he had been carrying around from the time he sprained his wrist, and now the pain had transformed itself into torpor. But she didn't feel as if she could sleep. She wanted to just lie, in the dark, away from the bunch of them.

Ann kept whining that it wasn't fair, Bethany could hear her.

Whining and sobbing. "Just because you guys can beat up on anybody you want without actually hurting them!" she was saying. Then John crawled into bed and issued almost a formal apology.

"Everybody's fuckin' drunk," he sighed afterwards.

"I know."

"Well, again, I'm sorry."

"Again, it's all right."

She could feel him picking up a handful of her hair and pressing it into the centre of his face.

"I'm lucky to have you," he said. "I don't tell you that enough— I know it."

Bethany wriggled her tooth and felt pleasure at the sudden bit of power. She smiled involuntarily, separating her split bottom lip and receiving a thread of pain. Perhaps she would be mad. Refuse to say another word. Keep him up all night with worry, her very need for him in question.

Reunion

I squirmed in the back seat, the 1975 high school yearbook open on my knees. The evening heat was syrupy and unfamiliar. I studied the back of Jane's tidy perm, but she was as impassive as always, untouched by temperature, while Winnie, who had gained considerable weight since high school, seemed to relish the sticky air. Although there was a brush of moisture along her hairline and her blue checkered dress pinched her tightly at the armpits, she was settled behind the wheel as though she had grown there, occupying that small space in the world as would a luxurious plant.

I was astonished by their matter-of-fact manner, their apparent lack of self-loathing; surely they were having second thoughts, as I was, en route to our twentieth high school reunion?

"I wish I wasn't here."

Jane turned and looked at me steadily, frowning. "You need to come out of the north more often, Yvonne," she declared. For two decades, *the north* had been Jane's way of referring to my home in Canada.

"No, what she needs is a drink," Winnie said. "Or a smoke," she added, rummaging through her handbag until she shook out a needle-thin joint, which she held aloft.

"That would destroy me," I said, peeved. Winnie didn't know me at all.

"How about one of these?" Jane asked, producing a roll of sugar-free breath-savers. Jane had grown so thin in anticipation of this event she nearly rattled. I thought enviously of her two children at home not far from here, rapt before the television.

I was suddenly annoyed with the extremes of both these women. They seemed to leave me in a no man's land of average weight and identity. And now they wanted to get me high and freshen my breath.

"I'd only think about Rudy, if I smoked that," I said.

There was a short silence before Jane asked, "How is he?"

"He's fine. He could be dead."

Jane turned and looked me over. "You look great."

"Sure," I said, because great was not how I looked. The dress I wore was an old Indian print, faded and tawdry; it could easily have passed for something salvaged from high school days. I picked up the yearbook and began to flip through it. Twenty years ago the three of us had been as satiny and resolute as marble, but unfinished, barely distinguishable from one another.

"Here's Teddy Lawson," I said, my finger pressed over the face of a boy with fine yellow hair scraggly on his neck in the fashion of the mid-seventies. "You know what he did to me in fifth grade? He stuck his finger in my ass."

Winnie gagged on her breath-saver and Jane's head shook as she laughed silently, which comforted me; sometimes it was hard to get a laugh out of Jane.

Winnie pounded her chest. "There's a nice walk down memory lane."

Jane handed the flask to me, insisting, "You really do look great." I stared at her until I understood.

"You too, Jane."

"Well—"

"I thought Teddy Lawson went to prep school," I said, looking back down at a boy the memory of whom I had managed to keep with me for over twenty years.

"You're right, he did," Jane said.

"So what's he doing in our graduating class?"

"Who was Teddy Lawson?"

"Winnie, you never remember anything," Jane said. "Ted Lawson's mother was from Denmark or Florida or somewhere. She lived in her bikini in one of the houses on the point. His father was not so nice."

"A mean bastard," suggested Winnie, who knew nothing about it.

"I'm not surprised he stuck his hand up Yvonne," Jane said and we laughed again.

"Show me his photo," Winnie demanded and I leaned over the seat with the book. "Looks harmless."

"Apparently not to Yvonne," Jane said.

"It was fifth grade," I reminded them.

Winnie turned into the parking lot. We sat in the dark with the windows up, despite the heat, and sipped on the flask. Cars were pulling in and couples getting out. We didn't recognize anyone.

"Are we the only ones without our spouses?" Winnie asked.

Jane sighed. "Makes you wonder."

"It never occurred to me," I said.

"Me either," Winnie said.

"Though someone had to stay home with Rudy," I added, but I said this gently because I no longer wanted to make this evening a failure.

"Let's go in," Jane said.

Inside the club the air was cold, the air conditioning presumably on bust. There was only a scattering of fluorescent lights overhead; it took me a moment to make out the swarms of unfamiliar faces. There was a bar at the far end and against one wall several tables had been pushed. Winnie and I took a seat while Jane bought drinks.

"You can't sit," Jane whispered when she returned. "You're being ignored."

She was right. There were few people sitting. Most were standing, mingling, catching up, and no one was approaching our table.

"I'm not standing," Winnie said loudly. "Not until they bring out some food."

I looked around. More than half the men were bald, paunchy; they seemed to have fared significantly less well than the women, the majority of whom wore spare dresses that nicely revealed tanned athletic limbs. I was willing to bet that most of these women weighed less now than they had twenty years ago. With the exception of Winnie, of course, but also of me.

"This is a nightmare," I said, and Jane gave me one of her looks as she rose, promising, "I'll be right back."

"This isn't so bad, Yvonne," Winnie assured me. "Who are all these people, anyway?"

"I hated high school," I said. "I hated everyone, everyone hated me."

Winnie laughed. "What about me and Jane?"

I stared at Winnie. "You and I weren't friends."

She stared back. "I thought we were."

"No, Winnie we were not," I told her, too overcome by my desire to flee to remind her that for the most part our relationship had been one of competition for Jane.

"I thought we hung out together," Winnie said.

I was smiling at her, trying to think of something to say, when I noticed a man moving rapidly towards me. He slid across the floor and landed kneeling at my side. "Yvonne," he said.

I glanced at Winnie but she shrugged massively. The man had tea-brown hair cut in a military style and his skin had a peeled-away look, scabrous with the remains of either bad acne or some kind of combat involving small knives. I looked down where his open collar revealed the upper reaches of what must have been quite a nest of chest hair. I thought of Jane's expression, *coming out of the north,* and felt unequal to the chit-chat required of me.

I shook my head apologetically. I didn't know him.

"Teddy Lawson," he said, less breezily, but putting his hand out for mine.

"Did you graduate with us?" I asked, puzzled; despite the clear evidence in the yearbook that he had attended graduation, I still believed Teddy Lawson had gone away to school.

He gave me a stern look. In that moment before he stood and walked away, I realized I had made a mistake.

"That's not Teddy Lawson," I tried to tell Winnie, who was laughing at me. "Look how long his legs are!"

"He grew."

"I thought he was sent to prep school," I persisted. "Where's Jane?"

"She's mingling."

I glanced around. Winnie and I were the only people in the entire room sitting. "Listen, Winnie," I said. "We have to get up. We have to talk to people, we can't just sit here."

"Why do we have to talk to people?"

I turned away from her and scanned the room and spotted Teddy Lawson surrounded by old buddies. He waved.

"Christ."

Jane returned with fresh drinks and the class scrapbook tucked under her arm. "Tequila sunrises!" she cried and almost missed her seat. "What did you say to Ted Lawson? He's going around telling everyone Yvonne Dearborn doesn't know who he is."

"Yvonne," Winnie said to me, opening the scrapbook. "You don't mean he actually put his finger into your …?"

"Yes, I do," I said primly. "We were walking down the hall, changing classes. I was wearing my fake leather jumper and red fish-net stockings and he was behind me."

"You had a fake leather jumper in fifth grade?" Jane asked. "You mean one of those plastic dresses? I don't remember that."

"Listen," I said. "I was very upset. It was a strange thing for him to do."

"No kidding it was a strange thing," Winnie howled, then added, "Here he is, Yvonne." She began reading from the scrapbook. "Career marine. Home: Texas. Married. Eight children, four adopted. That's a nice bundle."

She slid the book across the table. There he was in a recent snapshot taken at an amusement park. I counted eight children. Four were of Asian descent. His wife was blond and short—very short. Teddy was standing heads above them all, staring straight into the camera, his expression one of pride and honour.

"Oh barf." I stood. "Who wants what?"

Jane said, "Get me a pack of cigarettes."

But halfway across the room to the bar, I was intercepted by Teddy Lawson. He pointed a cigar at me and said, stooping, "Sorry for walking away on you, Yvonne. But I was a little hurt you didn't know me."

"I do know you. I just thought you went to prep school."

"That's right! Grades six through nine I went to Bellingham Academy. My parents were divorcing and it was rough at home. But I came back in tenth grade."

"Well, that explains it," I said, making a move to the bar.

"Yes."

But we both knew it didn't entirely. What I knew, simply, was that I had gone through high school with blinders on. Though the blinders were off now, I was still unable to make sense of what I saw. I looked around at the people my classmates had become. Who had I become?

"Yvonne." Teddy Lawson put a hand on my shoulder. "Do you remember the field trip to see *2001* in fifth grade?"

"Yes."

"Do you remember, I sat next to you?"

I stood, blinking from his cigar smoke. I had no recollection of anyone sitting beside me. What's more, I probably had no idea who was sitting beside me even at the time. Yet, this was what he remembered? This only?

"I guess I was sort of sweet on you," he told me.

It was a confession. I listened as he summarized his life, and gradually began to hate him and direct towards him all my anger of the past three years. I blamed him for everything, knowing he was not to blame.

"You have children?" he asked.

"One son." And in my mind's eye I saw Rudy at two, a roly-poly toddler at the back steps, picking wet leaves from the sides of his sneakers.

"How old?" Teddy asked.

"He's five now."

"That's a great age. Kindergarten, right?"

He was clearly an involved father. I burst out with an ugly noise—part giggle, part cry, and put my hand to my mouth. It occurred to me that the only way out of this conversation was by asking him what the hell he thought he was doing ramming his finger into my bottom in fifth grade, but he had pinned me with an earnest, level look and I realized I was stuck in no man's land again.

"He had meningitis two years ago," I explained. "So we're keeping him back a year. He's deaf. He's lucky."

Teddy was hunched over me, nodding.

"I don't know if you can imagine it," I said suddenly, still blaming him.

"I can imagine it."

"You want your child back no matter what. At any cost."

"Whatever remains of him," Teddy Lawson said.

"Yes."

"Like a war."

"Exactly." And I saw my spongy-skinned, bloated child, his organs failing as tubes persisted in feeding him, cleansing him, driving his pink tender lungs to inhale, exhale. "When it happened," I said, "all I could do was sit on his bedroom floor and wait."

Teddy Lawson put his arm around me, resting the cigar on my shoulder so that the smoke circled my head.

"I'm drunk," I said tiredly.

"Hey, we're all drunk." He released me and made a grand, sweeping gesture with his arms. I couldn't think who he was including.

"SO HE WAS SWEET ON YOU," Winnie joked on the way home. "That explains it."

From the back seat Jane said, "I'm seeing double, goddamn it."

"Listen, Jane," I said. "If you're going to go around at a third your recommended body weight, you might consider reducing your alcohol intake by at least as much." Winnie and I exchanged a smiling look of camaraderie. I felt light-hearted and rolled down the window and sucked in the fragrance that arose from the bogs and thickets, from the tangled woods where lianas hung from the trees as though curtaining off secrets from the world of humans.

Yet, I thought, Teddy Lawson remembered sitting beside me at the cinema. How could he and I have burdened ourselves with such opposing memories of each other? Twenty years had altered him, and all my classmates, in much the way one January month had Rudy. The people we had become bore traces of the children we had been, but these traces were negligible—almost ornamental. Sometimes Rudy looked up at me from his chair and for a moment I caught just that: a curious, ghostly trace of the baby he had been.

In twenty years, who would Rudy be? In what manner would his memories intersect with mine?

The heavy foliage beside the road lurched gold and black in the headlights of Winnie's car. I was suddenly overwhelmed by too much life coming at me from the sticky black soil, the clicking insects and ferocious bird life. Behind the wall of trees along the roadside was a world that was no longer mine, and could not be had I wanted it.

I pictured Rudy in his bedroom, the air dry and overheated against the cold at the windows, and longed to be there now to kiss him as I did every night, believing that through this touch my memories could be erased.

"Life's a bitch," Winnie suddenly offered.

Yes, I was about to say, it's one goddamn battle after another, but realized I no longer liked the dogged, angry bravery I had adopted as mine, or the woman it had made me. I closed my eyes tightly, as though the cigar smoke still stung them.

RAMONA DEARING

An Apology

The first day of the trial will be the hardest. Gerard Lundrigan arrives at the courthouse exactly one hour early, at nine o'clock. Even then the TV cameras are waiting, although they're not allowed inside the courtroom. He sits in that dark sanctuary, testing his chair. It will do. He's brought along the Graham Greene book he forgot to return to the library. But he can't read about the whisky priest, not just yet. Gerard makes sure the buttons on his blue cardigan are done up right. He holds the book open so it will look like he's doing something. Outside the tall windows, what looks to be the start of a March storm. He'd forgotten what it was like here. The wind is taking anything it can find. There's a good chance that by noon all of St. John's will be clamped in ice. Or it will be sunny, or raining, or snowing. You never know about this place, he does remember that. He thinks about his pup back in Ontario, and how it likes to nose through the snow. It would like it here, especially rolling in landwash after chasing gulls.

The jurors look nervous as they walk in. One woman giggles when she bumps into a chair on the way to the jury box, and her face stays red for a full hour. The other jurors' eyes swivel over the oak and mahogany scrollings, the ancient picture of the Queen, the thin, bunned judge in her red-sashed blue robe. A sheriff's officer walks around with one hand pressed to his ear piece, the other clamped at his hip to keep the keys on his belt from jingling. Two more sheriff's officers flank Gerard, tapping their fingers against their thighs. There can be trouble on the first day, apparently, scenes. The lawyers look edgy and clear their throats a lot. Gerard isn't sure how many spectators there are—he won't let himself look back. But there are eyes on him, of course—he can feel them. And he can see the jurors studying him. They've relaxed a bit, are sitting more deeply in their chairs. Not one of them looks like a leader. Not one of them looks to be well-studied. Only one man wears a tie. There's even a girl in jeans, chewing gum. They listen hard as the crown prosecutor outlines his case. During the preliminary inquiry, he'd been soft-spoken, methodical. Now he is playing to the jury, and there is insincerity and filth coming out his mouth. Absolute filth.

You're probably nervous, ladies and gentlemen of the jury. I know you are because I myself am nervous right now and I've been at this racket for a long time now. But there's no need to worry. All you have to do is sort through the facts, and I believe those facts are very clearly set out. You are the judge of the facts and as such, you will hear direct testimony that Brother Lundrigan beat little boys. Sodomized little boys. Ejaculated in their mouths as they gagged and struggled.

I know these are shocking things to say, sickening things to say. You probably wish you hadn't had breakfast. All I can say is get used to it, because you're going to hear about it from eleven different men over the course of the next six weeks or so.

Most of the jurors suction their arms across their stomachs and keep them there all morning. Gerard sits very tall and looks straight ahead.

THE AFTERNOON IS BETTER. The weather has settled somewhat. The first witness is called—the lead investigator from the Royal Newfoundland Constabulary. All he does is show a videotape of the orphanage, a long, long tape showing every room and closet and corridor and shed. The police shot the film before the wrecking ball knocked the place in on itself. There is the chapel, just as Gerard remembers it. The classrooms. The sleeping quarters. The gym. The old garden grounds. And so on, and on and on. All shot poorly, shakily, with bad lighting. But the courtroom has been darkened and therefore no one is staring at Gerard.

WHEN THE FIRST COMPLAINANT takes the stand, Gerard absorbs every word. He remembers the boy well. The one who'd wanted so badly to be on the gymnastics team but was disqualified because he failed math every year. He'd been a big boy then. Now he has the look of a withered drunk. Ridiculous in a burgundy velvet jacket. Soft-spoken—the judge doesn't ask the man to speak up nearly enough. He didn't get that mumbling habit from his time at the orphanage. They'd taught pride there. Pride and decency and right-living.

The fellow goes on for hours about how terrible the orphanage was, how he and his younger brother would steal buns and hide them in the little barn for the times when they couldn't sleep for hunger. How they got in trouble just for sitting still, and worse beatings when they actually did anything bad. How Bro. Lundrigan was the worst one for the strap, especially with the boys in his dorm. How he wouldn't tolerate any illness and wouldn't let a boy go to the sickroom even if he'd thrown up all night. How Bro. Lundrigan would toss any boy who wet the bed into the swimming pool, no matter the time of year. How if he saw a boy crying for any reason, he'd rub soap in the child's eyes so he'd have something to screech about.

Gerard wants to speak. It's physically painful not to be able to respond, acid burning his gut. But since he won't be testifying for at least a month, he's started a notebook outlining every single point he disagrees with, numbering each in case it will help his lawyer.

23) No child ever went hungry in my care.

24) The strap had nothing to do with me. Blame the era, not the man. Do you think your disobedience made me happy—do you think I liked it?

25) I remember personally taking you to the sickroom on at least two occasions.

26) Re: soap—whatever are you talking about?

"MAKE HIM STOP WATCHING ME," the first complainant says to the judge the fifth morning he's on the stand. The prosecutor has just started in on the buggery allegations. On the fire escape, one night. In the barn, many times. Many, many times. The witness's voice cracks. The judge orders a break.

117) The disgusting thing you allude to—where would I even have gotten the idea? What about my vows? Why would I do such a thing? You brought me here to watch your sickening tears and listen to you say these revolting things?

Gerard is thankful for his lawyer, who establishes in one efficient afternoon of cross-examination that the complainant has a long criminal record, including theft. He'd also attacked a man in a bar with a broken bottle. That's the kind of low-life he is. In and out of mental hospitals, with children spat out across northern Ontario like bits of gristle, and ex-wives lining up to get restraining orders.

THE NEXT WITNESS is a real crowd-pleaser. Makes the jury smile as he remembers stringing chestnuts to play conkers. As he describes skinning his shins against the rough concrete of the swimming pool. The time Bro. Superior came in for breakfast one morning dressed like Charlie Chaplin and kept pretending to fall off his chair. What it was like riding the hay wagon into St. John's and seeing all those mesmerizing lights and the houses where you could look in the windows at the moms and dads and pops and nannies and little kids sitting right nice and sweet at the table.

He has them all right. Even the judge looks choked up. And then less than half an hour later, he goes for a bull's-eye. His face is crazy red and he's dry-sobbing and beating one hand against the top of the witness box and pointing with the other: *That one, that one there. That bastard ruined me for everything. Your Honour, I'd as soon spit on him on his deathbed. That's a monster, that is. Not a man. Left me opened up and bleeding so's I couldn't shit for a week. Bite marks on my neck.*

The judge orders a break.

GERARD HAS BEGUN to put together some theories. These men are forty-five, fifty. They're all into the booze or the drugs. They've all done time. He knows—it all came out at the preliminary hearing.

They've got something else in common: they've disappointed anyone who ever came into their lives. Including Gerard.

Their fathers were alcoholics or thieves or dead and their mothers were sluts or mad or dead. Now they're men looking to blame, to make someone accountable for their empty spots.

And who better than Gerard? They remember him making them sit on their bleeding hands—as was common in those times—and they want revenge, they want to make him sit on his own bleeding hands and get a taste of himself. They'd do that to a sixty-four-year-old because all they want is this one chance in their lives to give out orders and have someone obey.

So, okay, Gerard is sitting on his hands. They've got him where they want him. They wag their fingers like he used to in math class, and now it's him who can't talk back. It's so straightforward eye-for-an-eye that it's almost comic. Except what they really want is for him to fix their lives and that's something he never, ever could do.

A man is not a mother. A twenty-two-year-old thinks he wants to get away from his slightly aristocratic parents. He thinks he wants to roll up his sleeves, get his hands dirty, serve. And so he does. And at first, God is everywhere. In the wind, in his ear, in the fellowship of the twenty-three-year-olds and the twenty-five-year-olds who also want nothing of society auctions and marriages and cigars. But there are fourteen boys in his charge. Two are just four years old, leggy babies with permanent ropes of snot hanging from their noses. Crying always for Mumma. The teen boys are revolting, with their acne and their smell and their trembling beds as they go at themselves in the dark. The middle ones are better, but still they hang off him, one on one arm, another on his back, another trying to get that one off. *Possums,* he'd called them, but he had to explain: no possums in Newfoundland.

Ripped off. Yes, they were. He always knew that. It wasn't easy for them. But it wasn't easy for him, either. Does anyone ever stop and think what it was like? Up at five-thirty for prayers with the other brothers. Getting the boys up at six and trying to get them to wash. Supervising breakfast. Teaching until four. Gymnastics coaching. Homework supervision. Somewhere in there making time to go over to the teachers' dorm and help out with the bed-bound ancient brothers. Then supervising his dorm, staying up all night if necessary with the croupy boys.

And those annual evaluations with the superior. Always getting on about the filth of the place, about how the boys needed to be pushed to do their chores properly. The lavatory like something out of India. How Bro. Superior wanted things pristine, the way they should be. And how the orphanage should be winning more trophies—how good it was for the boys to be the very best, to show them that adversity could be overcome.

One time Gerard muttered under his breath *Yes, Bro., but what about my needs?* It had struck him as funny—by rights he'd prayed them all away hadn't he? That wasn't so long before he left. He remembers it was a Tuesday, and he'd walked back over to the main building and announced to all the boys at supper that there'd be no homework that night. They'd see *Gold Rush* instead and each boy could go to the canteen and pick out chips *and* a soda *and* a bar. All evening he felt naughty and proud. But he tossed and turned in bed, worried he'd acted out of false pride.

AFTER THE THIRD MAN takes the stand, Gerard decides he can't keep thinking about the past. What good does it do, dredging up these old details? He's got things happening in his life right now that need attention, and all because of this trial. His lawyer has told him to keep taking notes. But everything that is being said has already been said twice before and presumably will go around nine more times. The jurors are starting to look bored. They get sent out of the courtroom a lot while the lawyers argue whether certain lines of questioning should be allowed. Gerard has heard the sheriff's officers say the women are knitting up a storm during the time they wait downstairs in the jury room and that one of them brought in this cappuccino machine they're all going mad for.

The lawyers have settled into a steadiness, a matter-of-factness. It has been five weeks now. They joke about being here for another three months.

Here I am just a bit taller than the door latch—I can feel it digging in back of my head—and here he is picking me up by my ears and telling me to clamp it or everything is going to hurt more.

More and more, all Gerard can think of is the pup and how it's doing. He remembers the little squeaky sound it makes when it yawns. He doesn't know why he got it with the trial coming up, but he did. He wasn't going to, but then the trial was postponed for the second time, some conflict with the judge's schedule. He just saw the pup—in a pet store, of all places—and took it home.

He'd felt like a new mother. Every sound led back to the pup. He was in the library one day when he was sure he could hear Brigus keening. Gerard had stood there waiting for claws to scrape white lines on his shins. But of course the dog wasn't there. The sound must have been a pencil sharpener or some such thing.

Walking home the long way, the pretty way—along the Avon and its low-waisted willows, past Tom Patterson Island, past the Stratford Festival Theatre, past the squirrels—another squeal from Brigus, except really it came from a gull. And the next false alarm was a scream of brakes from a bus.

When he'd returned home to the pup, a copy of *The Power and the Glory* warming his armpit, there was only the sound of his keys hitting the table and a metronome of tail hitting the sides of the crate. Thump thump thump thump, etc.

I never told no one until my lady put it on the line. She said, "Look, my honey, you've got something eating you all these years and it's eating me too and I'm falling apart and I don't even know why."

He wonders how the house-sitter is making out. He calls her a couple of times a week and she says everything's fine, but he wonders if that's really the case. It bothers him, having someone in his house. But what can he do? The pup can't be abandoned.

He'd put an ad in the paper for a caretaker. The girl answered and so did some older women and a boy maybe twenty-one. He interviewed the boy and liked him best, but decided against him on the basis of the trouble factor with boys. The women talked too much. The girl was quiet. He had her move in the week before he left just to make sure he could trust her. She didn't spend any time on the phone, which surprised him. She washed her dishes as soon as she finished eating. She spent all her time with the pup, mostly outside.

He'd told her he didn't know how long he'd be gone on business. Depended how the deal went. Not too long, he didn't think.

"You still working?" It was the only question she ever asked him. He'd nodded. At night, he could hear her drag the nightstand up against her door. She kept the pup in with her.

I said, "Lord Jesus, take me out of this." And then I tried with the razor. I really wanted it. I would picture Bro. Lundrigan walking past my casket getting all shaky.

Okay, he's not a saint. There are times he's picked Brigus up by the gruff and shook him and whacked him, once even in front of the girl. You can only trip down the stairs so many times with forty-eight ounces of stupidity skinning your heel. You can only pick up gummed toilet paper so many times off the living room floor, say good-bye to so many boots and tea towels. Gerard had taken to reading a book on dog training by some monks who raise and sell drug-sniffing German shepherds at their monastery in New York State. He'd read it at four-thirty in the morning, wide awake after taking the dog outside for its first shit of the day. While Gerard read, Brigus would curl tight, a potato bug on the floor next to the bedframe. The monks say to never give in to exasperation. Stay in control. *To stop biting, give the snout a firm but harmless shake. Expect a yelp of surprise. Hold the palm flat and ask for a lick instead. Praise your pup.*

Sometimes Gerard has grabbed the pup's snout just to make it cry out.

Brigus never seems to bite the girl. She's to dust and vacuum and scrub every week. No visitors. She'll be needing to keep the lawn cut and the garden tidy. "You understand everything I'm paying you to do?" he'd said. She'd nodded. It was his parents' house, he told her, and needed to be treated with that kind of respect. She'd nodded again. The pup was to be her first priority, though. Another nod, this time with a slight smile attached.

He wonders if she's having parties. If there are people fornicating in his house right now. In his parents' old bed. He decides to call again at the lunch break.

No answer, for the fourth day in a row.

THE FIFTH COMPLAINANT knocks the hell out of him. Gerard has no idea who he is. He knows he didn't recognize the name, but he thought when he saw the fellow it would all click. The man hadn't made it to the prelim, and now that Gerard is finally looking right at him, he can't place him at all.

At lunch he says to his lawyer, "How could I not know one of the children?"

His lawyer looks tired. "What's to remember when you're dealing with a liar?"

The records point to Gerard teaching the man for three years—he apparently failed grade seven math. He's convinced the man must have had another name back then. How could Gerard forget one of the boys?

THE LACK OF GIVING IN the dog really surprised him. He wishes he could talk to the New York State monks about that. They'd know what he means. It sits there insisting on being noticed, forever complaining. Something the orphans never would have dared. Fat Brigus, ears flopping back and forth as he pisses on the bathmat, wants chicken, wrestling matches, lap naps, and cheese.

Surely the dog will still know him when he gets back?

HE REMEMBERS the eleventh complainant in great detail. A sweet boy he was, needy but still sweet. Had these fat ringlets and a long skinny frame. Gerard's favourite possum, always leaning in, content. *Look what I got you, Brother.* And in his fist a wet stone, one side glowing an ashy red if the light hit it right. Gerard would pick him up and hold him tight.

He's grey now and has his hair clipped. Still thin, though. He would have loved Brigus, that boy, would have petted him bald. *If you pinches the pads on their feet they won't jump up no more, isn't that right? You gots to give them a big squirt of a squeeze whenever they does that. Can I touch his tail, Brother? I mean, may I, Bro.?*

THE MOTHER of the eleventh man gets herself in the paper. Apparently she's been in the public gallery through the whole trial. She waits until her boy's finished testifying. He has been crying softly for the last hour or so on the stand. But the mother doesn't go to her son. No, as soon as the judge leaves the courtroom, she walks up behind Gerard and tugs on the elbow of his cardigan and explains who she is.

No one else has spoken to him, aside from his lawyer. The reporters look down when he walks past them. The sheriff's officers never speak directly to him. "Does Mr Lundrigan want some water?" they'll ask his lawyer. The clerks don't look at him. Even in corner stores, if he's buying a paper or some chocolate, no one looks right at him. Sometimes the cashier won't hold her hand out to take the money, forcing him to leave it on the counter and forget about the change.

But the mother smiles. "I've forgiven you," she says.

Gerard's lawyer moves closer.

"I've thought about it and you're going to do your time and you should get at least one more little chance, you know. I mean, who in frig am I to rebuke you? I mean, I'm the one who handed over my boy, right?"

The spectators who are getting ready to put on their coats are like hares, all ears and eyes.

The woman's voice is getting louder, too. "I kept saying he's just a man, same as any other. Just a man. That's how I'm going to look at you, anyway. Others might not, but I'm going to. For me, you know. For myself. Important, you know?"

Gerard turns from her, reaches for his coat.

She comes around on the other side so that she's still facing him. The reporters are there now, too, holding out microphones. "I mean nothing can give back my Sean what you took, so why should we keep after you, really? I mean, jail, yes. Go to jail for a while, you definitely should do that. But hatred, that's no good."

"Okay, okay," the sheriff's officers say. "This courtroom's closed for the day." They have their hands on her elbows and are edging her back, gently.

She says, "Do you have a message I could bring to the boys for you?"

He puts his arms across his chest and hates himself for doing it.

"Len Stamps, Red Matthews, Tom Walsh. You remember them all, right? Plus my Sean, of course."

The officers are getting her closer to the door. She's pushing against them.

"Donnie Hawko. Bill Wheaton, John Cooke, Vince Rutherford. You heard them. You heard what they said."

The reporters are following her, trying to ask her questions. But she ignores them.

"Say you're sorry," she yells. "Say 'I apologize.' Just say that. You'll feel better."

THE NEXT AFTERNOON, Gerard is on the stand. The only witness for the defense. Some of the other Brothers wouldn't take the stand at their trials. But the juries didn't like that, apparently. Besides, Gerard doesn't mind talking. There's no way he can keep sitting on his hands.

The jury will see the authority he carries, the calm. The jury will remember the complainants and their mental illnesses, their criminal records. The roughness about them.

Except when he first gets on the stand, he feels like he might pass out. Everywhere he looks, he sees set faces.

He imagines the girl bringing Brigus here, coming in through the spectators' door and letting him off the lead at the back of the courtroom, a much bigger Brigus running at full hurl to cover Gerard with licks. He sees everyone smiling: the judge, the jury, the audience, himself.

After that, he gets his confidence back. *We wanted those boys to have a chance in the world. We pushed them. We made it clear everything was going to be hard for them. We didn't believe in pretending they weren't orphans.*

ON THE SUNDAY before cross-examination is to start, the girl answers the phone. She tells him she's seen his picture in the paper. She says she'll take care of the dog no matter what but she doesn't know if she can stay in the house because it is too sickening. She is thinking about going home to her parents and taking Brigus with her. "No," Gerard says. "You have to stay." If she leaves, she could steal everything on her way out. She could write things on the walls. She could set the house on fire. She could take Brigus and never give him back.

"Who exactly are you to be setting the rules?" she says, and he understands then her quietness is not as peaceful as he'd thought.

All he can say is, "Please, it's not whatever you're thinking." And offer extra money.

THE CROWN ATTORNEY mocks him. "You mean, you taught this man for three years but can't remember him? Therefore, if you can't remember him, we're to conclude you're innocent? Okay, let's look at that. Let's say you couldn't remember whether you'd filed your income taxes for last year. Let's say it turns out you didn't. Does that mean, in the eyes of Revenue Canada, that you're off the hook, Mr Lundrigan?"

Gerard can only repeat what he's already said several times: "I know the records indicate that man was in my classroom three years running, but I also know I'd never laid eyes on him before this trial started, so how could I have done these terrible things as he claims?"

The jury finds that amusing. The judge calls a break.

THERE'S ANOTHER BAD MOMENT on what turns out to be Gerard's last day of cross-examination. It involves the allegations of the last complainant, Sean.

"Did you ever, Mr Lundrigan, slip your tongue into his mouth as alleged?"

"No. But perhaps once when I kissed him there might have been an accident."

"You kissed the boy?"

"Yes, many times. Like a mother."

"On the lips?"

"Yes, sir. Like a mother would."

"Did you kiss the other boys?"

"No, sir."

"Why not?"

"He was special, very dear to me, innocent. He needed affection."

"So you kissed him on the lips?"

"I've already answered that."

"Like a mother?"

"Like a mother."

"Did you ever insert your penis into his mouth?"

"Of course not."

"Even by accident?"

Gerard's lawyer objects, and the judge agrees. She calls an early lunch break.

Gerard's lawyer says he can't eat with him today—he has to run to the dentist. A weak lie since normally they'd still be in session.

Gerard sees Sean's mother putting on her coat in the last row of benches in the public gallery. He wouldn't let himself look over that way when he was on the stand. Now she won't look at him.

THE JUDGE GIVES HER CHARGE to the jury. It takes two days for her to finish. Gerard spends the time working on an apology to the boys, but nothing comes out right.

I have no malice towards you. You came to us robbed. We were only boys ourselves, you forget that.

I'm sorry you made me come here.

I'm sorry you've made such a fuss.

I'm sorry you want my blood.

To think he wiped their asses.

A pity his lawyer would never let him send a letter. It might help them.

THE JURY IS OUT. Gerard's lawyer gives him a cell phone and tells him to stay within a ten-minute radius of the courtroom. The lawyer says not to fret if the deliberations take several days—the longer, the better. "I'd hang out with you," the lawyer says, "but I'm just snow-balled with work at the office."

At first Gerard stays in the little apartment he's rented. He knew the wait was going to be bad, but not this bad. If he lies on the bed, the ceiling comes down to a point just above his nose. The more he paces, the more he sees himself in the mirrors that are all over the room. If he looks out the window, he feels lonely.

THE HARBOUR IS QUIET. The *Astron* is in, and a fisheries patrol vessel. Some longliners. It is sunny, and even better, it's windy. Somehow the gusts comfort him. It's a clean wind here, a wind that leaves the good in you.

It licks at him as he starts winding up the road to Signal Hill. Maybe no one will recognize him with his ear flaps down. Not that he's hiding—it's the kind of cold that makes your ear drums ache.

The flags at Cabot Tower flap like tents in a blizzard. The few people walking around up here actually nod at him. It's a community of sorts, brought on by the elements.

He walks some more, looks down at Chain Rock. He could aim for it. There's no way he could even come close. But he could tell himself that's what he was doing. The wind would rub him against a rock face on the way down. If he waits until he's a bit colder he probably wouldn't feel a thing.

He remembers his last day with the dog. Not even that went right. He'd only meant to nudge Brigus toward the door with his foot but for some reason he'd kicked the pup good and hard. He'd spent forever trying to get it out from under the couch. In the end Gerard set up a semi-circle of cheese cubes, like stepping stones to the centre of the living room.

Outside, they'd passed through the art gallery grounds to get down to the river. Brigus barrelled through the steel sculpture that looks like an oversized napkin holder and then spun around, checking to make sure he could still see Gerard. When they got over the railroad tracks and down the hill, the dog hacked after studiously and sombrely licking a mound of dirt. Gerard had felt like whipping himself. "I'm no good for you," he'd said, and walked away, fast. But no matter where he stepped, he could hear the pup rushing the grass right behind.

What you do and what you mean. Two entirely different things. Gerard never meant anyone any trouble.

He does mean to push off right now, but he can't do it.

He heads down the footpath to the Interpretation Centre, where there are payphones—he's not allowed to tie up the cell phone. Gerard calls his house and, miraculously, she picks up.

"You're still there?" he says.

"I need the money, okay?"

"That's fine," he says, "I'm happy."

No response.

Gerard tries again. "He's your dog, okay? You take him. If you go."

The wind makes him cry on the way back down the hill. It keeps grinding bits of dirt right in there. He's hurrying because he's just now understanding it's not going to take the jury long.

There's so much wind he wonders whether he'll even hear the phone if it rings in his pocket.

But he does. He's surprised how relieved he feels.

MAVIS GALLANT

The Concert Party

O nce, long ago, for just a few minutes I tried to pretend I was
 Harry Lapwing. Not that I admired him or hoped to become a
minor Lapwing; in fact, my distaste was so overloaded that it seemed
to add weight to other troubles I was piling up then, at twenty-five. I
thought that if I could not keep my feelings cordial I might at least try
to flatten them out, and I remembered advice my Aunt Elspeth had
given me: "Put yourself in the other fellow's place, Steve. It saves wear."

I was in the South of France, walking along a quay battered by
autumn waves, as low in mind as I was ever likely to be. My marriage
had dropped from a height. There weren't two pieces left I could fit
together. Lapwing wasn't to blame, yet I kept wanting to hold him
responsible for something. Why? I still don't know. I said to myself,
O.K., imagine your name is Harry Lapwing. Harry Lapwing. You are
a prairie Socialist, a William Morris scholar. All your life this will make
you appear boring and dull. When you went to England in the late
forties and said you were Canadian, and Socialist, and working on
aspects of William Morris, people got a stiff, trapped look, as if you
were about to read them a poem. You had the same conversation
twenty-seven times, once for each year of your life:

"Which part of Canada are you from?"

"I was born in Manitoba."

"We have cousins in Victoria."

"I've never been out there."

"I believe it's quite pretty."

"I wouldn't know. Anyway, I haven't much eye."

One day, in France, at a shabby Mediterranean resort called Rivebelle (you had gone there because it was cheap) someone said, "I'd say you've got quite an eye—very much so," looking straight at Edie, your wife.

The speaker was a tall, slouched man with straight black hair, pale skin, and a limp. (It turned out that some kid at the beach had gouged him behind the knee with the point of a sunshade.) You met in the airless, shadowed salon of a Victorian villa, where an English novelist had invited everyone he could think of—friends and neighbors and strangers picked up in cafés—to hear a protégé of his playing Scriabin and Schubert through the hottest hours of the day.

You took one look at the ashy stranger and labeled him "the mooch." He had already said he was a playwright. No one had asked, but in those days, the late Truman era, travelers from North America felt bound to explain why they weren't back home and on the job. It seemed all right for a playwright to drift through Europe. You pictured him sitting in airports, taking down dialogue.

He had said, "What part of Canada are you from?"

You weren't expecting this, because he sounded as if he came from some part of Canada, too. He should have known before asking that your answer could be brief and direct or cautious and reserved; you might say, "That's hard to explain," or even "I'm not sure what you mean." You were so startled, in fact, that you missed four lines of the usual exchange and replied, "I wouldn't know. Anyway, I don't have much eye."

He said, "I'd say you've got quite an eye …" and then turned to Edie: "How about you?"

"Oh, I'm not from any part of anything," Edie said. "My people came from Poland."

Now, you have already told her not to say this without *also* mentioning that her father was big in cement. At that time Poland just meant

Polack. Chopin was dead. History hadn't got round to John Paul II. She looked over your head at the big guy, the mooch. Fergus Bray was his name; the accent you had spotted but couldn't place was Cape Breton Island. So that he wasn't asking the usual empty question (empty because for most people virtually any answer was bound to be unrevealing) but making a social remark—the only social remark he will ever address to you.

You are not tall. Your head is large—not abnormally but remarkably. Once, at the beach, someone placed a child's life belt with an inflated toy sea horse on your head, and it sat there, like Cleopatra's diadem. Your wife laughed, with her mouth wide open, uncovering a few of the iron fillings they plugged kids' teeth with during the Depression. You said, "Ah, that's enough, Edie," but your voice lacked authority. The first time you ever heard a recording of your own voice, you couldn't figure out who that squeaker might be. Some showoff in London said you had a voice like H.G. Wells'—all but the accent. You have no objection to sounding like Wells. Your voice is the product of two or three generations of advanced university education, not made for bawling orders.

Today, nearly forty years later, no one would dare crown you with a sea-horse life belt or criticize your voice. You are Dr. Lapwing, recently retired as president of a prairie university called Osier, after having been for a long time the head of its English department. You still travel and publish. You have been presented to the Queen, and have lunched with a prime minister. He urged you to accept a cigar, and frowned with displeasure when you started to smoke.

To the Queen you said, "... and I also write books."

"Oh?" said Her Majesty. "And do you earn a great deal of money from writing books?"

You started to give your opinion of the academic publishing crisis, but there were a number of other persons waiting, and the Queen was obliged to turn away. You found this exchange dazzling. For ten minutes you became a monarchist, until you discovered that Her Majesty often asks the same question: "Do you earn a great deal of money with your poems, vaulting poles, copper mines, music scores?" The reason for the question must be that the answer cannot drag much beyond "Yes" or "No." "Do you like writing books?" might bring on a full paragraph, and there isn't time. You are proud that you tried to furnish a complete and truthful answer. You are once more anti-monarchist, and will not be taken in a second time.

The subject of your studies is still William Morris. Your metaphor is "frontiers." You have published a number of volumes that elegantly combine your two preoccupations: "William Morris: Frontiers of Indifference." "Continuity of a Frontier: The Young William Morris." "Widening Frontiers: The Role of the Divine in William Morris." "Secondary Transformations in William Morris: A Double Frontier."

When you and Edie shook hands with the mooch for the first time, you were on a grant, pursuing your first Morris mirage. To be allowed to pursue anything for a year was a singular honor; grants were hard to come by. While you wrote and reflected, your books and papers spread over the kitchen table in the two-room dwelling you had rented in the oldest part of Rivebelle, your wife sat across from you, reading a novel. There was nowhere else for her to sit; the bedroom gave on a narrow medieval alley. You could not very well ask Edie to spend her life in the dark, or send her into the streets to be stared at by yokels. She didn't object to the staring, but it disturbed you. You couldn't concentrate, knowing that she was out there, alone, with men trying to guess what she looked like with her clothes off.

What was she reading? Not the thick, gray, cementlike Prix Goncourt novel you had chosen, had even cut the pages of, for her. You looked, and saw a French translation of "Forever Amber." She had been taught to read French by nuns—another problem; she was too Polish Catholic for your enlightened friends, and too flighty about religion to count as a mystic. To intellectual Protestants, she seemed to be one more lapsed Catholic without guilt or conviction.

"You shouldn't be reading that. It's trash."

"It's not trash. It's a classic. The woman in the bookstore said so. It's published in a classics series."

"Maybe in France. Nowhere else in the civilized world."

"Well, it's their own business, isn't it? It's French."

"Edie, it's American. There was even a movie."

"When?"

"I don't know. Last year. Five years ago. It's the kind of movie I wouldn't be caught dead at."

"Neither would I," said Edie staunchly.

"Only the French would call that a classic."

"Then what are we doing here?"

"Have you forgotten London? The bedbugs?"

"At least there was a scale in the room."

Oh, yes; she used to scramble out of bed in London saying, "If you have the right kind of experience, it makes you lose weight." The great innocence of her, crouched on the scale; hands on her knees, trying to read the British system. The best you could think of to say was "You'll catch cold."

"What's a stone?" she would ask, frowning.

"I've already told you. It's either seven or eleven or fourteen pounds."

"Whatever it is, I haven't lost anything."

For no reason you knew, she suddenly stopped washing your nylon shirts in the kitchen sink and letting them drip in melancholy folds on *France-Soir*. You will never again see a French newspaper without imagining it blistered, as sallow in color as the shirts. The words "nylon shirt" will remind you of a French municipal-bonds scandal, a page-one story of the time. She ceased to shop, light the fire in the coal-and-wood stove (the only kind of stove in your French kitchen), cook anything decent, wash the plates, carry out the ashes and garbage. She came to bed late, when she thought you had gone to sleep, put out her cigarette at your request, and hung on to her book, her thumb between the pages, while you tried to make love to her.

One night, speaking of Fergus Bray, you said, "Could you sleep with a creep like him?"

"Who, the mooch? I might, if he'd let me smoke."

With this man she made a monkey of you, crossed one of your favorite figures of speech ("frontiers") and vanished into Franco's Spain. You, of course, will not set foot in Franco territory—not even to reclaim your lazy, commonplace, ignorant, Polack, lower-middle-class, gorgeous rose garden of a wife. Not for the moment.

I am twenty-seven, you say to yourself. She is nearly twenty-nine. When I am only thirty-eight, she will be pushing forty, and fat and apathetic. Those blond Slavs turn into pumpkins.

Well, she is gone. Look at it this way: you can work in peace, cross a few frontiers of your own, visit the places your political development requires—Latvia, Estonia, Poland. You join a French touring group, with a guide moonlighting from a celebrated language institute in Paris. (He doesn't know Polish, it turns out; Edie might have been useful.) You make your Eastern rounds, eyes keen for the cultural flowering some of your friends have described to you. You see quite a bit of the beet harvest in Silesia, and return by way of London. At Canada House, you sign a fraudulent statement declaring the loss of your passport, and receive a new one. The idea is to get rid of every trace of your Socialist visas. Nothing has changed in the past few weeks. Your wife is still in Madrid. You know, now, that she has an address on Calle de Hortaleza, and that Fergus Bray has a wife named Monica in Glace Bay, Nova Scotia.

Your new passport announces, as the old one did, that a Canadian citizen is a British subject. You object, once again, to the high-handed assumption that a citizen doesn't care what he is called. You would like to cross the words out with indelible ink, but the willful defacement of a piece of government property, following close on to a false statement made under oath, won't do your career any good should it come to light. Besides, you may need the Brits. Canada still refuses to recognize the Franco regime. There is no embassy, no consulate in Madrid, just a man in an office trying to sell Canadian wheat. What if Fergus Bray belts you on the nose, breaks your glasses? You can always ring the British doorbell and ask for justice and revenge.

You pocket the clean passport and embark on a train journey requiring three changes. In Madrid you find Edie bedraggled, worn out, ready to be rescued. She is barelegged, with canvas sandals tied on her feet. The mooch has pawned her wedding ring and sold her shoes in the flea market. You discover that she has been supporting the bastard—she who never found your generous grant enough for two, who used to go shopping with the francs you had carefully counted into her hand and return with nothing but a few tomatoes. Her beauty has coarsened, which gives you faith in abstract justice. You remind yourself that you are not groveling before this woman; you are taking her back, greasy hair, chapped skin, skinny legs, and all. Even the superb breasts seem lower and flatter, as well as you can tell under the cheap cotton dress she has on.

The mooch is out, prowling the city. "He does that a lot," she says.

You choose a clean, reasonable restaurant and buy her a meal. With the first course (garlic soup) her beauty returns. While you talk, quietly, without a trace of rebuke, she goes on eating. She is listening, probably, but this steady gluttonous attention to food seems the equivalent of keeping her thumb between the pages of "Forever Amber." Color floods her cheeks and forehead. She finishes a portion of stewed chicken, licks her fingers, sweeps back her tangled hair. She seems much as before—cheerful, patient, glowing, just a little distracted.

Already, men at other tables are starting to glance at her—not just the Latins, who will stare at anyone, but decent tourists, the good kind, Swedes, Swiss, whose own wives are clean, smart, have better table manners. These men are gazing at Edie the way the mooch did that first time, when she looked back at him over your head. You think of Susanna and the Elders. You can't tell her to cover up: the dress is a gunnysack, nothing shows. You tell yourself that something must be showing.

All this on a bowl of soup, a helping of chicken, two glasses of wine. "I'm sure I look terrible," she says. If she could, she would curl up on her chair and go to sleep. You cannot allow her to sleep, even in imagination. There is too much to discuss. She resists discussion. The two of you were apart, now you are back together. That seems to be all she wants to hear. She sighs, as if you were keeping her from something she craves (sleep?), and says, "It's all right, Harry. Whatever it is you've done, I forgive you. I'll never throw anything up to you. I've never held a grudge in my life."

IN PLAIN TERMS, this is not a recollection but the memory of one, riddled with mistakes of false time and with hindsight. When Lapwing lost and found his wife, the Queen was a princess, John Paul II was barely out of a seminary, and Lapwing was edging crabwise toward his William Morris oeuvre—for some reason, by way of a study of St. Paul. Stories about the passport fraud and how Fergus Bray is supposed to have sold Edie's shoes had not begun to circulate. Lapwing's try at engaging Her Majesty in conversation—a favorite academic anecdote, perhaps of doubtful authenticity—was made some thirty years later.

Osier, when Lapwing started teaching, was a one-building college, designed by a nostalgic Old Country architect to reproduce a Glasgow train shed. In the library hung a map of Ulster and a photograph of Princess May of Teck on her wedding day; on the shelves was a history of England, in fifteen volumes, but none of Canada—or, indeed, of any part of North America. There were bound copies of *Maclean's*, loose copies of *The Saturday Evening Post*, and a row of prewar British novels in brown, plum, and deep-blue bindings, reinforced with tape—the legacy of an alumnus who had gone away to die in Bermuda. From the front windows, Lapwing could see mud and a provincial highway; from the back, a basketball court and the staff parking lot. Visiting Soviet agricultural experts were always shown round the lot, so that they could count the spoils of democracy. Lapwing was the second Canadian-educated teacher ever to be hired; the first, Miss Mary MacLeod, a brilliant Old Testament scholar, taught Nutrition and Health. She and Lapwing shared Kraft-cheese sandwiches and subversive minority conversation. After skinning alive the rest of the staff, Miss MacLeod would remember Universal Vision and say it was probably better to have a lot of Brits than a lot of Americans. Americans would never last a winter up here. They were too rich and spoiled.

In the nineteen-sixties, a worldwide tide of euphoric prosperity and love of country reached Osier, dislodging the British. When the tide receded, it was discovered that their places had been taken by teachers from Colorado, Wyoming, and Montana, who could stand the winters. By the seventies, Osier had buried Nutrition and Health (Miss MacLeod was recycled into Language Structure), invented a graduate-studies program, had the grounds landscaped—with vast undulating lawns that, owing to drought and the nature of the soil, soon took on the shade and texture of Virginia tobacco—ceased to offer tenure to the foreign-born, and was able to call itself a university.

Around this time I was invited to Osier twice, to deliver a guest lecture on Talleyrand and to receive an honorary degree. On the second occasion, Lapwing, wearing the maroon gown Osier had adopted in a further essay at smartening up, prodded my arm with his knuckle and whispered, "We both made it, eh, Burnet?"

To Lapwing I was simply an Easterner, Anglo-Quebec—a permanent indictment. Like many English-Canadians brought up to consider French an inferior dialect, visited on hotel maids and unprincipled politicians, he had taken up the cause of Quebec after nationalism became a vanguard idea and moved over from right to left. His loyalties, once he defined them, traveled easily: I remember a year when he and his wife would not eat lettuce grown in Ontario because agricultural workers in California were on strike. With the same constancy, he now dismissed as a racist any Easterner from as far down the seaboard as Maryland whose birth and surroundings caused him to speak English.

Our wives were friends; that was what threw us into each other's company for a year, in France. Some of the external, convivial life of men fades when they get married, except in places like Saudi Arabia. I can think of no friendship I could have maintained where another woman, the friend's wife or girlfriend, was uncongenial to Lily. Lapwing and I were both graduate students, stretching out grants and scholarships, for the first time in our lives responsible for someone else. That was what we had in common, and it was not enough. Left to ourselves, we could not have discussed a book or a movie or a civil war. He thought I was supercilious and rich; thought it when I was in my early twenties, and hard up for money, and unsure about most things. What I thought about him I probably never brought into focus, until the day I felt overburdened by dislike. I had been raised by my widowed aunt, cautioned to find in myself opinions that could be repeated without embarrassing anyone; that were not displeasing to God; on the whole, that saved wear.

In France, once we started to know people, we were often invited all four together, as a social unit. We went to dinner in rooms where there were eight layers of wallpaper, and for tea and drinks around cracked ornamental pools (Rivebelle had been badly shelled only a few years before), and Lapwing told strangers the story of his life; rather, what he thought about his life. He had been born into a tough-minded, hard-working, well-educated family. Saying so, he brought all other conversation to a standstill. It was like being stalled in an open, snowy plain, with nothing left to remind you of culture and its advantages but legends of the Lapwings—how they had studied and struggled, with what ease they had passed exams in medicine and law, how Dr. Porter Lapwing had discovered a cheap and ready antidote for wasp venom. (He blew cigar smoke on the sting.)

We met a novelist, Watt Chadwick, who invited us, all four, to a concert. None of us had known a writer before, and we observed him at first uneasily—wondering if he was going to store up detractory stuff about us—then with interest, trying to surmise if he wrote in longhand or on a typewriter, worked in the morning or the afternoon, and where he got his ideas. At the back of our wondering was the notion that writing novels was not a job for a man—a prejudice from which we had to exclude Dickens and others, and which we presently overcame. The conflict was more grueling for Lapwing, whose aim was to teach literature at a university. Mr. Chadwick's family had built a villa in Rivebelle in the eighteen-eighties which he still occupied much of the year. He was regarded highly in the local British colony, where his books were lent and passed around until the bindings collapsed.

Newcomers are always disposed to enter into local snobberies: the invitation delighted and flattered us.

"He finds us good-looking and interesting," Lily said to me, seriously, when we talked it over. Lapwing must have risen as an exception in her mind, because she added, "And Harry has lots to say."

Rivebelle was a sleepy place that woke up once a year for a festival of chamber music. The concerts were held in a square overlooking the harbor, a whole side of it open to a view of the sea. The entire coastal strip as far as the other side of Nice had been annexed to Italy, until about a year prior to the shelling I've mentioned, and the military commander of the region had shown more aptitude for improving the town than for fortifying its beaches. No one remembers his name or knows what became of him: his memorial is the Rivebelle square. He had the medieval houses on its south boundary torn down (their inhabitants were quartered God knows where) and set his engineering corps to build a curving staircase of stone, mosaic, and stucco, with a pattern of "V"s for "Viva" and "M"s for "Mussolini," to link the square and the harbor. In the meantime children went down to the shore and paddled in shallow water, careful not to catch their feet in a few strands of barbed wire. The commander did not believe an attack could come from that direction. Perhaps he thought it would never come at all.

On concert nights Lily and I often leaned on the low wall that replaced the vanished houses and watched, as they drifted up and down the steps and trod on the "V"s, visitors in evening dress. They did not look rich, as we understood the word, but indefinably beyond that. Their French, English, German, and Italian were not quite the same as the languages we heard on the beaches, spoken by tourists who smacked their children and buried the remains of pizzas in the sand. To me they looked a bit like extras in prewar films about Paris or Vienna, but Lily studied their clothes and manner. There was a difference between pulling out a mauled pack of cigarettes and opening a heavy cigarette case: the movement of hand and wrist was not the same. She noticed all that. She once said, leaning on the wall, that there was something unfinished about us, the Burnets and Lapwings. We had packed for our year abroad as if the world were a lakeside summer cottage. I still couldn't see myself removing my squashed Camels to a heavy case and snapping it open, like a gigolo.

"You've never seen a gigolo," said Lily. And, almost regretfully, "Neither have I."

She dressed with particular attention to detail for Mr. Chadwick's evening, in clothes I had never noticed before. Edie gave her a silk blouse that had got too tight. Lily wore it the way Italian girls did, with the collar raised and the sleeves pushed up and the buttons undone as far as she dared. I wondered about the crinoline skirt and the heart-shaped locket on a gold chain.

"They're from Mrs. Biesel," Lily said. "She went to a lot of trouble. She even shortened the skirt." The Biesels were an American couple who had rented a house that Queen Alexandra was supposed to have stayed in, seeking relief from her chronic rheumatism and the presence of Edward VII. Mr. Biesel, a former naval officer who had lost an arm in the North Africa landings, was known locally as the Admiral, though I don't think it was his rank. Mr. Chadwick always said, "Admiral Bessel." He often had trouble with names, probably because he had to make up so many.

The Biesels attracted gossip and rumors, simply by being American: if twenty British residents made up a colony, two Americans were a mysterious invasion. Some people believed the Admiral reported to Washington on Rivebelle affairs: there were a couple of diplomats' widows and an ex-military man who had run a tin-pot regiment for a sheikh or an emir. Others knew for certain that Americans who cooperated with the Central Intelligence Agency were let off paying income tax. Mr. Chadwick often dined and played bridge at Villa Delizia, but he had said to Lily and me, "I'm careful what I say. With Admiral Bessel, you never can tell."

He had invited a fifth guest to the concert—David Ogdoad, his part-time gardener, aged about nineteen, a student of music and an early drifter. His working agreement with Mr. Chadwick allowed him to use the piano, providing Mr. Chadwick was not at the same moment trying to write a novel upstairs. The piano was an ancient Pleyel that had belonged to Mr. Chadwick's mother; it was kept in a room called the winter salon, which jutted like a promontory from the rest of the house, with shuttered windows along two sides and a pair of French doors that were always locked. No one knew, and perhaps Mr. Chadwick had forgotten, if he kept the shutters closed because his mother had liked to play the piano in the dark or if he did not want sunlight further to fade and mar the old sofas and rugs. Here, from time to time, when Mr. Chadwick was out to lunch or dinner, or, for the time being, did not know what to do next with "Guy" and "Roderick" and "Marie-Louise," David would sit among a small woodland of deprived rubber plants and labor at getting the notes right. He was surprisingly painstaking for someone said to have a restless nature but badly in need of a teacher and a better instrument: the Pleyel had not been tuned since before the war.

Now, of course Mr. Chadwick could have managed all this differently. He could have made David an allowance instead of paying token wages; introduced David to his friends as an equal; found him a teacher, had the piano restored, or bought a new one; built a music studio in the garden. Why not? Male couples abounded on this part of the coast. There were distinguished precedents, who let themselves be photographed and interviewed. Mr. Maugham lived not far away. But Mr. Chadwick was smaller literary stuff, and he didn't want the gossip. The concert outing was a social trial balloon. Any of Mr. Chadwick's friends, seeing the six of us, were supposed to say, "Watt has invited a party of young people," and not the fatal, the final, "Watt has started going out with his gardener."

MR. CHADWICK had not been able to book six seats together, which was all to the good: it meant there was no chance of my having to sit next to Lapwing. He was opposed on principle to the performance of music and liked to say so while it was going on, and his habit of punching one in the arm to underscore his opinions always made me feel angry and helpless. I sat with Lily in the second row, with the Lapwings and Mr. Chadwick and his gardener just behind. The front row was kept for honored guests. Mr. Chadwick pointed them out to Edie: the local mayor, and Jean Cocteau, and some elderly Bavarian princesses.

People applauded as Cocteau was shown to his seat. He was all in white, with bright quick eyes. The Bavarians were stout and dignified, in blue or pink satin, with white fur stoles.

"How do you get to be a Bavarian princess?" I heard Edie say.

"You could be born one," said Mr. Chadwick. He kept his voice low, like a radio announcer describing an opera. "Or you could marry a Bavarian prince."

"What about the fantastic-looking Italians?" said Edie. "At the end of the row. The earrings! Those diamonds are diamonds."

Mr. Chadwick was willing to give the wearer of the earrings a niche in Italian nobility.

"Big money from Milan," said Lapwing, as if he knew all about both. "Cheese exporters." His tone became suspicious, accusing almost: "Do you actually know Cocteau?"

"I have met M. Cocteau," said Mr. Chadwick. "I make a distinction between meeting and knowing, particularly with someone so celebrated."

"That applause for him just now—was it ironic?"

I could imagine Lapwing holding his glasses on his blob of a nose, pressing his knuckle between his eyes. I felt responsible, the way you always do when a compatriot is making a fool of himself.

Of course not, Mr. Chadwick replied. Cocteau was adored in Rivebelle, where he had decorated an abandoned chapel, now used for weddings. It made everyone happy to know he was here, the guest of the town, and that the violinist Christian Ferras would soon emerge from the church, and that the weather could be trusted—no mistral, no tramontane to carry the notes away, no threat of rain.

I think he said some of this for David, so that David would be appreciative even if he could not be content, showing David he had reason upon reason for staying with Mr. Chadwick; for at any moment David might say he had had enough and was going home. Not home to Mr. Chadwick's villa, where he was said to occupy a wretched room—a nineteenth-century servant's room—but home to England. And here was the start of Mr. Chadwick's dilemma—his riddle that went round and round and carried back to the same point: What if David stopped playing gardener and was moved into the best spare bedroom—the room with Monet-like water lilies on three walls? What would be his claim on the room? What could he be called? Mr. Chadwick's adopted nephew? His gifted young friend? And how to explain the shift from watering the agapanthus to spending the morning at the piano and the afternoon on the beach?

"Do you know who the three most attractive men in the world are?" said Edie all of a sudden. "I'll tell you. Cary Grant, Ali Khan, and Prince Philip."

None of the three looked even remotely like Lapwing. I glanced at Lily, expecting a flash of complicity.

Instead she said softly, "Pablo Picasso, Isaac Stern, Juan Fangio."

"What about them?"

"The most attractive."

"Who's Fangio? You mean the racing driver? Have you ever seen him?"

"Just his pictures."

"I can't see what they've got in common."

"Great, dark eyes," said Lily.

I suppressed the mention that I did not have great, dark eyes, and decided that what she really must have meant was nerve and genius. I knew by now that nerve comes and goes, with no relation to circumstance; as for genius, I had never been near it. Probably genius grew stately and fat or gaunt and haunted, lost its hair, married the wrong person, died in its sleep. David Ogdoad, of whom I was still barely aware except as a problem belonging to Mr. Chadwick, had been described—by Mr. Chadwick, of course—as a potential genius. (I never heard his name again after that year.) He had small, gray eyes, and with his mouth shut looked like a whippet—something about the way he stretched his neck.

A string orchestra filed on stage, to grateful applause (the musicians were half an hour late), and an eerie hush settled over the square. For the next hour or so, both Lapwings held still.

At intermission Mr. Chadwick tried to persuade us to remain in our seats; he seemed afraid of losing us—or perhaps just of losing David— in the shuffling crowd. Some people were making for a bar across the square, others struggled in the opposite direction, toward the church. I imagined Christian Ferras and the other musicians at bay in the vestry, their hands cramped from signing programs. David was already in the aisle, next to Lily.

"The intermission lasts a whole hour," said Lapwing, lifting his glasses and bringing the program close to his face. "Why don't we just say we'll meet at the bar?"

"And I'll look after Mr. Chadwick," said Edie, taking him by the arm. But it was not Edie he wanted.

Lily turned to David, smiling. She loved being carried along by this crowd of players from old black-and-white movies, hearing the different languages mingling and overlapping.

"Glorious, isn't he?" said David, about Ferras.

Lily answered something I could not hear but took to be more enthusiastic small talk, and slipped a hand under her collar, fingering the gold chain. As we edged past the cheaper seats, she said, "This is where Steve and I usually sit. It's so far back that you don't see the musicians. We're very grateful to Mr. Chadwick for tonight." No one could say she had undermined David's sense of thankfulness; he had been given a spring and summer in the South, and it hadn't cost him a centime. I thought we should not discuss Mr. Chadwick with David at all, but my reasons were confused and obscure. I believed David liked Lily because she took him seriously as a musician and not as someone's gardener. I thought the constant company of an older, nervous man must be stifling, even though I could not imagine him with a young one: he wanted to be looked after and to be rebellious, all at once. The natural companion for David was someone like Lily—attractive, and charming, and married to another man. I knew he was restless and had talked to her about London. That was all I thought I knew.

At the grocery store that served as theater bar, wine and French gin and whiskey and soft drinks were being dispensed, at triple price. The wine was sour and undrinkable. David asked for tonic; Lily and I usually had Cokes. The French she had learned in her Catholic boarding school allowed her to negotiate this, timidly. She liked ordering, enjoyed taking over sometimes, but Mr. Chadwick had corrected her Canadian accent and made her shy. David, merely impressed, asked if she had been educated in Switzerland.

The possibility of becoming a different person must have occurred to her. She picked up the bottle of tonic, as if she had never heard of Coca-Cola, still less ordered it, and demanded a glass. No more straws; no more drinking from bottles. She then handed David a tepid Coke, and he was too struck by love to do anything but swallow it down.

Lapwing in only a few minutes had managed to summon and consume large quantities of wine. His private reasoning had Mr. Chadwick paying for everything: after all, he had brought Lapwing up here to be belabored by Mozart. Edie, who had somehow lost Mr. Chadwick, was drinking wine, too. I noticed that Lily wanted me to foot the bill: the small wave of her hand was an imperial gesture. Distancing herself from me, the graduate of a Swiss finishing school forgot we had no money, or nearly none. I fished a wad of francs out of my pocket and dropped them on the counter. Lapwing punched me twice on the shoulder, perhaps his way of showing thanks.

"I don't know about you," he said, "but I'm one of those people for whom music is wave after wave of disjointed noise." He made "those people" sound like a superior selection.

Mr. Chadwick, last to arrive, looked crumpled and mortified, as if he had been put through some indignity. All I could do was offer him a drink. He looked silently and rather desperately at the grocery shelves, the cans of green peas, the cartons leaking sugar, the French gin with the false label.

"It's very kind of you," he said.

Lily and Edie linked arms and started back toward the church. They wanted to see the musicians at close quarters. Mr. Chadwick had recaptured David, which left me saddled with Lapwing.

"I don't have primitive anti-Catholic feelings," said Lapwing. "Edie was a Catholic, of course, being a Pole. A middle-class Pole. I encouraged her to keep it up. A woman should have a moral basis, especially if she doesn't have an intellectual one. Is Lily still Catholic?"

"It's her business." We had been over this ground before.

"And you?"

"I'm not anything."

"You must have started out as something. We all do."

"My parents are Anglican missionaries," I said. "I'm nothing in particular."

"I'm sorry to hear that," Lapwing said.

"Why?"

I hoped he would say he didn't know, which would have raised him a notch. Instead he drank the wine left in Edie's glass and hurried after the two women.

In the bright church, where every light had been turned on and banks of votive candles blazed, our wives wandered from saint to saint. Edie had tied a bolero jacket around her head. The two were behaving like little girls, laughing and giggling, displaying ex-Catholic behavior of a particular kind, making it known that they took nothing in this place seriously but that they were perfectly at home. Lapwing responded with Protestant prudence and gravity, making the remark that Lily should cover her hair. I looked around and saw no red glow, no Presence. For the sake of the concert the church had been turned into a public hall; in any case, what Lily chose to do was her business. Either God existed and was not offended by women and their hair or He did not; it came to the same thing.

Mr. Chadwick was telling David about design and decoration. He pointed to the ceiling and to the floor. I heard him say some interesting things about the original pagan site, the Roman shrine, the early Christian chapel, and the present rickety Baroque—a piece of nonsense, he said. Lapwing and I, stranded under a nineteenth-century portrayal of St. Paul, given the face of a hanging judge, kept up an exchange that to an outsider might have resembled conversation. I was so hard up for something to say that I translated the inscription under the picture: "St. Paul, Apostle to the Gentiles, put to death as a martyr in Rome, A.D. 67."

"I've been working on him," Lapwing said. "I've written a lot of stuff." He tipped his head to look at the portrait, frowning. "Saul is the name, of course. The whole thing is a fake. The whole story."

"What do you mean? He never existed?"

"Oh, he existed, all right. Saul existed. But that seizure on the road to Damascus can be explained in medical terms of our time." Lapwing paused, and then said rather formally, "I've got doctors in the family. I've read the books. There's a condition called eclampsia. Toxemia of pregnancy, in other words. Say Lily was pregnant—say she was carrying the bacteria of diphtheria, or typhoid, or even tetanus ..."

"Why couldn't it be Edie?"

"O.K., then, Edie. I'm not superstitious. I don't imagine the gods are up there listening, waiting for me to make a slip. Say it's Edie. Well, she could have these seizures, she could hallucinate. I'm not saying it's a common condition. I'm not saying it often happens in the civilized world. I'm saying it could have happened in very early A.D."

"Only if Paul was a pregnant woman."

"Men show female symptoms. It's been known to happen—the male equivalent of hysterical pregnancy. Oh, not deliberately. I'm not saying it's common behavior. I don't want you to misquote me, if you decide to research my topic. I'm only saying that Saul, Paul, was on his way to Damascus, probably to be treated by a renowned physician, and he had this convulsion. He heard a voice. You know the voice I mean." Lapwing dropped his tone, as though nothing to do with Christianity should ever be mentioned in a church. "He hallucinated. It was a mystical hallucination. In other words, he did a Joan of Arc."

It was impossible to say if Lapwing was trying to be funny. I thought it safer to follow along: "If it's true, it could account for his hostility to women. He had to share a condition he wasn't born to."

"I've gone into that. If you ever research my premise, remember I've gone into everything. I think I may drop it, actually. It won't get me far. There's no demand."

"I don't see the complete field," I said. That sounded all right—inoffensive.

"Well, literature. But I may have strayed. I may be over the line." He dropped his gaze from the portrait to me, but still had to look up. "I don't really want to say more."

I think he was afraid I might encroach on his idea, try to pick his brain. I assured him that I was committed to French history and politics, but even that may have seemed too close, and he turned away to look for Edie, to find out for certain what she was doing, and ask her to stop.

MR. CHADWICK had found the evening so successful that he decided on a bolder social move: David must give a piano recital in the villa, with a distinguished audience in attendance. A reception would follow—white-wine cup, petits fours—after which some of us would be taken to a restaurant, as Mr. Chadwick's guests, for a dinner in David's honor. The event was meant to be a long jump in his progress from gardener to favored house guest.

He was let off gardening duty and spent much of his time now at the Biesels', where they offered him a cool room with a piano in it and left him in peace. Meanwhile the winter salon was torn apart and cleaned, dustcovers were removed from the sofas, the windows and shutters opened and washed and sealed tight again. The expert brought in from Nice to restore the Pleyel had a hard time putting it to rights, and asked for an extra fee. Mr. Chadwick would not give it, and for a time it looked as if there would be no recital at all. Mrs. Biesel quietly intervened and paid the difference. Mr. Chadwick never knew. One result of the conflict and its solution, apart from the piano's having been fixed, was that Mr. Chadwick began to tell stories about how he had, in the past, showed great firmness with workmen and tradesmen. They were boring stories, but, as Lily said, it was better than hearing the stories about his mother.

It seemed to me that the recital could end in nothing but disgrace and ridicule. I wondered why David went along with the idea.

"Amateurs have a lot of self-confidence," said Mrs. Biesel, when I asked what she thought. "A professional would be scared." I had come round to her house to call for Lily: she was spending a lot of time there, too, encouraging David.

Mrs. Biesel had a soft Southern voice and was not always easy to understand. (I was amazed when I discovered that to Mr. Chadwick all North Americans sounded alike.) I recall Mrs. Biesel with her head to one side, poised to listen, and her curved way of sitting, as if she were too tall and too thin for most chairs. I could say she was like a Modigliani, but it's too easy, and I am not sure I had heard of Modigliani then. The Biesels were rich, by which I mean that they had always lived with money, and when they spent any they always gave themselves a moral excuse. The day Lily decided she wanted to go to London without me, the Biesels paid her way. They saw morality on that occasion as a matter of happiness, Lily's in particular. Any suggestion that they might have conspired to harm and deceive was below their view of human nature. Conversation on the subject soon became like a long talk in a dream, with no words remembered, just an impression of things intended.

Mr. Chadwick pored over stacks of yellowed sheet music his mother had kept in a rosewood Canterbury. He wanted David to play short pieces with frequent changes in mood. "None of your all-Schubert," he said. "It just puts people to sleep."

Mrs. Biesel supplied printed programs on thick ivory paper. We were supposed to keep them as souvenirs, but the printer had left off the date. She apologized to Mr. Chadwick, as though it were her own fault. (It is curious how David was overlooked; the recital seemed to have become a social arrangement between Mrs. Biesel and Mr. Chadwick.) Mr. Chadwick ran his eye down the page and said, "But he's not doing the Debussy. He's doing the Ravel."

"It's a long, hard program," said Mrs. Biesel, in just above a whisper. "It might have been easier if he had simply worked up some Bach."

At three o'clock on one of the hottest afternoons since the start of recorded temperatures, David sat down to the restored Pleyel. On the end wall behind him was a large Helleu drawing of Mr. Chadwick's mother playing the piano, with her head thrown back and a bunch of violets tied to her wrist. The winter carpets, rolled up and stacked next to the fireplace, smelled of old dust and moth repellent. Still Mr. Chadwick would not let the room be aired. To open the windows meant letting in heat. "You must all sit very still," he announced, as David got ready to start. "It's moving about, stirring up the atmosphere, that makes one feel warm."

Who was there? Mr. Chadwick's friends and neighbors, and a number of people I suspect he brought in on short acquaintance. I remember his doctor, a dour Alsatian who had the complete confidence of the British colony; he had acquired a few reassuring expressions in English, such as "It's just a little chill on the liver" and "Port's the thing." People liked that. When I think of the Canadians in the winter salon—the Lapwings, and Lily and me, and Fergus Bray, and an acquaintance of Lapwing's called Michael Hagen-Beck—it occurs to me that abroad, outside embassy premises or official functions, I never saw that many in one room again. Hagen-Beck was an elderly-looking undergraduate of nineteen to twenty, dressed in scant European-style shorts, a khaki shirt, knee socks, and gym shoes. Near the end of the recital, he walked out of the house and did not come back.

Lily mooned at David, as she had at Christian Ferras. I supposed it must be her way of contemplating musicians. There was nothing wrong with it; I had just never thought of her as a mooner of any kind. Once she sprang from her chair and pushed open a shutter: the room was so dim that David had to strain to read the music. Mr. Chadwick left the shutter ajar, but latched the window once more, murmuring again his objection to stirring up the atmosphere.

During the Chopin Edie went to sleep, wearing one of those triangular smiles that convey infinite secret satisfaction. Her husband wiped his forehead with a cotton scarf he took out of her handbag and returned carefully, without waking her up. I had the feeling they got along better when one of them was unconscious. He adjusted his glasses and frowned at a gilt Buddha sitting in front of the cold fireplace, as if he were trying to assess its place in Mr. Chadwick's spiritual universe. During the pause between the Chopin and the Albéniz, he unlocked the French doors, left them wide, and went out to the baking terrace, half covered by the branches of a jacaranda; into the hot shade of the tree he dragged a wrought-iron chair and a chintz-covered pillow (the chair looked as if it had not been moved since the reign of Edward VII), making a great scraping sound over the flagstones. The scraping blended with the first bars of the Albéniz; those of us in the salon who were still awake pretended not to hear.

I envied Lapwing, settled comfortably in iron and chintz, in the path of a breeze, however tepid, with trumpet-shaped blue flowers falling on his neck and shoulders. He seemed to be sizing up over the chalkier blue of a plumbago hedge the private beach and white umbrellas of the Pratincole, Rivebelle's only smart hotel—surviving evidence that this part of the coast had been fashionable before the war. In an open court couples were dancing to a windup gramophone, as they did every day at this hour. We could hear one of those tinny French voices, all vivacity, but with an important ingredient missing—true vitality, I think—singing an old American show tune with sentimental French lyrics: *pour toi, pour moi, pour toujours.* It reminded me of home, all but the words, and finally I recognized a song my aunt had on a record, with "She Didn't Say 'Yes'" on the other side. Perhaps she used to dance to it, before she decided to save her energy for bringing me up. I remembered just some of the words: "new luck, new love." I wondered if there was any sense to them—if luck and love ever changed course after moving on. Mr. Chadwick was old enough to know, but it wasn't a thing I could ask.

Lapwing sat between two currents of music. Perhaps he didn't hear: the Pratincole had his whole attention. Our wives longed to dance, just once, in that open court, under the great white awning, among the lemon trees in tubs, and to drink champagne mixed with something at the white-and-chromium bar, but we could not afford so much as a Pratincole drink of water. I don't know how, but Lapwing had gained the impression that Mr. Chadwick was taking us for dinner there. He sat at his ease under the jacaranda, choosing his table. (A later review of events had Lapwing urging Hagen-Beck to join us for dinner, even though his share of the day was supposed to end with the petits fours: a story that Lapwing continued to evoke years after in order to deny it.)

The rest of us sat indoors, silent and sweating. We seemed to be suffocating under layers of dark-green gauze, what with the closed shutters, and the vines pressing on them, and the verd-antique incrustation in the ancient bronze ornaments and candelabra. The air that came in from the terrace, now that Lapwing had opened the French doors, was like the emanation from a furnace, and the sealed windows cut off any hope of a crossbreeze. Mrs. Biesel fanned herself with a program, when she was not using it to beat time. Fergus Bray slid from his sofa to the marble floor and lay stretched, propped on an elbow. I noticed he had concealed under the sofa a full tumbler of whiskey, which he quietly sipped. Once, sinking into a deep sleep and pulling myself up just in time, I caught sight of Lapwing leaning into the room, with his eyes and glasses glittering, looking—in memory—like the jealous husband he was about to become.

If a flash of prophecy could occur to two men who have no use for each other, he and I would have shared the revelation that our wives were soon to travel—his to Madrid with one of that day's guests, mine to London on the same train as our host's gardener and friend. (It was Mrs. Biesel's opinion that Lily had just wanted company on the train.) Mentioning two capital cities makes their adventure sound remote, tinged with fiction, like so many shabby events that occur in foreign parts. If I could say that Lily had skipped to Detroit and Edie to Moose Jaw, leaving Lapwing and me stranded in a motel, we would come out of it like a couple of gulls. But "Madrid," and "London," and "the Mediterranean," and a musician, a playwright, a novelist, a recital in a winter salon lend us an alien glow. We seem to belong to a generation before our own time. Lapwing and I come on as actors in a film. The opening shot of a lively morning street and a jaunty pastiche of circus tunes set the tone, and all the rest is expected to unfold to the same pulse, with the same nostalgia. In fact, there was nothing to unfold except men's humiliation, which is bleached and toneless.

The compliments and applause David received at the end of the recital were not only an expression of release and relief. We admired his stamina and courage. The varied program, and David's dogged and reliable style, made me think of an anthology of fragments from world literature translated so as to make it seem that everyone writes in the same way. Between fleeting naps, we had listened and had found no jarring mistakes, and Mr. Chadwick was close to tears of the humblest kind of happiness.

David looked drawn and distant, and very young—an exhausted sixteen. I felt sorry for him, because so much that was impossible was expected from him; although his habitual manner, at once sulky and superior, and his floppy English haircut got on my nerves. He resembled the English poets of about ten years before, already ensconced as archetypes of a class and a kind. Lily liked him; but, then, she had been nice to Hagen-Beck, even smiling at him kindly as he walked out. I decided that to try to guess what attracted women, or to devise some rule from temporary evidence, was a waste of time. On the whole, Hagen-Beck—oaf and clodhopper—was somehow easier to place. I could imagine him against a setting where he looked like everybody else, whereas David seemed to me everywhere and forever out of joint.

LATE IN THE EVENING Mr. Chadwick's dinner guests, chosen by David, climbed the Mussolini staircase to the square, now cleared of stage and chairs, and half filled with a wash of restaurant tables. A few children wheeled round on bikes. Old people and lovers sat on the church steps and along the low wall. Over the dark of the sky, just above the church, was the faintest lingering trace of pink.

The party was not proceeding as it should: Mr. Chadwick had particularly asked to be given a round table, and the one reserved for us was definitely oblong. "A round table is better for conversation," he kept saying, "and there is less trouble about the seating."

"It doesn't matter, Mr. Chadwick," said Edie, in the appeasing tone she often used with her husband. "This one is fine." She stroked the pink-and-white tablecloth, as if to show that it was harmless.

"They promised the round table. I shall never come here again."

At the table Mr. Chadwick wanted, a well-dressed Italian in his fifties was entertaining his daughter and her four small children. The eldest child might have been seven; the youngest had a large table napkin tied around his neck, and was eating morsels of Parma ham and melon with his fingers. But presently I saw that the striking good looks of the children were drawn from both adults equally, and that the young mother was the wife of that much older man. The charm and intelligence of the children had somehow overshot that of the parents, as if they had arrived at a degree of bloom that was not likely to vary for a long time, leaving the adults at some intermediate stage. I kept this observation to myself. English-speaking people do not as a rule remark on the physical grace of children, although points are allowed for cooperative behavior. There is, or used to be, a belief that beauty is something that has to be paid for and that a lovely child may live to regret.

A whole generation between two parents was new to me. Mr. Chadwick, I supposed, could still marry a young wife. It seemed unlikely; and yet he was shot through with parental anguish. His desire to educate David, to raise his station, to show him off, had a paternal tone. At the recital he had been like a father hoping for the finest sort of accomplishment but not quite expecting it.

We continued to stand while he counted chairs and place settings. "Ten," he said. "I told them we'd be nine."

"Hagen-Beck may turn up," said Lapwing. "I think he went to the wrong place."

"He was not invited," said Mr. Chadwick. "At least, not by me."

"He wasn't anywhere around to be invited," said Mrs. Biesel. "He left before the Ravel."

"I told him where we were going," said Edie. "I'm sorry. I thought David had asked him."

"What are you sorry about?" said Lapwing. "He didn't hear what you said, that's all."

"Mr. Chadwick," said Lily. "Where do you want us to sit?"

The Italian had taken his youngest child on his lap. He wore a look of alert and careful indulgence, from which all anxiety had been drained. Anxiety had once been there; you could see the imprint. Mr. Chadwick could not glance at David without filling up with mistrust. Perhaps, for an older man, it was easier to live with a young wife and several infants than to try to hold on to one restless boy.

"Sit wherever you like," said Mr. Chadwick. "Perhaps David would like to sit here," indicating the chair on his left. (Lapwing had already occupied the one on the right.) Protocol would have given him Mrs. Biesel and Edie. Lily and the Biesels moved to the far end of the table. Edie started to sit down next to David, but he put his hand on the chair, as if he were keeping it for someone else. She settled one place over, without fuss; she was endlessly good-tempered, taking rudeness to be a mishap, toughened by her husband's slights and snubs.

"It's going to be all English again," she said, looking around, smiling. I remember her round, cheerful face and slightly slanted blue eyes. "Doesn't anyone know any French people? Here I am in France, forgetting all my French."

"There was that French doctor this afternoon," said Mrs. Biesel. "You could have said something to him."

"No, she couldn't," said Lapwing. "She was sound asleep."

"You would be obliged to go a long way from here to hear proper French," said Mr. Chadwick. "Perhaps as far as Lyons. Every second person in Rivebelle is from Sicily."

Lapwing leaned into the conversation, as if drawn by the weight of his own head. "Edie doesn't have to hear proper French," he said. "She can read it. She's been reading a French classic all summer— 'Forever Amber.'"

I glanced at Lily. It was the only time that evening I was able to catch her eye. Yes, I know, he's humiliating her, she signaled back.

"There are the Spann-Monticules," said Mr. Chadwick to Edie. "They have French blood, and they can chatter away in French, when they want to. They never come down here except at Easter. The villa is shut the rest of the year. Sometimes they let the mayor use it for garden parties. Hugo Spann-Monticule's great-great-grandmother was the daughter of Arnaud Monticule, who was said to have sacked the Bologna library for Napoleon. Monticule kept a number of priceless treasures for himself, and decided he would be safer in England. He married a Miss Spann. The Spanns had important wool interests, and the family have continued to prosper. Some of the Bologna loot is still in their hands. Lately, because of Labour, they have started smuggling some things back into France."

"Museum pieces belong in museums, where people can see them," said Lapwing.

"They shouldn't be kept in an empty house," said the Admiral.

Lapwing was so unused to having anyone agree with him that he looked offended. "I wouldn't mind seeing some of the collection," he said. "They might let one person in. I don't mean a whole crowd."

"The day France goes Communist they'll be sorry they ever brought anything here," said Mrs. Biesel.

"France will never go Communist," said her husband. "Stalin doesn't want it. A Communist France would be too independent for the Kremlin. The last thing Stalin wants is another Tito on his hands."

I was surprised to hear four sentences from the Admiral. As a rule he drank quietly and said very little, like Fergus Bray. He gave me the impression that he did not care where he lived or what might happen next. He still drove a car, and seemed to have great strength in his remaining arm, but a number of things had to be done for him. He had sounded just now as if he knew what he was talking about. I remembered the rumor that he was here for an underground purpose, but it was hard to see what it might be, in this seedy border resort. According to Lily, his wife had wanted to live abroad for a while. So perhaps it really was as simple as that.

"You're right," Mrs. Biesel said. "Even French Communists must know what the Russians did in Berlin."

"Liberated the Berliners, you mean?" said Lapwing, getting pink in the face.

"Our neighbors are all French," said Edie, speaking to Mr. Chadwick across David and the empty chair. "They aren't Sicilians. I've never met a Sicilian. I'm not even sure where they come from. I was really thinking of a different kind of French person—someone Harry might want to talk to. He gets bored sometimes. There's nobody around here on his level. Those Spanns you mentioned—couldn't we meet them? I think Harry might enjoy them."

"They never meet anyone," said Mr. Chadwick. "Although if you stay until next Easter you might see them driving to church. They drive to St. George's on Easter Sunday."

"We don't go to church, except to look at the art," said Edie. "I just gradually gave it up. Harry started life as a Baptist. Can you believe it? He was fully immersed, with a new suit on."

"In France, it's best to mix either with peasants or the very top level," said Mrs. Biesel. "Nothing in between." Her expression suggested that she had been offered and had turned down a wide variety of native French.

I sat between Fergus Bray and the Admiral. Edie, across the table, was midway between Fergus and me, so that we formed a triangle, unlikely and ill-assorted. To mention Fergus Bray now sounds like a cheap form of name-dropping. His work has somehow been preserved from decay. There always seems to be something, somewhere, about to go into production. But in those days he was no one in particular, and he was there. He had been silent since the start of the concert and had taken his place at table without a word, and was now working through a bottle of white wine intended for at least three of us. He began to slide down in his chair, stretching his legs. I saw that he was trying to capture Edie's attention, perhaps her foot. She looked across sharply, first at me. When his eyes were level with hers, he said, "Do you want to spend the rest of your life with that shrimp?"

I think no one but me could hear. Lapwing, on the far side of Fergus, was calling some new argument to the Biesels; Mr. Chadwick was busy with a waiter; and David was lost in his private climate of drizzle and mist.

"What shrimp?" said Edie. "You mean Harry?"

"If I say 'the rest of your life,' I must mean your husband."

"We're not really married," Edie said. "I'm his common-law wife, but only in places where they recognize common law. Like, I can have 'Lapwing' in my passport, but I couldn't be a Lapwing in Quebec. That's because in Quebec they just have civil law. I'm still married to Morrie Ringer there. Legally, I mean. You've never heard of him? You're a Canadian, and you've never heard of Morrie Ringer? The radio personality? 'The Ringer Singalong'? That's his most famous program. They even pick it up in Cleveland. Well, he can't live with me, can't forget me, won't divorce me. Anyway, the three of us put together haven't got enough money for a real divorce. You can't get a divorce in Quebec. You have to do some complicated, expensive thing. When you break up one marriage and set up another, it takes money. It's expensive to live by the rules—I don't care what you say." So far, he had said scarcely anything, and not about that. "In a way, it's as if I was Morrie's girl and Harry's wife. Morrie could never stand having meals in the house. We ate out. I lived for about two years on smoked meat and pickles. With Harry, I've been more the wife type. It's all twisted around."

"That's not what you're like," said Fergus.

"Twisted around?"

"Wife type. I've been married. I never could stand them. Wife types." He made a scooping movement with his hand and spread his palm flat.

In the falsetto men assume when they try to imitate a woman's voice, he addressed a miniature captive husband:

"From now on, you've got to work for me, and no more girlfriends."

"Some women are like that," said Edie. "I'm not."

"Does the shrimp work for you?"

"We don't think that way. He works for himself. In a sense, for me. He wants me to have my own intellectual life. I've been studying. I've studied a few things." She looked past him, like a cat.

"What few things?"

"Well … I learned a few things about the Cistercians. There was a book in a room Harry and I rented in London. Someone left it behind. So, I know a few things."

"Just keep those few things to yourself, whatever they may be. Was your father one?"

"A monk? You must be a Catholic, or you wouldn't make that sort of a joke. My father—I hardly know what to think about him. He won't have anything to do with me. Morrie was Jewish, and my father didn't like that. Then I left Morrie for a sort of Baptist Communist. That was even worse. He used to invite Morrie for Christmas dinner, but he won't have Harry in the house. I can't help what my father feels. You can't live on someone else's idea of what's right."

"You say all those things as though they were simple," he said. "Look, can you get away?"

She glanced once round the table; her eyes swept past me. She looked back at Fergus and said, "I'll try." She lifted her hair with both hands. "I'll tell Harry the truth. I'll say I want to show you the inside of the church. We were in it the other night. That's the truth."

"I didn't mean that. I meant, leave him and come to me."

"Leave Harry?"

"You aren't married to him," Fergus said. "I'm not talking about a few minutes or a week or a vacation. I mean, leave him and come to Spain and live with me."

"Whereabouts in Spain?" she said.

"Madrid. I've got a place. You'll be all right."

"As what? Wife or girlfriend?"

"Anything you want."

She let go her hair, and laughed, and said, "I was just kidding. I don't know you. I've already left somebody. You can't keep doing that, on and on. Besides, Harry loves me."

We were joined now by Michael Hagen-Beck. The stir caused by his arrival may have seemed welcoming, but it was merely surprise. On the way to the restaurant Mrs. Biesel had set forth considerable disapproval of the way he had left the concert before the Ravel. Lily had defended him (she believed he had gone to look for a bathroom and felt too shy to come back), but Lapwing had said gravely, "I'm afraid Hagen-Beck will have to be wiped off the board," and I had pictured him turning in a badge of some kind and slinking out of class.

He nodded in the curt way that is supposed to conceal diffidence but that usually means a sour nature, removed the empty chair next to David, dragged it to the far end of the table, and wedged it between Mrs. Biesel and Lily.

"Hey, there's Hagen-Beck," said Lapwing, as if he were astonished to find him this side of the Atlantic.

"I'm afraid he is too late for the soup," said Mr. Chadwick.

"He won't care," said Lapwing. "He'd sooner talk than eat. He's brilliant. He's going to show us all up, one day. Well, he may show some people up. Not everybody."

Lily sat listening to Hagen-Beck, her cheek on her hand. In the dying light her hair looked silvery. I could hear him telling her that he had been somewhere around the North Sea, to the home of his ancestors, a fishing village of superior poverty. He spoke of herrings— how many are caught and sold in a year, how many devoured by seagulls. Beauty is in the economics of Nature, he said. Nowhere else.

"But isn't what people build beautiful, too?" said Lily, pleading for the cracked and faded church.

A waiter brought candles, deepening the color of the night and altering the shade and tone of the women's skin and hair.

"This calls for champagne," Mr. Chadwick said, in a despairing voice.

David had not touched the fish soup or the fresh langouste especially ordered for him. He stared at his plate, and sometimes down the table to the wall of candlelight, behind which Lily and Hagen-Beck sat talking quietly. Mr. Chadwick looked where David was looking. I saw that he had just made a complex and understandable mistake; he thought that David was watching Hagen-Beck, that it was for Hagen-Beck he had tried to keep the empty chair.

"Great idea, champagne," said Lapwing, once he had made certain Mr. Chadwick was paying for it. "We haven't toasted David's wonderful performance this afternoon." From a man who detested the very idea of music, this was a remarkable sign of good will.

Hagen-Beck would not drink wine, probably because it had been unknown to his ancestors. Summoning a waiter, who had better things to do, he asked for water—not false, bottled water but the real kind, God's kind, out of a tap. It was brought to him, in a wine-stained carafe. Two buckets of ice containing champagne had meanwhile been placed on the table, one of them fatally close to Fergus. The wine was opened and poured. Hagen-Beck swallowed water. Mr. Chadwick struck his glass with a knife: he was about to estrange David still further by making a speech.

Fergus and Edie, deep in some exchange, failed to hear the call for silence. In the sudden hush at our table Edie said distinctly, "When I was a kid, we made our own Christmas garlands and decorations. We'd start in November, the whole family. We made birds out of colored paper, and tied them to branches, and hung the branches all over the house. We spent our evenings that way, making these things. Now my father won't even open my Christmas cards. My mother writes to me, and she sends me money. I wouldn't have anything to wear if she didn't. My father doesn't know. Harry doesn't know. I've never told it to anybody, until now."

She must have meant "to any man," because she had told it to Lily.

"It's boring," said Fergus. "That's why you don't tell it. Nobody cares. If you were playing an old woman, slopping on in a bathrobe and some old slippers, it might work. But here you are—golden hair, golden skin. You look carved in butter. The dress is too tight for you, though. I wouldn't let you wear it if I had any say. And those god-awful earrings—where do they come from?"

"London, Woolworth's."

"Well, get rid of them. And your hair should be longer. And nobody cares about your bloody garlands. Don't talk. Just be golden, be quiet."

I suppose the others thought he had insulted her. I was the only one who knew what had gone on before, and how easily she had said, "Wife or girlfriend?" Lapwing merely looked interested. Another man might have challenged Fergus, or, thinking he was drunk, drawn his attention away from Edie and let it die. But Lapwing squeaked, "That's what I keep telling her, Bray. Nobody cares! Nobody cares! Be quiet! Be quiet!"

I saw Lapwing's heavy head bowing and lifting, and Edie's slow expression of shock, and Fergus pouring himself, and nobody else, champagne. This time there surely must have been a flash of telepathy between two people with nothing in common. Fergus and I must have shared at least one thought: Lapwing had just opened his palm, revealing a miniature golden wife, and handed her over.

Then Edie looked at Fergus, and Fergus at Edie, and I watched her make up her mind. The spirit of William Morris surrounded the new lovers, evading his most hardworking academic snoop. Lapwing ought to have stood and quoted, "Fear shall not alter these lips and these eyes of the loved and the lover," but he seemed to see nothing, notice nothing; or like Mr. Chadwick he continued to see and notice the wrong things.

Three of the future delinquents at our table were ex-Catholics. They took it for granted that the universe was eternal and they could gamble their lives. Whatever thin faith they still had was in endless renewal—new luck, new love. Nothing worked out for them, but even now I can see what they were after. Remembering Edie at the split second when she came to a decision, I can find it in me to envy them. The rest of us were born knowing better, which means we were stuck. When I finally looked away from her it was at another pool of candlelight, and the glowing, blooming children. I wonder now if there was anything about us for the children to remember, if they ever later on reminded one another: There was that long table of English-speaking people, still in bud.

The Nature of Pure Evil

Hedy reaches for the telephone to make another bomb threat. In minutes, from the corner windows of this office on the nineteenth floor of the TD Tower, she will see people empty like ants from the art gallery across the way. Last week it was her own building, the week before an entire city block—including the Hotel Georgia, Albear Jewellers and the Nightcourt Pub—and before that the Four Seasons Hotel. She knows it's illegal, but has convinced herself that it's not wrong, nor even harmful. It's a disruption of commerce, nothing more. Even the city gallery, with its reproductions shop and elegant little café, is a place of commerce. Hedy is like Jesus in the temple, screaming, "Get out!"

Only, Jesus most likely wasn't seized with mirth after ordering the people out of the temple. Although Hedy's major acquaintance with the Saviour is not by way of the Bible, but through the rock opera *Jesus Christ Superstar*, she can well imagine that Jesus didn't shake with uncontrollable laughter after knocking over tables of dovecotes and chasing the money-changers and their customers into the street. And what would Jesus think of the temples of today anyway, some of them as violently rococo as the court of the Sun King, shamelessly passing their gilded collection plates at every opportunity? Her next target would be Christ Church Cathedral, no question about it.

Hedy has to admit that her original impetus for disrupting daily commerce had not been half so noble as Jesus's. His was the sanctity of prayer. Hers was Stanley.

HEDY IRONED THE PLEATS of Stanley's white tuxedo shirt as he stood in the kitchen alcove in his undershirt, shaking Nuts 'n' Bolts into his mouth from the box and trying not to get any onto his freshly creased tuxedo pants. Hedy lifted the iron and it hissed like a small dragon. She pressed it down one more time. Stanley came over and traced her spine lightly with his hand. "That's perfect, honey. Bang-on job."

After Hedy helped adjust Stanley's bow tie, she asked him one more time, "So how come I don't get to come to this wedding with you?"

"Aw, Hedy, come on. Don't start with that again."

"I'm not starting with anything. It just seems funny."

Stanley shrugged. "I told you, I'm the only one invited."

"In that case, we'll see who has a better time. I'm going to curl up with a fat novel, my box of Quality Street and some Bessie Smith. I hate borscht, anyways."

"Atta girl," Stanley said and chucked her affectionately under the chin.

The next day, Hedy showed up at work with swollen eyes bulging like tennis balls. Tiny blood vessels had burst in her nose from a night of crying. "Allergies," Hedy said brightly in response to the reception-ist's concerned look. Brigit, the salesperson at the next desk who had taken it upon herself to become Hedy's best friend, took one look at her and led her into the Ladies. When Hedy told her Stanley had come home after the wedding, packed a suitcase and left because it had been his *own* wedding, Brigit put her hands over her mouth and looked like she'd stopped breathing.

"Oh, Hedy!"

"It's all right," Hedy sniffed.

"It's terrible. It's so weird. He must be insane."

Hedy shook her head. "He's quite normal."

"If he's not crazy, then he's pure evil."

HEDY LOOKS TO SEE if there's anyone within hearing distance and then starts to dial. At the time management company she works for, the employees pride themselves on organizing their days effectively, conquering gridlock of the mind. They talk of things like Time Bandits and the Time Crunch Decade. By prioritizing their activities, they are seldom stuck working at their desks through the lunch hour. Instead, they are at liberty to go shop for the perfect wedding gift, pick up their dry cleaning, or stroll the mall, a hot dog in hand, pretending to be free spirits while dodging skateboards piloted by heavily pierced and tattooed waifs. As a result, there is usually no one in the office at the tail end of the lunch hour, except for the substitute receptionist and employees organizing house parties who don't want to be caught squandering company time.

The first time Hedy called in a bomb threat, she did it without any forethought. She was on the telephone to a potential client, a paint wholesaler, on the verge of selling him a seminar package for his office staff, when through the big plate-glass windows of the nineteenth floor she saw Stanley walk into the Four Seasons, arm in arm with a woman. She was sure it was Stanley. His red bomber jacket, his bouncy gait. This was one week after she had carefully ironed his white tuxedo shirt and sent him off to his own wedding. The iron had hissed with that reassuring sound she loved. She had even straightened his bow tie.

She told the potential client that a colleague had just collapsed—heart attack, cholesterol, angina, epilepsy, fish bone—it was hard to see from where she was sitting, and she had better go. Her St. John Ambulance training might be needed. Hedy surprised herself with her quick, bubbly lie. She had always been the carefully honest one, the one who admitted to the bus driver that her handful of change was a penny short of the fare, the one who had always come home at least half an hour before curfew.

Her throat tightened at the thought of Stanley taking his bride to lunch at Chartwell. They had gone to Chartwell, once, after they first moved in together. The tomato-gin soup had tickled her nose and Stanley had made a big show of choosing a martini "like Roger Moore would of drunk." In that dark room, with fox-hunt wallpaper and sturdy chairs upholstered in tapestry, Hedy had imagined they were now legitimately in love. What if Stanley and his bride, his *wife*, now sat at the same table, toying with the same cutlery? What if his wife put the very same silver fork into her mouth that Hedy had used to pierce the crisp skin of her stuffed quail seven years ago?

Hedy opened the telephone book, looked up the Four Seasons, and dialled.

She had been surprised how easy it was. People pouring out onto Georgia and Howe streets, dodging traffic and then standing, craning their necks from across the road, waiting for the explosion. The police cars and fire trucks whirring up from all directions, and Hedy standing alongside her colleagues who anxiously lined the office windows wondering what in the world was going on down there. She had pinched her forearms to keep from laughing. All those people milling around on the sidewalks, scared, excited, all because of her one little phone call. And there was Stanley, standing by himself in the crowd, practically right below her window, goosenecking for a better view, his new bride momentarily forgotten.

The newspapers wrote righteous and relieved editorials about the false alarm. But Hedy realized that people had enjoyed the incident. They got to go home and say, "You wouldn't believe what happened today!" People had something to discuss while they waited at bus stops and SkyTrain stations. They were *talking* to each other. By casting them out into the street, Hedy had done them all a favour. Like Jesus.

AS HEDY'S BEST FRIEND, Brigit felt compelled to launch a crusade to prove Stanley was evil. Whenever Hedy insisted Stanley had never been the slightest bit crazy, Brigit said, "Then he must be pure evil. There's no other explanation for that kind of behaviour." Hedy found her friend's efforts on her behalf embarrassing. Brigit would haul her up to a colleague's desk and say, "Tell Tina/Shaffin/Morgan/Pascal, et cetera, exactly what Stanley did." After Hedy finished the *Reader's Digest* version, with much prodding from Brigit, Brigit would say, "Now, don't you find that insane?" The colleague would agree, after glancing at Hedy, that yes, Stanley's actions sounded a touch insane. "But if he's not crazy, then what?" Brigit would ask. "If he's perfectly normal, wouldn't you say he was pure evil?"

Brigit showed Hedy magazine articles about people without consciences—people who, on a mere whim, crushed children's heads like melons, sold fake and fatal remedies to the elderly, or were secretly polygamous. None of them showed any remorse. "It's not just the deed itself, it's the lack of remorse that makes them evil," Brigit said.

It was true Stanley had shown no remorse. "Gotta go, kiddo, Steph's waiting in the car," he had said as Hedy handed him his folded shirts, which he carefully laid into the largest of their burgundy Samsonite bags, along with a handful of the fresh-smelling cedar eggs they kept in the underwear drawer. The luggage was a gift from her mother, who had felt sorry for them when they showed up at the airport one Christmas years ago with their clothes in an old Adidas hockey bag mended with silver duct tape. Hedy considered the set of luggage theirs as opposed to just hers. That's what happens with things after you live together for seven years. She had wanted to ask what "their" song had been at the wedding. She needed to know it wasn't their song, Rod Stewart's "You're in My Heart, You're in My Soul." She sort of doubted it—Rod Stewart didn't seem to be held in high regard these days. Still, some things remain sacred.

She wanted to ask whether Steph—or was it Stephanie?—knew about her, but she realized of course she must; he's up here packing his clothes and has asked her to wait downstairs. Hedy had felt giddy, almost hurrying him along, thinking, *His wife's waiting downstairs,* as if she was anxious not to be labelled the other woman, some dame spread-eagled across the bed in filmy lingerie, cooing B-movie enticements.

Hedy had wanted to ask him why he was doing this. But she believed that if he knew, he probably would have told her.

"Hitler, Clifford Olson, David Koresh, those blond monsters in St. Catharines, all anonymous albino hitmen everywhere," Brigit said, "and Stanley."

HEDY HAS IT ALL down pat now. If she's not creepily specific, this may be the time they decide the caller is crying wolf. They might call her bluff. But then, perhaps they can't afford to take that chance. Not with all those children in the art gallery, Hedy thinks, the ones there for the regular Wednesday children's tour.

Last time, she detailed the type of bomb and the group responsible, which resulted in an even quicker evacuation and a SWAT team—*a SWAT team!* The entire TD Tower and adjoining mall had been emptied out. They weren't allowed to take the elevators, for fear that might trigger the bomb, so everyone in the tower trooped down the stairs, some barely concealing their panic, others skeptical and cursing about sales they'd be losing to competitors. As Hedy was jostled down the stairs, she thought of the adulterers who might not be at work that day due to an illicit rendezvous at Horseshoe Bay or the Reifel Bird Sanctuary. "Bob!" "Sue!" their innocent loves would say when they arrived home. "I was so worried about you because of that bomb threat. I tried to phone but all the lines kept ringing busy." The adulterers, still in a postcoital haze, would let slip, "Bomb threat? What bomb threat?" And the cat, claws and all, would tumble out of the bag.

"Plastic explosives," Hedy says to the hysterical gallery attendant on the other end of the line. "Even trained dogs can't smell them." She knows enough to keep it short so the call can't be traced. Last week the employee who answered the phone at the TD branch downstairs had maintained the presence of mind to try to keep her on the line. "I have two little children," the woman had said. "Louise and Adrienne, two lovely girls. Do you happen to have any children, ma'am?" Hedy had hung up, admiring the woman's outward calm.

But this giddy gallery attendant has already dropped the receiver and is yelling something wildly in the background. Hedy hears the receiver bump against the counter, once, twice, three times, and pictures it dangling on the end of its line, twisting a little like a freshly hooked fish. Someone picks up the receiver and Hedy hears the carefully varnished tones of a Kerrisdale matron, "Who do you think you are?"

Didn't Jesus say, Let he who is without sin cast the first stone? Everyone knows that from their elementary school catechism. And Hedy, well, she is without sin. She is the lamb.

"IT'S NOT LIKE it was the love affair of the century," Hedy told Brigit. "We were just comfortable."

"That's still no excuse to treat you like that."

Hedy and Brigit entered the Frog & Peach, a lovely, rustic little French restaurant on the west side of the city.

"These women you're about to meet, they're very good people," Brigit said. "You'll like them. You spend way too much time alone. Women need female friends."

"Please promise you won't bring up Stanley."

Brigit made as if she was zipping up her mouth with her fingers and then tossing the key over her shoulder. She made such a show of it that Hedy could almost hear the key tinkle on the restaurant's terra-cotta tiles.

Hedy had finished her trout with persimmon chutney and sweet potato gratin, and was toying with her fudge cake on raspberry coulis when Brigit brought up the subject of evil. To be fair, she didn't exactly bring it up, but grasped the opportunity when it arose. Mary Tam, who was a French immersion teacher, looked at the praline slice she'd ordered and said, "Oh, c'est diabolique, c'est mauvais, je l'aime." Then she automatically translated, out of habit: "It's devilish, it's evil, I love it."

"Would you say that people who do unspeakable things are plain crazy?" Brigit asked as if the thought just happened to descend on her from the pastoral fresco overhead. Her fork swayed dreamily above her lemon mousse. "Or is there such a thing as pure evil?" Hedy picked up her knife and made a quick sawing motion across her throat. Brigit ignored her.

"It depends on what you mean by evil," said Donna von something, who was unbelievably thin despite her seven-month pregnancy. She had attended university in the States and throughout dinner she fumed about an American professor of hers named Bloom who had decried moral relativism. He had even published a book on the topic, *The Closing of the American Mind,* or something like that. When Hedy weakly joked that she thought the American mind was already closed, Donna had looked at her with pity.

"What's evil in some cultures isn't considered evil in others." Donna's tone implied she would mentally thrash all dissenters.

"By evil, I mean doing something that causes irreparable pain or harm to innocent people," Brigit said. "I don't think it's relative at all."

"Female circumcision. That's brutal any way you look at it."

"Please, I'm still eating."

Mary put down her fork and took a big swallow of red wine. "Hurting children is evil, rape is evil, eating people is evil."

"What if you eat someone to survive, like those rugby players that crashed in the Andes? And look at how curious everyone was, wanting to know what it tasted like." Hedy thought Donna's smile looked wickedly jejune, as if she had just scored a point at a high school debating tournament.

"When you've come into contact with pure evil, there's no mistaking it," Claudia, a practising family therapist, said slowly. She had been rather quiet all through dinner and now the unexpected sound of her voice commanded attention. "When I was living in Ottawa a few years ago, I went to an open house one Sunday. It was a beautiful place in Sandy Hill, right near the University of Ottawa. A three-storey sandstone, with enormous red maple leaves brushing against the front windows because it was fall."

"Fall in Ottawa is fabulous," Brigit said. Everyone shushed her.

"It was full of people, and the real estate agent had put out a platter of petits fours and was serving coffee in real china cups. It felt like some exquisite afternoon salon as people wandered in and out of rooms, chatting, sipping at coffee and nibbling little cakes. But there was this one room on the third floor, sort of an attic bedroom, that people seemed to walk out of really quickly. They came hurrying down the stairs, dribbling coffee and crumbs."

Mary refilled the wineglasses. "I don't know if I can listen to this."

"I went up the stairs behind the real estate agent, who seemed almost hesitant to show me that room. I walked right into it and immediately I felt the hairs rise on the back of my neck and arms. The real estate agent stood in the doorway, just outside the room, and tried to direct my view out the window toward the Ottawa River. But something made me look up. The ceiling was painted black, with thin red lines connected to form a pentagram."

"Look, the hairs on my arms are standing up right now!" Mary held her thin arms out over the table. The black hairs glistened silver in the candlelight. The hairs on Hedy's arms were rising, too. She felt like she used to at sleepover parties when the girls tried to outdo each other with horror stories just before falling off to sleep. Maybe that's what evil was, just another party game.

Donna looked disdainful. "I find it really hard to believe they wouldn't have painted the ceiling over before attempting to sell such a prime piece of real estate."

"That's what I thought, too," Claudia said. "But I found out they had tried. They went through half a dozen professional painters and a couple of university students. Nobody could stay in that room more than five minutes. There was something evil in there, I could feel it. I've never come across a feeling like that before or since."

"I was talking about evil people," Brigit said, sounding irritated. "Not *spirits*."

Hedy looked up at the fresco and saw a bucolic scene of little satyrs chasing plump nymphs across faux-distressed plaster. The candlelight flicked shadows across it, creating the illusion that the creatures were moving, darting in and out of flames. She thought of Stanley and his bride, Stephanie, tousling on a king-size brass bed with jungle-motif sheets and decided that if Brigit brought up the subject of Stanley she would be forced to tip a burning candle into her lap.

"What about that person who's been calling in all those fake bomb threats?" Mary asked.

"Oh, that person," Brigit said. "That person's just nuts."

"I think we're talking about someone who desperately craves attention. Someone deprived of adequate affection in childhood."

"Original. I don't think you need a psych degree to figure that one out."

"I think it's pretty harmless."

"What if someone gets hurt, gets so scared they have a fatal heart attack right there on the street in front of their building?"

Hedy drifted in and out of the conversation. She thought about her childhood, a textbook case of love and understanding. Pork chops and applesauce, Snakes and Ladders, backyard swing sets, and a mother who hadn't been too embarrassed to hold a snowy white cotton pad in her hand and carefully explain what womanhood had to do with Hedy. She thought about Stanley, her affection for the springy rust-coloured hairs on his chest and his ability to bluster through most awkward social situations in an amiably anti-intellectual manner. But was that love?

"If hurting someone wasn't the intent, I would say it wasn't evil."

"Especially if they're sorry."

"What if they say they're sorry, but they're not."

"It's easy to *say* you're sorry."

"Only God really knows."

"What if you don't believe in God, or any gods?"

"Right."

God could really make people scurry, Hedy thought. God of Thunder, God of Lightning. Raining frogs down from the sky, now there was a feat. Where had she heard that? How could a booming giant like God have had a gentle son like Jesus? But it was always the quiet ones who surprised everyone when they finally opened their mouths to roar, wasn't it? Or perhaps she was putting too much stock in the Jesus of Tim Rice and Andrew Lloyd Webber.

"Evil has nothing to do with what's legal or illegal."

"I agree, I mean, there are so many unjust laws."

"Like which ones, for instance?"

"Always the devil's advocate."

"There's that word again."

"What word?"

"Devil."

"Ha ha."

HEDY STANDS AT THE WINDOW across the room from her desk, looking out toward the art gallery. A small person with green hair skateboards down the granite steps. The Iranians are there, passing out their pamphlets, counting on the milk of human kindness. Others steal a moment from a busy day to sit on the steps and hold their faces to the sun. She feels happy, although she would never tell Brigit that. In Brigit's judgment, she has every right to feel paralysed with unhappiness, catatonic with indignation. But Hedy has combed her heart and found no detritus, no coiled reddish hairs, no rust flakes.

Brigit would find some fault with happiness, anyways. Yesterday, she showed Hedy a magazine article about a British psychiatrist who thinks happiness should be classified as a mental condition—because it's a highly *abnormal* state of being. The psychiatrist wasn't referring to bliss, but a plain, old-fashioned level of contentment and calm. In which case perhaps Stanley is crazy after all, not evil, because he seemed so happy the last time Hedy saw him, unapologetically happy.

She wonders why people haven't started pouring out of the art gallery yet. It's been almost ten minutes since her phone call, yet there are no signs of panic, no sirens piercing the air, no men in stiff black coveralls stealthily slipping through the side entrances of the gallery, their intricate bomb diffusion kits strapped to their belts. Hedy's mood loses a little of its fine buoyancy. She decides she must make the call again. She glances toward her telephone, but sees that Brigit is back at the neighbouring desk.

"I was just listening to the CBC news in the car," Brigit says, as Hedy roots around in her top drawer for a quarter, "and did you know that there's a trend away from accepting pleas of insanity in cases of aggravated assault? It's an acknowledgement of man's baser instincts. I mean men *and* women, of course." Hedy nods as if she's paying attention, and then smiles as her fingers close around a quarter that's been nesting in a pile of paper clips. She tells Brigit that she's forgotten to pay an important bill and has to run down to the bank for a few minutes, just in case anyone asks. Brigit tut tuts, "Oh, those darn Time Bandits!" and waves her off with a conspiratorial wink.

Hedy starts counting as she enters the elevator, needing to know how long it will take to get back upstairs. She wants to be there in time to watch all the people streaming out of the gallery, the panicked milling around with the merely curious, the emergency vehicles dramatically screeching to a halt, the children noisily demanding to be told what's going on. As she walks through the shiny lobby toward the row of pay phones, Hedy feels positively grand. She is the one without sin striding quickly across the burning desert, thin sandals moulded to her calloused feet, the quarter hot and round and flat in the hollow of her hand.

Between Wars

He's given up the smell of mangoes, their sticky sweetness carried on grey clouds of diesel smoke, for an alien world of tar, cement, and heavy green weighted down with round drops of rain. He is strung taut like a washing line between two worlds, his hopes, his dreams, his fidelity and obligations all hanging limp, like wet laundry, like flags of united nations on a windless day.

It is New York, 1967, and Amir is dipping a hard-boiled egg in Tabasco sauce. Taking bite after small bite, thinking of war, thinking of home. "Learn the law," his mother, with her gold teeth and lame leg, had insisted.

"But I need to be here to be of help," he had said. His mother had been saying this for years.

"Your brothers are here."

Amir had looked around the table at his brothers and sighed. Shakil, his elder brother, had lost an eye in an explosion at a ceramics factory, Anwar was too eager to fight, and Sami was only eleven years old.

"For Daddy," his mother had said, patting his hand.

FOR DADDY, Amir left the West Bank for New York City to take up the offer of a graduate scholarship at Columbia. He arrived at JFK in the late summer of 1967 carrying a cardboard box and a briefcase and wearing his best pair of shoes. The box contained two suits his mother had sewn together under the tin roof of their makeshift home, a grey one of Egyptian cotton for summer, and a heavy brown wool suit for a winter harsher than the bounds of her imagination would permit. He hugged the briefcase that his father and his father's brothers had presented to him with as much ceremony as a gift to a bride at a Palestinian wedding, against his chest, as if it were a child. It was black Italian leather and had been specially ordered, his name, Amir Mahmoud, embossed in gold in italicized Roman script. It kept his passport, his visa, his maps, and photos of his family—his mother's gold smile at the centre of her world of men—safe and secure.

He slept on a mildewed mattress in a hostel beside six other men who had all come to New York seeking fortune, fame, refuge, or anonymity. Black, white, and Asian. First names only. He was the only Arab, the only Muslim among them, and they snickered when he bent down on all fours to pray. A man named Dave from Arkansas called him Swami, asked him what kind of shit magic lantern he'd rubbed to end up in this hellhole. Amir picked the lumps of pork byproduct from his plate of wieners and beans and prayed in the toilet, his knees sticking on dried urine, his head nearly smacking the porcelain bowl.

A week after his arrival, Amir plucked a pink index card off a bulletin board outside the Columbia housing registry. "Room for good Muslim brother," the notice read. He took photos of his family to the appointment. A gap-toothed Nigerian man answered the door of the top apartment in a five-story walkup in Greenwich Village. The Nigerian man was once a prince, but now, here in New York, where he lived with his two wives, he drove a taxi. Black and yellow. Pimps and diplomats and cops and ex-cons all asking the same thing: "Where you from?"

"I thought they didn't allow that in America," said Amir, puzzled. The younger wife offered tea, the elder offered cake. "How is it you could bring them both?"

"They are sisters," the man laughed conspiratorially. "So one has sponsored the other. You see? There are ways around every system. Even in America."

The older one had a bedroom, the younger one slept on a pullout couch in the living room that was also the kitchen. The other bedroom, with a mattress on the floor and a chair by a barred window overlooking a dark alleyway, was Amir's to rent, if he wanted it, which he did. For ten dollars extra, he could take his dinner with them, eat okra till the end of time.

"Delicious?" the younger one asked him.

"Mmm," Amir piped through gummy lips, scraping back his chair after the first seven nights of okra. He closed the door to his room, lay down on his mattress, and cracked open a shiny new American history textbook that had cost him more than six pairs of shoes would have cost at home.

ON HIS FIRST DAY of classes, Amir sat quietly in a seminar on Middle Eastern politics, sandwiched between a bookish woman who'd never left America and a young man with a yarmulke sitting on his bald head. The professor pegged the Arab and the Jew immediately, inviting them to stage a debate at the end of term. Amir would defend Zionism; Shel would argue that Zionism was racist.

Amir was shocked and confused. He couldn't possibly. *Is this what they do in America? Play games? Don costumes? Make puppet shows out of wars?* It seemed to be, because as soon as he'd dropped the course and enrolled in American political history, the professor decided they were going to stage the Civil War. Black students defending the interests of slave owners, white students fighting for emancipation. Amir, obviously more black than white in his professor's eyes, was lumped in with the slave owners.

Strange games. Bloodless wars in American classrooms. He'd make a mockery of their war, if it was required, but there was no way he could do that to his own.

"They have no idea what it is to live through a war!" he said to his Nigerian friend over dinner. "They have no idea that it is not just an exercise in philosophical debate. It has its own logic, unarticulated momentum. It has fuel—fury and hate."

"We're in America now, my man," said the Nigerian. "We left that behind us. We came for this better life." He shrugged. "Peace."

"FOR THIS BETTER LIFE," Amir mutters to himself on a cold morning in November at a coffee shop near the campus where he eats breakfast now, and sometimes dinner too, when he can't force down any more okra.

"You Italian or something?" the waitress asks him. He normally hates this kind of question, all the variations on this question that have been asked of him in the months since his arrival. But he hears something different this time. He hears a twang like a harp at the back of her throat when she speaks, he hears a voice that matters more than the words it speaks.

"Greek?" she asks, trying again.

"Palestinian," he says quietly to his grilled cheese sandwich.

"I've never heard of that."

"It's in the Middle East."

"You gotta war going on there, right?"

He nods.

"That why you're here? I mean in New York, not this dump specifically."

He nods again, in lieu of offering an explanation.

She refills his coffee cup. He looks at the pale freckled skin of her forearm as she pours and watches as she wanders down the rest of the counter, sideways, doing the same for the other customers. She is plain, she is pretty, she has braces on her top teeth but she is not ashamed to smile. Her nametag says Marianne.

HE GOES BACK to the coffee shop the following Thursday for a glimpse of the girl and the Thursday special. She greets him with a mouthful of facts about Palestine. He looks at her with surprise.

"Funk and Wagnalls," she says, smiling coyly.

He's still confused.

"Encyclopedia," she says.

He's touched by her curiosity. "Most people don't know that much about Palestine," he says.

"Well, it's all there in the book. Except the thing is, it was published in the fifties so it's not exactly up to date."

"But you know something about the background then."

"I was kind of hoping you could fill me in on what's happened since."

"It's not a very happy story."

"Who needs happy?" she says, gesturing wildly. "You think I do, just because I'm a girl?"

"I didn't mean that ..."

"So why won't you tell me?"

"I will tell you," he says, lowering his voice. "But not here."

"Are you asking me out then?"

"Uh—" he stammers.

"OK," she says. "Name the time and place."

"I can name the time. But I don't know any place."

"What time then?"

"Tomorrow?" he says. "Five o'clock?"

"Fine. At my place."

He swallows hard while she writes the directions down on a paper napkin.

HE WEARS HIS SUMMER SUIT the next day, with a white shirt but no tie, like an American. He doesn't know what to bring—an appropriate gift—so he asks the younger wife and she says, "Take some candy, take something sweet. The girls, they like sweet things," and when he closes the door behind him, he hears the two women laughing together. They're laughing at him. They must think him a fool, and he does feel like a fool today, but his self-consciousness abates when he enters a Lebanese bakery that he's found in the Yellow Pages and speaks Arabic to the woman at the counter as she wraps up a paper box full of sweeter than sweet baklava trembling in honey. She wraps the box in pink paper tied with a bow.

"For a girl?" the woman asks him.

He nods in embarrassment.

"A nice Arab girl?" she persists.

"American."

The Lebanese woman tsks with disapproval. "Loose morals," she says. "If I were your mother," she says, wagging a crooked finger and sending him on his way.

MARIANNE LOOKS DIFFERENT out of her uniform. Her hair is loose and golden and she's wearing a short dress covered in polka dots.

He presents his gift to her and she blushes. "Come in," she says, gesturing toward the couch. "My mother," she says, introducing him to a woman in a wheelchair by the window.

"You've grown," her mother says.

"Uh—" he stammers.

"Just ignore her. She's had a stroke. Gets things all mixed up."

He smiles politely, uncomfortably, and sits down on the sofa. He pulls at his trouser leg because he's gained twenty pounds since the suit was made.

"What pretty pastries," Marianne exclaims from the kitchen. "I'm making tea. Or would you like something stronger?"

"Tea is fine," he says and smiles again at the confused woman in the wheelchair.

Marianne brings in a tray and sets it down on the coffee table. "Tea, Mother?" she asks, raising the teapot.

Her mother sticks out her tongue and pulls a face like a child. "Vodka," she says.

"Ma, it's too early for that. Before dinner, OK? I'll give you a vodka before dinner."

Her mother winces and looks away.

"She had a stroke two years ago," Marianne explains. "So I brought her up here to live with me. I'm from Kansas, you know, like Dorothy. Somewhere over the rainbow."

Amir looks at her blankly.

"Wow," says Marianne. "It's a movie. Well, anyway, I moved up here about five years ago. Long story. I wanted to be an actress, but, well, it's my teeth," she says, pointing at her mouth. "I only managed to get one commercial and it was for Tide and I had to play this ugly house-wife who uses some inferior brand of laundry soap and my husband leaves me for this new woman on the block who uses Tide. I didn't know they were casting me for the part of the ugly one until I got to the set and they kept saying 'Show us your teeth.' Nice, huh?"

"But you're not ugly at all," says Amir.

"That's sweet of you to say, but these teeth," she says, pointing at her mouth again. "So now I've got to wear these for two years and that means I can't do any acting at all."

"That is a shame," says Amir, amazed by America.

"What do you call these?" she asks, lifting the plate off the coffee table.

"Baklava."

"Pretty. Don't you think so, Mother? Would you like to try one of these?"

Her mother sticks her tongue out again and repeats, "Vodka."

Marianne rolls her eyes and stands up. "I want to show you some-thing," she says, gesturing to Amir. "Come on."

He follows her into the lavender den of her bedroom. She has a white lace bedspread over her bed and a large stuffed animal that looks part dog, part dinosaur perched upon her pillow. She's taped a map to the wall, a large map of the Middle East.

"I bought this the other day," she says, tapping the map. "I was hoping you might show me Palestine."

He's surprised again by her openness, her curiosity.

"Well," he begins, putting his fingertips on the map. "Here is east Jerusalem, which we claim as ours. Here is Jordan, most of which we consider Palestine. The West Bank, the Golan Heights, both of which were seized by Israel in June—"

"Draw the borders for me," Marianne says, handing him a pen.

"OK," he says, hesitantly taking the pen. He draws a bold black line, a line he knows from memory, a line he knows by heart; he draws Palestine onto a map in the lavender bedroom of a girl from Kansas and it gives him more satisfaction, more relief than he has felt in months. He feels better in New York at this moment than he has felt since he arrived.

"There," he says with satisfaction. "But all these borders are contested. War here, war here, and war here."

"War," she repeats. "What's the worst thing that ever happened to you?" she asks him then.

He lifts his shirt and shows her a belly riddled with scars.

She gasps because she is a girl who loves tough men, because she is a girl who longs for a hero, she gasps and falls in love in that instant, wants to kiss his stomach and see him punch out one of the assholes who sits in the coffee shop after his shift and drinks until he cannot restrain himself from trying to untie her apron string, to drag her down onto his lap.

Because he is a man who didn't grow up with this American romance, Amir doesn't know what to make of her reaction. *Is she horrified? Is she sickened? Does she think he is at fault?* He is embarrassed to have been so bold. But she puts her palms against his shoulders then and leans her whole body against him. He remains still while she kisses him tenderly between the sparse black hairs on his chest.

He wants to laugh. He is stunned. He doesn't understand her reaction.

"What's the worst thing that ever happened to you?" he asks her, finally recovering, the pink of her lipstick still wet at the nape of his neck.

"Vodka!" her mother shouts from the other room.

They both laugh and she leans back against the map where contested borders frame her like a halo. She pulls him into her polka dots. He leans into her, so close her spots are no longer black and white but one undulating field, a no man's land of grey where the pepper and the sweet of worlds colliding invoke a sense of déjà-vu.

DUMB!

My Husband's Jump

My husband was an Olympic ski jumper. (*Is* an Olympic ski jumper?) But in the last Olympics, he never landed.

It began like any other jump. His speed was exactly what it should be. His height was impressive, as always. Up, up he went, into a perfect sky that held its breath for him. He soared. Past the ninety- and hundred-metre marks, past every mark, past the marks that weren't really marks at all, just marks for decoration, impossible reference points, marks nobody ever expected to hit. Up. Over the crowd, slicing the sky. Every cheer in every language stopped; every flag in every colour dropped.

It was a wondrous sight.

Then he was gone, and they came after me. Desperate to make sense of it. And what could I tell them? He'd always warned me ski jumping was his life. I'd assumed he meant metaphorically. I didn't know he meant to spend (*sus*pend) his life mid-jump.

How did I feel? Honestly, and I swear this is true, at first I felt only wonder. It was pure, even as I watched him disappear. I wasn't worried about him, not then. I didn't begrudge him, not then. I didn't feel jealous, suspicious, forsaken.

I was pure as that sky.

But through a crack in the blue, in slithered Iago and Cassius and every troublemaker, doubt-planter, and doomsayer there ever was. In slithered the faithless.

Family, friends, teammates, the bloody IOC—they had "thoughts" they wanted to share with me.

The first, from the IOC, was drugs. What did I think about drugs? Of course he must have been taking something, they said. Something their tests had overlooked? They were charming, disarming.

It was not a proud moment for me, shaking my head in public, saying no, no, no in my heart, and secretly checking every pocket, shoe, ski boot, cabinet, canister, and drawer in the house. I found nothing. Neither did the IOC. They tested and retested his blood, his urine, his hair. (They still had these *pieces* of him? Could I have them, I wondered, when they were done?)

The drug theory fizzled, for lack of evidence. Besides, the experts said (and why had they not spoken earlier?) such a drug did not, *could not,* exist. Yet. Though no doubt somebody somewhere was working on it.

A SWISS SKI JUMPER, exhausted and slippery-looking, a rival of my husband's, took me to dinner.

He told me the story of a French man whose hang glider had caught a bizarre air current. An insidious Alpine wind, he said, one wind in a billion (what were the chances?) had scooped up his wings and lifted him to a cold, airless altitude that could not support life.

Ah. So my husband's skis had caught a similarly rare and determined air current? He had been carried off, against his will, into the stratosphere?

The Swiss ski jumper nodded enthusiastically.

You believe, then, that my husband is dead?

He nodded again, but with less gusto. He was not heartless—just nervous and desperate to persuade me of something he didn't quite believe himself. I watched him fumble helplessly with his fork.

Have you slept recently? I asked. You seem jumpy—excuse the pun.

He frowned. You don't believe it was the wind?

I shook my head. I'd been doing that a lot lately.

His fist hit the table. Then how? He looked around, as if he expected my husband to step out from behind the coatrack. *Ta da!*

I invited him to check under the table.

Was it jealousy? Had my husband achieved what every ski jumper ultimately longs for, but dares not articulate? A dream that lies dormant, the sleeping back of a ski hill, beneath every jump. A silent, monstrous wish.

Yes, it was jealousy—and I pitied the Swiss ski jumper. I pitied them all. For any jump to follow my husband's, any jump *with a landing,* was now pointless. A hundred metres, a hundred and ten, twenty, thirty metres. Who cared? I had heard the IOC was planning to scrap ski jumping from the next Olympics. How could they hold a new event when the last one had never officially ended?

They needed closure, they said. Until they had it, they couldn't move on.

Neither, apparently, could my Swiss friend. He continued to take me to dinner, to lecture me about winds and aerodynamics. He produced weather maps. He insisted, he impressed upon me … couldn't I see the veracity, the validity of … look here … put your finger here on this line and follow it to its logical end. Don't you see how it might have happened?

I shook my head—no. But I did. After the fifth dinner, how could I help but see, even if I couldn't believe?

I caught sleeplessness like an air current. It coiled and uncoiled beneath my blankets, a tiny tornado of worry, fraying the edges of sleep. I would wake, gasping—the *enormity* of what had happened: My husband had never landed. Where was he, *now,* at this instant? Was he dead? Pinned to the side of some unskiable mountain? Had he been carried out to sea and dropped like Icarus, with no witnesses, no one to congratulate him, no one to grieve?

I had an undersea image of him: A slow-motion landing through a fish-suspended world—his skis still in perfect V formation.

Meanwhile the media were attributing my husband's incredible jump to an extramarital affair. They failed to elaborate, or offer proof, or to draw any logical connection between the affair and the feat itself. But this, I understand, is what the media do: They attribute the inexplicable to extramarital affairs. So I tried not to take it personally.

I did, however, tell one reporter that while adultery may break the law of *marriage*, it has never been known to break the law of *gravity*. I was quite pleased with my quip, but they never published it.

My husband's family adopted a more distressing theory. While they didn't believe he was having an affair, they believed he was trying to escape *me*. To jump ship, so to speak. Evidently the marriage was bad. Look at the lengths he'd gone to. Literally, the *lengths*.

In my heart of hearts I knew it wasn't true. I had only to remember the way he proposed, spontaneously, on a chair lift in New Mexico. Or the way he littered our bed with Hershey's Kisses every Valentine's Day. Or the way he taught me to snowplow with my beginner's skis, making an upside-down V in the snow, the reverse of his in the air.

But their suspicions hurt nonetheless and, I confess, sometimes they were my suspicions too. Sometimes my life was a country-and-western song: Had he really loved me? How could he just fly away? Not a word, no goodbye. Couldn't he have shared his sky ... with me?

But these were surface doubts. They came, they went. Like I said, where it counted, in my heart of hearts, I never faltered.

The world was not interested in *my* theory, however. When I mentioned God, eyes glazed or were quickly averted, the subject politely changed. I tried to explain that my husband's jump had made a believer out of me. Out of *me*. That in itself was a miracle.

So where were the religious zealots, now that I'd joined their ranks? I'd spent my life feeling outnumbered by them—how dare they all defect? Now they screamed *Stunt*, or *Affair*, or *Air current*, or *Fraud*. Only I screamed *God*. Mine was the lone voice, howling *God* at the moon, night after night, half expecting to see my husband's silhouette pass before it like Santa Claus.

God was mine. He belonged to me now. I felt the weight of responsibility. Lost a husband, gained a deity. What did it mean? It was like inheriting a pet, unexpectedly. A very large Saint Bernard. What would I feed him? Where would he sleep? Could he cure me of loneliness, bring me a hot beverage when I was sick?

I WENT TO SEE Sister Perpetua, my old high school principal. She coughed frequently—and her coughs were bigger than she was. Vast, hungry coughs.

Her room was spare: a bed, a table, a chair. Through a gabled window I could see the overpass linking the convent to the school. Tall black triangles drifted to and fro behind the glass.

You've found your faith, Sister Perpetua said.

I couldn't help it.

And then she said what I most dreaded to hear: that she had lost hers.

I left the window and went to her. The bed groaned beneath my weight. Beside me, Sister Perpetua scarcely dented the blanket.

She had lost her faith the night she saw my husband jump. She and the other sisters had been gathered around the television in the common room. When he failed to land, she said, they felt something yanked from them, something sucked from the room, from the world entire—something irrevocably lost.

God?

She shrugged. What we had *thought* was God.

His failure to land, she continued, but I didn't hear the rest. His failure to land. *His failure to land.*

Why not miracle of flight? Why not leap of faith?

I told her I was sure of God's existence now, as sure as if he were tied up in my backyard. I could smell him on my hands. That's how close he was. How real, how tangible, how furry.

She lifted her hands to her face, inhaled deeply, and coughed. For a good three minutes she coughed, and I crouched beneath the swirling air in the room, afraid.

IT WAS A WARM NIGHT in July. A plaintive wind sang under my sleep. I woke, went to the window, lifted the screen. In the yard below, the dog was softly whining. It was not the wind after all. When he saw me, he was quiet. He had such great sad eyes—they broke the heart, they really did.

I sank to my knees beside the window.

I was content, I told him, when everyone else believed and I did not. Why is that?

He shook his great floppy head. Spittle flew like stars around him.

And now all I'm left with is a dog—forgive me, but you are a very silent partner.

I knelt there for a long time, watching him, watching the sky. I thought about the word *jump*. My husband's word.

I considered it first as a noun, the lesser of its forms. As a noun, it was already over. A completed thing. *A* jump. A half-circle you could trace with your finger, follow on the screen, measure against lines on the ground. Here is where you took off, here is where you landed.

But my husband's *jump* was a verb, not a noun. Forever unfinished. What must it be like, I wondered, to hang your life on a single word? To *jump*. A verb ridden into the sunset. One verb to end all others.

To *jump*. Not to doubt, to pity, to worry, to prove or disprove. Not to remember, to howl, to ask, to answer. Not to love. Not even to *be*.

And not to *land*. Never, ever to land.

ELISABETH HARVOR

One Whole Hour (Or Even More) with Proust and Novocaine

S wishing past a service station in the middle of a wood—an appari-
tion in all this dripping greenery, a whiff of diesel oil or gas taint-
ing the green-twig smell of the rain—she caught a rushed glimpse of a
tourist family whose three shivery children were hopping and hugging
themselves while taking shelter under the concrete canopy housing the
gas tanks. It was the youngest child who most caught her attention: a
fleeting back view of a sleeveless blouse cut into a white cotton butterfly, the overhang of the butterfly hiding the bony wings of the small
shoulder-blades while exposing the band of pale skin above the puffy
lilac jut of the shorts. Which made her remember the absolute mood-
iness of being that young again: dull Monday morning ruined by rain.
Also the games she had played on just such dim, rainy mornings under
the blankets with her brothers. Tummie Touch. Doctor. Rubbies.
Father and Mother. There were also—but this was not until five or six
years later—the books: *Great Expectations* and *A Tale of Two Cities* and
The Nymph and the Lamp and *The Wind in the Willows*. But by the
time she'd turned thirteen, reading had become clandestine, furtive,
because although her mother "adored" books, she did not like to see

her children reading books on their own, and if she saw one of them reading a book, she would start handing out chores.

And so she used to hide to read the books she was sure her mother wouldn't want her to read. Even if she was sure a book was acceptable she would feel a frantic compulsion to rush to finish it before her mother came into any room where she happened to be reading, and one afternoon when her parents were away at the dentist's she went down to one of the parlour bookshelves and pulled out Volume Two of *Remembrance of Things Past.* She chose it over Volume One because she so much preferred the titles of the smaller books it contained—*Cities of the Plain, The Captive, The Sweet Cheat Gone, The Past Recaptured*— but as she was carrying it up the stairs to her room she could hear a door above her being creaked to click shut. She knew it was the door of the bedroom temporarily occupied by Eric, a friend of one of her brothers, and she knew this because on this particular afternoon they were the only ones at home.

She went into her own room, closed her door, primly sat at her desk like a student about to begin a history assignment, then opened the first page of *Cities of the Plain.* She was hoping for a story about horses, a story about someone riding on horseback and seeing, across a vast plain, a golden city. But instead, making her way through a thicket of difficult words and French names (*campanile,* Marquis de Frécourt), she was introduced to a narrator who seemed to be close to her own age but who had a much larger vocabulary—but then he was French— and this boy was spying on two men (a Baron and a tailor) by peeking between the slats of a pair of shutters, then there was a description of the tailor, a man who had "placed his hand with a grotesque impertinence on his hip, stuck out his behind, posed himself with the coquetry that the orchid might have adopted on the providential arrival of the bee ..." She felt a powerful throb of excitement on reading this, and after the two men had gone into the tailor's shop and closed the door she raced on ahead, rushing through the narrator's plan to eavesdrop by passing through a kitchen to descend a service stair so he could hurry under the breadth of the courtyard to the place where there was a stairway up into a room next door to the tailor's shop. But now he was changing his mind and was instead reaching the shop by a more public and quicker route, and now he was even already here and overhearing (from behind a partition) what sounded like one person strangling another at close range, a sound that made her start to tick even though she was still seated at her desk; a sound that turned her into a ticking little time-bomb reading a book, she was sexually ticking, regular ticks and then a series of throbs, and now and then she would feel the need to shrug sideways and squirm a little in her chair, then she would feel the need to shrug sideways—but in the opposite direction—then squirm in her chair again. It seemed to have something to do with the kind of afternoon it was too, it was such a muggy, still afternoon, but then there was a conversation between the Baron and the tailor that was very silly and dull and so she put down the book and stepped out of her jeans to pull on her red corduroy shorts and a black T-shirt that was a little too tight for her, then went over to the long mirror on her closet door and stood next to it to study her body in profile. She stuck out her behind as the tailor had done and let her mouth fall open, then decided to go down to the back of the house and sit under the tree that grew next to the fence that walled in the back garden. She went down and out, longing to be seen, to be admired, longing for Eric to come to his window and look down and see her. She let the back door slam behind her and walked over to the fence to sit under the tree, then posed her legs and leaned back on her hands in a way that made her breasts aim perfectly up. But after a few minutes had passed, it felt too weird to be on display, especially since she didn't know if Eric was even bothering to look, and her legs were beginning to get restless too—she would draw one of them up, then bring it down to draw up the other and toss back her hair. But she soon tired of this and so she stood up to slap at the bits of grass that had attached themselves to the back of her shorts, and it was while she was hitting at herself that a whistle—thrilling, piercing, sure of itself, male—came down from above. She didn't need to look up, she knew who was whistling, but she had seen older girls act aloof when they were being whistled at and so she decided to act aloof too. A-*loof*: she liked the word, but once she'd stepped into the cool of the house again, there was nothing she could think of that she really wanted to do, and so she walked her fingers past books whose titles made her think of books for babies in kindergarten (*The Book of Small, Growing Pains, The House of All Sorts*), then she pulled out the copy of *Growing Pains* and opened it near its middle so she could smell it. It smelled of a mushroomy old-book smell, but not mildewed because there was no damp in it, only a smell of raw and very old mushrooms. She turned the pages of waxy paper that looked as if they had tiny worms of light pressed into them, but she didn't really want to look at pictures or read or even to go out for a ride on her bike, and so she picked up a pair of carved ivory chopsticks and began to hit at things as she wandered from room to room, making a perky but lonely sort of xylophone music: a ping to a glass goblet here, two clicks each to two glass candlesticks there. She turned on a lamp, turned it off again, did a sweep down the piano keys with all her fingers. But as she was passing under the poster of the rosy *Shrimp Girl* she had an inspiration: she could ask Eric to play Scrabble with her. And so she got out the box of letter tiles, and after peeking at herself one more time in one of the downstairs mirrors she went up the stairs with the Scrabble board pressed to her breasts like a school book.

Music was coming from Eric's room when she knocked on his door. The squeak of bedsprings came next, then the sound of someone hopping on one foot, then the footsteps of two feet, and when Eric opened his door to her his face looked flushed on one side, as if he had been sleeping on it, and he smiled at her oddly, then told her that he knew how to play a much better game. To her "What's that, then?" he would only say, "Come on in and I'll show you ..." And so she stepped inside, breathing in the curious smell in his room: dirty socks and something else. Cheese, she thought; her brothers' rooms also mostly smelled of cheese, and then he was saying that his game was called Grabble, and that the first rule of this game was that she had to guess what number he was thinking of.

She said, "Nine."

He wasn't all that much taller than she was and his dark hair looked damp and his shorts seemed to be breathing all on their own and made her think of an elephant, they were so grey and wrinkled. "No," he said. "But that was close. So I'm going to have to give you one more chance."

Of course the whole point was to guess wrong. Even she knew that. You won by losing. She thought of older girls at school saying to boys in Grade 12, "See you tomorrow ..." and then the boys in Grade 12 tilting back in their chairs to say "Is that a threat or a promise?"

She said, "Fourteen hundred and ninety-two ..."

"Even closer." He smiled. "But that isn't it either." He was still watching her in a thinking sort of way and so she wasn't really all that surprised when he shoved her (but jokingly) against the wall by his door. Then he lightly tapped her on a shoulder. "Rule number two: you have to hit my hand away."

She lightly pushed at it.

He touched her left elbow.

But this time, instead of batting him away, she pouted up at him, feeling insolent and plump in every part of her body. His hand went lower down then, and right away began a slow and almost unbearably tremendous massage while taunts from her childhood began to sing themselves up inside her head. So make me then. So I bet you wouldn't dare to. So I dare you. And by the time his hand, and then his whole body, had rubbed hard against her for however long they'd imagined it would take for her mother's appointment at the dentist's to be over, the corduroy ribs had been rubbed off the fabric of her shorts until it had become—but she didn't see this until later—as see-through and hazy as a red veil. But while it was all still going on she was only drunk on what was happening, she was a hundred times more drunk than any flower after a visit from any Baron or bee, then he was starting to walk her backwards toward his bed—and she wanted him to, she wanted to go wherever his guiding hand pushed her, but at the same time she was worried that once they were lying down she wouldn't at all know what to do with her own hands—when they heard the warning gouge of tires in gravel, then the slam of a car door followed by the tinier gouge of high-heels walking fast across the wet yard of pebbles, then the dangerously innocent but also dangerously probing voice calling up: "Hullo, hullo!" And so she was sure that her mother must know; she was sure she knew everything. And besides, Eric was talking to her, he was saying in a low voice, "Go to your room now, *hurry ...*" and so she did, but her heart was by now violently beating down where the ticking had been and she was feeling sullen because they'd been interrupted and so she thrashed around on her bed trying to make one of her hands be Eric's hand, but her hand was too small (and also too much hers) and then that night he didn't come down to join the family for dinner, and when her sunburned father, scrubbed and pink as the Shrimp Girl, asked her if she knew where he was, she said no, and when her mother asked her how she had spent her afternoon she was quite honestly able to tell her that she had spent it reading a book by Marcel Prowst. Her brothers had all laughed. *"Proost!"* they had shouted. While their mother—flushed and upset, her lower lip still slightly swollen from the novocaine—had turned to appeal to her pink husband, "Don't you think that a girl of thirteen is too young to be reading Proust?"

FRANCES ITANI

Clayton

I n the morning, he heard their cries. He lay on his bed and for a long time thought of nothing, allowing the cries to wash over him like waves, soothing. And when the sun rose, silvery on the water, he stood at his window in the attic room to which he had carried a narrow spring bed. Zeta had objected to this, knowing that if he took a mattress to the attic, he would also sleep there. But he had taken it anyway, ignoring her. There was a table there, too, a lamp, and electricity. He had run an extension cord up the attic stairs—Pa's cord. He smiled as he thought of it. Morgan, the undertaker, had left an extension behind when Clayton's father died and they had needed a lamp up front by the coffin. Clayton had returned to the empty room alone after Pa was carried out and, seeing the forgotten extension on the floor, picked it up and pocketed it, no hesitation. Morgan's fee had been too high anyway. And Clayton felt a foolish affection for the cord. It had supplied Pa's last light, hadn't it?

At first, Clayton could not see their wide dark backs. But when the double blow, the high bushy blow, rose above the waterline, and when he heard them answering one to another, he felt the quick surge of joy. He knew with certainty they were humpbacks, feeding and playing in the Gulf. Frisking on their way north.

It had been seven years since he'd seen a whale, although last year he'd come close. He'd heard them through the fog. He'd even stood with raised binoculars many winter hours at the attic window, hoping to catch a glimpse of them on their return, late December, early January. They seemed to stay closer to shore on the home journey, though for what reason Clayton could only guess. Currents? Or maybe food supply. Perhaps, if this was a good year, he'd see the sperm whales, too. Old bulls that left their families every summer and headed for polar waters. These he would recognize by their forward slanting blows and their deep moaning sighs. When he was a boy, he'd learned to differentiate. His father had taught him what to look for. Just as Clayton, in turn, had taught his own children—William, Latham, and his daughter, Maureen. But he and Zeta were alone now. And there were fewer whales. Most years, he saw none at all. You could thank the ships for that, and the whalers, and the oil spills. What was the use even thinking about it?

Clayton dressed and went downstairs. He shook the fire, waking Zeta, and she entered the kitchen still fastening the tie of her maroon dressing gown. She was silent, and put bowls on the table while he filled the kettle.

"I'll be doing the road fill today," he said.

She didn't answer; she was sullen and hostile. She hated him taking the bed to the attic, but what did she do if he stayed in the house, if he did sleep in their room? She ignored him. She wanted to have him around, but didn't pay any attention when he was there. She didn't know how to please him anymore. For that matter, what did he do to please her? Nothing, that he could think of.

But despite the fleeting misgivings he had about his relations with Zeta and where they had gone wrong, after breakfast, Clayton was aware of the spring in his step when he left the house, binoculars swinging from his neck. He headed for the shed to get the tractor, and felt Zeta at his back, standing at the half-open screen, though she did not call after him. He hitched to the tractor a low wagon he and Latham had built to hold sand and gravel. Latham had his own farm now, and sons of his own. Clayton sat high on the tractor and bumped along the knotted dirt road that crossed his fields and led along the swells of land, rising, falling, to the creek bed that emptied into the pond, and even farther to the cliffs and then, to the gently sloping beach that tilted into the Gulf. It was the kind of day that made him push back his hat and look around in every direction. Clear skies, an occasional puff of cloud on the horizon, gulls soaring high, the early summer sea lapping and calm, barely a noise. He had to hush, remind himself to listen, face the slightness of the waves to watch rather than hear them as they slipped on shore.

It was at the creek bed that he began to dig for fill. The road was so full of holes, it was dangerous to have the tractor on it. He would work all week, a little each day. He began to toss sand with his shovel, listening to the spatter against the floor of the shallow wagon. He thought of how he'd always kept a mound of coarse sand at the side of the house for cleaning the bottoms of kitchen pots—especially in summer when the pots were black from the wood stove. He and Zeta and the children used to kneel at the edge of the mound, rotating pots and pans back and forth against the grating, cleansing sand, until the bottoms and part way up the sides were scratched and silvery. Clayton thought about Pa's cord again, and smiled. If that were the worst thing he had to live with, he'd have a clear conscience indeed. But being a man who still had an occasional song in his heart, there were, of course, other things.

ON THE NORTHWEST EDGE of Clayton's farm, along the cliff, stood a skimpy row of unused one-room cabins. Beside those stood an abandoned barn, both doors off. He could see through to the water, in one doorway and out the next—by standing in the field above it. Inside, there were rotting timbers and tangled grass, but the roof was sound and the ladder nailed firmly to the wall. It was this ladder that Clayton climbed for the first time in fifteen years, his binoculars still on a strap about his neck. At the top, he tested, and saw that he could walk a wide beam from one end to the other, even though the attic floor had fallen through. He could perch on a cross beam and look out either way, north to the beginning expanse of ocean, and south up the slope to the house.

At the south peak, he held the binoculars to his eyes, wondering, the knowledge of Zeta at the door still in his memory. She was there, yes, but he saw William, too. William, the eldest. Darkness had fallen around him. William had forgotten to take out the ashes, bring in the coal. A bitter winter night, and William was in bed.

"Don't wake him," Zeta said. "I'll do it myself. He's only nine and he has school in the morning. Let him make a mistake."

But no, if William hadn't been made to dress and go out to the barn in the dark, he'd have forgotten again. Wouldn't he?

Zeta drew her lips together, looking helplessly at Willy's back. She held the storm door open to give the child light, though she and Clayton and William had known that the coal bin would be in blackness at the end of the yard.

Oh, Willy, do you still have nightmares about standing on the steps, falling into that pool of fluid darkness?

Clayton allowed the binoculars to fall back on his chest. William was in his thirties, thirty-six, thirty-seven; Clayton could not remember which. What had he seen? He climbed down and went back to the tractor, and drove to the south field. He inspected his fences along the boundary of the clay road, and spent the rest of the day doing repairs.

IN THE MORNING, Zeta stood at the door looking out after him. He had slept in the attic again, but not restfully. There was something wrong and he did not know what it was. He drove down to the old barn, climbed the ladder and again lifted the binoculars towards the house. He was shocked when Zeta stepped suddenly into focus, pointing a pistol at his face. She aimed, but did not pull the trigger. Instead, she turned towards the poplar and aimed at it. Then, at the stoop from which she hung the clothes. Then, at the birdhouse. Smiling, she turned quickly and went back into the house.

Feeling weak and perspiring, Clayton realized that she could not have seen him. From the ground below, he could not even see the back door. What had Zeta been doing? What was it about her that had changed so startlingly since he'd left her a half hour ago, standing at the back door like a shadow of his stricken conscience? He remembered that in the glasses her lips had been moving. Singing! She must have been singing. He thought of her smile as she'd turned to go inside. A self-satisfied smile, undisturbed. And her brisk step. He had not seen her move that quickly since before Maureen had left to marry Johnny Cheney from down the road. Johnny was a good ball player but not much good at anything else. Zeta had wanted to open one of the old cabins for the wedding. They had invited Reverend Orland and a few neighbours back after the ceremony. Zeta made lunch and served it on the open cabin veranda, and Maureen and Johnny stayed on and honeymooned in the cabin. No money to go anywhere else. Clayton still held some of the pain he'd felt when he'd driven down to the cabin after leaving the church and had seen what someone had strung up on the veranda post as a joke—a pair of ladies' violet-coloured panties. Probably one of Johnny's ball-playing friends. Clayton had ripped down the panties and thrown them into the back of his truck. No joke. Not for his Maureen.

Clayton climbed down and stood on the cliff before the doorless, gaping barn. His boots smothered some of the early wild strawberries at his feet. Zeta's little get-together for Maureen had been awkward, a failure. The half-dozen cars had to be driven across the fields to get there, and the occupants had stood around, cheerless in Sunday suits and ties, on the raw wood of the veranda. Maureen and Johnny posed for a camera in the long grass on the cliff, a rough surf behind them. And the veil Maureen had sewn herself lifted beautifully, in one quick swoop of wind, and blew out to sea. Seven and a half months later, their son had been named Clayton, after him.

But Zeta. What was she up to? He turned to walk back to the creek where he had left the tractor and, as he did so, his ears caught a smart cracking sound, sharp as a rifle shot. He searched the horizon for signs of whales, but could see nothing in the rolling sea. One had probably breached, or smacked its huge flukes against the water. He would not have mistaken the sound.

WHEN CLAYTON RETURNED to the house for lunch, Zeta served him
and sat in the rocker by the stove with her cup of tea. Hardly a word
passed between them. She was so like the uncommunicative woman he
had left at the door in the morning, he did not, *could not* ask about
what had intervened. He had not, after all, been meant to see. She
would accuse him of spying.

After lunch, he went upstairs to check the bureau drawer, where he
kept his .38. It was there, but it looked as if it hadn't been touched for
years. Unloaded. He replaced it in the drawer and went downstairs to
have his nap on the kitchen sofa.

While he slept, he dreamed. He dreamed that he had gone to
Honest Albert's—the Island Furniture Warehouse—and that Albert
was trying to sell him a sofa. The colour was apple green.

"It's just what you need for your naps, Clayton. I tell you, Zeta will
love it in the kitchen."

Albert kept pushing Clayton towards the end of a long, low room
that was barnlike and musty. Sofas and daybeds were stacked there, and
an enormous SALE sign hung from the ceiling. Beneath that, on the
floor, was a black coffin filled with nickels.

"It's the hottest sale this Island has ever seen," Honest Albert said.
He was laughing and wheezing, and kept pointing to the coffin.

"Put both those big hands of yours into the box, Clayton, and pull
out as many nickels as you can carry."

Clayton hesitated. He took a deep breath and dug both hands deep
down until he touched the bottom of the coffin. He came up dripping
nickels, and emptied his hands of them onto a spotted cloth which
Albert had spread out over an Arborite table. The two men counted the
nickels—two hundred and thirty-three.

"Not bad, Clayton! That's more'n anybody's got yet. You did all
right for yourself. Let me see a minute—that's eleven dollars and
sixty-five cents off the price of the sofa. Zeta'll be some proud of
you."

When Clayton drove home with the sofa in the back of the truck,
Zeta was standing at the back door with the .38.

"You've been made a fool of again, Clayton," she shouted. "You're a damned fool."

She took a shot at him and missed. She took another and he ducked behind the sofa that was halfway off the truck. She filled the sofa full of bullets until the gun clicked, empty, and then she began to hum a little tune and turned to go back inside the house. Maureen and Willy and Latham were standing under the poplar, watching.

"Don't you think you've slept long enough?" Zeta said, standing over him. "I've got work to do in here."

Clayton looked down at the sofa, but it was a faded blue-grey and the only holes in it were the ones where the springs stuck through. He got up, and splashed water on his face at the kitchen sink, and went back out to the tractor.

IN THE MORNING there was a cool, light drizzle, and Clayton went out in his shirt sleeves to work on the road. A cloud cover hung low over the surface of an indifferent sea; the waves were the darkest blue. Apart from Clayton and an occasional screeching gull, there wasn't another living thing in sight. He thought of Latham who had always loved every living thing. Latham, second son, released from the bondage of being eldest.

Latham and Maureen had been outdoor companions to each other throughout their childhood. Following the tracks of the dune fox, sitting silent for hours in the cove watching the great blue heron. Latham had been one to scramble around shore, overturning rocks, collecting shells and sand saucers, trapping what he could in tidal pools, examining, sometimes bringing his finds home to raise in the aquarium he kept in his room. Clayton and Zeta had never worried about Latham around the water because he had been born with a second sense for it, a fearlessness that neither of the others had. But he was easily hurt in other ways. One time, he'd caught a hermit crab that had made its home in a moon shell, and he kept it as a pet. It had been doing badly and Latham had suspected it was dying, but couldn't let it go. He'd come to the door of his parents' room in the night, holding two narrow pieces of wood he had nailed together.

"If the crab is dying," he said, "I have a cross ready. The only thing is, I love it dearly."

After it had died and been buried under the roots of the poplar, Latham came to their room in the night again, and stood by their bed. Clayton and Zeta had been making love. Clayton was angry at first, not knowing how long the child had been standing there.

"Dad," said Latham. "I'm having trouble sleeping. I hear the spirit of my crab crawling around the aquarium. It's clacking against the glass."

What could you tell a child like that? What did Latham tell his own sons?

Clayton filled three more deep-pitted ruts in the road, but his mind kept going back to the rotting barn, to Zeta and the .38. He took the binoculars from the edge of the wagon where they'd been hanging, and headed back to the spot where he'd been the day before. Crazy. He must be crazy to spy on Zeta. For it could not be called anything else. He climbed the ladder and walked the beam, admitting to himself that spying was exactly what he had come to do.

But he felt a safety, a surety, hidden away up there in the peak of the barn. For a long time he just sat, looking out into the Gulf. The clouds were breaking up and the sun flashed through linear folds of sky. As if they, too, were pleased, the whales suddenly began their songs, echoing far, far out. Clayton held his binoculars to his eyes and saw a large herd, moving and playing, keeping close. They were turning lazily, spouting through the haze. The sounds drifted past as if the whales were swimming just below him, beneath the cliff. He knew there had been a time when they would have come this close, but that would have been in his grandfather's day, when his grandfather had been a boy, scoping out the whales. Clayton had heard the stories often enough during his own boyhood.

Far off, the humpbacks called to one another with eerie repetitive cries—long, low echoing sighs and high-pitched squeals. The herd noises rolled in as patterned bursts of sound, followed by long silences. Clayton did not focus his glasses on the house. He felt peace such as he had not experienced for a long time, and he climbed down the ladder and went back to work, trying to hold that peace around him.

THE NEXT MORNING, Clayton managed to stay out of the barn, but when he woke from his after-lunch nap, he went directly there, climbed the south peak and raised his glasses to see if Zeta had come out of the house. He had scarcely looked at Zeta across the lunch table, so anxious had he been to get away from her to see what she would do. Now, he was startled, frightened, unprepared, as he caught sight of himself running across his own visual field, running and calling for Maureen. Yes, it was he, Clayton. Looking everywhere for Maureen, who was lost. He was at the picnic fair and the boys were with him and they were small. Clayton was younger, had dark brown hair, more of it than the hand now knew against the familiar scalp as he felt instinctively for it there.

He was running everywhere, looking for Maureen. Although the fair was held at the exhibition field in town where the local farmers shopped, Clayton saw not a single familiar face. Where could she have gone? Zeta had told the children that morning to stay with their father, not to get lost. After the pony rides and the outdoor tightrope walk, he had taken them to a new event, the pig races, which had been held in the livestock building. But the event had not been what he had expected—greased pigs and tumbling overgrown boys in overalls, slipping and sliding and laughing. No, there had been a small narrow stretch of cement floor around which metal chairs had been placed in rows, and here he had sat with the children, waiting. A truck backed in through the parting crowd and stopped at the end of the row of chairs. A man stepped out and called to some of his boys to give him a hand. They unloaded eight of the puniest, most frightened, squealing piglets that Clayton had ever set eyes on. And then, on cue, eight local girls, all contestants in the fair's Beauty Contest, came forward, awkward and shy and disgusted, but each determined, Clayton could see, to get through this initiation rite, which could lead to a year's reign over the other seven. Each girl slipped into a pair of overalls, and each pig had a leash snapped to its collar. Although the girls were supposed to hold their charges in their arms to await the starter pistol, the legs of the pigs kept shooting out from the girls' grasp, and the pigs and the pigshit were flying high. By the time the gun went off, the girls were smeared from the neck down and the pigs were criss-crossed and tangled, their leashes knotted and uncooperative. Yet, somehow, in their fright, two of the pigs managed to cry their way diagonally up the marked area of floor, prodded and pulled by their own Beauty Queens. The other six pigs ran helter skelter in all directions, and were cowering behind booths and under chairs. Two of the girls were crying. Clayton made a move to get the children away, but saw that Maureen had already run out of the building.

"Stay here!" he shouted to William and Latham. Too sternly? Their small round faces stared up at him. "Don't move until I get back."

He ran all over the grounds and found her, finally, perched in the crotch of a tree, sobbing against its bark.

"They were mean to the pigs, Daddy," she yelled, accusing him. "They were cruel to those pigs."

When Clayton got her calmed down, he carried her back to the building where his boys were standing in the doorway, looking out. He gave them each a dime and sent them across the path for a soft drink, and they wandered ahead, confused and hazy-hot.

Clayton rubbed his eyes. He had come up here like an old fool trying to spy on Zeta, and now for the life of him he did not know why he had come or what he'd expected to see.

"He who digs a pit for another will himself fall into it," was one of Zeta's favourite expressions, and now it repeated itself in his head. He had been surprised all through the years of his marriage to discover in Zeta a part of self that was unbending, that would never yield. And powerful as he sometimes thought he was, he had never been able to budge that core of Zeta.

The waves below the cliff on the other side of the barn were lashing in on a rising wind. The sky was clouding over. Clayton felt a reluctance to lift the glasses to his eyes once more, a reluctance to watch the unfolding of detail and fantasy—if indeed he had imagined what had come before. And there was fear, fear that all of his past would somehow present itself, come tumbling out. He did not want that. He allowed the binocular strap to slip from his hands, and he heard the thud on the ground below. He walked the wide beam and climbed down the ladder. Drove the tractor back up the slope and into the shed, and closed the big double doors behind him.

WHILE ZETA SET THE TABLE for supper, Clayton stretched out on the kitchen sofa, his feet pointed towards the stove. He was thinking of a story he had once read to the children at bedtime. It was a Japanese story in a collection called *Animal Tales for Children Around the World,* and was called "Kachi-Kachi-Yama." He had never forgotten. The principal animal was a crafty badger that sneaked up to an old woman's farm while the old man was in the fields. The badger cut the old woman into pieces and made soup from her bones. The badger then dressed in the old woman's clothing and served the soup to the old man when he came in for his midday meal. The old man sat clicking his tongue to show how delicious was the soup, and ate bowl after bowl of—his wife.

The children had asked suspiciously, "Dad, are you changing the story?" as he'd floundered with the ending. Why did the grotesque endure? Was he a fool for imagining that if his own past would settle he might get on with his present, even look to what might be left to him of future?

Although it had not escaped his notice that scalloped potatoes, his favourite, were on the table, he pushed back his chair after eating and mumbled in Zeta's direction that he was going for a walk before it got too dark.

"The wind's coming up," she said, without looking at him. "You'd better wear your heavy jacket."

IN THE DECLINING LIGHT, Clayton saw the massive grey-black form as a huge silhouette, when he reached the edge of the cliff. His heart gave a jump inside his chest and he wondered for a second if he were imagining what he saw below. He took the path down to the beach, seeing and hearing the white-tipped waves as they battered the shore. As each wave broke, its curl ran along the surface of the water. The wind was softer in shelter of the cliffs.

The whale had come in head-on up the gently sloping beach. It was almost as long as the old barn, and had a huge squarish head and a great flat forehead that was scarred and glistening. Its skin was black and sleek, and Clayton knew before he stood beside it that it was a sperm. He'd heard of whales stranding, but had never seen such a thing; all his memory could supply was that they sometimes came in in large numbers. He looked up and down the beach and out into the waves, but this was the only whale to be seen. It gave a sudden shudder, and slammed its flukes against the sand. As the reverberation went through Clayton's body, he jumped three feet back, knowing it was alive. An eye, a purplish-dark eye as big as a grapefruit, opened and looked straight at Clayton. Clayton felt an immense surge of pity for the creature and was not afraid. The whale had come in to die on Clayton's land.

He did not know what to do, whether he should go to get Zeta or get help. But how could he help? It was useless to think that anyone could get this old whale back into the water. The sea had begun to ebb, and the huge body had already made a deep impression in the sand. And the whale itself seemed to be ebbing. Clayton put his hand on the side of the whale's head and wondered at the feel of it. The great eye closed, and the blowhole high up on the left released a soft moan of air. For a long time, Clayton stood with his hand on the whale. At times, it made clicking sounds. After long intervals, it released air from its lungs and snapped its blowhole shut with a soft sucking sound.

Clayton took off his plaid jacket and waded into the water in trousers and boots, the icy water numbing his legs. He soaked the jacket through and brought it back to the whale and tried to spread it along part of the whale's head and back. It was like putting a postage stamp on a boxcar but Clayton somehow felt, rather than knew, that the whale was more comfortable because of it. The narrow lower jaw had flattened into the sand, and there were small pools of water around its astonishing white mouth. The whale had begun to bleed, and the blood was trickling into these little pools. The sky was almost completely dark.

Clayton removed the jacket and soaked it in the sea again, bringing it back to the whale. Although for the rest of his life he would never know how he did it, he felt himself slipping and sliding and climbing up onto the massive rippled back. The whale made no sound. Clayton stretched his length out over the huge long back, and lay his head near the blowhole. A wide whoosh of humid warm air blew back strands of Clayton's grey hair. Clayton put his face down, and mourned.

THE HOUSE WAS IN DARKNESS when he returned. He was cold and soaked and bloody, and he stripped in the kitchen and washed there, at the sink. He rolled up his clothes and left them by the door. Tomorrow, he would phone his neighbours, and they would try to bury or burn the remains.

And if hundreds of years from now, the earth was pushed back, churned up, would anything be found? Of the whale, of him, of Zeta? Would there be no rag, no bone, no trace of themselves?

"Zeta," he called softly through the bedroom door. "Zeta, you awake?"

No answer.

"Zeta, I'm back."

"I know," she said. "You've been upset, haven't you." She lifted the covers for him and he slid into bed beside her, in the dark.

NANCY LEE

Associated Press

That boy works as a photographer for the Associated Press. He is at home in a suite at the Marriott Hotel, in a city whose name sounds like machine-gun fire. You keep in touch through e-mail. He sends you photos of human rights violations: the scarred backs of Chinese women, a severed hand at the side of the road, a secret mass grave. You send him photos of local atrocities: your father's retirement cake in the shape of breasts, the words "Jesus Sucks" graffitied in etching gel across the windows of a church.

That boy is more social conscience than you can bear. His love letters are diatribes, global history lessons. He woos you with the blood of political unrest, the testimonials of broken refugees. Devotion disguised as the pain of strangers, something coded and hidden in newspaper clippings, wire-service announcements. When he does think to mention the curve of your back, the smell of your skin, his words are few and precious, grains of rice, drops of clean water.

In your last message, you wrote: *A terrible thing has happened here. I've been selected for jury duty—a man accused of killing prostitutes and burying them in his backyard. There will be crime scene photos.*

You sent this message three days ago. You have not heard from that boy in over a month, since he responded to the retirement cake photo with a curt, "ha, ha." You know he isn't dead; every day he checks in with a supervisor at the AP. You want to call it irresponsible, selfish, but he risks his life to expose terror and oppression in the world, and you live in a two-bedroom condominium with heated tile floors. Everything he does seems forgivable.

THERE ARE NO NEW MESSAGES *on the server.*

THIS BOY, with his high-rise-view suite, black leather furniture and state-of-the-art home theatre system, is seducing you the old-fashioned way. South African Chardonnay in hand-blown glasses, Nina Simone in quadraphonic sound. You let your head loll back against the sofa, indulge in the ease of its smooth surface. You watch him lounge in his custom-ordered chair, polished black hide pulled tight over a chrome skeleton.

Earlier that day, you had chosen the perfect outfit for court, a tailored black suit, a steel-grey blouse, serious, but impartial. Your make-up was decidedly neutral.

The air in the jury room was warm and overused. The room itself, dismal and dated—a concrete box, walls panelled in worn gold velveteen, red modular furniture from the seventies.

The other jurors chatted, drank coffee from Styrofoam cups. You fanned yourself with your notepad, tried to picture the accused. You had seen his photo months ago, in newspapers, a balding, dough-faced man with small eyes that receded like pressed raisins. You wondered if he would appear in regular clothes, if he would be handcuffed and shackled.

The door opened and a sheriff walked in; he was older and short, stocky in his tan uniform and black vest, his gun belt pulled tight around his gut. He called for everyone's attention and the room hushed. He announced that the accused had changed his plea to guilty, thanked you for your time.

You were confused. Some of the jurors cheered and clapped, others hurried into their coats, dialled cell phones. You looked to the man beside you, a well-dressed electronics salesman with perfect posture. He was softened by your alarm, tried to reassure you. "It's a little-known fact that most criminal cases are settled before lunch."

Outside the jury room, you stalled, studied the geometric patterns in the carpet, considered sneaking into another trial. You imagined opening statements, objections, false testimony, bloodstained evidence. Things you could e-mail about later.

He felt responsible for you, you could tell. As he stretched into his raincoat, he hovered, as if waiting to see how long you would stay. When only the two of you were left, he offered to walk you to your car; then, at your car, to buy you lunch. Lunch stretched out past dark and now you are in his apartment.

He has the bright, smooth face of someone well scrubbed. You suspect he showers too often, gets his hair cut before it needs cutting, tries clothes on in a change room before buying them. You already know everything about him. You tell yourself he isn't your type; you don't like dark-haired men, men with skin so clean looking, you can be sure they are without scent or heat.

He reaches under the coffee table and pulls out a box. "Do you like trivia?"

You smile despite yourself. "Yes."

"We'll have a contest. First to get ten in a row wins." He hands you a stack of cards.

The idea of competing engages you; you could use a victory, even a small one. You shuffle the cards in your hands. "Wins what?"

He smiles. "We'll decide that after."

You reach for your wineglass, bring it to your lips as he flips the top card in his deck. "What is the capital of Indonesia?"

You try to swallow before you laugh and end up coughing. The wine rises up into your nasal cavity. The alcohol burns. You snort, then, embarrassed, start to giggle uncontrollably. He laughs with you, his eyes curious. "Boy," he says, "you must really know this one." This makes you laugh harder. You curl over yourself, your hand at your stomach. He waits. The moment you feel tears in your eyes, you know you will let yourself lose this game, sleep with this boy.

THERE ARE NO NEW MESSAGES *on the server.*

MONTHS OF ABSENCE made that boy a perfect lover. Distance times longing times uncertainty. You had both learned that love at its best was slow and drawn out, stretched thin for sadness to show through. Each moment you spent together carried within itself a nagging seed, a small, hard reminder of what you would inevitably lose. The sensation of your fingertips touching, life vibrating from one skin to another seemed at once an immeasurable gift, an unbearable injustice. Sometimes you took days to undress one another.

Your bodies moved with calculated stealth, a careful invasion. You lingered wherever the territory seemed foreign, the damp skin behind his knees, the pale insides of his wrists. He unfolded you like a map. Searched for changes in the landscape, new tan lines, a scratch from your neighbour's cat. The couplings remained wordless. Although he hadn't told you directly, you knew there were things he did not want to hear, things that would burden him, that he would never say in return. You kept them to yourself. If you felt those words rising inside you, you held them back like stale breath. Sometimes they found a way out, as mewing when you cried, as gasps when you were ecstatic.

You were someone else when that boy was in town. You took vacation time from your job at the library and forgot you worked there. You attended political lectures and rallies, watched slide shows of hidden, anonymous suffering. Your legs and underarms were waxed. Your hair was trimmed and highlighted in a way that made you look, you thought, more optimistic, proactive. You read at least two newspapers a day. You went to basketball games, and drank beer, watched him sit forward in his seat and nod silently while everyone around you stood and cheered. You listened as he rattled off player stats and conference rankings, as he talked about free throws and penalties; you heard him say that basketball was the one thing he missed about the Western world.

You lay stretched and naked in front of his camera, stared into the eye of his lens, tried to project who you were with him. Hoped that later, in the darkroom, it would bloom on the paper as something disturbing and spectacular, something from which he would try, but fail, to turn away.

You had a habit of going through that boy's things when he was in town. While he went out for coffees or newspapers, you would flip through his plane tickets and itinerary, read his date book, empty his toiletry bag onto your bed. You would piece together his life without you, names of co-workers and guides, addresses of consulates and labs, appointments, deadlines. Once you found his toiletry bag stuffed with condoms. You clutched them in a fist when he came back in the door. "What are these for?" you asked him.

He laughed. "You don't know what those are for?"

"What do you need them for?"

He walked over to you and peeled a silver square off the strip. "The AP gives them out by the bushel. Look," he said, holding the square close to his face to read the fine print on the wrapper. "They've probably expired."

He looked at you and shook his head, slid his hand under your chin and kissed you firmly on the mouth. "God," he said. "You're tougher than customs."

THERE ARE NO NEW MESSAGES *on the server.*

THIS BOY WANTS to tell you he loves you even though it's only been a couple of weeks. You see it in the sad edges of his smile when he says goodnight. But you know by the thoughtful way he makes dinner reservations, by his gracious habit of being on time, he will wait until you are ready to hear the words, five weeks, maybe seven.

The first night he is in your apartment, he cooks dinner. He is confident in your kitchen, doesn't panic when he cannot find turmeric in the cupboard. He interrogates you as he dices and juliennes, his slender hand working your knife into the hearts of vegetables. You dodge his questions. Duck and cover. You are accustomed to listening and thinking carefully, painfully about what has been said; answering makes you nervous. "Who was your first best friend?" he asks, handing you a vellumous slice of jicama. "I don't know," you shrug. He looks at you as if you are strange.

You chew, your mind sifting for something erudite, articulate. "What do you think of East Timor?" you ask.

He shakes his head. "It's awful. I guess."

You nod. He smiles without looking at you, which, you've learned, is the physical cue that he's about to make a joke. "I'll start researching it tomorrow if it's important to you."

You pick up a garlic clove and hurl it at his head; it bounces off his forehead.

He slams down the knife. "Okay, that's it." He chases you around the counter until he has you pinned against a wall with your wrists behind you. He presses into you, you press back. He brushes the hair out of your face, moves his open lips to your neck and whispers slowly, "Tell me. The name. Of your first. Best. Friend."

WHILE YOU ARE BRUSHING your teeth and he is shaving, this boy asks whose clothing takes up a third of your bedroom closet, whose boxes and equipment fill your hallway storage space. You say they belong to a man, a friend.

"What kind of friend?" he asks.

"The kind that works overseas," you reply.

You stare at his reflection in the mirror and watch hard lines cut down to his jaw, a pained tension in his mouth as he rinses his razor under the tap. You are surprised to see that expression on someone else. You've worn it yourself so often, you sometimes slip into it for no reason, catch it reflected in the windows of cars, in glass doors.

Your own face is slack, as if your muscles have gone to sleep. This too is unfamiliar.

He sees your face in the mirror and stops shaving. "What?" His voice is sharp.

You continue brushing, very slowly as you weigh the pros and cons of saying simply, "Nothing." You slide the toothbrush out of your mouth and spit into the sink. "I know what you're thinking."

He snickers. "What am I thinking?"

You turn and look straight at him, wanting him to know that you are connecting with him, relating to him, not mocking him. "You're telling yourself, leave it alone, leave it alone."

He stares at you. Shakes his head, throws his razor into the sink and walks out of the bathroom.

THERE ARE NO NEW MESSAGES *on the server.*

TO BE HONEST, you weren't really interested in that boy until he told you he was leaving town. He was the too casual and tousled blond beside you in the rodeo-bar-turned-trendy-hangout. A going-away party for a fashion reporter, a button-down Ralph Lauren gay friend named Marcel who was, at that moment, riding a sluggish mechanical bull and twirling his camel-coloured suit jacket above his head.

You were drunk and unamused. The conversation with "Runs Hands Through Hair," the indigenous nickname you had thought up for that boy in an epic moment of boredom, was stilted and depressing. He wanted to talk about Pinochet. You wanted to talk about why you hated country music, all those lost wives and dogs. After several attempts at attack, you both capitulated, nodded when the other spoke, sipped your drinks in armistice.

After an hour, you cut in on Marcel's account of his latest nineteen-year-old, a Scottish model with "alarmingly strong hands and a delicious Italy-shaped birthmark on his hip." You Euro-kissed Marcel goodbye and pulled on your coat as you walked to the exit. That boy was standing on the sidewalk, finishing a cigarette. He offered to share a cab.

When he mentioned returning to Mexico, you imagined white sand beaches, blended drinks, ceviche; cheap hotels and burning tequila. You rested your head against the taxi window, let his voice dissolve into the drone of the road, and thought about slipping into a bath, washing away the smell of rodeos and politics. You were surprised when the cab pulled up to his building, a new brick townhouse near the centre of the city. You had cast him in a less cosmopolitan setting, a low-rent ethnic neighbourhood popular with the college crowd, an old house, a single room. He invited you in for coffee, to look at his photographs. He was being polite. You were curious. You assumed something *National Geographic:* majestic cliff-scapes, waterfalls, the craggy faces of friendly market vendors. Instead, you found a small, one-legged Mexican boy, shirtless with a bandana around his forehead, kissing the barrel of an automatic rifle. The decapitated bodies of three freedom fighters, their heads snatched as trophies, the hand of one victim making the shape of a gun. An old woman crying, cradling the body of a young woman whose torso had been blown open by explosives, the brilliant midday sun catching the young woman's wound, the centre of her body glistening like an oozing tropical fruit.

He placed a mug of coffee on the table in front of you. "It isn't how most people think of the world," he said.

You nodded, half agreeing with him, half acknowledging the embarrassing truth about yourself: you never really thought about the world. You rarely watched the evening news, only read the entertainment section of the paper. It wasn't that you didn't want to know what was going on, but that you couldn't make sense of it. The world had become too tangled for you to unravel in the hour before dinner, coups, rebellions, interventions, peacekeeping. Complex systems to manage hunger and murder and exploitation, but nothing to end them. That is what bothered you most, that there was no conceivable end.

You caught him looking at his own photographs, hands on his hips, chin lowered, chest dented into his body; you saw that the cost of these images went far beyond airfare and film. The blond hair above his ears was peppered with grey, incongruous with his age—which you had noted as you admired the numerous stamps in his passport—thirty-three. He struck you as someone who would grow old overnight. Perhaps after a long journey, an extended time away, he would return and seem closer to expiration: sudden creases in his face, a remoteness in the way he paused before speaking. The thought made you sad.

He straightened and asked if you wanted more coffee. You shook your head. You hesitated for a moment, then reached out your arm and slipped your hand inside his. The skin of his palm was tender and damp. He glanced at you sidelong for just a second, his eyes inquisitive, his smile small and private. You felt yourself blushing. As he turned back to his photos, he squeezed your hand.

You sat together on the couch. He explained each photograph, his voice quiet, but animated. His arm rested on the cushions behind your neck, his body inches from yours. He watched you as you studied his pictures, which made it difficult for you to study him. You imagined that under his white shirt, his frame was taut, trained. When he smiled, the angles of his face relaxed, his eyes warmed and you noticed for the first time that his lips were smooth and fleshy, like a boy's.

By three a.m. you had heard all about the Zapatistas and their struggle for independence. You were drawn in by their covered faces, their cunning tactics in the night.

You called in sick five days in a row; you spent every hour with him. The weekend before he left, the two of you drove to a bed and breakfast in the mountains. On a late-nineteenth-century silk brocade divan, in front of a window overlooking a glacier lake, you asked if you could meet him in Mexico. You made it sound casual, like you were planning to go there anyway. And you were, some day. He stared at the lake as if out on the water there were something familiar, something he knew he would see at this place. You breathed as slowly and quietly as you could. He seemed at ease, his mouth turned up slightly at the corners, a half smile. You took that as a good sign. He had been thinking about it, too. His eyes stayed on the water as he spoke. "This is something I do alone." You made an effort at a smile, then shifted your gaze away from him, to the dark hills that loomed around the lake's edge. You didn't want him to see the tension in your face, to read your insecure thoughts.

THERE ARE NO NEW MESSAGES *on the server.*

YOU CALL THIS BOY because you should, because you haven't been completely honest. He arrives with flowers, birds of paradise. You've set the coffee table with two bottles of red wine and two glasses. You each sit on opposite ends of the couch. You tell him the entire story from beginning to end. Sometimes he nods, other times he sits motionless. Twice you cry. You are surprised; he is not. He says nothing, does not console you or try to hold you, but gently pries the soggy tissues out of your palm, replaces them with fresh ones. He refills the wineglasses. You both fall asleep on the couch. In the middle of the night, he wakes you, guides you to bed, his arm around your waist. He folds you into the blankets, then lies on top of the covers in his clothes. You pull him towards you, press your face into his neck. You are comforted by the feel of his cheek against your forehead, the collar of his shirt against your chin. You fall asleep, your head full of the scent of his laundry detergent. Something bright and lemony that makes everything smell new.

THE NEXT DAY you send the following message: *I can't compete with all the trouble in the world.*

SEEING THIS BOY as often as you do, you worry about the dense scrub of relationship, an overgrowth of tenderness that will choke you into apathy, bind you towards contempt. You know sex is the place it will germinate, root itself. You are vigilant. You read women's magazines for advice on frequency, intensity, variety: *the trick to keeping a relationship hot is to save your tricks; every third time incorporate something new.*

But it is by accident, not during one of your "every third" times that you strike the mainline to this boy's desire, expose what is raw and eager in him with the slip of your hand.

It begins when you undress him one night and jokingly wrap his leather belt around your wrists. He moves on you swiftly, one hand at his zipper. He pushes your arms above your head, draws the belt so tight it bites your skin. He opens your legs with his knees, shifts his weight to one side, works himself past the crotch of your panties. He covers your eyes with his hand.

Nights later, he turns you naked on your stomach. Traps you between his legs while he loops his belt around your neck, enters you slowly from behind. His body on you and over you again and again. You lose your heartbeat in his rhythm, then feel its return, an urgent throb in your neck and head as the belt tightens. He curls the leather tail around his fist, once, twice. You watch the bedroom wall advance, retreat, as your vision narrows, then brightens. You wonder in a moment of swoon if you will die here, a willing captive in your own bed. You wonder how many women in the world die this way, blind and tied. He finishes abruptly; the belt goes slack. You watch colours turn on the insides of your eyelids as he kisses your neck, strokes your breast, slides down your body to finish you off.

This is how sex evolves between you. Loving torture. You invest in equipment: blindfolds, restraints. He practises cracking a belt so that it stings without breaking the skin. You learn to admire the marks across your back, around your ankles and wrists. There is something divine and surprising in the mercy you show each other afterward. A sincere caretaking that is ciphered into everyday language as you soothe your limbs against the cool of the sheets, fluff pillows for one another, check for any true harm. Something as simple as this boy offering to get out of bed and make coffee warms you like an unexpected gift.

YOU ARE LYING on your side in the predawn morning, lulling between the blue light of your bedroom and a dream about microfiche. The phone rings. And though you usually let the machine pick it up at this hour, you reach for it in your half sleep, bring it to your ear. There is a buzz and a click, then the sound of an open tunnel.

"Tell me you don't have cancer." It is that boy.

"What?" you ask, struggling to ground yourself in time, space, and context. "What?"

"Cancer."

You sit up. This boy lies still in the bed, far away in sleep, his back to you. You speak softly, your lips close to the receiver. "I don't have cancer."

That boy sighs. "Thank God." He laughs. "While I was in Aceh I had this awful dream that you were dying and not going to tell me." His voice is forced. This, you think, is his best effort at being light.

You are silent.

"I'm sorry," he says. "For not writing."

You hear the echo of your own uneven breath.

"Aceh's a mess. It's East Timor all over again. Worse. They're making an example of the Acehnese. They're—"

"Do you know what time it is here?" you ask.

You hear him tap something in a broken rhythm, his finger or a pencil against a hard surface. He coughs. When he speaks again, he sounds tired. "Is he there?"

You swallow to mask your voice. "Who?"

"I don't know." He laughs. "Anyone." The casual tone is awkward on him.

You cannot think of where to begin, how to explain, so you just say, "Yes."

The click when that boy hangs up is so quiet, you don't realize he's gone until you hear the hum of empty air, feel the useless weight of the receiver in your hand.

You place the phone into its cradle, turn and press against this boy's body, your face between his shoulders, your chest to his back. You pull the comforter to your neck. Your right foot brushes against the bed in small circles, a nightmare remedy left over from childhood. His hand reaches behind for your waist and pulls you closer. You hunker down behind his shoulder, hide from the sun, a sliver of light above the windowsill.

YOU TRY TO SEPARATE that boy from your life. The surgery is messy, like something severed in the jungle without anaesthetic. You mistrust your preferences, your habits, your usuals, wonder which ones you adopted because of him. When did you start preferring americanos to cappuccinos? When did you decide fifty dollars was too much to pay for dinner?

In a grocery store line-up, you dig through your purse for your chequebook. You have already asked yourself if it was his suggestion to buy organic, to skip the cereal aisle and never buy peanut butter or oranges from Florida. Inside your purse, your palm catches the tip of an open lipstick. The checkout girl drums the counter with a pen. The man behind you mutters something rude. You stare at the deep maroon smear across your hand, a painless wound. Ask yourself, did I buy that for him?

THIS BOY'S APARTMENT is a refuge, a high glass tank that shields you from the world. While you work your days in the stacks, pulling books for inter-library loan, you dream of the view from his balcony, the dark water of the inlet, the city lights laid out like a jewelled carpet. You imagine your reflection in the sliding glass door, a version of yourself that is cool and smooth to the touch.

Inside these glass walls, you are frivolous and happy to be so. The two of you make dinner, drink wine, watch *Jeopardy!*, have sex. You tell each other the same animal bar jokes over and over, and pretend each time you've never heard them before. *A bear walks into a bar. Three pigs walk into a bar ... An octopus walks into a bar ...*

The two of you sneak down to the indoor pool and you swim naked for him, lap after lap, your body turning a slippery somersault at each end. He kneels at the pool edge, leans to kiss you as you approach. You wrap your arms around his neck and his lips brush your eyebrow. "I love you," he whispers. You hold him against you, your wet hair soaking his cheek. He loosens your arms to look at your face. You raise your feet and push against the pool wall, glide away from him. He pulls off his t-shirt and dives in. His body is silent under water. In a few strokes, he is beside you. You face each other, tread water in the middle of the pool. The laps have made you tired; you try to ignore the aching in your legs and shoulders. His eyes are bright and wide and wet. You feel your bottom lip touching the surface, struggle to keep your chin up. He is smiling. "Do you love me?" he asks. You laugh out loud, your body contracting, your head dipping under. You come up with a mouthful of water and spit it in his face. He wipes his eyes, then reaches his hand out and grabs your arm, pulls you toward him. You expect him to force you under, to hold you thrashing and airless as punishment for your dirty play. Instead, he moves his hand to the top of your back, buoys you up, allows you to float without having to move.

THAT BOY CAME to your work once. He had been taking photographs of heroin addicts in the downtown eastside, part of a photo essay for a community gallery. You ate sandwiches outside the library, perched together on the edge of a concrete planter, the June sun easy against your back. You watched some kids in baggy shorts lounge in an alcove, their skateboards leaned up against the wall. A girl with cherry-red hair used a thick permanent marker to sign her curvy name on a boy's naked calf.

While you ate, that boy took photographs: the girl with her cheek against the boy's bare leg, a homeless man in front of the library's towering postmodern facade, your thin shadow on the sidewalk below the cement planter.

A group of pre-school children passed by, a parade of handmade paper hats and knapsacks, swinging arms, profuse smiles, luscious and heartbreaking. That boy nudged you, pointed at the children, "How 'bout a couple of them?" You turned to see if he was joking; a dry piece of sandwich scraped down your throat. His face was attentive, awaiting your response. You felt yourself flush, and smiled, nodded slowly, your body very still. He pulled away from you then, the strap of his camera slapping your bare arm.

The children posed for him as a group, three rows of coloured hats, hands in mouths, eyes at the clouds, their teacher grinning and proud in a flowery dress that threatened to rise with the wind. You sat, hot and nauseated, embarrassed by what you thought he had meant, unable to look at him. He walked back toward you and you watched the children instead, moving away, their plump, lively bodies flattening into two dimensions, daubs of colour below the vast city sky.

YOU GROW TIRED of this boy's apartment sooner than you expect. You tell him things are busy at the library. You stay late and roam the stacks, search for books that would interest you if you were the type to have interests. The history of carousel horses, small engine repair, winter gardening, the complete works of Dorothy Parker, Japanese paper art, the concise dictionary of Eastern mysticism, the songs of Bruce Springsteen, a century of fashion, a hundred and one metalwork ideas, the encyclopaedia of Victorian upholstery. You bring them home, their weight somehow comforting in your arms. The books pile up on your floor like clumsy pagodas, an obstacle course of precarious possibilities. In many you find things left by previous readers: bus transfers, an unused teabag, shopping lists, two fettuccini noodles, and once, a fifty-dollar bill folded between two diagrams of origami frogs. Sometimes, shockingly, in the margins of books, you find doodles, random sketches of geometric shapes or cartoon faces in pencil or pen. Messages scratched into a dirt wall, the impenetrable hieroglyphs of those who came before you and searched for something in this same place.

In a book on kosher cooking you find a piece of paper folded as a bookmark. A list of names: six nuns and two priests. You recognize the list; you used to carry it around in your purse; abominable murders posted on the Internet. And now you wonder if these were real names, real deaths, or simply an Internet hoax to manipulate political sympathy. You tell yourself you never really cared about those people, that love and propaganda are not the same thing.

In your own apartment, you monitor your autonomy. You have boxed that boy's clothes and camera equipment and moved them to a storage locker. And now, even the smallest infringements set you off. You balk when this boy brings over breakfast cereal without consulting you. You return the CDs he buys for your meagre collection. You are cautious about decisions and choices; the integrity of the border can no longer be compromised. To establish definite boundaries, you refuse to have extra keys made, dig a trench in the comforter when you sleep in the same bed at night. You sometimes imagine a halo of white chalk around your body as you walk through your apartment, feel it between this boy's fingertips and your skin when he touches you, something dusty and smooth. He is understanding. Tells you he respects independent women. Wonders aloud if the two of you should move in together. You point to the piles of books on your floor and tell him, there is hardly room.

IF YOU HAD IMAGINED a life for you and that boy, it was not the one you had. If you could do it over, you would be the kind of girl he would want to take with him. You would be stronger or smarter or harder. You remember his photos of female Zapatistas, skinny, rigid women in fatigues and bandana masks, their eyes fiery with disobedience. Look in the mirror at your own eyes, vague, watery. Your body, still young but softening, curving gently in and out on itself, womanly. A home body.

You've been unusually tired in the mornings and evenings, prone to crying in the afternoon. You decide to join a gym. Start in the class that combines kickboxing and aerobics. A sinewy man several inches shorter than you shouts in your face as you force your limbs out into fierce upper cuts, jabs, hooks. You feel both keenly charged and on the verge of collapse as you dodge, fake and swing, dodge, fake and swing. Sweat gathers in a stream between your shoulder blades; you watch your arms lash out in front of you, tell yourself, this is useful. This will come in handy some day.

YOU JOIN THIS BOY for dinner at a trendy, upscale restaurant, this boy and his friends. You are out of sorts when you arrive, a combination of agitation and fatigue. You pace the foyer, smile at the wait staff as they pass, scratch at the fake gold leaf with your thumbnail until this boy comes out into the lobby. "I was just going to call you," he says, waving his cell phone, all surprise and relief.

"I just got here," you say.

He guides you through the restaurant. Everything is dark red: the carpet, the velvet upholstery, the heavy satin curtains that drip down the sides of walls, and the walls themselves, reddened with a paint so dark and matte, it sucks away the room's already dim light.

The friends, three men arranged around a table, are easy to look at, the type who use hair products, wear dry-clean–only clothes. Two of them look a little younger than this boy; the third, older. This boy moves to fill your glass with wine. The older friend stops him. "Give her the good stuff." This boy fills his own glass with the remains of a local Gamay, christens your glass with an imported Cabernet Sauvignon.

The banter is light and energetic. Each friend draws you into alliance—a nod in your direction, a sidelong glance, a more direct, "Am I right?" from the older friend. You trail on the fringe of conversation, swallow your wine in mouthfuls. All the friends are attractive, all the friends are funny and sharp. This generic quality makes you stare at this boy until he is nothing but a blur between two faux-finished pillars. You see that his hazy face is smiling broadly at you, but then again, so are the others. Men like this are not uncommon in the world.

You wonder if his friends share the same proclivities in bed. You think that you could probably sleep with any of them. Apart from minor differences, age, hair colour, height, they are interchangeable. You suspect that they would also like to sleep with you. Two of them bump wrists in a bungled attempt to fill your wineglass. They laugh at your quips, mistake your apathy for keen wit. At intervals, they each turn from the conversation to smile at you, hold your gaze for as long as they can, create the brief illusion of intimacy. The message is clear, "If it doesn't work out for you two, we're just as good."

You peruse the menu. One of the younger ones touches your arm. "The decor in this place is something else, hey?"

"Yes," you say, dryly. "I believe they call this period Early Haemorrhaging." The friend chuckles. This boy stares at you with more than a hint of annoyance; you feel, momentarily, like a child.

After you've ordered, the conversation turns to electronics, DVDs, amps. You rearrange the napkin on your lap, study the other restaurant patrons: couples and groups who look far too young and coutured to be real. You wonder if they all give to Amnesty International.

You wish that you had met that boy's friends, anonymous phone voices who called at night and beckoned him out for drinks and card games.

"You wouldn't enjoy it," he told you. "They're crusty old photographers and pressmen. It's all shop talk."

"There aren't any women?" you asked.

"Sure there's women," he told you. "But they're crusty, too."

On those nights, you thought about calling your own friends. Girls from the college library program, girls who worked with you. Friends you ran into on the street and exchanged phone numbers with, knowing full well neither of you had any intention of getting together. You couldn't be bothered to keep in touch; you ignored invitations, forgot birthdays. When you did call, you found yourself rambling to answering machines or friends who were already in pyjamas.

You spent those nights alone, imagined that boy in a smoky room, laughing, rested back, his ankle on his knee. Relaxed in a way he never was with you. The people in the room were sarcastic and funny and informed. The women were never crusty.

The food arrives and the smell of it, garlic, anchovies, olive oil, causes a turn in your stomach. You excuse yourself from the table, move calmly through the restaurant to the ladies' room, a den of mirrors and chrome washed in a lighter, pinker red. In the stall, you grip the cold tank of the toilet, lean your face down to the bowl and catch a whiff of bleach and air freshener. Your body unleashes two and a half glasses of sanguine wine.

At the sink, you rinse your mouth and wash your face with cold water. Pat your skin dry with a paper towel. As you reapply lipstick, you feel relieved that the alcohol is out of you. You tell yourself, it's better this way. This is no time to take up drinking.

BY THE WEEK'S END, this boy is frustrated with your cultivated despondency. He suggests a trip, somewhere warm. His coffee table is covered with travel brochures, glossy pages of vacant beaches, crystal tides. You are afraid to pick them up. You wander around his apartment, look under cushions, behind the television. You flip through fashion magazines to watch the pages fan. He offers to fix you a drink, but you decline, pacing instead a track around his coffee table. He fixes himself one, three fingers of gin, no ice; you haven't had sex for days now and he is antsy. He carries his drink to the table and stands in your way. "We could go for a swim?" You stop in front of him, shake your head. He runs his hand around the back of your neck, up into your hair; he massages the base of your skull. "I know what'll make you feel better."

He pulls gently on your hair. You feel your skin loosening its grip on your bones. You lay your head into his palm and let him hold you. Your shoulder blades relax back and down. His lips land on your neck, soft, brushing kisses. His fingertips unbutton your blouse, trace the edges of your bra. You feel yourself hanging in air, your head tipped back, and wonder when he will let go, when you will fall. He keeps your head cradled in one hand as the other moves to your skirt, crawls under the hem. You stop him there, your hand grabbing down for his wrist and wrenching his arm up between the two of you. He smiles at the speed and severity of your gesture.

You look at him as directly as you can. "I'm late."

THERE ARE NO NEW MESSAGES *on the server.*

THIS BOY HOLDS YOUR HAND in the waiting room. Whispers he loves you. Gets up to check with the nurse about the time. Shakes his foot while he reads a magazine. You breathe deeply into your stomach, sure you can feel something there, something floating in a liquid pouch. You tell yourself there are already too many people in the world, too many hungry children. You sift through a stack of old newspapers on the waiting-room table, pull out the international news sections. Wars, atrocities, disasters calm you. It is exactly as you suspected, the world is no place to raise a child.

You stare at the colour photograph that fronts a world news section already a few days old: *Army helicopter hit by rebel ground fire crashes in jungle outside Aceh.* The image is the view from the jungle floor. Leafy trees and vines decorated with glinting pieces of fuselage. Here and there, dark red blooms hang from branches like great weeping flowers.

THE DOCTOR who performs your procedure is cheerful, tells a joke about three men with Alzheimer's who share a house; he makes the nurses laugh. He gives instructions in a tender voice. *Slide down to the end of the table, good, good, feet on here.* He stops for a moment with your heel in his hand, the paper bootie crinkling, turns your leg to examine the fading marks. Looks at you kindly, his eyebrows raised as if asking if he should be concerned. You push a weak smile, he smiles back, and sets your paper foot in the stirrup.

Let your knees relax outward, that's it, good, you'll feel a little pressure, just my hand, good, perfect. His voice is hypnotic in its rhythm, its soothing timbre. The gown is crisp against your skin, the table cool and hard beneath you. A nurse strokes your forearm as the doctor moves a needle between your legs. *Just a pinch,* he says before you feel it.

You close your eyes and feel the glow of the examination lamps on your body. You try to draw in that focused warmth, absorb it, as if it were the sun. The lip of the table underneath your backside drops with a metallic click. Your legs tense. *Just relax,* the doctor's hand on the inside of your calf, your lower body flushed and heavy. The table seems softer, you are sinking into it. The noises of the room slip away in gentle increments. The chatter of nurses fades out to a distant twitter, grows dim and cottony as if they have left the room, then comes back slowly, sparkles into the chatter of young girls on a beach, their busy hands spreading oils and lotions, adjusting straps and sunglasses. The whir of a machine vibrates into the engine of a seaplane as it parts with the water, leaving a bright white cleft in the cyan tide. You are lying on sand, the earth's warm pressure against your back, the heat of the sun penetrating points deep in your centre. Every now and then, a young brown boy selling cold drinks comes by to ask if you are alright, you tell him, yes, yes. As he moves away from you, your head is filled with the perfume of jasmine and tropical fruit. There are other sounds: the music of handmade instruments, the easy laughter of island wives, the clicks and clacks of an unknown language. And beneath all this, the deep and insistent surge of your own breath, the echo of a pulse in your belly. You are amazed to find that here you can sit up, stand, walk around. You push your feet into the sand, stare at painted birds, brilliant flowers. You watch as glassy waves crawl onto beach, play broken seashells like wind chimes. The taste in your mouth is salty sweet, sea air, cane sugar. There are no rebels here, you tell yourself, no guerrillas, no mercenaries. No one dies here, no priests, no women. No children die here.

THE SKY MELTS into a puddly horizon of pink and tangerine. This boy is silent as he drives, but holds your hand, rubs his thumb over your knuckles. You stop at a drugstore for painkillers. The nurse at the clinic assured you there would be almost no pain, but you are unconvinced.

Back at your apartment, this boy tucks you into bed, tells you he will stay on the couch so you can get some rest, leaves you with a glass of water and the bottle of pills.

You shake two white tablets into your hand, then place them on the nightstand, beside the phone. You want to feel the pain first without the drugs, to confront it dead-on before numbing it out. You wait for the muted ache in your abdomen to grow, think about the two teenage girls in the recovery room, their worried murmurs to the nurses, their uncertain smiles. All three of you had glanced over your blankets at each other, fleeting but polite looks of sympathy. You had all endured something, you had all survived.

Your body feels alarmingly normal, a fullness around your middle, but other than that, nothing. You had expected something traumatic, an unhealed wound, a permanent injury. You had expected to suffer.

The bedroom glows with the warm tones of dusk, the hard corners of walls and furniture rounded and smoothed by the light. A photograph of this scene would disturb no one. You reach your hand between your legs, touch the hospital pad, remind yourself there is still blood.

You reach into the drawer of the nightstand and pull out a folded piece of paper. You stare at the phone for a long time before picking up the receiver. You dial a series of numbers, listen for chimes, dial more numbers. A hotel switchboard operator connects your call.

You count the rings. You have decided to hang up after seven.

At six, he answers. "Hello?" That boy's voice is distant and curious. "Hello."

A pause and crackle on the line. "How are you?"

You slide your hand under the sheets, rub the flat of your stomach. "I saw the photo. In the paper. The helicopter."

"Yeah, what a mess." He sighs. "I've really wanted to call you, I just thought."

"I know." A twinge, small and sharp, flickers in your abdomen. "It's okay."

"I miss you."

You turn onto your side, push your hand into the sting. A cramp begins, a closed fist, a warm, twisting grip. Tears fall over the bridge of your nose.

"Something's happened here," he says. The connection falters; his words are delayed, then repeated in a digital stutter. "Happened here happened here."

"Something's happened here, too," you say, but he is already talking over you.

"I've applied for a new assignment in the Middle East. If I schedule it right, I might get a week or two off before I start." The ends of his sentences retreat into echo; the phone line is more like a vast space than a thin tunnel.

You and that boy are worlds apart, your closeness, an incidental by-product of technology, an illusion of satellites and fibre optics.

"Are you still there?"

You swallow to clear your throat. "Yeah." You look over at the pills, but the pain has disappeared, a fleeting and shadowy exit.

"Did you say something while I was talking? I couldn't hear you, this connection is terrible."

"No," you say.

THIS BOY SLEEPS with a clear mind, dreams in quadraphonic sound. In bed, with the lights off, you stare at his shoulder, the turns and curves of muscle and bone. You marvel that his body is so sharp against the fade of the room, so vividly distinguishable from the rest of the world. Your own skin seems to blur into the air around you, wash into the sheets. You watch the flutter beneath this boy's eyelids, run your fingers through his hair, damp around the temples like a feverish youth. You kiss the ridge of his brow.

Tomorrow you will tell him it is over. He will not believe you. He will negotiate, then shout, then cry. You will not know when to touch him. You will follow him around as he gathers his things, and beg him to look at you, to talk to you. He will shake his head and push you away. He will call you something horrible and you will slap him so hard his mouth will bleed. You will cry; he will take off his coat.

By the end of it, sometime between ten and midnight, after a full day of emotional hostage-taking, without food or water, while you are filling a glass with ice and he is dabbing hydrogen peroxide to his lip, you will look at each other and find someone so unfamiliar, you will wonder if you are in the right apartment, the right country.

It is then that the two of you will finally reach a settlement, decide to call a truce, lie down in each other's arms and, soon after, manoeuvre your way out, in the dark.

The Still

Jackson's bootleg business was open any hour you could rouse him. He lived an inner solitude so profound he remained untouched by the constant flow and swirl of his clientele. He sat to the side, said nothing, offered an enigmatic smile if pressed for an opinion. Jackson was an excellent bootlegger. He kept a reasonable selection of commercial product but realized his best profit from the manufacture and sale of untaxed alcohol. He kept half a dozen kegs full of homebrew and made wine that could light a barbecue. He was an alcoholic. He understood alcoholics.

The smell of bacon frying prodded Jackson awake. He wasn't alone in his cabin. He didn't care to think that through immediately. He buried his face into his pillow, eyes still closed, and took stock of his body. At twenty-eight years old it held up well to abuse, recovered quickly. He wasn't too bad. He shuffled himself around so he could lean over the edge of the bed and grope through the case of Keith's he kept under there. When his hand located a full bottle he sat up in bed, plumping the pillows behind him, and sipped back his hair-of-the-dog like a Victorian lady taking her tonic. It was Lori, he remembered, who was frying the bacon.

Lori always woke up first. She wanted a chance to fix her face. Not the whole story; she didn't want to appear desperate. Just enough to fix her colour, hide any bags under the eyes, maybe a touch of liner. She wanted to give her hair that sexy tousled look. She chose her blue flip-flops and a workshirt of Jackson's, carefully rolling up the sleeves and pulling it together with just the two middle buttons. She had seen Demi Moore in a magazine once in a workshirt. It looked like she had no underwear or anything and the shirt could fall off at any second.

Jackson sat over his breakfast trying to bring into focus an idea he had been working on yesterday. He piled his bacon onto the toast to build a sandwich. His eggs had all the whites cut off them, three golden buttons, cooked all the way through so they didn't run. He blinked in embarrassment that Lori knew this about him. The old Surge milking machine! That was what he had been thinking about. And copper piping looped around and around through cold water in that sink. His eyes shone.

Lori, leaning back against the sink, caught the hungry gleam in his eye. She raised her fingers to her hair. "I always look a fright in the morning," she giggled.

He had wine nearly ready. He could start with that, to try. Move to a cheaper mash later on. He licked his lips.

Lori giggled again. She sauntered over to him and wriggled her way onto his lap. "You were terrific last night."

Jackson noticed her there on his lap. He mumbled, as always, into his beard. "Good breakfast." Her chest was so close he had to turn his head to finish his toast. He could heat the mash on his hot plate. Or maybe a Coleman would be better?

"I cleaned up a bit," she said. "This is not a bad place. It's so cool that you built it yourself. I used to go out with this other guy, I mean like *years* ago, and he was so useless you wouldn't believe. He got a flat tire once and I had to change it for him ..."

Jackson was thinking about soldering. "I'd want a blowtorch for that job," he may have said. Lori slid onto her knees on the floor in front of him.

THE BARN WAS DOWN at the road, next to his mother's house where he and his nine brothers and sisters had been raised. His mom still kept an old Jersey and a couple of beef but mostly the pigeons had taken over, dropping long furrows of shit onto old hay beneath the beams. Piles of junk had grown up in the centre of the barn. Jackson picked through it, quickly coming across the main part of the milker, a large, round, stainless-steel container with a plate-sized hole in the top where the cover fit. Finding the cover was the hard part, it being so much smaller. An hour into the search the only things of value he had unearthed were a ball cap he had lost some years ago, a Robertson screwdriver, and his brother, Matthew, passed out on a bed of mouldy straw. He might have given up except that Matthew gave a groan and twisted his body. An arc of steel glinted from underneath his armpit. Jackson reached under his brother to pull out the missing piece. There was a hay fork under there too, which looked uncomfortable, so he pulled that out as well. Fitted together, the milker looked like a huge silver curling stone.

LORI PICKED UP the beer bottles and spot-cleaned the painted aspenite floor where there had been spills. She gathered up the piles of shavings in the corner where Jackson sat to whittle. She swept. She emptied the hubcap ashtrays. She wiped the table and little squares of counter at each end of the sink. Next time she would bring some vinegar to do the window, maybe borrow a brush from Rosie and give the floor a good scrub. Linoleum flooring would be better. The walls were yellow with tobacco smoke but it was hard to wash chipboard that hadn't been painted. She would wallpaper them if they were hers, and make some curtains for the window and put in a little cookstove there instead of that old pot belly. She made the bed but that was hard too because the bedroom was hardly bigger than the bed. She blushed a little at the grey pallor of the sheets. Jackson had a tiny bathroom with cold running water but he'd never got around to hooking up the toilet. So it sat there, taking up half the space, the bowl crammed with empty beer bottles, several cases of homebrew stacked on the tank. She wiped out the sink, rubbing the amber stains until they glowed.

It had been almost a year now that she had been "dropping by," visiting Rosie, wandering back to see Jackson, waiting around for successive tribes of boisterous drunks to finish their business and drive off, packed like sardines into the cabs of their rickety pickups. It had been almost a year since the first time, the night they had both been so drunk. It had been easier after that. If she was there when everyone else had left he might reach out and stroke her thigh or squeeze her waist. He had lovely big hands. Strong. He said so little it was hard to tell what he was thinking. But he had never been mean to her. Ever. And he had given her three of his carvings. She had a lonely-looking raven and a spruce tree and an odd one of a bottle with a gnarled old hand gripping it.

BY ELEVEN O'CLOCK Jackson's breathing was becoming laboured. It was the pressure against the emptiness. Jackson felt his ribcage harden into a tin cylinder. There was nothing inside. Nothing. Whenever he spoke to other people it was like climbing up out of a well. It was hard to focus on them, they were so far away, at the wrong end of a telescope. He had to put them together in his mind, piece by piece. He had to strain to hear them over the rush of nothingness. The muted mumblings he produced required great effort, as if he were shouting across a chasm, shouts usually lost in an echo before they reached anyone. It was too much work.

Jackson would have one beer when he woke up in the morning, two if he really needed them. After that, he held out for the rest of the morning, as long as he could, until his chest started to crinkle under an irresistible pressure, like an empty beer can in a closing fist. Then he would drink. It was like pouring water into that can, filling the vacuum, packing substance into the void, relieving the pressure.

He left his milker by the farmhouse, in the tool shack they had always flattered with the term "workshop." He headed back to his cabin. The seashell drone in his ears had become a roar. He drew himself a pitcher of homebrew from the keg, drank it straight down, draining the pitcher. Lori perched on the edge of a rickety chair, filing her nails and chattering away a mile a minute. Then she looked at him expectantly, waiting for a response. He smiled, hoping that would pass as an answer. He drew off another pitcher. Since Lori had washed all the glasses that had been lying around he had to search the shelves for some. He poured them each a beer.

She giggled, uncertain. "What's that smile supposed to mean?" She sounded rickety, half way between hopeful and humiliated. "Do you want to get married or not?" She had wanted it to sound strong and "no nonsense" like Rosie, but it came out more like a plea. And she could feel the tears welling up in her eyes.

Jackson understood that she was talking to him, about him. About them. But it was like overhearing a conversation in a laundromat. He took another long drink then picked up the owl he was carving.

She couldn't believe she had started this and wished to god she could go back. Then a whoop and a holler and a burst of ribald laughter rolled into the air between them. Jackson's first customers of the day had arrived. She had never felt so alone.

"I'm not hanging around while that crowd drools all over your floor! I'm going to Rosie's to call my sister to come and pick me up." She was leaking tears now. "Oh, Jacky, I love you!" She hugged his neck as he stood by the doorway waiting for his customers.

Jackson put his hands on her waist. He could see, dispassionately, how he could have bedded her all those times. 'Doggy style,' he thought and the expression brought a tiny smile to his lips. She looked up at him, into that faint, shy smile searching for her dignity. She grabbed her things and fled.

JACKSON STOOPED OVER his work in the tool shed by the farmhouse, forming a length of bendable copper piping, curling it around and around in perfect, even loops. While he worked he forced himself to think about Lori. It was like doing a school math problem, completely apart from him. Academic. It made no sense that she would want to marry him but she did. It didn't make any difference to him. Nothing did. He didn't want to upset anyone. If it would make her happy ...

He had no experience with this kind of thing. And he wasn't fond of metal work. Soldering and welding made him feel far from his hands.

He didn't notice his four- and five-year-old nephews until a little fist curled around the pipe.

"Jackson's making a giant-size slinky!"

Matthew sauntered along behind his boys. He leaned on the doorpost, watching progress. "Never you mind that, Old Man," he said to his son. "And don't you two get into any trouble or I'll whoop yez both." The boys paid no attention.

"I'll give you a hand with the solder later on if you want." Jackson nodded at his lap. When Jackson heard receding footsteps on the gravel he looked up and watched his brother stroll off, shoulders swaying gracefully on his lanky frame.

WHEN LORI STARTED her period she did her very best to feel relieved. The relief, though, floated on the surface of a deep pool of desperation. By the end of the day she had locked her sister out of their tiny room and lay across her bed weeping. She simply could not bear it if one more person looked past her to choose a bottle. Jackson had to love her. She did everything right. She never asked him for anything. Until today. Why did she say that? Why? 'I love you, Jacky. Want to marry me?' She spat the sentences out over and over in a stream of rarefied venom. She buried her face in her pillow where she sobbed. "Stupid-stupid-stupid. Stupid!" Eventually, her sister's angry pounding on the door roused her. She took her time getting up. Maybe my thighs are too fat, she thought. Nobody wants to marry a big fat cow.

MATTHEW SHOWED UP for the soldering and the inaugural run. When they'd finished tinkering with the joints, Matthew held the milker while Jackson poured in the wine. Soon the still had settled into operation and they sat back to wait and watch.

"Good thing it's you and me, b'y," Matthew crowed. "Cause brandy's too good for that regular crowd you got around here."

Jackson looked across the table at his brother, saw the way his hair twirled in a cowlick above his left eye, the tiny scar beside his nose where he'd been hit with a snowball filled with ice as a kid. He looked, for just a second, into his eyes. He couldn't remember the last time he'd looked into the eyes of another human being and the intensity of it stung him. He gathered himself up.

"Lori wants to get married."

"Wow. Is she pregnant?"

The question had never occurred to Jackson. Now that he thought of it he supposed it was possible.

"I don't know."

"Well, you better ask her, buddy! Jesus, Jackson, sometimes I think you're thick like that." He rapped on the wooden tabletop with his knuckles.

Jackson got up and checked the connections in the still.

"Married. Christ, I remember before me and Rosie got married, when we were going out. What a time we had. We went up to that barbecue in Scotsburn. Remember I told you that time ole stunned arse, Clifford, was selling hash in the parking lot? And he was so lit he thought he was putting it back in the glove compartment of his car but really it was the minister's car? And the minister and his wife came back and drove off and Clifford took off running down the road after them, cussing a blue streak? Rosie hates that fucker, Clifford. She near pissed herself that day she laughed so hard.

"And remember that time Barry Landry was working for Van Dyke and he got fired cause he fucked off and never fed the pigs? And he was pissed off because he never got his last day's pay. So we all rattled over there in Barry's old truck and stole those piglets and ran out of gas and the Mountie came up and Rosie had to convince him we're home late from the sale? Home from the cattle sale at three o'clock in the fuckin' morning!? She was beautiful. I didn't care when she got pregnant. I was glad. I'd've married her the first day I met her."

The still chortled and gave out a low hiss.

Matthew's voice turned oddly warm and delicate, not much above a whisper, "Make damn good and sure you love her. Or you'll both be fucked."

The first bright drop of shine slipped out the end of the copper piping, pinging into the waiting pitcher.

LORI DIDN'T VISIT HIM the next day or the next. Jackson could have just let it go. Most things will go away if you ignore them. His father had always said that, but his mom would always slam or bang something and proclaim that was *not* true of the bills. The following morning he looked up Lori's father's number in the phone book, dialled, and asked to speak to Lori. He waited a minute then heard the receiver being passed over with a whisper, "It's a man."

Lori answered with a question. "Hello?"

"Hi."

"Jackson!" She remembered the little smile he had given her before she left, the beers he poured for her, the wood carvings, the weight of his body on hers.

"How are you?" He had reminded himself to ask this, practised it.

"Good, Jackson. I'm really good. Gee, I don't think you've ever called here before. This is great. I was just doing my toenails. Geeky, eh? It's that really bright red shade I had on a couple of weeks ago. Wild. I was going out later, just to the store, I mean. You're lucky you caught me. How are you?"

"Okay."

Then Jackson wasn't sure exactly what was the polite way to ask a girl if she was pregnant. "I was wondering, cause you said you wanted to get married, I just wondered, if you were pregnant or anything."

Then it was Lori's turn to pause. He didn't care about her, he was only interested in himself. He cared enough to call, to ask her. He didn't just walk off like lots of them did. He wasn't interested in her for herself. He would only marry her if he had to. He would marry her if she was pregnant. If she was pregnant she could make a scene and he would comfort her and propose and they would fix up the cabin and he would hook up the toilet and build on another room or maybe two. She'd be out of this shit-hole and have a home of her own and a baby and Jackson looking after them all. And after the baby came he'd give up drinking, well not completely, but he'd move the bootlegging out into a shed or something and only drink on weekends, which wouldn't be bad. If she were pregnant. And she could *say* she was. And by the time he found out she probably *would* be and they'd laugh about it.

"Uh. No. I'm not pregnant. Or anything."

"Well. That's great then."

"Yeah. Thank god, eh?"

"Yeah."

Lori waited, wondering if he was going to ask her to come over. Since he was happy. Since she wasn't pregnant.

Jackson didn't have anything to go on. He tried to remember the lines they used on the soaps. "... 'cause I'm not ahh, really ready, you know, for uhmm, a relationship right now ...?"

There was silence.

"You're not mad, are you?" he asked.

"No."

"Okay then."

Lori was going to say goodbye but the receiver was already buzzing in her ear. Twenty-two years old she was. Twenty-two. She cradled the receiver in her lap. She didn't have the strength to hang up.

MATTHEW AND JACKSON recovered from the first batch of shine just as the experimental potato mash was ready for the still. Jackson set up the machine and they sat back in their chairs, watching droplets form on the cooling pipe that poked above the water in the sink. Jackson felt a shrug of feeling in his chest, a kind of gurgle bubbling up through the beer. It was strange, and frightening after all this time. His brother, Matthew, had helped him out. Not that he'd said anything that great, just that he'd said something. He had heard his brother's voice. For a second he thought he might reach over and touch him. He swallowed. The bubble was almost painful. Matthew, he thought, thank you.

"Matthew," he said. The word pierced the air between them, stark naked. He cringed at the intimacy of it. He felt a bit dizzy and had to gulp a breath. Matthew was looking at him. "This is going to be a great batch," Jackson said.

ANNABEL LYON

Black

T he old woman upstairs is taking a long time to die. Downstairs, Jones is making some phone calls. Jones calls Barry and Edith, and Tom and Anna, and Jack and Ruby and Glen. He calls Denise. He calls Larry and Kate and Bridget and Amy. He calls Foster. He calls Suzy and Morris.

"God, Jones," Morris says. "I'm so sorry."

"But will you come?" Jones asks.

Morris pulls on the phone cord, stretching Jones's voice out and letting it seize back to coils, a kid with bubblegum, finger to tongue. "Do you really think," Morris says. "At this point, I mean."

"Yes," Jones says.

"I mean, considering."

"Yes."

"Will Lorelei be there?"

"Lorelei, Lorelei," Jones says. "Are you coming or not?"

"Is this really the right time?" Morris says.

"I want to see everything go up in the air and come down again different," Jones says. "I think this is the thing I've been waiting for."

"This thing is your mother dying."

"Morris," Jones says. "You have to at least think about it."

"Suzy won't want to."

"I think you should be here for this," Jones says.

SUZY DOESN'T want to go.

"Come on, Suzy," Morris says. "Why are you being so difficult?"

"I just don't want to," Suzy says.

"You'll regret it later in life."

"No."

"We're going and that's final."

Morris is forty-three and Suzy is five.

THERE ARE COMPLICATIONS. First, Suzy needs a dress.

"A dress!" Suzy shrieks, as though he has suggested a crucifixion or a gentle roasting. She runs around the house, flapping her arms. A dress!

Morris is dark but Suzy is blond. She has never worn a dress a day in her life.

"Come on, Suzy," Morris says. "It's not so bad."

"Have you ever worn a dress?" she asks.

"Yes," he says.

"How was it?"

"You get used to it," Morris says. "You have to get the right kind, that's all."

"What's the right kind?"

Black satin bias-cut with skinny little straps and a velvet train. Did he really, all those years ago? "Well, now," Morris says. "Let's see."

MORRIS AND SUZY take the bus downtown. He pays and she looks out the window.

Morris thinks about dresses and little girls in dresses. He thinks about sturdy cotton, blue and white stripes, dresses Suzy could fall down in and people would worry about her first. Morris loves Suzy and wants her to be pretty and happy. He knows this is a contradiction and it distresses him pleasantly, like love. It draws his love for her out ahead of him in a long ribbon, trailing him along, flustered and anxious and determined to get things right.

Suzy thinks about construction paper and glue. She thinks about spreading a thin pool of glue into her palm and letting it dry and peeling it off again and how it makes a print of her skin, and how her palm is cool and sticky-dry afterwards. She thinks about scissors and the heavy feel of cutting and the sound, like a lion's snarling purr. She thinks about looping noodles of white glue all over the world.

They find Suzy's dress on a hanger on a rack in a large department store. Morris knows it when he sees it. The dress is plain yellow with a green satin sash and a bow above the bum. He selects yellow running shoes to go with the dress. Suzy steps from the cubicle, pretty as May, and lets the saleslady zip her up. Morris is delighted.

"What do you say?" he says to the saleslady. "I mean, what do you say?"

The saleslady looks at Suzy, who is kicking at herself in the mirror with the toe of her new running shoe.

"Thank you, Morris," Suzy says.

ANOTHER COMPLICATION: will Suzy have to kiss the corpse? It happens that way in films. Angelic white-blond child is led to the open casket; creamy blond woman splinters, twenty years on, into something unrecognizable. Sometimes she will wear black, sometimes white; sometimes she will smoke, sometimes not. Morris doesn't like to think of Suzy smoking, although he likes to think of the elegance of smoke in black and white.

He gives her a colour bath. Yellow hair, blue mat, orange towel, white hooded robe. A happy child's bath.

Morris sits on the toilet seat and watches Suzy play with her fish, a fat orange fish with yellow sunglasses. Inside its mouth sits a smaller blue fish with the pleasing form of a nut. Suzy pulls the blue fish out of the orange fish's mouth and lets them go in the water. The orange fish gobbles at the bathwater, eventually closing on the blue fish with a click.

Suzy has forty-seven bath toys—Morris has counted them. Today, she pulls the blue fish too hard and the ratchet jams, snapping the string. She pales, a fish in each fist.

"We'll find another one," Morris says quickly, wondering where Lorelei procured such a hideous toy. He offers Suzy one of the neglected forty-six, a turtle. She tries to stuff the turtle into the orange fish's mouth.

Tonight, and every night after tonight, Suzy must sleep with the fish. The orange fish does not worry her so much any more, but the blue fish weighs upon her heart like a stone. She puts it in her mouth, gags, takes it out. She sleeps with it against her lips, hoping her breath will keep it warm.

THE HOUSE OF JONES and his mother has the feel of a party, a laid-back Sunday-afternoon extended family get-together with stocking feet and beer cans and sports on TV for those that want it, but hushed in deference to the woman dying upstairs. It feels like a house full of people who just happen not to be in any of the rooms Morris wanders into. It hums, it buzzes, it breathes. Morris is surprised that Jones, being Jones, has achieved such a thing.

Morris divests Suzy of her coat and tells her to go play. He finds Jones and hands him a foil-wrapped banana loaf. Jones leads him into the kitchen, where a woman is talking on the phone.

"String him along," the woman says to the phone. To Morris she says, "Where's Suzy?"

"Hello, Lorelei," Morris says.

"Fuck that," Lorelei says. "Where is my child?"

Morris goes to find Suzy. She's in the den, playing with a beagle. "Time to go, Suzy," he says.

Back in the kitchen, the only person he sees is Jones, spiking ice cubes from a tray.

"Where did Lorelei go?" Morris asks. He looks around the room again in case she is hiding, but there is only Jones. Morris feels the phone staring at him suspiciously, as though it still holds her breath.

"She left," Jones says. "She had to go shopping." Jones and Lorelei are brother and sister.

Suzy got her blond from Lorelei, but Morris hopes that is the extent of it. Suzy blinks at Morris, waiting. She got her blue eyes from her real father, who is dead in Michigan. She got her vocabulary from Morris.

"Is everything okay out there?" Jones asks. "I don't know a lot about parties. Are we doing all right?"

"Smashing, Jones," Morris says. "Smashing."

Suzy soars back to the den, where the puppy is waiting for her. She pets the puppy. The puppy blinks. She scratches the puppy under the collar. The puppy likes that, too. She touches the puppy's ear with a fingertip. The ear flicks quick as a bug's wing, quicker than seeing. The puppy sneezes and Suzy is in love.

Outside, as the drinks go down, the guests start to slump a little less and throng a little more. A man standing near Morris points at the ceiling. "Have I got this right?" he asks Morris. "Is she actually dead up there?"

"I'm unclear on that point myself," Morris says. "You could ask Jones."

"The guy in the kitchen?"

Morris nods.

"That man."

Morris mingles. He meets the housekeeper, an Iranian girl with a long pour of hair on her like black honey. In the course of their conversation he learns she has no complete language. She was born in Tehran, but her family moved to Hamburg when she was two. At seven she was taken to Montreal, at twelve to Vancouver. Each language—Persian, German, French, English—was a box she tried to break out of, boxes nested each inside the next, like a Chinese puzzle. She is a delicious horror. Morris longs to lie beside her, to cage her like ivory in his arms and to whisper in her ear, beautiful things she will not understand.

Jones tugs on Morris's sleeve.

"Yes, Jones," Morris says.

"She's dead."

"What. You mean, now?"

Jones nods. "What do I do?"

"What do you mean, what do you do?"

"With—it."

They look at each other.

"That's a damn good question," Morris says. "Did you make plans?"

"Rio," Jones says.

Morris stares.

"The other part, it kind of slipped my mind," Jones says. "Maybe if I get some more ice."

"Suzy?" Morris calls. "Honey? Start saying goodbye."

He goes to find Shiraz—he has an idea that is her name—and asks her to come home with him and Suzy, but she says no.

Morris goes to find Suzy. When he picks her up, her breath in his ear is a thick whisper about chocolate. "You and me both," he says.

He is turning her into her blue raincoat when she stops, fists still poking the fabric for daylight. "I want to see grandma," Suzy says.

There is an interesting silence.

"Grandma's sleeping, pretty," Jones says.

Morris can't believe it. Jones has a brain.

But Suzy is adamant, she is iron. She makes a break for the stairs and is snatched back by strangers.

"I know," Morris says. "Let's go for Chinese."

"Hurray!" Suzy roars.

"Sssh," Jones says, pointing upstairs and looking annoyed.

THE FIRST TIME Morris went for Chinese, he was six days old. His mother wore him on her chest in a tomato-coloured canvas sling. His parents were pathologically gentle people, walkers, sippers, smilers, tree-loving rainy-day pacifists, born fading. By the time he arrived, their lives were peanut-coloured, almost nude. In a baptismal moment his mother dripped sweet-and-sour sauce on his head, but she and his father were too engrossed in their respective fortune cookies to suspect meaning.

HIS MOST VIVID CHILDHOOD MEMORY was of sickness, which he loved. He loved staying in bed all day, reading books, eating Jell-O, flesh broth, globs of honey and aspirin crushed between two spoons. He loved the natural disorders of his body—vomiting, diarrhoea, infections, swellings, fevers, pale sleeps and altered appetites. Because his parents did not believe in TV and because he had a window, Morris watched weather. He saw blushing sunrises, curtains of rain holding in the night, snow in the blue afternoons. He missed prodigious amounts of school, was top of his class, and never wore a hat, in the hopes of catching something special.

IN HIS BACHELORHOOD, Morris would watch sports on TV. He watched blunt-headed events, car rallies and football. He watched women's triathlons from Hawaii, sun-slick virgins with space goggles and citrus neoprene and the strength of men. He watched figure skating. He listened to the hiss of skates, the music that didn't seem to fit with anything anyone was doing, the monsoons of applause. One afternoon he approached the TV and crouched before it, poked the skater gently with his finger and felt the prickling bite of static. She swooped and slithered. He studied her pixels. He imagined her laid out in his palm, a handful of dust. He imagined blowing her away. He backed away until she was a woman again, coronet and plumage. She glittered like sugar, like glass, spinning first one way, then the other. He couldn't turn her off. He let the afternoon go.

MORRIS ONCE ATTENDED seminar in drag to see if anyone would notice. After graduation he got a job as a legal secretary. Eighteen years later he got stuck in an elevator with a crazy woman and her two-year-old daughter. He told them his joke about the zebra. It was the beginning of the end.

LORELEI THE BEAUTY QUEEN had butterfly brains and the prettiest damn fingernails Morris had ever seen. She also had a baby girl who looked like she'd stepped off the top of a Christmas tree and was still floating down. They were like something from a magazine, and Morris wanted to cut and paste himself right into their lives. He braided himself then and there into their histories, so that a year later, when Lorelei, who was mad as a star, took off, Morris and Suzy were left in a twist.

SOMETIMES SUZY is pie-happy. Other times she is the pale queen on the dark shore, watching for stone ships that never return. At four she ties her shoes, recites the alphabet and dreams of winged men with glass hands that shatter and bleed. Ice is her favourite food. Morris puts food colouring in the ice cubes they eat together for a bedtime snack. He watches Suzy suck, then bite down. Her pyjamas still have feet. She is the black queen, pale and dolorous in her steel crown, mouth running with colours.

WHEN SUZY IS FIVE, she and Morris attend a party given in honour of, or in spite of, the death or dying of Suzy's maternal grandmother, Lenore. Death happens; trauma is narrowly avoided; bruised souls are slicked over with the balm of a good Chinese takeout and the inimitable joy of chopsticks in the hands of the uninitiated. Puppies are discussed.

WHEN SUZY IS THIRTEEN, she and Morris will go to Jones's funeral. The service will be short and mercifully lacking in foolery—no poetry readings, mucus-riddled reminiscences or favourite pieces of cello music. Jones will lie quietly in his casket at the front of the church. On top of the casket will be propped a large black-and-white glossy, taken about fifteen years earlier, of Jones with a movie-star grin, syrupy eyes and feathered frosted hair. Morris will spend most of the service pondering this photograph. He will conclude that Jones, being Jones, had it taken all those years ago with just this occasion in mind. Morris will surprise himself, at this point, by weeping.

Suzy will not cry. "I don't get this," she will say.

Jones will leave Suzy fifty thousand dollars, to be given over to her in a lump at the age of forty-four years. Jones will leave Morris wondering what space, if any, Jones's passing has left in the world.

WHEN SUZY IS SIXTEEN and into black, Morris will overhear her talking on the phone. "This guy I live with," she will say, meaning himself, Morris. This will startle him, unduly, since it is only true.

Suzy will spend months of daytime in her room, door closed, blinds drawn. She never goes out; she never plays music. She has no boyfriends, girlfriends, clubs, interests or hobbies.

Morris asks her what she does in there.

"Think," Suzy says.

"I'm trying," Morris says. "Yoga? Taxes?"

"No, that's what I do. I think."

IN UNIVERSITY, Suzy will have a room-mate who dyes her hair black every two weeks to hide her red roots. The room-mate will have had an old Irish granny who told her she was damned to hell because she hadn't been christened. She said her hair was stained all the colours of sin because devils had crept into her mother's womb through the umbilical cord and kissed her scalp with mouths bloody from eating the flesh of the newly dead. The room-mate's parents used to go away for the weekend, leaving granny to babysit.

Suzy will tell Morris about her frantic spice-haired room-mate. He will tell her how he had always wanted a band called Dropdead Redhead.

"Was I christened?" she will ask.

"Absolutely," he will say, wondering.

Suzy will write away for a copy of the parish records. One day a letter will come and she will burst upon Morris like a star, hurling a ball of crumpled paper in his face. "They called me Candace," she will spit.

"Well, look at it this way," Morris will say. "You're still a Pisces."

"I am a fucking fish named Candace," Suzy will say, her voice warped to a queerness, the closest she ever comes to tears.

Morris will wonder if he has ever loved her more than at this moment, his beautiful misnamed undaughter.

IN GRADUATE SCHOOL Suzy will thrive, in a sick way, in her philosophy of science seminar. She will tell Morris how every scientific phenomenon has an infinite number of logically possible explanations. She will liken facts about the world to dots on a graph, which can be joined by any number of different lines, representing theories. She will tell Morris how human relationships are like scientific theories, where every fact one person has about another is a dot, but the connecting lines exist only in one's head. No two lines are identical: love; a theorem; lines connecting lives; invisible threads looping through the universe, weaving a fabric of uncertainty and certain ignorance.

Morris will watch Suzy talk, Suzy of the black tunic and black leggings and the fine baby's hair. He will remember Suzy going into black, but he won't ever remember her coming out.

IT IS A FACT about Suzy that she will never fall in love. People will come to her in fragments—a pleasing glance, the width of a hand, a tone of voice, a cast of thought—from which she cannot seem to cobble a passion. Or maybe it is that Suzy herself is fragmented, all shards and splinters, shivered by a world of farce and darkness. Or just that she is flawed: hair thinning like a banker's, and a coldness of bearing she cannot sense and cannot lose.

DURING A BOUT of food poisoning, Morris will come over to make Suzy ruby Jell-O and hold her hand. While she is in the bathroom throwing up he will look at her chick's hair on the pillow. Her hair is falling out.

When Suzy comes back she will look at the pillow. "Oh, that Candace," she will say.

WHEN SUZY IS THIRTY-SIX she will go to Morris's funeral. She will wear a baseball cap because her hair is many different lengths, and in some places absent. She will not change her clothes for the occasion. She will smell strongly of herself. She will not cry.

FIFTY YEARS LATER Suzy will be in her garden, weeding her borders. She will be remembering a time when she couldn't breathe if she saw a flower, when they were evil mouths that talked to her when she was alone, laughing and hissing, coloured cups brimming venom. How they waved their petals, furling and unfurling, blind twisting mouths, thrusting petulant lips. Now they will fill her head with a rush like rain, a song of threading voices. She will feel the grass about her, the looming blades, for she will have fallen—a stroke, they will say, sudden, they will say—and she will realize there was a time when she could look at a person's eyes and it was like looking into a house through an open window, and then when it was like looking through glass.

Days will pass before they find her. It will have been a slow death. Eighty-six years is a slow death.

SUZY AND MORRIS in the Chinese restaurant, blue and gold. Through the window, the oriental filigree of traffic on a late afternoon down-town, after rain.

"This is how you eat an egg roll," Suzy says. "This is how you eat chow mein."

Suzy is discovering chopsticks. She chews with her mouth open, concentrating. "Oh, peas!" she says.

Morris looks at the goop in Suzy's open mouth. "Here," he says, passing her a plate. "Some more of the green stuff."

"Why?"

"It's good for you."

"Why?"

"Eat."

Suzy giggles and throws a pea at his head.

Morris giggles. Truly, he thinks, I am a terrible parent.

She throws all her peas at him, then pokes at her plate with the chopsticks for something golden and crunchy. "Can I have a puppy?" she asks.

"Sure," Morris says.

Always here, always now, he thinks, watching her eyes pool to glory. Always remember me this way. Because the day I am dust this is all you will have, and it will not be enough.

"Doggy bag?" the waiter says.

Suzy, alarmed, looks at Morris.

"Yes," he says. "Yes, please."

ALICE MUNRO

Wenlock Edge

My mother had a bachelor cousin a good deal younger than her,
who used to visit us on the farm every summer. He brought
along his mother, Aunt Nell Botts. His own name was Ernie Botts. He
was a tall, florid man with a good-natured expression, a big square face,
and fair curly hair springing straight up from his forehead. His hands,
his fingernails were as clean as soap itself; his hips were a little plump.
My name for him—when he was not around—was Earnest Bottom.
I had a mean tongue.

But I meant no harm. Or hardly any harm.

After Aunt Nell Botts died Ernie did not come to visit anymore, but
he always sent a Christmas card.

When I started college in the city where he lived, he began a custom
of taking me out to dinner every other Sunday evening. He did this
because I was a relative—it's unlikely that he even considered whether we
were suited to spending time together. He always took me to the same
place, a restaurant called the Old Chelsea, which was on the second floor
of a building, looking down on Dundas Street. It had velvet curtains,
white tablecloths, little rose-shaded lamps on the tables. It probably
cost more, strictly speaking, than he could afford, but I did not think of
that, having a country girl's notion that all men who lived in the city,
wore a suit every day, and sported such clean fingernails had reached a
level of prosperity where indulgences like this were a matter of course.

I always ordered the most exotic offering on the menu—chicken vol au vent or duck *à l'orange*—while he always ate roast beef. Desserts were wheeled up to the table on a dinner wagon: a tall coconut cake, custard tarts topped with strawberries, even out of season, chocolate-coated pastry horns full of whipped cream. I took a long time choosing, like a five-year-old trying to decide between flavors of ice cream, and then on Monday I had to fast all day, to make up for such gorging.

Ernie looked a little too young to be my father. I hoped that nobody from the college would see us and think that he was my boyfriend.

He inquired about my courses, and nodded solemnly when I told him, or reminded him, that I was in Honors English and Philosophy. He didn't roll his eyes at the information, the way people at home did. He told me that he had a great respect for education and regretted that he hadn't had the means to continue, after high school. Instead, he had got a job working for the Canadian National Railway, as a ticket salesman. Now he was a supervisor.

He liked serious reading, he said, but it was not a substitute for a college education.

I was pretty sure that his idea of serious reading would be the Condensed Books of the *Reader's Digest,* and to get him off the subject of my studies I told him about my rooming house. In those days, the college had no dormitories—we all lived in rooming houses or in cheap apartments or in fraternity or sorority houses. My room was the attic of an old house, with generous floor space and not much headroom. But, being the former maid's quarters, it had its own bathroom. Two other scholarship students, who were in their final year in Modern Languages, lived on the second floor. Their names were Kay and Beverly. In the high-ceilinged but chopped-up rooms of the ground floor lived a medical student who was hardly ever home, and his wife, Beth, who was home all the time, because they had two very young children. Beth was the house manager and rent collector, and she was often feuding with the second-floor girls over the way they washed their clothes in the bathroom and hung them there to dry. When Beth's husband, Blake, was home he sometimes had to use that bathroom because of all the baby stuff in the one downstairs, and Beth said that he shouldn't have to cope with stockings and other intimate doodads in his face. Kay and Beverly retorted that use of their own bathroom had been promised when they moved in.

Why did I choose to tell this to Ernie, who flushed and said that they should have got it in writing?

KAY AND BEVERLY were a disappointment to me. They worked hard at Modern Languages, but their conversation and preoccupations seemed hardly different from those of girls who worked in banks or offices. They did their hair up in pincurls and polished their fingernails on Saturdays, because that was the night they had dates with their special boyfriends. On Sundays, they had to soothe their faces with lotion because of the whisker-burns the boyfriends had inflicted on them. I didn't find either boyfriend in the least desirable and I wondered how they could.

They said that they had once had some crazy idea of working as interpreters at the United Nations but now they figured they would teach high school, and with any luck get married.

They gave me unwelcome advice.

I had got a job in the college cafeteria. I pushed a cart around collecting dirty dishes and wiping the tables clean.

They warned me that this job was not a good idea.

"You won't get asked out if people see you at a job like that."

I told Ernie about this and he said, "So, what did you say?"

I told him that I'd said I wouldn't want to go out with anybody who would make such a judgment, so what was the problem?

Now I'd hit the right note. Ernie glowed; he chopped his hands up and down in the air.

"Absolutely right," he said. "That is absolutely the attitude to take. Honest work. Never listen to anybody who wants to put you down for doing honest work. Just go right ahead and ignore them. Keep your pride. Anybody that doesn't like it, you tell them they can lump it."

This speech of his, the righteousness and approval lighting his large face, the jerky enthusiasm of his movements, roused the first doubts in me, the first gloomy suspicion that the warning might have some weight to it after all.

When I got home that night, there was a note from Beth under my door, asking to talk to me. I guessed that it would be about my hanging my coat over the bannister to dry, or making too much noise on the stairs when Blake (sometimes) and the babies (always) had to sleep in the daytime.

The door opened on the scene of misery and confusion in which it seemed that all Beth's days were passed. Wet laundry—diapers and smelly baby woollens—was hanging from ceiling racks; bottles bubbled and rattled in a sterilizer on the stove. The windows were steamed up, and the chairs were covered with soggy cloths and soiled stuffed toys. The bigger baby was clinging to the bars of a playpen and letting out an accusing howl—Beth had obviously just set him in there—and the smaller one was in a high chair, with some mushy pumpkin-colored food spread like a rash across his mouth and chin.

Beth peered out from all this with a tight expression of superiority on her small flat face, as if to say that not many people could put up with such a nightmare as well as she could, even if the world wasn't generous enough to give her the least bit of credit.

"You know when you moved in," she said, then raised her voice to be heard over the bigger baby's cries, "when you moved in I mentioned to you that there was enough space up there for two?"

Another girl was moving in, she informed me. The new girl would be there Tuesdays to Fridays, while she audited some courses at the college.

"Blake will bring the daybed up tonight. She won't take up much room. I don't imagine she'll bring many clothes—she lives in town. You've had it all to yourself for six weeks now, and you'll still have it that way on weekends."

No mention of any reduction in the rent.

Nina actually did not take up much room. She was small, and thoughtful in her movements—she never bumped her head against the rafters, as I did. She spent a lot of her time sitting cross-legged on the daybed, her brownish-blond hair falling over her face, a Japanese kimono loose over her childish white underwear. She had beautiful clothes—a camel-hair coat, cashmere sweaters, a pleated tartan skirt with a large silver pin—the sort of clothes you would see in a magazine layout, under the headline "Outfitting Your Junior Miss for Her New Life on Campus." But the moment she got back from the college she discarded her costume for the kimono. I also changed out of my school clothes, but in my case it was to keep the press in my skirt and preserve a reasonable freshness in my blouse or sweater, so I hung everything up carefully. Nina tossed her clothes anywhere. I ate an early supper at the college as part of my wages, and Nina always seemed to have eaten, too, though I didn't know where. Perhaps her supper was just what she ate all evening—almonds and oranges and a supply of little chocolate kisses wrapped in red or gold or purple foil.

I asked her if she didn't get cold, in that light kimono.

"Unh-unh," she said. She grabbed my hand and pressed it to her neck. "I'm permanently warm," she said, and in fact she was. Her skin even looked warm, though she said that was just a tan, and it was fading. And connected with this skin warmth was a particular odor that was nutty or spicy, not displeasing but not the odor of a body that was constantly bathed and showered. (Nor was I entirely fresh myself, owing to Beth's rule of two baths a week.)

I usually read until late at night. I'd thought that it might be harder to read, with someone else in the room, but Nina was an easy presence. She peeled her oranges and chocolates; she laid out games of solitaire. When she had to stretch to move a card she'd sometimes make a little noise, a groan or grunt, as if complaining about this slight adjustment of her body but taking pleasure in it, all the same. Otherwise she was content, and curled up to sleep with the light on whenever she was ready. And because there was no special need for us to talk we soon began to talk, and tell about our lives.

Nina was twenty-two years old and this was what had happened to her since she was fifteen:

First, she had got herself pregnant (that was how she put it) and married the father, who wasn't much older than she was. This was in a town somewhere outside Chicago. The name of the town was Laneyville, and the only jobs there were at the grain elevator or fixing machinery, for the boys, and working in stores, for the girls. Nina's ambition was to be a hairdresser but you had to go away and train for that. Laneyville wasn't where she had always lived—it was where her grandmother lived, and she lived with her grandmother because her father had died and her mother had got married again and her stepfather had kicked her out.

She had a second baby, another boy, and her husband was supposed to have a job lined up in another town so he went off there. He was going to send for her but he never did. So she left both children with her grandmother and took the bus to Chicago.

On the bus she met a girl named Marcy, who, like her, was headed for Chicago. Marcy knew a man there who owned a restaurant and she said he would give them jobs. But when they got to Chicago and located the restaurant it turned out that the man didn't own it—he'd only worked there and he'd quit some time before. The man who did own it had an empty room upstairs and he let them stay there in return for their cleaning the place up every night. They had to use the ladies' room in the restaurant but they weren't supposed to spend too much time there in the daytime—they had to wash themselves at night.

They didn't sleep hardly at all. They made friends with the barman in the place across the street—he was a queer but nice—and he let them drink ginger ale for free. They met a man there who invited them to a party and after that they got asked to other parties and it was during this time that Nina met Mr. Purvis. It was he, in fact, who gave her the name Nina. Before that, she had been June. She went to live at Mr. Purvis's place in Chicago.

She waited a little while before bringing up the subject of her boys. There was so much room in Mr. Purvis's house that she was hoping they could live with her there. But when she mentioned it Mr. Purvis

told her that he despised children. He did not want her to get pregnant, ever. But somehow she did, and she and Mr. Purvis went to
Japan, to get her an abortion.

At least up until the last minute that was what she thought she
would do, but then she decided, no. She would go ahead and have the
baby.

"All right," he said. He would pay her way back to Chicago, but
from then on she was on her own.

She knew her way around a bit by this time, and she went to a place
where they looked after you till the baby was born, and you could have
it adopted. It was born and it was a girl and Nina named her Gemma
and decided to keep her, after all.

She knew another girl who had had a baby in this place and kept
it, and she and this girl made an arrangement that they would work
shifts and live together and raise their babies. They got an apartment
that they could afford and they got jobs—Nina's in a cocktail
lounge—and everything was all right. Then Nina came home just
before Christmas—Gemma was eight months old—and found the
other mother half drunk and fooling around with a man, and the
baby, Gemma, burning up with fever, too sick to even cry.

Nina wrapped her up and took her to the hospital in a cab. Traffic
was all snarled up because of Christmas, and when she finally got there
they told her that it was the wrong hospital, for some reason, and sent
her off to another hospital. On the way there, Gemma had a convulsion and died.

Nina wanted to have a real burial for Gemma, not just have her put
in with some old pauper who had died (that was what she'd heard
happened to a baby's body when you didn't have any money), so she
went to Mr. Purvis. He was nicer to her than she'd expected, and he
paid for the casket and the gravestone with Gemma's name, and after
it was all over he took Nina back. He took her on a long trip to London
and Paris and a lot of other places, to cheer her up. When they got
home he shut up the house in Chicago and moved here. He owned
some property out in the country nearby; he owned racehorses.

He asked her if she would like to get an education, and she said she would. He said she should just sit in on some courses to see what she'd like to study. She told him that she'd like to live part of the time the way ordinary students lived, and he said he thought that that could be arranged.

Hearing about Nina's life made me feel like a simpleton.

I asked her what Mr. Purvis's first name was.

"Arthur."

"Why don't you call him that?"

"It wouldn't sound natural."

NINA WAS NOT supposed to go out at night, except to the college for certain specified events, such as a play or a concert or a lecture. She was supposed to eat lunch and dinner at the cafeteria. Though, as I said, I don't know whether she ever did. Breakfast was Nescafé in our room, and day-old doughnuts I brought home from the cafeteria. Mr. Purvis did not like the sound of this but he accepted it as part of Nina's imitation of the college student's life—as long as she ate a good hot meal once a day and a sandwich and soup at another meal, and this was what he thought she did. She always checked what the cafeteria was offering, so that she could tell him she'd had the sausages or the Salisbury steak, and the salmon or the egg-salad sandwich.

"So how would he know if you did go out?"

Nina got to her feet, with that little sound of complaint or pleasure, and padded over to the attic window.

"Come here," she said. "And stay behind the curtain. See?"

A black car, parked not right across the street but a few doors down. A streetlight caught the gleaming white hair of the driver.

"Mrs. Winner," Nina said. "She'll be there till midnight. Or later, I don't know. If I went out, she'd follow me and hang around wherever I went, then follow me back."

"What if she went to sleep?"

"Not her. Or if she did and I tried anything she'd be awake like a shot."

JUST TO GIVE Mrs. Winner some practice, as Nina put it, we left the house one evening and took a bus to the city library. From the bus window we watched the long black car having to slow and dawdle at every bus stop, then speed up to stay with us. We had to walk a block to the library, and Mrs. Winner passed us and parked beyond the front entrance, and watched us—we believed—in her rearview mirror.

I wanted to see if I could check out a copy of "The Scarlet Letter," which was required for one of my courses. I could not afford to buy one, and the copies at the college library were all checked out. Also I wanted to take a book out for Nina—the sort of book that showed simplified charts of history.

Nina had bought the textbooks for the courses she was auditing. She had bought notebooks and pens—the best fountain pens of that time— in matching colors. Red for Pre-Columbian Civilizations, blue for the Romantic Poets, green for Victorian and Georgian English Novelists, yellow for Fairy Tales from Basile to Andersen. She sat in the back row at every lecture, because she thought that that was the proper place for her. She spoke as if she enjoyed walking through the Arts Building with the throng of other students, finding her seat, opening her textbook at the specified page, taking out her pen. But her notebooks remained empty.

The trouble was, as I saw it, that she had no pegs to hang anything on. She did not know what Victorian meant, or Romantic, or Pre-Columbian. She had been to Japan, and Barbados, and many of the countries in Europe, but she could never have found those places on a map. She wouldn't have known whether the French Revolution came before or after the First World War.

I wondered how these courses had been chosen for her. Had she liked the sound of them? Had Mr. Purvis thought that she could master them? Or had he perhaps chosen them cynically, so that she would soon get her fill of being a student?

While I was looking for the book I wanted, I caught sight of Ernie Botts. He had an armful of mysteries, which he was picking up for an old friend of his mother's. He had told me that he always did that, just as he always played checkers, on Saturday mornings, with a crony of his father's out in the War Veterans' Home.

I introduced him to Nina. I had told him about her moving in, but nothing about her former or even her present life.

He shook Nina's hand and said that he was pleased to meet her and asked at once if he could give us a ride home.

I was about to say no, thanks, we'd take the bus, when Nina asked him where his car was parked.

"In the back," he said.

"Is there a back door?"

"Yes, yes. It's a sedan."

"No, I meant in the library," Nina said. "In the building."

"Yes. Yes there is," Ernie said, flustered. "I'm sorry, I thought you meant the car. Yes. A back door in the library. I came in that way myself. I'm sorry." Now he was blushing, and he would have gone on apologizing if Nina had not broken in with a kind laugh.

"Well, then," she said. "We can go out the back door. So that's settled. Thanks."

Ernie drove us home. He asked if we would like to detour to his place, for a cup of coffee or a hot chocolate.

"Sorry, we're sort of in a rush," Nina said. "But thanks for asking."

"I guess you've got homework."

"Homework, yes," she said. "We sure do."

I was thinking that he had never once asked me to his house. Propriety. One girl, no. Two girls, O.K.

No black car across the street, when we said our thanks and good nights. No black car when we looked out the attic window. In a short time, the phone rang, for Nina, and I heard her saying, on the landing, "Oh, no, we just went in the library and got a book and came straight home on the bus. There was one right away, yes. I'm fine. Absolutely. Night-night." She came swaying and smiling up the stairs. "Mrs. Winner's got herself in hot water tonight."

ONE MORNING, Nina did not get out of bed. She said she had a sore throat, a fever. "Touch me."

"You always feel hot to me."

"Today I'm hotter."

It was a Friday. She asked me to call Mr. Purvis, to tell him that she wanted to stay here for the weekend.

"He'll let me. He can't stand anybody being sick around him—he's a nut that way."

Mr. Purvis wondered if he should send a doctor. Nina had foreseen that, and told me to say that she just needed to rest, and she'd phone him, or I would, if she got any worse. "Well, then, tell her to take care," he said, and thanked me for phoning, and for being a good friend to Nina. And then, as an afterthought, he asked me if I would like to join him for Saturday night's dinner. He said he found it boring to eat alone. Nina had thought of that, too.

"If he asks you to go and eat with him tomorrow night, why don't you go? There's always something good to eat on Saturday nights—it's special."

The cafeteria was closed on Saturdays. The possibility of meeting Mr. Purvis both disturbed and intrigued me.

So I agreed to dine with him—he had actually said "dine." When I went back upstairs, I asked Nina what I should wear. "Why worry now? It's not till tomorrow night."

Why worry, indeed? I had only one good dress, the turquoise crêpe that I had bought with some of my scholarship money, to wear when I gave the valedictory address at my high-school commencement exercises.

MRS. WINNER CAME to get me. Her hair was not white but platinum blond, a color that to me certified a hard heart, immoral dealings, and a long bumpy ride through the sordid back alleys of life. Nevertheless, I opened the front door of the car to ride beside her, because I thought that that was the decent and democratic thing to do. She let me do this, standing beside me, then briskly opened the back door.

I had thought that Mr. Purvis would live in one of the stodgy mansions surrounded by acres of lawns and unfarmed fields north of the city. It was probably the racehorses that had made me think so. Instead, we travelled east through prosperous but not lordly streets, past brick and mock-Tudor houses with their lights on in the early dark and their Christmas lights already blinking out of the snowcapped shrubbery. We turned in at a narrow driveway between high hedges and parked in front of a house that I recognized as "modern" by its flat roof and long wall of windows and the fact that the building material appeared to be concrete. No Christmas lights here, no lights of any kind.

No sign of Mr. Purvis, either. The car slid down a ramp into a cavernous basement garage; we rode an elevator up one floor and emerged into a hallway that was dimly lit and furnished like a living room, with upholstered straight-backed chairs and little polished tables and mirrors and rugs.

Mrs. Winner waved me ahead of her through one of the doors that opened off this hallway, into a windowless room with a bench and hooks around the walls. It was just like a school cloakroom, except for the polish on the wood and the carpet on the floor. "Here is where you leave your clothes," Mrs. Winner said.

I removed my top boots. I stuffed my mittens into my coat pockets. I hung my coat up. Mrs. Winner stayed with me. There was a comb in my pocket and I wanted to fix my hair, but not with her watching. And I did not see a mirror.

"Now the rest," she said.

She looked straight at me to see if I understood, and, when I appeared not to (though, in a sense, I did—I understood but hoped I had made a mistake), she said, "Don't worry, you won't be cold. The house is well heated throughout."

I did not move to obey, and she spoke to me casually, as if she could not be bothered with contempt. "I hope you're not a baby."

I could have reached for my coat, at that point. I could have demanded to be driven back to the rooming house. I could even have walked back on my own. I remembered the way we had come and, though it would have been cold, it would have taken me less than an hour.

"Oh, no," Mrs. Winner said, when I still did not move. "So you're just a bookworm. That's all you are."

I sat down. I removed my shoes. I unfastened and peeled down my stockings. I stood up and unzipped then yanked off the dress in which I had delivered the valedictory address with its final words of Latin. *Ave atque vale.*

Still covered by my slip, I reached back and unhooked my brassiere, then somehow hauled it free of my arms and around to the front to be discarded. Next came my garter belt, then my panties—when they were off I balled them up and hid them under the brassiere. I put my feet back into my shoes.

"Bare feet," Mrs. Winner said, sighing. It seemed that the slip was too tiresome for her to mention, but after I had again taken my shoes off she said, "Bare. Do you know the meaning of the word? *Bare.*"

I pulled the slip over my head, and she handed me a bottle of lotion and said, "Rub yourself with this."

It smelled like Nina. I rubbed some on my arms and shoulders, the only parts of myself that I could touch, with Mrs. Winner standing there watching, and then we went out into the hall, my eyes avoiding the mirrors, and she opened another door and I went into the next room alone.

It had not occurred to me that Mr. Purvis might be waiting in the same naked condition as myself, and he was not. He wore a dark-blue blazer, a white shirt, an ascot scarf (though I did not know it was called that at the time), and gray slacks. He was hardly taller than I was, and he was thin and old, mostly bald, with wrinkles in his forehead when he smiled.

It had not occurred to me, either, that the undressing might be a prelude to rape, or to any ceremony but supper. (And indeed it was not, to judge by the appetizing smells in the room and the silver-lidded dishes on the sideboard.) But why hadn't I thought of such a thing? Why wasn't I more apprehensive? It had something to do with my ideas about old men. I thought that they were not only incapable, owing to their unsavory physical decline, but too worn down—or depressed— by their various trials and experiences to have any interest left. I wasn't stupid enough to think that my being undressed had nothing to do with the sexual uses of my body, but I took it more as a dare than as a preliminary to further trespass, and my going along with it finally had more to do with pride or some shaky recklessness than with anything else. And that word. "Bookworm."

Here I am, I might have wished to say, in the skin of my body which does not shame me any more than the bareness of my teeth. Of course that was not true, and in fact I had broken out in a sweat, but not for fear of any violation.

Mr. Purvis shook my hand, making no sign of awareness that I lacked clothing. He said that it was a pleasure for him to meet Nina's friend. Just as if I were somebody Nina had brought home from school. Which, in a way, was true. An inspiration to Nina, he said I was.

"She admires you very much. Now, you must be hungry. Shall we see what they've provided for us?"

He lifted the lids and set about serving me. Cornish hens, which I took to be pygmy chickens, saffron rice with raisins, various finely cut vegetables fanned out at an angle and preserving their color more faithfully than the vegetables that I regularly saw. A dish of muddy-green pickles and a dish of dark-red preserve.

"Not too much of these," Mr. Purvis said of the pickles and the preserve. "A bit hot to start with."

He ushered me back to the table, turned again to the sideboard and served himself sparingly, and sat down.

There was a pitcher of water on the table, and a bottle of wine. I got the water. Serving me wine in his house, he said, would probably be classed as a capital offense. I was a little disappointed, as I had never had a chance to drink wine. When Ernie and I went to the Old Chelsea, he always expressed his satisfaction that no wine or liquor was served on Sundays. Not only did he refuse to drink, on Sunday or on any other day, but he disliked seeing others do it.

"Now, Nina tells me," Mr. Purvis said, "Nina tells me that you are studying English Philosophy, but I think it must be English *and* Philosophy, am I right? Because surely there is not so great a supply of English philosophers?"

In spite of his warning, I had taken a dollop of green pickle on my tongue and was too stunned to reply. He waited courteously while I gulped down water.

"We start with the Greeks. It's a survey course," I said, when I could speak.

"Oh yes. Greece. Well, who is your favorite Greek so far—Oh, no, just a minute. It will fall apart more easily like this."

There followed a demonstration of how to separate and remove the meat from the bones of a Cornish hen—nicely done, and without condescension, rather as if it were a joke we might share. "Your favorite?"

"We haven't got to him yet—we're doing the pre-Socratics," I said. "But Plato."

"Plato is your favorite. So you read ahead, you don't just stay where you're supposed to? Plato. Yes, I could have guessed that. You like the cave?"

"Yes."

"Yes, of course. The cave. It's beautiful, isn't it?"

When I was sitting down, the most flagrant part of me was out of sight. If my breasts had been tiny and ornamental, like Nina's, I could have been almost at ease. Instead, they were large and lollopy; they were like bald night creatures dumbfounded by the light. I tried to look at him when I spoke, but against my will I suffered waves of flushing. When this happened, I thought I sensed his voice changing slightly, becoming more soothing and politely satisfied, as if he'd just made a winning move in a game. But he went on talking nimbly and entertainingly, telling me about a trip he had made to Greece. Delphi, the Acropolis, the famous light that you didn't believe could be true but was true, the bare bones of the Peloponnesus.

· "And then to Crete—do you know about the Minoan civilization?"

"Yes."

"Of course you do. Of course. And you know the way the Minoan ladies dressed?"

"Yes."

I looked into his face this time, his eyes. I was determined not to squirm away, not even when I felt the heat on my throat.

"Very nice, that style," he said almost sadly. "Very nice. It's odd the different things that are hidden in different eras. And the things that are displayed."

Dessert was vanilla custard and whipped cream, with bits of cake in it, and raspberries. He ate only a few bites of his. But, after failing to settle down enough to enjoy the first course, I was determined not to miss out on anything rich and sweet, and I fixed my appetite and attention on every spoonful.

He poured coffee into small cups and invited me to drink it in the library.

My buttocks made a slapping noise, as I loosened myself from the sleek upholstery of the dining-room chair. But this was almost covered up by the clatter of the delicate coffee cups on the tray, in his shaky old grasp.

Libraries in houses were known to me only from books. This one was entered through a panel in the dining-room wall. The panel swung open without a sound, at a touch of his raised foot. He apologized for going ahead of me, as he had to do when he carried the coffee. To me it was a relief. I thought that the back of the body—not just mine but anyone's—was the most beastly part.

When I was seated in the chair he indicated, he gave me my coffee. It was not as easy to sit here, out in the open, as it had been at the dining-room table. That chair had been covered with smooth striped silk but this one was upholstered in some dark plush material, which prickled me, setting off an intimate agitation.

The light in this room was brighter and the books lining the walls seemed more prying and reproving than the dim dining room, with its landscape paintings and light-absorbing panels.

For a moment, as we moved from one room to the other, I'd had some notion of a story—the sort of story I'd heard of but that few people then got the chance to read—in which the room referred to as a library would turn out to be a bedroom, with soft lights and puffy cushions and all manner of downy coverings. But the room we were in was plainly a library. The reading lights, the books on the glass-enclosed shelves, the invigorating smell of the coffee. Mr. Purvis pulling out a book, riffling through its leaves, finding what he wanted.

"It would be very kind if you would read to me. My eyes are tired in the evenings. You know this book?"

"'A Shropshire Lad.'"

I knew it. In fact, I knew many of the poems by heart.

"And may I ask you please—may I ask you please—not to cross your legs?"

My hands were trembling when I took the book from him.

"Yes," he said. "Yes."

He chose a chair in front of the bookcase, facing me.

"Now—"

"'On Wenlock Edge the wood's in trouble,'—"

The familiar words and rhythms calmed me down. They took me over. Gradually I began to feel more at peace.

The gale, it plies the saplings double,
It blows so hard, 'twill soon be gone:
To-day the Roman and his trouble
Are ashes under Uricon.

Where was Uricon? Who knew?

It wasn't really that I forgot where I was or whom I was with or in what condition I sat there. But I had come to feel somewhat remote and philosophical. The thought came to me that everybody in the world was naked, in a way. Mr. Purvis was naked, though he wore clothes. We were all sad bare creatures. Shame receded. I just kept turning the pages, reading one poem and then another, then another.

Liking the sound of my voice. Until to my surprise and almost to my disappointment—there were still wonderful lines to come—Mr. Purvis interrupted me. He stood up; he sighed.

"Enough, enough," he said. "That was very nice. Thank you. Your country accent is quite suitable. Now it's my bedtime."

I handed him the book. He replaced it on the shelf and closed the glass doors. The country accent was news to me. "And I'm afraid it's time to send you home."

He opened another door, into the hallway I had seen so long ago, at the beginning of the evening. I passed in front of him and the door closed behind me. I may have said good night. It is even possible that I thanked him for dinner, and that he spoke to me a few dry words (*not at all, thank you for your company, it was very kind of you, thank you for reading Housman*) in a suddenly tired, old, crumpled, and indifferent voice. He did not lay a hand on me.

The same dimly lit cloakroom. The turquoise dress, my stockings, my slip. Mrs. Winner appeared as I was fastening my stockings. She said only one thing to me, as I was ready to leave. "You forgot your scarf."

And there indeed was the scarf I had knitted in Home Economics class, the only thing I would ever knit in my life. I had come close to abandoning it, in this place.

AS I GOT OUT of the car, Mrs. Winner said, "Mr. Purvis would like to speak to Nina before he goes to bed. If you would remind her."

But there was no Nina waiting to receive this message. Her bed was made up. Her coat and boots were gone. A few of her clothes were still hanging in the closet.

Beverly and Kay had both gone home for the weekend, so I ran downstairs to see if Beth had any information. "I'm sorry," Beth, whom I never saw sorry about anything, said. "I can't keep track of all your comings and goings." Then, as I turned away, "I've asked you several times not to thump so much on the stairs. I just got Christopher to sleep."

I had not made up my mind what I would say to Nina when I got home. Would I ask her if she, too, was required to be naked in that house—if she had known perfectly well what sort of an evening was waiting for me? Or would I say nothing and wait for her to ask me? And, even then, would I say innocently that I'd eaten Cornish hen and yellow rice, and that it was very good? That I'd read from "A Shropshire Lad"?

Would I just let her wonder?

Now that she was gone, none of this mattered. The focus was shifted. Mrs. Winner phoned after ten o'clock—breaking another of Beth's rules—and when I told her that Nina was not there she said, "Are you sure of that?"

She said the same thing when I told her that I had no idea where Nina had gone. "Are you sure?"

I asked her not to phone again till morning, because of Beth's rules and the babies' sleep, and she said, "Well. I don't know. This is serious."

When I got up in the morning, the car was parked across the street. Later, Mrs. Winner rang the bell and told Beth that she had been sent to check Nina's room. Even Beth was quelled by Mrs. Winner, who looked all around our room, in the bathroom and the closet, even shaking out a couple of blankets that were folded on the closet floor.

I was still in my pajamas, writing an essay on "Sir Gawain and the Green Knight," and drinking Nescafé.

Mrs. Winner said that she had phoned the hospitals, to see if Nina had been taken ill, and that Mr. Purvis himself had gone out to check several other places where she might be.

"If you know anything, it would be better to tell us," she said. "Anything at all."

Then as she started down the stairs she turned and said in a voice that was less menacing, "Is there anybody at the college she was friendly with? Anybody you know?"

I said that I didn't think so.

I had seen Nina at the college only a couple of times. Once, she was walking down the lower corridor of the Arts Building, in the crush between classes, probably on her way to a class of her own. The other time, she was in the cafeteria. Both times she was alone. It was not particularly unusual to be alone when you were hurrying from one class to another but it was a little strange to sit alone with a cup of coffee in the cafeteria at quarter to four in the afternoon, when that space was practically deserted. She sat with a smile on her face, as if to say how pleased, how privileged, she felt to be there, how alert and ready she was to respond to the demands of this life—as soon as she understood what they were.

In the afternoon it began to snow. The car across the street had to move, to make way for the snowplow. When I went into the bathroom and caught the flutter of Nina's kimono on its hook on the door, I finally felt what I had been suppressing—a true fear for Nina. I could see her, disoriented, weeping into her loose hair, wandering around in the snow in her white underwear instead of her camel-hair coat, though I knew perfectly well that she had taken the coat with her.

THE PHONE RANG just as I was about to leave for my first class on Monday morning.

"It's me," Nina said, in a rushed warning, but with something like triumph in her voice. "Listen. Please. Could you please do me a favor?"

"Where are you? They're looking for you."

"Who is?"

"Mr. Purvis. Mrs. Winner."

"Well, you're not to tell them. Don't tell them anything. I'm here."

"Where?"

"Ernest's."

"Ernest's?" I said. "*Ernie's?*"

"Sh-h-h. Did anybody there hear you?"

"No."

"Listen, could you please, please get on a bus and bring me the rest of my stuff? I need my shampoo. I need my kimono. I'm going around in Ernest's bathrobe. You should see me—I look like an old woolly brown dog. Is the car still outside?"

I went and looked.

"Yes."

"O.K. then, you should get on the bus and ride up to the college just like you normally do. And then catch the bus downtown. You know where to get off. Dundas and Richmond. Then walk over here. Carlisle Street. Three sixty-three. You know it, don't you?"

"Is Ernie there?"

"No, dum-dum. He's at work. He's got to support us, doesn't he?"

Us? Was Ernie to support Nina and me?

No. *Ernie and Nina.* Ernie was to support Ernie and Nina.

Nina said, "Oh, please. You're the only friend I've got."

I did as directed. To fool Mrs. Winner, I stuffed Nina's things into my satchel. I caught the college bus, then the downtown bus. I got off at Dundas and Richmond and walked west to Carlisle Street. The snowstorm was over, the sky was clear, it was a bright, windless, deep-frozen day. The light hurt my eyes and the fresh snow squeaked under my feet.

Half a block north, on Carlisle Street, I found the house where Ernie had lived with his mother and father and then with his mother and then alone. And now—how was it possible?—with Nina.

The house looked exactly as it had when I had gone there once or twice with my mother. A brick bungalow with a tiny front yard, an arched living-room window with an upper pane of colored glass. Cramped and genteel.

Nina was wrapped, just as she had said, in a man's brown woolly tasselled dressing gown, with the manly but innocent Ernie smell of shaving cream and Lifebuoy soap.

She grabbed my hands, which were stiff with cold inside my mittens.

"Frozen," she said. "Come on, we'll get them into some warm water."

"They're not *frozen*," I said. "Just freezing."

But she went ahead and helped me off with my things, and took me into the kitchen and ran a bowlful of water, and then as the blood returned painfully to my fingers she told me how Ernest (Ernie) had come to the rooming house on Saturday night. He was bringing a magazine that had a lot of pictures of old ruins and castles and things that he thought might interest me. She got herself out of bed and came downstairs, because, of course, he would not go upstairs, and when he saw how sick she was he said she had to come home with him so that he could look after her. Which he had done so well that her sore throat was practically gone and her fever completely gone. And then they had decided that she would stay here. She would just stay with him and never go back to where she was before.

She seemed unwilling even to mention Mr. Purvis's name.

"But it has to be a big huge secret," she said. "You're the only one to know. Because you're our friend and you're the reason we met."

She was making coffee. "Look up there," she said, waving at the open cupboard. "Look at the way he keeps things. Mugs here. Cups and saucers here. Every cup has got its own hook. Isn't it tidy? The house is just like that all over. I love it.

"You're the reason we met," she repeated. "If we have a baby and it's a girl, we could name it after you."

I held my hands round the mug, still feeling a throb in my fingers. There were African violets on the windowsill over the sink. His mother's order in the cupboards, his mother's houseplants. The big fern was probably still in front of the living-room window, and the doilies on the armchairs. What Nina had said, in regard to herself and Ernie, seemed brazen and—especially when I thought of the Ernie part of it—abundantly distasteful.

"You're going to get married?"

"Well."

"You said if you have a baby."

"Well, you never know, we might have started that without being married," Nina said, ducking her head mischievously.

"With Ernie?" I said. "With *Ernie?*"

"Well, there's *Ernie,*" she said. "And then there's Er-*nest.*" She hugged the bathrobe around herself. "Might be something happening already, you never know."

"What about Mr. Purvis?"

"What about him?"

"Well, if it's something happening already, couldn't it be his?"

Everything about Nina changed. Her face turned mean and sour. *"Him,"* she said with contempt. "What do you want to talk about him for? He never had it in him."

"Oh? What about Gemma?"

"What do you want to talk about the past for? Don't make me sick. That's all dead and gone. It doesn't matter to me and Ernest. We're together now. We're in love now."

In love. With Ernie. Ernest. Now.

"O.K.," I said.

"Sorry I yelled at you. Did I yell? I'm sorry. You're our friend and you brought me my things and I appreciate it. You're Ernest's cousin and you're our family."

She slipped behind me and her fingers darted into my armpits and she began to tickle me, at first lazily and then furiously.

"Aren't you? Aren't you?"

I tried to get free but I couldn't. I went into spasms of suffering laughter and wriggled and cried out and begged her to stop. Which she did, when she had me quite helpless, and both of us were out of breath.

"You're the ticklishest person I ever met," she said.

I HAD TO WAIT a long time for the bus, stamping my feet on the pavement. When I got to the college, I had missed my second class, as well as the first, and I was late for my work in the cafeteria. I changed into my green cotton uniform in the broom closet and pushed my mop of black hair (the worst hair in the world for showing up in food, the manager had warned me) under a cotton snood.

I was supposed to get the sandwiches and salads out on the shelves before the doors opened for lunch, but now I had to do it with an impatient line of people watching me.

I thought of what Beverly and Kay had said, about spoiling my chances with men, marking myself off in the wrong way. How scornful

I'd been when they said it, but maybe they'd been right, after all. It appeared that, except in examinations, I got many things wrong.

AFTER I'D FINISHED cleaning up the cafeteria tables, I changed back into my ordinary clothes and went to the college library to work on my essay.

An underground tunnel fed from the Arts Building to the library, and on bulletin boards around the entrance to this tunnel were posted advertisements for movies and restaurants and used bicycles and type-writers, as well as notices for plays and concerts. The Music Department announced that a free recital of songs composed to fit the poems of the English country poets would be presented on a date that had now passed. I had seen this notice before, and did not have to look at it to be reminded of the names: Herrick, Housman, Tennyson. A few steps into the tunnel the lines began to assault me:

On Wenlock Edge the wood's in trouble.

Had he known? Had he known that I would never think of those lines again without feeling the prickle of the upholstery on my bare haunches? The sticky prickly shame. A far greater shame it seemed now than at the time. He had got me, in spite of myself.

> *From far, from eve and morning*
> *And yon twelve-winded sky,*
> *The stuff of life to knit me*
> *Blew hither: here am I.*

No.

> *What are those blue remembered hills,*
> *What spires, what farms are those?*

No, never.

> *White in the moon the long road lies*
> *That leads me from my love.*

No. No. No.

I would always be reminded of what I had done. What I had agreed to do. Not been forced, not ordered, not even persuaded. Agreed to do.

Nina would know. She would be laughing about it. Not cruelly, but just the way she laughed at so many things. She would always remind me.

Nina and Ernie. In my life from now on.

THE COLLEGE LIBRARY was a high beautiful space, designed and built and paid for by people who believed that those who sat at its long tables in front of open books—even those who were hungover, sleepy, resentful, and uncomprehending—should have space above them, panels of dark gleaming wood around them, high windows bordered with Latin admonitions through which to look at the sky. For a few years before they went into schoolteaching or business or began to rear children, they should have that. And now it was my turn and I would have it, too.

"Sir Gawain and the Green Knight."

I was writing a good essay. I would probably get an A. I would go on writing essays and getting A's because that was what I could do. The people who awarded scholarships, who built universities and libraries, would continue to dribble out money so that I could do it.

People like Mr. Purvis.

Still, those dribbles, that charity, did not make me amount to anything in their eyes. What I was doing here did not really matter. Somehow I had not known that. Nina knew it now and probably she had always known it. Ernie, too, though he had thought it his duty to pretend otherwise. Mr. Purvis and Mrs. Winner. Even Beth and Kay and Beverly knew that you had to get a footing somewhere else. This was only a game.

And I had thought it was the other way round.

Just as I had made myself believe that it was a challenge with Mr. Purvis and that I had won, or come off equal.

Equal?

NINA DID NOT STAY with Ernie for even one week. One day he came home and found her gone. Gone her coat and boots, her lovely clothes and the kimono that I had brought over. Gone her taffy hair and her tickling and the extra warmth of her skin and the little *unh-unhs* when she moved. All gone with no explanation, not a word on paper.

Ernie was not one, however, to shut himself up and mourn. He said so, when he phoned to tell me the news and check on my availability for Sunday dinner. We climbed the stairs to the Old Chelsea and he commented on the fact that this was our last dinner before the Christmas holidays. He helped me off with my coat and I smelled Nina's smell. Could it still be on his skin?

No. The source was revealed when he passed something to me. Something like a large handkerchief.

"Just put it in your coat pocket," he said.

Not a handkerchief. The texture was sturdier, with a slight ribbing. An undershirt.

"I don't want it around," he said, and by his voice you might have thought that it was just underwear in general that he did not want around, never mind that it was Nina's and smelled of Nina.

He ordered the roast beef, and cut and chewed it with his normal efficiency and polite appetite. I gave him the news from home, which as usual at this time of year consisted of the size of the snowdrifts, the number of blocked roads, the winter havoc that gave us distinction.

After some time, Ernie said, "I went round to his house. But there was nobody in it."

"Whose house?"

"Her uncle's," he said. He knew which house it was, because he and Nina had driven past it, after dark. There was nobody there now, he said. They had packed up and gone.

It had been her choice, after all. "It's a woman's privilege," he said. "Like they say, it's a woman's privilege to change her mind."

His eyes, now that I looked into them, had a dry famished look, and the skin around them was dark and wrinkled. He pursed his mouth, controlling a tremor, then talked on, with an air of trying to see all sides, trying to understand.

"It wasn't the money. It was just that he was old and senile and she has a soft heart. And the fact that he looked after her when her parents were killed."

If I stared for a moment, he didn't notice.

"I wouldn't have objected to us taking him in. I told her I was used to old people. But I guess she didn't want to put that on me.

"It was a shock, all right, when I came home and she was gone. But you just have to roll with the punches. Better not to expect too much. You can't take everything personally."

When I went past the coats on my way to the ladies' room, I got the shirt out of my pocket. I stuffed it in with the used towels.

THAT DAY in the library I had been unable to go on with Sir Gawain. I had torn a page from my notebook and picked up my pen and walked out. On the landing outside the library doors there was a pay phone, and beside that hung a phone book. I looked through the phone book and on the piece of paper I wrote two things. They were not phone numbers but addresses.

1648 Henfryn Street.

The other address, which I needed only to confirm, was 363 Carlisle Street.

I walked back through the tunnel to the Arts Building and entered the little shop across from the Common Room. I had enough change in my pocket to buy an envelope and a stamp. I tore off the part of the paper with the Carlisle Street address on it and put that scrap into the envelope. I sealed the envelope and on the front of it I wrote the name of Mr. Purvis and the address on Henfryn Street. All in block capitals. Then I licked and fixed the stamp. I think that in those days it would have been a four-cent stamp.

Just outside the shop was a mail chute. I slipped the envelope into it, there in the wide lower corridor of the Arts Building, with people passing me on their way to classes, on their way to have a smoke and maybe a game of bridge in the Common Room.

Most of them on a course, as I was, of getting to know the ways of their own wickedness.

I kept on learning things. I learned that Uricon, the Roman camp, is now Wroxeter, a town on the Severn River.

EMMA RICHLER

Sister Crazy

We just moved to a new country. It's my dad's country, where he comes from, and our house is at the end of a street which is a cul-de-sac, a bum-of-the-bag as Jude likes to call it in select company. It's not poetic but these are the facts, cul-de-sac = bum-of-the-bag and frankly, this creases me up. It creases Ben up too. Harriet has no idea what we are talking about, but if her two big brothers and her one big sister are creasing up with mirth, she's likely to go for it too and start laughing in a big-hearted hysterical fashion, like she has just heard the funniest thing on earth.

So Jude saves this joke for us; he is pretty sure Mum and Dad will not find it very witty. It's hard to explain this kind of thing to our parents. Some things are just not worth going into, that's what you learn as you move along, and saying bum-of-the-bag is one of them. It strikes us as funny most of all when we are felled by kid-type pressures, for instance, we are lying around in a heap on the floor and it is late afternoon and flying through our heads are kid-type pressures like, bloody, I have a load of homework. And why does that weird kid follow me around at school. Or, will I get to watch the whole film tonight before Mum comes in and says "Bedtime." I know the first half of a lot of films by now and I am keen to see some endings, I really am. There are other pressures, like what shall I have for a snack and is there time for it between now and dinner, and what is this new country we are in and how long are we here for. When you are beset by worries like these, you get a bit weak, and if Jude then says let's go see what's up in the bum-of-the-bag, Jem, it's no wonder I crease up with mirth and get that helpless feeling.

The word bum is not a problem. You can say just about anything you like in our house as long as you know what you are talking about and you use your imagination. Otherwise, Mum and Dad are pretty quick to clear you up on the matter. Sometimes it is a good idea to check separately with each one of them if you want a fuller picture. If you want the bare facts about a word and it is not very likely to take up a large space in your regular vocabulary, you go see my dad. If you want some associated news, like images and etymology and poetic examples of usage of this word, you go to Mum. When Mum tells a story, I can just about sit there all day.

Harriet is a bit reckless when it comes to words, however. I keep telling her when she starts wandering around muttering some word to pass it by me first. If I don't know it and feel it may be a dodgy one, I'll take it to Ben, who is the oldest, and more patient with research and dictionaries than I am. She won't listen, though. I believe there is a daredevil within. If this were an age before flight, my little sister Harriet would have been up there, the first woman, sitting bolt upright and gleeful in a rickety biplane with a leather flying hat on and a pair of goggles and maybe a long white scarf.

When Harriet feels the urge to test out a word she picks dinnertime. There she is, sitting up so straight her back is swaying in a little at her waist, she can't help it. She learns ballet and she takes this posture thing to heart. She thinks, Sit straight! Pile each vertebra right on top of one another, no messing up! She thinks it so hard, her little body seems electrified and she'll even look around at me or Jude if we are a bit slouchy due to the weight of kid-type pressures and give us a ballet-mistress glare of disapproval, involving a sharp turn of her head, a whip of blond ponytail and a wide-eyed expression. It can be annoying.

Then Harriet starts her muttering. She says something real quiet in between mini ballet-type bites of supper and she darts furtive looks in all directions and keeps repeating whatever she is saying in this little whisper, just inviting every single one of us to ask,

"Well, what is it, Harriet? What did you say? What's going on?"

"Fuck me," she says.

Oh-oh.

I am not surprised by my sister, not really, but Jude looks all around, waiting to see what will happen next, and Ben has a worried, responsible expression and fiddles with his cutlery, while Gus doesn't care because he is still a baby and is deeply involved with a crispy piece of potato. My dad bursts into hysterics and this is bad news for Harriet, who is going to cry any second now, her face starting to shimmer and break up. Then Mum smiles that smile and Harriet's eyes widen and she zooms in on Mum and her smile, just for some relief, and I understand this instinct of hers, this desire to shut out the whole world in a gruesome moment and latch on to Mum's smile.

I have examined this smile quite a bit, trying to see how it has the effect it does. Mum is very beautiful. It does not mean smiling has to be her thing. For instance, I have noted some women in old films who are beautiful and haven't the first idea about smiling and can look frankly terrifying or terrified themselves once they start moving the little muscles around the mouth and separating the lips. This woman Greta Garbo, for one. I watched her in a film called *Camille*, where she wore very big dresses and when she laughed and smiled at the man she loved, I thought, if I were him, I would run away or at least ask her if she was okay, did she need a glass of water or something. I really think there is some kind of art in the smiling and laughing business.

Sometimes I check myself out in the mirror and I note that I have a sort of lopsided thing going on when it comes to smiles. Also, the side of my mouth that wants to smile does not necessarily curl upward like it should but downward, which may be a little spooky for some observers. Most of all, I can be in company and have a big feeling for a smile but it just doesn't show up on my face. I am learning to make up for this so that even if I think I'm smiling like a clown in a circus, it's really only quite a normal-size smile. It's important to make these little adjustments when you get to know stuff about yourself. I frown a lot and not everybody likes this, but it is just that I have a lot to think about, a lot of things to work out, although now I try to be aware of my forehead and relax the muscles up there when there are a lot of people around, or even just Harriet, when we walk to school together. I know I am frowning if her head is hanging a little instead of being really perky. She bows her head and walks in front of me, or behind, and keeps checking my face and looking away, like she is some kind of small animal no one wants to play with. I have to watch out and be aware of things. It is more important to be careful when I am with Harriet because Harriet is my sister.

It makes me wonder though, what happens to a person's face—physiognomy is a word I heard from Ben—if they are crazy and have a lot of crazy thoughts and not much of an impulse to smile in a regular fashion. We saw this film once, *The Hunchback of Notre Dame*, which is a favorite film of my dad's of course, because there are a lot of crazy people in it, shouting and throwing things and looking in serious need of a bath. My dad loves films featuring this sort of person, he laughs and laughs. My dad loves this film so much that for about three weeks after we watched it, he escorted some of his kids to bed, loping behind us in the hall all hunched over and with a messed-up expression on his face, sometimes calling out "The bells, the bells." It was extremely annoying and I am glad no one from outside the family was around to see him during this three-week period.

In this film, Charles Laughton plays a hunchback called Quasimodo, a name so strange and fun to say that Harriet spoke it about eighty-two times that night while I was trying to get to sleep.

"Quasi-modo," she says over and over, trying out a different emphasis now and then and finally sticking with one, which involves a slow, horror-movie type delivery of the first two syllables and a quick-fire pronunciation of the "modo" bit. It's working, because even though she acts like this is a game she is playing by herself and I am no part of it, she knows perfectly well it's getting to me, which is what this game is all about. Each time she says "modo" in that gunfire fashion, my heart starts jumping, although I know it's coming. I have to shout at Harriet to please shut up, despite the risk she will get horrible sulks and not talk to me the next morning, building a wall of cereal boxes or something between our places at breakfast so as not to see me. I will have to live with this possibility due to my need for sleep.

"Harriet! Stop it!" I rise up from bed and glare at her in the dark and she starts whimpering a little.

"Quasimodo," she says, turning over in bed and making a cave out of her sheets and blankets. "Quasimodo," she tries, one final time, in the quietest voice I ever heard. It's a bit heartbreaking. Harriet has a heartbreaking way about her.

I think some more about this film concerning a French hunchback in the Middle Ages. Quasimodo is pretty ugly. Is this the face of a crazy person whose thoughts are wild and do not come out right, like when you have had anesthetic at the dentist and you want to do things, say things, move your face a certain way, and it just does not happen? Then I saw that Quasimodo is probably not at all crazy, the least crazy one in the film. When he rescues the boring Gypsy woman, Esmeralda, and he has her all safe in his bell tower, he explains that although he cannot hear, he can understand sign language. Esmeralda has clearly not been to sign-language school or maybe it was not all that developed in the Middle Ages. She wants to know why Quasimodo rescued her and she repeats the question along with some sign language so he can understand. Her idea of sign language is to ask, "Why did you rescue me?" in words, and swish her hand with one pointed finger in front of her chest twice, depicting, I guess, her own self swinging on the rope Quasimodo rescued her on. To me it's not really enough, but Quasimodo says straight away, really calm,

"Why did I rescue you?"

Quasimodo is a smart guy and very sensitive. He can just about guess what you are saying even if you are hopeless at sign language. He is very ugly and sad but he is okay and not crazy, so I have decided that signs of craziness will not always show up in the face. In the physiognomy of a person. You have to look a lot closer than that.

I am pretty sure there can be craziness lurking inside a person and it does not show up at all, and that in the same confusing manner, some signs of behavior look crazy but the person is not. My dad is a really good example of this.

When Harriet has said fuck me, at dinner, I understand the way she holds out for Mum's smile, how her big blue watering eyes just go all out for Mum in a desperate fashion. That smile of hers is really useful for solving problems and making you feel okay when you never thought you would again, but sometimes that smile can be pretty bloody. This is when. You rise up on a school morning and get very clean and even comb your hair until it flies around in a really stupid way and you barely recognize your own self in the mirror. You haul on your school uniform and it is stiff and refuses to fit your body right like your jeans do, and Jude's old rugby top from the country we lived in before, the top that is now too small for him and that you love wearing because it was his and still smells of him and of the country you lived in before. You do not want to go to school today, not in the least. What is the point. What is the point of anything.

"What's wrong, Jem?" Mum says although she does not sound all that worried. She is paying a lot of attention to Gus, our baby. She's on to me.

"I think I am sick," I say, speaking low and like words themselves are difficult to throw together into a sentence, like I could faint any second now. "I don't—I think—I might—maybe I should stay home today."

"Why don't you step outside first, and take some DEEP BREATHS!"

Then she smiles at me. She looks right at me and one eyebrow raises up a little and she smiles.

"Oh forget it," I say, a bit sharp and grumpy. "I'll go. Bloody." I don't even bother with the deep breaths business.

That is when Mum's smile is kind of crafty, making you do a thing you ought to be doing but definitely don't want to do.

It's too late for Harriet now, because Dad is laughing big time and he is drowning out Mum. Everyone perks up at the table and the ends of Harriet's mouth go all wiggly and here it comes, tears, lots of them.

You have to be really careful with laughter around my sister. She does not have a big thing for laughter even though she looks so merry, like everything in the world goes just right for her and she cannot understand why anyone could have a problem, which is why she looks so crushed if I am frowning on our way to school, why it is so scary for her, just like a big storm with lightning and thunder which is something else she cannot understand, the suddenness and angry noise of it, making her run around the house closing all the windows with great strength and decision even though she is such a small person, as if Harriet herself, my little sister with a big thing for dancing but not laughter, can hold off chaos all on her own, just by showing you how much it freaks her out, like that is enough.

It is enough for me. I stop frowning when I take note of her shivering small-beast expression. I let her close the windows of our room if the trees are too whooshy in the wind at night and she can't sleep, and I hate the windows to be shut at night. I let her, though.

And I understand her problem with laughs. I understood how it is for Harriet when I heard Greta Garbo in those films, it's the same thing, it can be a shock you feel right inside your body and all through it, as if someone you are crazy about turns around and hits you out of nowhere. It's a bad feeling.

I remember a birthday party for Harriet once, when she was a little kid, after the bit where all her chirping friends came and tossed balloons and wore little hats and separated smarties and other sweets into color codes and so on, clearly little kids quite like Harriet in some ways with a lot of peculiarities in their behavior, involving methodical reorganizing of their immediate surroundings. Nothing any one of those little kids did seemed to surprise any other kid. Okay. There was lots of chirping going on and it struck me they were like a row of starlings on a telephone wire, when they all sit squashed up together, usually late in the afternoon, like this is a really good time to meet and talk about their day all at once.

Maybe Harriet was a little tired after all that, but when it was time for grown-up dinner and we all sat together at the white oak table, which had been cleared of party stuff, it was soon time to bring on Harriet's cake so she could blow out her candles and then make the first cut, Mum holding her hand over Harriet's very small one grasping the knife like it was the weirdest most fearsome object she had ever held on to, and guiding her, the knife upside down for wish power. You close your eyes, you cut upside down slowly, in time with your wish that you make with your eyes closed, slowly, so you don't cut all the way through the cake and you are only about halfway into your wish. Ben, for instance, cuts real fast on his birthday and it is very aggravating to behold because I keep thinking he did not, he could not, have made his wish in that time and I worry he will lose out for a whole year. I can't help it. I worry about things like that.

Harriet, though, must make the longest wish in history because when she gets to the cutting bit, her eyes are squeezed tight and she cuts in slow motion, occasionally opening up her eyes and checking with Mum, and I know Harriet wants to tell her what she is wishing and I have an urge to warn her not to, because otherwise the wish will not work, but I do not need to as Harriet is well informed when it comes to all that stuff, magic and wishes and all types of things that are not everyday things, that are a bit weird. I am pretty sure she wishes something weird, too, like the power to fly or that all her stuffed animals would turn into real ones or that she could eat chocolate only, forever, at all mealtimes.

My sister loves chocolate and this is another weird thing, that on her birthday she asks for cheese pie. But cheese is not Harriet's thing. She has a big thing for chocolate, not cheese at all. I am the one with a big thing for cheese, but on my birthday I ask for another great cake of Mum's, a chocolate one with melted After Eight icing. It's a pretty cool cake but I wonder about it now, and I think that on our birthdays, it is as if my sister and I were standing face to face and my big thing became her big thing and hers became mine, just for these days, our separate birthdays, like a mirror game, a crazy-type mirror like the ones they have at fun fairs. One day when Harriet is bigger, I'll tell her this idea I had because I know she will like it, but she may be too young right now and get confused.

Before Harriet gets to cut upside down with Mum's hand over her own, she has to blow out the candles. This is what happens. We all huddle close to her and she sits up in that ballet way and takes in just about all the air available in the big kitchen and looks around for a second with that posh ballet expression on her face. She looks like a bird on a lawn with her chest all puffed up, she looks like a bird when it is gearing up for a song and you feel special watching, as if the tune coming soon were aimed at you, a message, an announcement. It's so funny seeing Harriet all poised to blow that we laugh. All of us. And Harriet deflates, a party balloon, and the edges of her mouth tremble and the tears come down. This is funny, too.

Laughter. Mum tries again, she has explained to Harriet over and over, this distinction, a word I like because it means different and special at the same time, she explains that there is a distinction between laughing at and laughing with. She gives examples, she explains it well, in the gentlest voice, so that you will not ever forget the meaning. When Mum explains a thing, you get this picture in your head and you don't ever need anyone to explain it again. That's how it is. But Harriet, she knows, is still not ready. She tries hard, I can see the thoughts moving around in her eyes, but I know for Harriet, just now in her life, what hits her first off is the sound, and she feels it physically and it hurts her, like she thinks we are laughing because she has done something crazy. You didn't, Harriet. You didn't.

I thought that maybe when Harriet hears laughter, it's like when a storm is coming and she wants to close all the windows because it's too noisy too quickly out there in the world.

I also looked up ear in my dad's encyclopedia, the big set Mum gave him one Christmas. There was a really good diagram in it and names of parts and little arrows and so on. The eardrum separates the outer ear from the middle ear, where three bones connect it to the inner ear. The inner ear has two things. One. The cochlea, which is responsible for balance and turns sound into nerve impulses. It tells Harriet's brain about her place in the world, the movements she is making. It must work really hard in Harriet and is maybe extremely sensitive due to her big thing for dance. Two. The hearing part, called the labyrinth. I looked up labyrinth: complicated structure with many passages hard to find way through or without guidance, maze. That's what I thought. It sounds like Harriet to me, she has a maze inside her. And this is what I worked out about Harriet soon after that birthday party.

So on the night my sister tries out her new expression, on the night she says fuck me, after a lot of the usual coaxing from everyone at the table, she cannot be saved by Mum's smile because of Dad and his kind of mountain-lion laugh, his shoulders and chest shaking like he is in a small car on a very bumpy road. My dad can't help it, having this laugh and being the biggest person in our family, and Harriet can't help crying and looking helpless like one of those dying ballerinas, all loose and in a heap but getting up about eight more times to do a few more steps, because dying is a really slow and delicate process for ballerinas, unlike for soldiers in war films, where one shot is usually enough to keep them lying down for good, no death throes at all.

Harriet has heard this new expression in my dad's country, but I don't know where. I have uneasy feelings about this new country, but most of all I worry about Harriet here, because she is not a suspicious type, she is really open and friendly and this place may be too big and too noisy. I am going to have to watch out for her even more than usual. That's my plan.

Harriet is not silly, she is open and friendly and I do not mean that she will go right up to a person and hang on to their cuff or anything, but if you are a stranger and you take a look at Harriet, she will have an open and friendly gaze, she will not frown and scare you off the way I do. Harriet is inviting and although that is a much nicer way to be than the way I am, it is not always safe. Next, Harriet has a habit of going astray, not quite lost, just sort of wandering free of you like a kite does in the air when it is first of all flapping and fighting in your arms and suddenly it's aloft and graceful and offering up some resistance, connected to you still but doing its own thing. I have noticed that when Mum is out with all her kids in a park or a museum or zoo or somewhere, she turns around at regular intervals, real cool though, not anxious or anything and not even searching Harriet out directly but she will say her name in a very soft fashion, "Harriet," she says just like that, as if Harriet were still right next to her, and I see that when Mum does this, Harriet moves in closer from wherever she is, she skips in toward us a little without joining us exactly. It is a bit like a homing signal for a bird and very reassuring.

I am not as calm as Mum. If I lose sight of Harriet I get cross with her because she has made me picture her at the bottom of an old pit or under a fallen tree or lost in a huddle of shops or having tea with a stranger, but usually I find her quite easily and she is perched on her little haunches talking to a bird or feeding a squirrel. She has a really big thing for animals and they have a really big thing for Harriet, kind of following her around like she is one of them. Sometimes I walk into our bedroom and she is sitting in the window and talking away merrily. You might think she is crazy, but she is not. She is having a conversation with a small animal who has come into the space she left by opening the window a little and they are having a snack together, sharing an apple or a nice roll with butter. It's weird in a good way, and I stay quiet, watching them. Harriet will never be alone, I think, not ever.

Fuck me, she said. Bloody.

Dad says to my sister, "It's okay, Harriet. It's not serious. I'll explain this word to you later, okay? We'll have talkies, how about that?" He wants her to stop crying. He feels bad.

Harriet takes in two sharp half-breaths and says, "O-kay," with another gulpy half-breath right in the middle. Then Dad tries to cheer her up and takes her plate and gets ready to serve her some more chicken and vegetables. At the time, Harriet was still eating things that had been birds or furry animals before they were meals, because she had not really made the connection yet, she couldn't see that shepherd's pie started out as a big friendly cow or that lamb stew was made from one of her all-time favorite animals.

Harriet cannot eat very much but my dad offers her more partly to make up for the tears situation and also because Harriet does not like a lot of food crowding up her plate at once. She might aim to have two slices of chicken breast plus a little wing and two pieces of broccoli and two crispy potato bits, but you cannot give her this straight off, you have to serve it bit by bit.

"Not touching!" Harriet nearly screams. She has been so offended tonight, she is almost fierce. How could my dad do this, especially after making her cry, how could he pass her plate back with the chicken wing touching the broccoli? I am amazed as well. I feel for Harriet. Next he makes it worse. He is a bit startled, so he just moves the food around with his finger, separating the chicken and the broccoli, and now Harriet is crying again because that is not right, you have to start all over again, put the food back, pick some different bits and lay them out properly on the plate. Shuffling it around when the pieces have already touched is no good at all.

Jude says, "It mixes up in your stomach. Even in your mouth it'll be touching."

"No!" wails Harriet. "Not touching! Not touching!"

It's not a good night for Harriet and I know why she likes her types of food separate on a plate; it's because up to the point when it mixes up within she can choose, she can control her world and how things go inside her. She can organize it, make it all neat and pretty before the chaos of chewing and digesting. I see her point. Also, she eats bit by bit because she is like one of the small birds she talks to and that I have read about in a book on bird life in a chapter called "The Care and Feeding of the Young Bird." Some really small birds can only take a little at a time. For instance, the pied flycatcher grown-up has to feed its baby thirty-three times an hour. Really big birds may only eat two or three times in a week and other birds, like the nighthawk, have little bills but very big mouths and they can store a lot of stuff for later inside their mouth. That is quite a good method, I think. Then there is the Eurasian swift, who will fly for hundreds of miles just to get one supper for its young who might have to wait about two days to eat. They are probably very fussy eaters and only like certain things that are hard to find. Other baby birds eat food that the grown-ups have already chewed. I am really glad Harriet is not into this way of feeding. The business of feeding chicks is pretty hard work and I read that often the parents get really tired and thin by the time the chicks are ready to sort themselves out at mealtimes without a lot of help. I read this about the mother birds, how "weight loss and mortality increased linearly with brood size." I looked up linearly. Then I numbered us all up, counting Harriet twice due to her special care and feeding needs, and came up with a brood of 5 + 1. I thought about Mum and mortality, and this is another reason I need to watch out for Harriet. She needs special care and feeding right now, and I know I can help out. No one is going to get too thin or tired around here if I look out for Harriet, who is not crazy but more like a small chick in ways that you might not think about just by looking at her.

JUST BEFORE YOU LEFT ME for the first time I had a dream and you were in it. This was before I pierced my hand with a knife, the little wound in my palm like the mouth of a fish feeding on the surface of a pond, opening and closing, opening and closing, and as I fainted I thought, my hand is talking to me, it is trying to tell me something. Later I thought how embarrassing my wound was, being in a classical spot for a stigmatist, even though Jesus was no doubt nailed through the wrists and not the palms at all and he was only one of many cruci-fied types, crucifixion being a very low form of capital punishment and regularly inflicted on pirates and slaves and agitators of any kind. Constantine the Great abolished crucifixion in the fourth century, and I like him for that, I do. Before the wound, came the dream that you were in, that is, I think it was you, it seemed like you, although I hardly knew you, I still don't, fifty minutes, five times a week is never enough, but when I woke up I felt it must be you, although I cannot swear to it, or to anything at all just now, not really.

In the dream I am walking away from a building of medical arts. I don't feel well and someone passes by me and pauses and looks back, and moves on. Good, I think. I feel worse, though, and walking on, I realize my legs no longer support me. I grab a lamppost and I am furious and ashamed at my weakness. I am determined to stay on my feet, but someone, my passerby, grips my hand firmly.

"Go away," I hiss, "I'll be okay in a minute!"

No you will not, this person conveys to me without speaking. No, not in a minute.

Now I am losing my sight and it is frightening.

"Okay!" I scream at this person. "So hold on! But don't *fucking let go!*"

"FUCKING-BLOODY!" my sister says.

Harriet has been following me all day and copying me, doing whatever I do and daring me to get upset about it by glancing right into my face with wide-open blue eyes and her mouth all pursed up and her little chin in the air in anticipation of some kind of big reaction I just can't be bothered to give her. Mum says I should be flattered when Harriet traipses after me all over the house doing whatever I do. I don't know. Anyway, I am too tired to get upset due to the terrible wound that I have and which Harriet keeps poking at with her index finger, approaching my temple in kind of slow motion, like she is about to get poisoned by my wound or something, then touching it and pulling her hand back like she has just had an electric shock. She does this about eighteen times.

I am lying on my stomach reading a Tintin book. So is Harriet, even though she can't read French yet. Every time I turn a page, hovering near the page corner, thinking about it, she does the same. I don't care. I am recovering from my terrible wound and I am tired. Every now and again, in between pokes, Harriet says, in an amazed type voice,

"Fucking-bloody!"

This is how I got my wound. Ben, Jude and I are trying to learn something about this new country we are in and sometimes the best way is to play a typical sport, so we are doing some baseball, which is like cricket but not like cricket. For instance, the bowler does not run in toward the batsman but stands around on this little hill thinking about things and suddenly he lifts one leg and bowls at you. It's weird. Also, in cricket you can hit the ball but you do not have to run, but in baseball if you hit the ball frontward, you have to run like crazy, and you let go of the bat too, and this strikes me as pretty typical of this new country, a kind of noisy, crazed way to play a sport.

Ben, Jude and I are playing in our bum-of-the-bag, our cul-de-sac. We do not have a bat but we did find an old iron rod down the hill at the end of our bum-of-the-bag. It was lying in a lot of scrub around the trees and bushes on the slope and we decided it would make a good baseball bat. I am the wicket-keeper, although it is called something else, I don't know what. Jude is batting and Ben is bowling, or whatever they call it in Dad's country. We don't let Harriet play but we tell her she is the umpire, just to keep her happy. She is not very good at team sports due to not having a big thing for rules written by people other than her. In our old country she was always kicking our football out of play or picking it up right in the middle of things and doing some kind of ballet with it. This would leave us speechless. She is definitely not good at team sports but you can't tell her this, I have learned, you just have to create a position for her where she can't really mess things up.

Today Harriet is the umpire. I am not sure they have one in baseball. Never mind.

It is possible I am sitting too close to the batsman, I don't know. I remember thinking this before Jude swipes at the ball and hits me in the temple with the iron rod. That's how I got my wound, which Harriet keeps poking while saying her new favorite swear word.

"Harriet?" I say.

"Harriet?" Harriet says.

"Stop it for a minute!"

Harriet repeats this too, and I drop my head into my Tintin book and Harriet does the same.

"Harriet, didn't Dad talk to you about that word?"

"Yes! Talkies," Harriet says.

"Well? Don't you think you could just say bloody by itself, I don't know, what do you think?"

"Fuck is *not* a bad thing, Daddy said. Why can't Harriet say it? Fucking-bloody."

"Okay, Harriet."

I borrowed a book of Ben's and there was a chapter in it about the brain and it had some really good pictures and diagrams. Here is what I read. The left side and the right side of the brain have different jobs. The right = creative, the left = analytical. Right and left parts are called hemispheres. I like that, hemisphere. I copied all of this out. Left hemisphere skills = analytical thinking, digital computation, rational thinking, sequential ordering, temporal thinking, verbal skills. Right hemisphere skills = artistic ability, holistic thinking, intuition, simul-taneous thinking, synthetic reasoning, visual and spatial ability. I asked Mum to explain some of these words, which is a lot easier than looking them all up. I definitely did not understand everything she said and the more I frowned the more she smiled at me. I don't think she gave me all the details. Never mind. I have enough. This is what I suspect about Harriet. All the skills in her left hemisphere, the analytical part, are also creative. Her whole brain, both hemispheres, is creative and I think that is cool, why can't everyone see that?

ON THE LAST DAY, before the second time you leave me, which will be for thirty-nine days and forty nights, I follow you down the hallway toward the room where we will talk for a while, and I notice how slowly you walk, this warm-weather walk that you have in almost all weathers, and I think today it is like the walk of a person who has some very bad news to tell and is not in a hurry to tell it. I also notice a stain on your left shoulder, not so much a stain as a discoloration, and I think, this is not your shirt, it belongs to a loved one and you wear it a lot probably although I have never seen it before, and I suddenly want to clasp you gently from behind and lay my right cheek just there over the stain and maybe rest there for thirty-nine days and forty nights, until I can wake up somewhere safe where I cannot hurt myself with all the deliberate energy of a crazy person.

I read that alcohol suppresses normal sleep brain waves and impairs the quality and quantity of sleep, and I don't care about this at all. Fuck it. Fucking-bloody. On the first night, I stand in the dimming light of my living room and I walk across it with my wineglass and I notice a strange blob of darkness at my feet, on the floor, and near it, two or three more dark stains. I remember the stain on your shirt, on your left shoulder, and I bend down to touch the stain and I realize it is blood. I look up at the ceiling, maybe it is coming from there. Then I see my hand, and the cut I made earlier has reopened and has been bleeding without my noticing. I hold my hand up in the air, but this is what I do first. I wash the stain out of the carpet and then I wipe the hardwood floor, I try to remove all the stains and the last thing I do is wash my wound. That is the last thing that I do.

During the summer of 1224, two years before Francis of Assisi died, he went into the mountains at La Verna to fast for forty days. He was celebrating the Assumption of the Blessed Virgin Mary and preparing for St. Michael's Day, and round about the fourteenth of September, the feast of Exaltation of the Cross, he had a vision of a beautiful crucified half-man, half-seraph with six wings. When the vision disappeared, Francis was marked with the stigmata, but he was very shy about this and was very careful thereafter to conceal the wounds. Francis was the first stigmatist, but he was reluctant, it was not his big thing, his big thing was goodness and that is so quaint, I think, so much weirder than stigmata, and now I am thinking about Harriet and how I would like to call her, but I feel too ashamed of the chaos I am making.

I do not sleep much on this night. I dream of Harriet. I watch her from the edge of a frozen night garden, brittle and starlit with shimmering snow and crystalline trees with shapes of animals carved out of the icy foliage. My sister is barefoot in a gauzy dress and she is dancing all around and she is so merry and so private I can't disturb her. I want to tell her to put some shoes on or she will catch cold. It is possible she is sleepdancing and although there is a fiction about sleepwalkers, they are not conscious and they can hurt themselves and you must watch out for them if you can. Only in REM sleep, the dream place, is the body paralyzed to prevent disaster, but in sleepwalking you are free, you are open to danger. In my dream, Harriet may be sleepdancing but she is so happy, she is okay and she has carved all these animals out of the trees. She is with all her friends and she does not need me.

I READ SOMETHING ELSE in Ben's science book which is really interesting. I copy this out into a notebook because it has to do with Harriet. SYNESTHESIA/SYNESTHETICS. "These people taste words, feel flavors, and see letters in colors. Most synesthetics are women who have had synesthesia since birth. Synesthetics' brains may be structurally different, containing unusual neural pathways that carry messages to more than just one sensory cortex in the brain." The book says that you *suffer* from synesthesia but I don't think it is a bad thing at all, something you suffer from. Maybe I do not really understand it, but I think Harriet has a kind of synesthesia. I think so. Here are two examples.

We are in our old country and it is a Saturday and Harriet is five. I am eight. Harriet has been following me around all day, copying me, which is supposed to be a compliment but is driving me crazy, especially since Jude has gone off with some friends and I am in a pretty bad mood due to being left by Jude. I am sorting out some of my Action Man stuff, tidying it up and so on, even though I don't really need to, and I have it all spread out in front of me on the floor. After that I am going to read my book, *The Eagle of the Ninth* by Rosemary Sutcliff, which is really good and is about Roman soldiers, and then I will have a snack and then maybe Jude will be home. I hope so because Harriet is driving me crazy, hanging around even though I am ignoring her completely.

Harriet is playing with my little penknife which Mum bought for me in Scotland. On the hilt of the knife is a painting of Edinburgh Castle plus a whole troop of soldiers from the Black Watch in front walking up and down. I like it a lot.

"Be careful with that," I say.

"Be careful with that," Harriet repeats in a miserable voice.

I roll my eyes big time. Harriet opens up the knife, pulling out the blade, and she looks all startled when it snaps into place.

"Don't do that," I say darkly.

"Don't do that," she says, and then she throws the knife at me, just missing my left ear. Wow. Wow. Look what she did. Harriet's eyes are real spooked now and there is a silence between us as we sit cross-legged on the floor, face to face.

Mum passes by our room and she looks in and Harriet swivels her little body toward Mum and she starts wailing right away, that's what she does, and she says,

"Jem threw the knife! Jem threw the knife at Harriet!"

I am eleven now and when I read Ben's book, I remember this knife-throwing act and I know this is synesthesia. Harriet was not lying, it is just how she saw things, that I was throwing a knife at her, all Saturday morning, because I was not looking out for her that day when she wanted me to.

Example number two. It is night and Harriet is eight. We are asleep but Harriet wakes me up. She rises up from her bed and her little white nightdress glows in the dark. She is very straight up, all the vertebrae piled properly and so on, then she leaps up into the windowsill, which is quite a bit smaller than the one in the old bedroom we shared in our old country, and she flaps her featherweight arms and bats them lightly against the windowpanes. Now I am worried and I am aware of my heart thumping and I climb onto the sill but I try not to show I am worried she will fall right out of the window so I push it closed slowly and take hold of her ankle in the softest grip I can manage.

"Harriet?"

"Yes," she says in a strange voice, kind of anxious and loud.

"What are you doing?"

"Going outside," she says, much more awake now, because she sounds like Harriet again and the tears are coming. "I'm flying," she says. "Playing with the birds. Fly. Fly."

"Shall we do a card game, Harriet? Do you want to?" That's what we usually do when Harriet sleepwalks or just can't sleep, we play card games she never knows the rules to, or we make bird shadows on the wall, birds that go "gloo-gloo, gloo-gloo" for some reason I can't remember just now, or else I sing to her, quite badly, but she likes it anyway.

"Sing," says Harriet.

Okay, baby. Okay.

That is example number two. Harriet feels like a bird. So Harriet can fly.

"IS IT A MAN or a woman?" my friend asks me in a parked car in my street, also a cul-de-sac, a bum-of-the-bag, where I live now, grown up and on my own. I just want to go home. I hate questions and I feel like Harriet who rarely had time for questions, not seeing the point of them at all and never really answering them in the way most people expect you to, with some kind of immediacy and logic, most of all, logic.

At the first convent where Harriet and I both went, there was once a changeover of order, and gray nuns we knew so well became blue nuns we did not know at all, and with them came new rules, such as the option of bringing your own lunch. This was the very best bit about the new order and Mum packed lunches for us that were full of marvels, including little notes written in her elegant script that always sloped diagonally across a page with maybe, "Hello, little goose!" or "See you soon, darling," and these notes would be tucked in amongst leftover dinner-party food, smoked salmon, deviled eggs, lovely things that other kids gathered round us to stare at.

Today Harriet has lost her lunch and I do not ask her anything about it because she will not answer me. She looks hungry and she tugs at my sleeve and I let her scoot in next to me, even though she is not supposed to sit at my table, she should be at the table with the little kids. Never mind.

Sister Lucille says, "Harriet, where is your lunch?" She doesn't ask very patiently. She is not curious, she is cross.

Harriet squeezes in closer to me, burying her chin in her chest but twisting around a little to glance at me from the corner of her eye.

"She—" I start to answer for Harriet.

"Jemima Weiss! I asked your sister!"

Bloody.

"The badger went in the hole. Little badgers inside!" says Harriet without looking at Sister Lucille. Harriet is going to start crying any second, I can feel her body shivering. I wish Sister Lucille would go away and I think how Mum would guess right off what happened, how she would understand that Harriet was playing in an out-of-bounds area in the playground, that she had gone astray without being quite lost and had found some animals, a badger going into his house, and she had left her lunch for the badger and his family. It's not hard to see this. You can easily upset Harriet with questions and it is best to avoid them unless you understand Harriet the way I do and do not think she is crazy, which she is not, no.

"Is it a man or a woman?"

"A woman." Who cares. Leave me alone.

"Is it working for you?"

Fuck off. "I don't know. Yes, I mean. Maybe."

"What is her name?"

Why are you asking me this. "I am not going to tell you," I say quietly.

"Fine," my friend says, glancing at me the way you do at a danger-ous person, a deranged person.

I won't share you, I can't share you because right now I can't tell the difference between sharing and outright loss and I might lose you, someone might take you away from me before I even know who you are and why I need you. I think of Harriet and how she went into the world out of my sight, to be shared, I guess, and she went places where I couldn't look out for her and I lost it, my special job of looking out for her. I want it back.

WHEN HARRIET WAKES UP in the morning, her hair flying all around, she is happy because she realizes breakfast is coming up pretty soon and breakfast is her favorite meal. Saturday is Harriet's favorite day because after the breakfast thought she has another big happy jolt and that has to do with not having to haul on a lot of clothes she does not feel like wearing, like gloves and a hat, a tie, tunic, pullover, stripy pinafore and the right color socks depending on the season, which is another complication for Harriet, a different uniform according to the season. On a sunny winter morning Harriet wants to wear white gloves and a straw hat but she is not allowed, it's in the rules. Also, she has to wear a hat on the way to school or you can get reported and some days she hates this.

"No hat! Can't see the sky! Stop it! Get off!"

When it is really bad with Harriet, I hold the hat and hover near her, ready to clap it right onto her head when we get too close to school.

Often when I let go of Harriet and shove her gently toward the little kids' entrance in the courtyard, she turns around and gives me a painful look, like maybe I have made a big mistake and she should stay with me, go where I go, because really bad things are going to happen to her now, but I have to leave her, it's what I have to do.

"See you tomorrow," she says.

"Right here at the gates, Harriet."

"Okay."

Harriet knows we meet at ten to four p.m., she knows it, but it is so long until she is free again that it will feel like tomorrow, and that is another thing about Harriet, that it is whatever time she feels, which can be a pretty good way to be, having your own way with time, especially on Saturdays for instance. On Saturday she feels so happy, all she will eat that day is breakfast, like she is waking up on a Saturday, all day long. Even at supper, Harriet will have Baby Familia, her favorite cereal, a Swiss muesli type cereal that comes in very tiny bits with dusted raisins. This is what she will eat when we are all having something like shepherd's pie or fish or sausages with mashed potatoes. It's cool and nobody minds at all.

DO YOU THINK it's cruel that in the hour you have for me there are only fifty minutes? When you say, rather softly, "Well," and then you pause and you add, "it's time," and then you stand up, watching me in my crazed flurry of leave-taking, that awful moment, do you mean, "I am sorry, it's not me, it's time," like telling me to fuck off out of here is not your fault at all, sending me out into the world where I came from, where up to the first minute and from the fifty-first minute, all my hours contain sixty whole minutes, some endless and others frighteningly brief? Or do you just mean to remind me with these three words, "Well, it's time," that this is one way I can measure my life, just one way to do it?

One day I think you should take me home and let me sit at your table, a stranger there, to watch you with your family and learn stuff. I think you should. I know one thing though, I know that a family can start with one fantasy you have nothing to do with and end in another, your own, and the problem is the space between, and maybe you do take me home, for a little bit every day, making me take a look at things I don't want to see, like Harriet sick, near dying and me not there, me not there at all.

I was not there because we were not Harriet and Jem, we were strangers, and the distance between her country and mine was the least of it and so I could not really know how bad it was with her, how she lay nearly lifeless, so unlike Harriet, with tubes going in and out and a lot of poison flooding her body and a great wound in her side. Peritonitis, they said, one of the worst cases they had ever seen. Maybe the tubes were the worst thing because when Mum told me how Harriet tried to shrug them off, pull them out, Mum seeing in this Harriet's first signs of return to life, I thought about Jude's red cardinals. Jude had a lot of birds once, doves, finches, canaries and then he saved and saved and bought a red cardinal and mostly he let them fly all about in one room which we converted for the birds, and only at night, when he could not be watching out for them, he'd lock them in their cages. He found his red cardinal dead three days after he bought it, his neck all twisted, and he bought one more and the same thing happened. Then he was told by someone who knew about birds that cardinals cannot be caged. They can't stand it and they will die, which is exactly what happened.

I keep thinking about Harriet's awful wound and I have this particular idea, which may be a crazy one, it's possible. This is it. Even though Harriet is healed now, I want to put my hands in her wound, in her side, I want to put my hands inside and wash them there and then maybe I will be okay for all time. I see it very clearly, this hand-washing inside Harriet.

"Why do you wear that?" you ask, indicating the bracelet I have fashioned out of surgical bandaging, cutting a piece to size and stapling it together to fit my wrist, with, as you pointed out to me, the scratchy ends of the staples against my skin.

Haircloth/hairshirt, worn by religious penitents, becoming a popular upholstery material in the nineteenth century.

"People might see the cuts and think I am crazy," I said.

"Oh. I thought maybe *you* do not want to see."

I think Francis of Assisi had a sense of humor. He saw all things as a reflection of God, the elements, people, disasters, illness, parts of the body, all things. He called everyone and everything Brother this and Sister that, and he even gave his illnesses nicknames, apologizing to "Brother Ass the Body" for all the pain it had to endure, including a horrible eye disease near the end of his life. He definitely had a sense of humor. You might not have had a fine dinner in his hut, due to his big thing for austerity, but you would have been entertained, I think so.

Tonight I walk all around my flat, and I talk aloud. I look at the knife that cut me.

"Brother Knife!" I say.

I see my blood. "Sister Blood, hello!"

"Brother Pasta Sauce, Sister Telephone, Brother Books, Brother Mirror, Sister Soap!"

I am laughing now. Is this crazy or what?

"Sister Crazy!" I announce. "Sister Crazy."

NOW WE ARE Harriet and Jem again, her scar is nearly nine years old and I think maybe I have synesthesia too, when it comes to Harriet, that is, because sometime, I don't know when, I looked at Harriet and she became my big sister and she looked back at me and I am the baby sister and it is like when we were little kids and her big thing for chocolate became my big thing and my big thing for cheese became hers but only on birthdays, in a cake situation.

For a few days during your break, I am in Harriet's house, which is gracious, inviting, elegant, and has peculiarities such as this. You open a door and across the room, at a point your eye is naturally drawn to, is a stuffed animal sitting on a radiator or in a windowsill or somewhere, a lamb or a mouse, a dog, a bear, and it makes you smile, it really does. My sister draws animals for a living. She paints in her own time, working all night or just for a morning, in her own house, a place she made, a space she knows.

I am in the spare bedroom and Harriet comes in with her dog who gets in bed with me and starts licking my wrists. The dog, Harriet says, knows when you are upset and licks and licks until you rise up out of it. It has to be true because usually this dog ignores me completely, knowing, I guess, that I do not have a big thing for pets.

"Harriet?"

Harriet sits on the bed and looks right at me.

"Harriet. Sometimes—do you ever get—you know—a big urge to just get up and pack a small bag and go home but you don't know where that is anymore, you don't know which way to go?"

And Harriet does not answer, not with immediacy and logic, anyway, but she tells me all the things she made for lunch, the pea soup that has been cooking in fresh stock for days and that she will serve in white bowls with carved lion heads on the sides; the pissaladière she will lay on colorful plates with hand-painted birds on them, keeping aside my favorite plate for me, the one with the blood-red bird like a cardinal. As she tells me this she strokes away a wisp of my hair which is wet because I am crying like an idiot, like a crazy person, and my hair is tangling up in my eyelashes. She does this really gently.

Crazy is not a person, it is a place you go, it is the maze inside Harriet without Harriet to guide you, it is standing in the eye of a storm with all the windows open, because you think you ought to take it, something Harriet always knew not to do. Please let me out of here. Please come back.

Harriet has a big thing for animals but she knows the difference between an animal and a person. She is not crazy. Harriet gets up off the bed and she walks out of my room and her dog follows.

EDEN ROBINSON

Traplines

D ad takes the white marten from the trap.
"Look at that, Will," he says.

It is limp in his hands. It hasn't been dead that long.

We tramp through the snow to the end of our trapline. Dad whistles. The goner marten is over his shoulder. From here, it looks like Dad is wearing it. There is nothing else in the other traps. We head back to the truck. The snow crunches. This is the best time for trapping, Dad told me a while ago. This is when the animals are hungry.

Our truck rests by the roadside at an angle. Dad rolls the white marten in a gray canvas cover separate from the others. The marten is flawless, which is rare in these parts. I put my animals beside his and cover them. We get in the truck. Dad turns the radio on and country twang fills the cab. We smell like sweat and oil and pine. Dad hums. I stare out the window. Mrs. Smythe would say the trees here are like the ones on Christmas postcards, tall and heavy with snow. They crowd close to the road. When the wind blows strong enough, the older trees snap and fall on the power lines.

"Well, there's our Christmas money," Dad says, snatching a peek at the rearview mirror.

I look back. The wind ruffles the canvases that cover the martens. Dad is smiling. He sits back, steering with one hand. He doesn't even mind when we are passed by three cars. The lines in his face are loose now. He sings along with a woman who left her husband—even that doesn't make him mad. We have our Christmas money. At least for now, there'll be no shouting in the house. It will take Mom and Dad a few days to find something else to fight about.

The drive home is a long one. Dad changes the radio station twice. I search my brain for something to say but my headache is spreading and I don't feel like talking. He watches the road, though he keeps stealing looks at the back of the truck. I watch the trees and the cars passing us.

One of the cars has two women in it. The woman that isn't driving waves her hands around as she talks. She reminds me of Mrs. Smythe. They are beside us, then ahead of us, then gone.

Tucca is still as we drive into it. The snow drugs it, makes it lazy. Houses puff cedar smoke and the sweet, sharp smell gets in everyone's clothes. At school in town, I can close my eyes and tell who's from the village and who isn't just by smelling them.

When we get home, we go straight to the basement. Dad gives me the ratty martens and keeps the good ones. He made me start on squirrels when I was in grade five. He put the knife in my hand, saying, "For Christ's sake, it's just a squirrel. It's dead, you stupid knucklehead. It can't feel anything."

He made the first cut for me. I swallowed, closed my eyes, and lifted the knife.

"Jesus," Dad muttered. "Are you a sissy? I got a sissy for a son. Look. It's just like cutting up a chicken. See? Pretend you're skinning a chicken."

Dad showed me, then put another squirrel in front of me, and we didn't leave the basement until I got it right.

Now Dad is skinning the flawless white marten, using his best knife. His tongue is sticking out the corner of his mouth. He straightens up and shakes his skinning hand. I quickly start on the next marten. It's perfect except for a scar across its back. It was probably in a fight. We won't get much for the skin. Dad goes back to work. I stop, clench, unclench my hands. They are stiff.

"Goddamn," Dad says quietly. I look up, tensing, but Dad starts to smile. He's finished the marten. It's ready to be dried and sold. I've finished mine too. I look at my hands. They know what to do now without my having to tell them. Dad sings as we go up the creaking stairs. When we get into the hallway I breathe in, smelling fresh baked bread.

Mom is sprawled in front of the TV. Her apron is smudged with flour and she is licking her fingers. When she sees us, she stops and puts her hands in her apron pockets.

"Well?" she says.

Dad grabs her at the waist and whirls her around the living room.

"Greg! Stop it!" she says, laughing.

Flour gets on Dad and cedar chips get on Mom. They talk and I leave, sneaking into the kitchen. I swallow three aspirins for my headache, snatch two buns, and go to my room. I stop in the doorway. Eric is there, plugged into his electric guitar. He looks at the buns and pulls out an earphone.

"Give me one," he says.

I throw him the smaller bun, and he finishes it in three bites.

"The other one," he says.

I give him the finger and sit on my bed. I see him thinking about tackling me, but he shrugs and plugs himself back in. I chew on the bun, roll bits of it around in my mouth. It's still warm, and I wish I had some honey for it or some blueberry jam.

Eric leaves and comes back with six buns. He wolfs them down, cramming them into his mouth. I stick my fingers in my ears and glare at him. He can't hear himself eat. He notices me and grins. Opens his mouth so I can see. I pull out a mag and turn the pages.

Dad comes in. Eric's jaw clenches. I go into the kitchen, grabbing another bun. Mom smacks my hand. We hear Eric and Dad starting to yell. Mom rolls her eyes and puts three more loaves in the oven.

"Back later," I say.

She nods, frowning at her hands.

I walk. Think about going to Billy's house. He is seeing Elaine, though, and is getting weird. He wrote her a poem yesterday. He couldn't find anything nice to rhyme with "Elaine" so he didn't finish it.

"Pain," Craig said. "Elaine, you pain."

"Plain Elaine," Tony said.

Billy smacked Tony and they went at it in the snow. Billy gave him a face wash. That ended it, and we let Billy sit on the steps and write in peace.

"Elaine in the rain," I say. "Elaine, a flame. Cranes. Danes. Trains. My main Elaine." I kick at the slush on the ground. Billy is on his own.

I let my feet take me down the street. It starts to snow, tiny ladybug flakes. It is only four but already getting dark. Streetlights flicker on. No one but me is out walking. Snot in my nose freezes. The air is starting to burn my throat. I turn and head home. Eric and Dad should be tired by now.

Another postcard picture. The houses lining the street look snug. I hunch into my jacket. In a few weeks, Christmas lights will go up all over the village. Dad will put ours up two weeks before Christmas. We use the same set every year. We'll get a tree a week later. Mom'll decorate it. On Christmas Eve, she'll put our presents under it. Some of the presents will be wrapped in aluminum because she never buys enough wrapping paper. We'll eat turkey. Mom and Dad will go to a lot of parties and get really drunk. Eric will go to a lot of parties and get really stoned. Maybe this year I will too. Anything would be better than sitting around with Tony and Craig, listening to them gripe.

I stamp the snow off my sneakers and jeans. I open the door quietly. The TV is on loud. I can tell that it's a hockey game by the announcer's voice. I take off my shoes and jacket. The house feels really hot to me after being outside. My face starts to tingle as the skin thaws. I go into the kitchen and take another aspirin.

The kitchen could use some plants. It gets good light in the winter. Mrs. Smythe has filled her kitchen with plants, hanging the ferns by the window where the cats can't eat them. The Smythes have pictures all over their walls of places they have been—Europe, Africa, Australia. They've been everywhere. They can afford it, she says, because they don't have kids. They had one, a while ago. On the TV there's a wallet-sized picture of a dark-haired boy with his front teeth missing. He was their kid but he disappeared. Mrs. Smythe fiddles with the picture a lot.

Eric tries to sneak up behind me. His socks make a slithering sound on the floor. I duck just in time and hit him in the stomach.

He doubles over. He has a towel stretched between his hands. His choking game. He punches at me, but I hop out of the way. His fist hits the hot stove. Yelling, he jerks his hand back. I race out of the kitchen and down to the basement. Eric follows me, screaming my name. "Come out, you chicken," he says. "Come on out and fight."

I keep still behind a stack of plywood. Eric has the towel ready. After a while, he goes back upstairs and locks the door behind him.

I stand. I can't hear Mom and Dad. They must have gone out to celebrate the big catch. They'll probably find a party and go on a bender until Monday, when Dad has to go back to work. I'm alone with Eric, but he'll leave the house around ten. I can stay out of his way until then.

The basement door bursts open. I scramble under Dad's tool table. Eric must be stoned. He's probably been toking up since Mom and Dad left. Pot always makes him mean.

He laughs. "You baby. You fucking baby." He doesn't look for me that hard. He thumps loudly up the stairs, slams the door shut, then tiptoes back down and waits. He must think I'm really stupid.

We stay like this for a long time. Eric lights up. In a few minutes, the whole basement smells like pot. Dad will be pissed off if the smoke ruins the white marten. I smile, hoping it does. Eric will really get it then.

"Fuck," he says and disappears upstairs, not locking the door. I crawl out. My legs are stiff. The pot is making me dizzy.

The woodstove is cooling. I don't open it because the hinges squeal. It'll be freezing down here soon. Breathing fast, I climb the stairs. I crack the door open. There are no lights on except in our bedroom. I pull on my jacket and sneakers. I grab some bread and stuff it in my jacket, then run for the door but Eric is blocking it, leering.

"Thought you were sneaky, hey," he says.

I back into the kitchen. He follows. I wait until he is near before I bend over and ram him. He's slow because of the pot and slips to the floor. He grabs my ankle, but I kick him in the head and am out the door before he can catch me. I take the steps two at a time. Eric stands on the porch and laughs. I can't wait until I'm bigger. I'd like to smear him against a wall. Let him see what it feels like. I'd like to smear him so bad.

I munch on some bread as I head for the exit to the highway. Now the snow is coming down in thick, large flakes that melt when they touch my skin. I stand at the exit and wait.

I hear One Eye's beat-up Ford long before I see it. It clunks down the road and stalls when One Eye stops for me.

"You again. What you doing out here?" he yells at me.

"Waiting for Princess fucking Di," I say.

"Smart mouth. You keep it up and you can stay out there."

The back door opens anyway. Snooker and Jim are there. One Eye and Don Wilson are in the front. They all have silver lunch buckets at their feet.

We get into town and I say, "Could you drop me off here?"

One Eye looks back, surprised. He has forgotten about me. He frowns. "Where you going this time of night?"

"Disneyland," I say.

"Smart mouth," he says. "Don't be like your brother. You stay out of trouble."

I laugh. One Eye slows the car and pulls over. It chokes and sputters. I get out and thank him for the ride. One Eye grunts. He pulls away and I walk to Mrs. Smythe's.

THE FIRST TIME I saw her house was last spring, when she invited the English class there for a barbecue. The lawn was neat and green and I only saw one dandelion. There were rose bushes in the front and raspberry bushes in the back. I went with Tony and Craig, who got high on the way there. Mrs. Smythe noticed right away. She took them aside and talked to them. They stayed in the poolroom downstairs until the high wore off.

There weren't any other kids from the village there. Only townies. Kids that Dad says will never dirty their pink hands. They were split into little groups. They talked and ate and laughed and I wandered around alone, feeling like a dork. I was going to go downstairs to Tony and Craig when Mrs. Smythe came up to me, carrying a hot dog. I never noticed her smile until then. Her blue sundress swayed as she walked.

"You weren't in class yesterday," she said.

"Stomachache."

"I was going to tell you how much I liked your essay. You must have done a lot of work on it."

"Yeah." I tried to remember what I had written.

"Which part was the hardest?" she said.

I cleared my throat. "Starting it."

"I walked right into that one," she said, laughing. I smiled.

A tall man came up and hugged her. She kissed him. "Sam," she said. "This is the student I was telling you about."

"Well, hello," Mr. Smythe said. "Great paper."

"Thanks," I said.

"Is it William or Will?" Mr. Smythe said.

"Will," I said. He held out his hand and shook mine.

"That big, huh?" he said.

Oh no, I thought, remembering what I'd written. Dad, Eric, Grandpa, and I had gone out halibut fishing once and caught a huge one. It took forever to get it in the boat and we all took turns clubbing it. But it wouldn't die, so Dad shot it. In the essay I said it was seven hundred pounds, but Mrs. Smythe had pointed out to the whole class that halibut didn't get much bigger than five hundred. Tony and Craig bugged me about that.

"Karen tells me you've written a lot about fishing," Mr. Smythe said, sounding really cheerful.

"Excuse me," Mrs. Smythe said. "That's my cue to leave. If you're smart, you'll do the same. Once you get Sam going with his stupid fish stories you can't get a word—"

Mr. Smythe goosed her. She poked him with her hot dog and left quickly. Mr. Smythe put his arm around my shoulder, shaking his head. We sat out on the patio and he told me about the time he caught a marlin and about scuba diving on the Great Barrier Reef. He went down in a shark cage once to try to film a great white eating. I told him about Uncle Bernie's gillnetter. He wanted to know if Uncle Bernie would take him out, and what gear he was going to need. We ended up in the kitchen, me using a flounder to show him how to clean a halibut.

I finally looked at the clock around eleven. Dad had said he would pick me and Tony and Craig up around eight. I didn't even know where Tony and Craig were anymore. I couldn't believe it had gotten so late without my noticing. Mrs. Smythe had gone to bed. Mr. Smythe said he would drive me home. I said that was okay, I'd hitch.

He snorted. "Karen would kill me. No, I'll drive you. Let's phone your parents and tell them you're coming home."

No one answered the phone. I said they were probably asleep. He dialed again. Still no answer.

"Looks like you've got the spare bedroom tonight," he said.

"Let me try," I said, picking up the phone. There was no answer, but after six rings I pretended Dad was on the other end. I didn't want to spend the night at my English teacher's house. Tony and Craig would never shut up about it.

"Hi, Dad," I said. "How come? I see. Car trouble. No problem. Mr. Smythe is going to drive me home. What? Sure, I—"

"Let me talk to him," Mr. Smythe said, snatching the phone. "Hello! Mr. Tate! How are you? My, my, my. Your son is a lousy liar, isn't he?" He hung up. "It's amazing how much your father sounds like a dial tone."

I picked up the phone again. "They're sleeping, that's all." Mr. Smythe watched me as I dialed. There wasn't any answer.

"Why'd you lie?" he said quietly.

We were alone in the kitchen. I swallowed. He was a lot bigger than me. When he reached over, I put my hands up and covered my face. He stopped, then took the phone out of my hands.

"It's okay," he said. "I won't hurt you. It's okay."

I put my hands down. He looked sad. That annoyed me. I shrugged, backing away. "I'll hitch," I said.

Mr. Smythe shook his head. "No, really, Karen would kill me, then she'd go after you. Come on. We'll be safer if you sleep in the spare room."

In the morning Mr. Smythe was up before I could sneak out. He was making bacon and pancakes. He asked if I'd ever done any freshwater fishing. I said no. He started talking about fishing in the Black Sea and I listened to him. He's a good cook.

Mrs. Smythe came into the kitchen dressed in some sweats and a T-shirt. She ate without saying anything and didn't look awake until she finished her coffee. Mr. Smythe phoned my house but no one answered. He asked if I wanted to go up to Old Timer's Lake with them. He had a new Sona reel he wanted to try out. I didn't have anything better to do.

The Smythes have a twenty-foot speedboat. They let me drive it around the lake a few times while Mrs. Smythe baked in the sun and Mr. Smythe put the rod together. We lazed around the beach in the afternoon, watching the people go by. Sipping their beers, the Smythes argued about who was going to drive back. We rode around the lake some more and roasted hot dogs for dinner.

THEIR PORCH LIGHT is on. I go up the walk and ring the bell. Mrs. Smythe said just come in, don't bother knocking, but I can't do that. It doesn't feel right. She opens the door, smiling when she sees me. She is wearing a fluffy pink sweater. "Hi, Will. Sam was hoping you'd drop by. He says he's looking forward to beating you."

"Dream on," I say.

She laughs. "Go right in." She heads down the hall to the washroom.

I go into the living room. Mr. Smythe isn't there. The TV is on, some documentary about whales.

He's in the kitchen, scrunched over a game of solitaire. His new glasses are sliding off his nose and he looks more like a teacher than Mrs. Smythe. He scratches the beard he's trying to grow.

"Come on in," he says, patting the chair beside him.

I take a seat and watch him finish the game. He pushes his glasses up. "What's your pleasure?" he says.

"Pool," I say.

"Feeling lucky, huh?" We go down to the poolroom. "How about a little extra this week?" he says, not looking at me.

I shrug. "Sure. Dishes?"

He shakes his head. "Bigger."

"I'm not shoveling the walk," I say.

He shakes his head again. "Bigger."

"Money?"

"Bigger."

"What?"

He racks up the balls. Sets the cue ball. Wipes his hands on his jeans. "What?" I say again.

Mr. Smythe takes out a quarter. "Heads or tails?" he says, tossing it.

"Heads," I say.

He slaps the quarter on the back of his hand. "I break."

"Where? Let me see that," I say, laughing. He holds it up. The quarter is tails.

He breaks. "How'd you like to stay with us?" he says, very quietly.

"Sure," I say. "But I got to go back on Tuesday. We got to check the traplines again."

He is quiet. The balls make thunking sounds as they bounce around the table. "Do you like it here?"

"Sure," I say.

"Enough to live here?"

I'm not sure I heard him right. Maybe he's asking a different question from the one I think he's asking. I open my mouth. I don't know what to say. I say nothing.

"Those are the stakes, then," he says. "I win, you stay. You win, you stay."

He's joking. I laugh. He doesn't laugh. "You serious?" I ask.

He stands up straight. "I don't think I've ever been more serious."

The room is suddenly very small.

"Your turn," he says. "Stripes."

I scratch, missing the ball by a mile. He takes his turn.

"We don't want to push you," he says. He leans over the table, squints at a ball. "We just think that you'd be safer here. Hell, you practically live with us already." I watch my sneakers. He keeps playing. "We aren't rich. We aren't perfect. We ..." He looks at me. "We thought maybe you'd like to try it for a couple of weeks first."

"I can't."

"You don't have to decide right now," he says. "Think about it. Take a few days."

It's my turn again but I don't feel like playing anymore. Mr. Smythe is waiting, though. I pick a ball. Aim, shoot, miss.

The game goes on in silence. Mr. Smythe wins easily. He smiles. "Well, I win. You stay."

If I wanted to get out of the room, there is only one door and Mr. Smythe is blocking it. He watches me. "Let's go upstairs," he says.

Mrs. Smythe has shut off the TV. She stands up when we come into the living room. "Will—"

"I asked him already," Mr. Smythe says.

Her head snaps around. "You what?"

"I asked him."

Her hands clench at her sides. "We were supposed to do it together, Sam." Her voice is flat. She turns to me. "You said no."

I can't look at her. I look at the walls, at the floor, at her slippers. I shouldn't have come tonight. I should have waited for Eric to leave.

She stands in front of me, trying to smile. Her hands are warm on my face. "Look at me," she says. "Will? Look at me." She is trying to smile. "Hungry?" she says.

I nod. She makes a motion with her head for Mr. Smythe to follow her into the kitchen. When they're gone I sit down. It should be easy. It should be easy. I watch TV without seeing it. I wonder what they're saying about me in the kitchen.

It's now almost seven and my ribs hurt. Mostly, I can ignore it, but Eric hit me pretty hard and they're bruised. Eric got hit pretty hard by Dad, so we're even, I guess. I'm counting the days until Eric moves out. The rate he's going, he'll be busted soon anyway. Tony says the police are starting to ask questions.

It's a strange night. We all pretend that nothing has happened and Mrs. Smythe fixes some nachos. Mr. Smythe gets out a pack of Uno cards and we play a few rounds and watch the Discovery Channel. We go to bed.

I lie awake. My room. This could be my room. I already have most of my books here. It's hard to study with Eric around. I still have a headache. I couldn't get away from them long enough to sneak into the kitchen for an aspirin. I pull my T-shirt up and take a look. There's a long bruise under my ribs and five smaller ones above it. I think Eric was trying to hit my stomach but he was so wasted he kept missing. It isn't too bad. Tony's dad broke three of his ribs once. Billy got a concussion a couple of weeks ago. My dad is pretty easy. It's only Eric who really bothers me.

The Smythes keep the aspirin by the spices. I grab six, three for now and three for the morning. I'm swallowing the last one when Mr. Smythe grabs my hand. I didn't even hear him come in. I must be sleepy.

"Where'd they hit you this time?" he says.

"I got a headache," I say. "A bad one."

He pries open the hand with the aspirins in it. "How many do you plan on taking?"

"These are for later."

He sighs. I get ready for a lecture. "Go back to bed" is all he says. "It'll be okay." He sounds very tired.

"Sure," I say.

I get up around five. I leave a note saying I have things to do at home. I catch a ride with some guys coming off the graveyard shift.

NO ONE IS HOME. Eric had a party last night. I'm glad I wasn't around. They've wrecked the coffee table and the rug smells like stale beer and cigarettes. Our bedroom is even worse. Someone puked all over Eric's bed and there are two used condoms on mine. At least none of the windows were broken this time. I start to clean my side of the room, then stop. I sit on my bed.

Mr. Smythe will be getting up soon. It's Sunday, so there'll be waffles or french toast. He'll fix a plate of bacon, and eat it before Mrs. Smythe comes downstairs. He thinks she doesn't know that he does this. She'll get up around ten or eleven and won't talk to anyone until she's had about three coffees. She starts to wake up around one or two. They'll argue about something. Whose turn to take out the garbage or do the laundry. They'll read the paper.

I crawl into bed. The aspirin isn't working. I try to sleep but it really reeks in here. I have a biology test tomorrow. I forgot to bring the book back from their place. I lie there awake until our truck pulls into the driveway. Mom and Dad are fighting. They sound plastered. Mom is bitching about something. Dad is not saying anything. Doors slam.

Mom comes in first and goes straight to bed. She doesn't seem to notice the house is a mess. Dad comes in a lot slower.

"What the—Eric!" he yells. "Eric!"

I pretend to sleep. The door bangs open.

"Eric, you little bastard," Dad says, looking around. He shakes me. "Where the fuck is Eric?"

His breath is lethal. You can tell he likes his rye straight.

"How should I know?"

He rips Eric's amplifiers off the walls. He throws them down and give them a good kick. He tips Eric's bed over. Eric is smart. He won't come home for a while. Dad will have cooled off by then and Eric can give him some money without Dad's getting pissed off. I don't move. I wait until he's out of the room before I put on a sweater. I can hear him down in the basement chopping wood. It should be around eight by now. The RinkyDink will be open in an hour.

When I go into the kitchen, Mom is there. She sees me and makes a shushing motion with her hands. She pulls out a bottle from behind the stove and sits down at the kitchen table.

"You're a good boy," she says, giggling. "You're a good boy. Help your old mother back to bed, hey."

"Sure," I say, putting an arm around her. She stands, holding onto the bottle with one hand and me with the other. "This way, my lady."

"You making fun of me?" she says, her eyes going small. "You laughing at me?" Then she laughs and we go to their room. She flops onto the bed. She takes a long drink. "You're fucking laughing at me, aren't you?"

"Mom, you're paranoid. I was making a joke."

"Yeah, you're really funny. A laugh a minute," she says, giggling again. "Real comedian."

"Yeah, that's me."

She throws the bottle at me. I duck. She rolls over and starts to cry. I cover her with the blanket and leave. The floor is sticky. Dad's still chopping wood. They wouldn't notice if I wasn't here. Maybe people would talk for a week or two, but after a while they wouldn't notice. The only people who would miss me are Tony and Craig and Billy and maybe Eric, when he got toked up and didn't have anything for target practice.

Billy is playing Mortal Kombat at the RinkyDink. He's chain-smoking. As I walk up to him, he turns around quickly.

"Oh, it's you," he says, going back to the game.

"Hi to you too," I say.

"You seen Elaine?" he says.

"Nope."

He crushes out his cigarette in the ashtray beside him. He plays for a while, loses a life, then shakes another cigarette out one-handed. He sticks it in his mouth, loses another man, then lights up. He sucks deep. "Relax," I say. "Her majesty's limo is probably stuck in traffic. She'll come."

He glares at me. "Shut up."

I go play pool with Craig, who's decided that he's James Dean. He's wearing a white T-shirt, jeans, and a black leather jacket that looks like his brother's. His hair is blow-dried and a cigarette dangles from the corner of his mouth.

"What a loser," he says.

"Who you calling a loser?"

"Billy. What a loser." He struts to the other side of the pool table.

"He's okay."

"That babe," he says. "What's-her-face. Ellen? Irma?"

"Elaine."

"Yeah, her. She's going out with him 'cause she's got a bet."

"What?"

"She's got to go out with him a month, and her friend will give her some coke."

"Billy's already giving her coke."

"Yeah. He's a loser."

I look over at Billy. He's lighting another cigarette.

"Can you imagine a townie wanting anything to do with him?" Craig says. "She's just doing it as a joke. She's going to dump him in a week. She's going to put all his stupid poems in the paper."

I see it now. There's a space around Billy. No one is going near him. He doesn't notice. Same with me. I catch some guys I used to hang out with grinning at me. When they see me looking at them, they look away.

Craig wins the game. I'm losing a lot this week.

Elaine gets to the RinkyDink after lunch. She's got some townie girlfriends with her who are tiptoeing around like they're going to get jumped. Elaine leads them right up to Billy. Everyone's watching.

Billy gives her his latest poem. I wonder what he found to rhyme with "Elaine."

The girls leave. Billy holds the door open for Elaine. Her friends start to giggle. The guys standing around start to howl. They're laughing so hard they're crying. I feel sick. I think about telling Billy but I know he won't listen.

I leave the RinkyDink and go for a walk. I walk and walk and end up back in front of the RinkyDink. There's nowhere else to go. I hang out with Craig, who hasn't left the pool table.

I spend the night on his floor. Craig's parents are Jehovah's Witnesses and preach at me before I go to bed. I sit and listen because I need a place to sleep. I'm not going home until tomorrow, when Mom and Dad are sober. Craig's mom gets us up two hours before the bus that takes the village kids to school comes. They pray before we eat. Craig looks at me and rolls his eyes. People are always making fun of Craig because his parents stand on the corner downtown every Friday and hold up the *Watchtower* mags. When his parents start to bug him, he says he'll take up devil worship or astrology if they don't lay off. I think I'll ask him if he wants to hang out with me on Christmas. His parents don't believe in it.

Between classes I pass Mrs. Smythe in the hall. Craig nudges me. "Go on," he says, making sucking noises. "Go get your A."

"Fuck off," I say, pushing him.

She's talking to some girl and doesn't see me. I think about skipping English but know that she'll call home and ask where I am.

At lunch no one talks to me. I can't find Craig or Tony or Billy. The village guys who hang out by the science wing snicker as I go past. I don't stop until I get to the gym doors, where the headbangers have taken over. I don't have any money and I didn't bring a lunch, so I bum a cigarette off this girl with really tight jeans. To get my mind off my stomach I try to get her to go out with me. She looks at me like I'm crazy. When she walks away, the fringe on her leather jacket swings.

I flunk my biology test. It's multiple choice. I stare at the paper and kick myself. I know I could have passed if I'd read the chapter.

Mr. Kellerman reads out the scores from lowest to highest. My name is called out third.

"Mr. Tate," he says. "Three out of thirty."

"All riiight," Craig says, slapping my back.

"Mr. Davis," Mr. Kellerman says to Craig, "three and a half."

Craig stands up and bows. The guys in the back clap. The kids in the front laugh. Mr. Kellerman reads out the rest of the scores. Craig turns to me. "Looks like I beat the Brain," he says.

"Yeah," I say. "Pretty soon you're going to be getting the Nobel Prize."

The bell rings for English. I go to my locker and take out my jacket. If she calls home no one's going to answer anyway.

I walk downtown. The snow is starting to slack off and it's even sunning a bit. My stomach growls. I haven't eaten anything since breakfast. I wish I'd gone to English. Mrs. Smythe would have given me something to eat. She always has something left over from lunch. I hunch down into my jacket.

Downtown, I go to the Paradise Arcade. All the heads hang out there. Maybe Eric'll give me some money. More like a belt, but it's worth a try. I don't see him anywhere, though. In fact, no one much is there. Just some burnouts by the pinball machines. I see Mitch and go over to him, but he's soaring, laughing at the ball going around the machine. I walk away, head for the highway, and hitch home. Mom will have passed out by now, and Dad'll be at work.

SURE ENOUGH, Mom is on the living room floor. I get her a blanket. The stove has gone out and it's freezing in here. I go into the kitchen and look through the fridge. There's one jar of pickles, some really pathetic-looking celery, and some milk that's so old it smells like cheese. There's no bread left over from Saturday. I find some Rice-A-Roni and cook it. Mom comes to and asks for some water. I bring her a glass and give her a little Rice-A-Roni. She makes a face but slowly eats it.

At six Dad comes home with Eric. They've made up. Eric has bought Dad a six-pack and they watch the hockey game together. I stay in my room. Eric has cleaned his bed by dumping his mattress outside and stealing mine. I haul my mattress back onto my bed frame. I pull out my English book. We have a grammar test this Friday. I know Mrs. Smythe will be unhappy if she has to fail me. I read the chapter on nouns and get through most of the one on verbs before Eric comes in and kicks me off the bed.

He tries to take the mattress but I punch him in the side. Eric turns and grabs my hair. "This is my bed," he says. "Understand?"

"Fuck you," I say. "You had the party. Your fucked-up friends trashed the room. You sleep on the floor."

Dad comes in and sees Eric push me against the wall and smack my face. He yells at Eric, who turns around, his fist frozen in the air. Dad rolls his sleeves up.

"You always take his side!" Eric yells. "You never take mine!"

"Pick on someone your own size," Dad says. "Unless you want to deal with me."

Eric gives me a look that says he'll settle with me later. I pick up my English book and get out. I walk around the village, staying away from the RinkyDink. It's the first place Eric will look.

I'm at the village exit. The sky is clear and the stars are popping out. Mr. Smythe will be at his telescope trying to map the Pleiades. Mrs. Smythe will be marking papers while she watches TV.

"Need a ride?" this guys says. There's a blue pickup stopped in front of me. The driver is wearing a hunting cap.

I take my hand out of my mouth. I've been chewing my knuckles like a baby. I shake my head. "I'm waiting for someone," I say.

He shrugs and takes off. I stand there and watch his headlights disappear.

They didn't really mean it. They'd get bored of me quick when they found out what I'm like. I should have just said yes. I could have stayed until they got fed up and then come home when Eric had cooled off.

Two cars pass me as I walk back to the village. I can hide at Tony's until Eric goes out with his friends and forgets this afternoon. My feet are frozen by the time I get to the RinkyDink. Tony is there.

"So. I heard Craig beat you in biology," he says.

I laugh. "Didn't it just impress you?"

"A whole half a point. Way to go," he says. "For a while there we thought you were getting townie."

"Yeah, right," I say. "Listen, I pissed Eric off—"

"Surprise, surprise."

"—and I need a place to crash. Can I sleep over?"

"Sure," he says. Mitch wanders into the RinkyDink, and a crowd of kids slowly drifts over to him. He looks around, eyeing everybody. Then he starts giving something out. Me and Tony go over.

"Wow," Tony says, after Mitch gives him something too.

We leave and go behind the RinkyDink, where other kids are gathered. "Fucking all right," I hear Craig say, even though I can't see him.

"What?" I say. Tony opens his hand. He's holding a little vial with white crystals in it.

"Crack," he says. "Man, is he stupid. He could have made a fortune and he's just giving it away."

We don't have a pipe, and Tony wants to do this right the first time. He decides to save it for tomorrow, after he buys the right equipment. I'm hungry again. I'm about to tell him that I'm going to Billy's when I see Eric.

"Shit," I say and hide behind him.

Tony looks up. "Someone's in trou-ble," he sings.

Eric's looking for me. I hunch down behind Tony, who tries to look innocent. Eric spots him and starts to come over. "Better run," Tony whispers.

I sneak behind some other people but Eric sees me and I have to run for it anyway. Tony starts to cheer and the kids behind the RinkyDink join in. Some of the guys follow us so they'll see what happens when Eric catches up with me. I don't want to find out so I pump as hard as I can.

Eric used to be fast. I'm glad he's a dopehead now because he can't really run anymore. I'm panting and my legs are cramping but the house is in sight. I run up the stairs. The door is locked.

I stand there, hand on the knob. Eric rounds the corner to our block. There's no one behind him. I bang on the door but now I see that our truck is gone. I run around to the back but the basement door is locked too. Even the windows are locked.

Eric pops his head around the corner of the house. He grins when he sees me, then disappears. I grit my teeth and start running across our backyard. Head for Billy's. "You shithead," Eric yells. He has a friend with him, maybe Brent. I duck behind our neighbor's house. There's snow in my sneakers and all the way up my leg, but I'm sweating. I stop. I can't hear Eric. I hope I've lost him, but Eric is really pissed off and when he's pissed off he doesn't let go. I look down. My footprints are clear in the snow. I start to run again, but I hit a thick spot and have to wade through thigh-high snow. I look back. Eric is nowhere. I keep slogging. I make it to the road again and run down to the exit.

I've lost him. I'm shaking because it's cold. I can feel the sweat cooling on my skin. My breath goes back to normal. I wait for a car to come by. I've missed the night shift and the graveyard crew won't be by until midnight. It's too cold to wait that long.

A car, a red car. A little Toyota. Brent's car. I run off the road and head for a clump of trees. The Toyota pulls over and Eric gets out, yelling. I reach the trees and rest. They're waiting by the roadside. Eric is peering into the trees, trying to see me. Brent is smoking in the car. Eric crosses his arms over his chest and blows into his hands. My legs are frozen.

After a long time, a cop car cruises to a stop beside the Toyota. I wade out and wave at the two policemen. They look startled. One of them turns to Eric and Brent and asks them something. I see Eric shrug. It takes me a while to get over to where they're standing because my legs are slow.

The cop is watching me. I swear I'll never call them pigs again. I swear it. He leans over to Brent, who digs around in the glove compartment. The cop says something to his partner. I scramble down the embankment.

Eric has no marks on his face. Dad probably hit him on the back and stomach. Dad has been careful since the social worker came to our house. Eric suddenly smiles at me and holds out his hand. I move behind the police car.

"Is there a problem here?" the policeman says.

"No," Eric says. "No probulum. Li'l misunnerstanin'."

Oh, shit. He's as high as a kite. The policeman looks hard at Eric. I look at the car. Brent is staring at me, glassy-eyed. He's high too.

Eric tries again to reach out to me. I put the police car between us. The policeman grabs Eric by the arm and his partner goes and gets Brent. The policeman says something about driving under the influence but none of us are listening. Eric's eyes are on me. I'm going to pay for this. Brent is swearing. He wants a lawyer. He stumbles out of the Toyota and slips on the road. Brent and Eric are put in the backseat of the police car. The policeman comes up to me and says, "Can you make it home?"

I nod.

"Good. Go," he says.

They drive away. When I get home, I walk around the house, trying to figure out a way to break in. I find a stick and jimmy the basement door open. Just in case Eric gets out tonight, I make a bed under the tool table and go to sleep.

No one is home when I wake up. I scramble an egg and get ready for school. I sit beside Tony on the bus.

"I was expecting to see you with black eyes," he says.

My legs are still raw from last night. I have something due today but I can't remember what. If Eric is in the drunk tank, they'll let him out later.

The village guys are talking to me again. I skip gym. I skip history. I hang out with Craig and Tony in the Paradise Arcade. I'm not sure if I want to be friends with them after they joined in the chase last night, but it's better to have them on my side than not. They get a two-for-one pizza special for lunch and I'm glad I stuck with them because I'm starved. They also got some five-finger specials from

Safeway. Tony is proud because he swiped a couple of bags of chips
and two Pepsis and no one even noticed.

Mitch comes over to me in the bathroom.

"That was a really cheap thing to do," he says.

"What?" I haven't done anything to him.

"What? What? Getting your brother thrown in jail. Pretty crummy."

"He got himself thrown in jail. He got caught when he was high."

"That's not what he says." Mitch frowns. "He says you set him up."

"Fuck." I try to sound calm. "When'd he tell you that?"

"This morning," he says. "He's waiting for you at school."

"I didn't set him up. How could I?"

Mitch nods. He hands me some crack and says, "Hey, I'm sorry,"
and leaves. I look at it. I'll give it to Tony and maybe he'll let me stay
with him tonight.

Billy comes into the Paradise with Elaine and her friends. He's
getting some glances but he doesn't notice. He holds the chair out for
Elaine, who sits down without looking at him. I don't want to be
around for this. I go over to Tony.

"I'm leaving," I say.

Tony shushes me. "Watch," he says.

Elaine orders a beer. Frankie shakes his head and points to the sign
that says WE DO NOT SERVE MINORS. Elaine frowns. She says something
to Billy. He shrugs. She orders a Coke. Billy pays. When their Cokes
come, Elaine dumps hers over Billy's head. Billy stares at her, more
puzzled than anything else. Her friends start to laugh, and I get up and
walk out.

I lean against the wall of the Paradise. Billy comes out a few minutes
later. His face is still and pale. Elaine and her friends follow him, recit-
ing lines from the poems he wrote her. Tony and the rest spill out too,
laughing. I go back inside and trade the crack for some quarters for the
video games. I keep losing. Tony wants to go now and we hitch back
to the village. We raid his fridge and have chocolate ice cream coconut
sundaes. Angela comes in with Di and says that Eric is looking for me.
I look at Tony and he looks at me.

"Boy, are you in for it," Tony says. "You'd better stay here tonight."

When everyone is asleep, Tony pulls out a weird-looking pipe and does the crack. His face goes very dreamy and far away. A few minutes later he says, "Christ, that's great. I wonder how much Mitch has?"

I turn over and go to sleep.

THE NEXT MORNING Billy is alone on the bus. No one wants to sit with him so there are empty seats all around him. He looks like he hasn't slept. Tony goes up to him and punches him in the arm.

"So how's Shakespeare this morning?" Tony says.

I hope Eric isn't at the school. I don't know where else I can hide.

Mrs. Smythe is waiting at the school bus stop. I sneak out the back door of the bus, with Tony and the guys pretending to fight to cover me.

We head back to the Paradise. I'm starting to smell bad. I haven't had a shower in days. I wish I had some clean clothes. I wish I had some money to buy a toothbrush. I hate the scummy feeling on my teeth. I wish I had enough for a taco or a hamburger.

Dad is at the Paradise, looking for me.

"Let's go to the Dairy Queen," he says.

He orders a coffee, a chocolate milk shake, and a cheeseburger. We take the coffee and milk shake to a back table, and I pocket the order slip. We sit there. Dad folds and unfolds a napkin.

"One of your teachers called," he says.

"Mrs. Smythe?"

"Yeah." He looks up. "Says she'd like you to stay there."

I try to read his face. His eyes are bloodshot and red-rimmed. He must have a big hangover.

The cashier calls out our number. I go up and get the cheeseburger and we split it. Dad always eats slow to make it last longer.

"Did you tell her you wanted to?"

"No," I say. "They asked me, but I said I couldn't."

Dad nods. "Did you tell them anything?"

"Like what?"

"Don't get smart," he says, sounding beat.

"I didn't say anything."

He stops chewing. "Then why'd they ask you?"

"Don't know."

"You must have told them something."

"Nope. They just asked."

"Did Eric tell them?"

I snort. "Eric? No way. They would … He wouldn't go anywhere near them. They're okay, Dad. They won't tell anybody."

"So you did tell them."

"I didn't. I swear I didn't. Look, Eric got me on the face a couple of times and they just figured it out."

"You're lying."

I finished my half of the cheeseburger. "I'm not lying. I didn't say anything and they won't either."

"I never touched you."

"Yeah, Eric took care of that," I say. "You seen him?"

"I kicked him out."

"You what?"

"Party. Ruined the basement," Dad says grimly. "He's old enough. Had to leave sooner or later."

He chews his last mouthful of cheeseburger. Eric will really be out of his mind now.

We drive out to check the trapline. The first trap has been tripped with a stick. Dad curses, blaming the other trappers who have lines near ours. "I'll skunk them," he says. But the last three traps have got some more martens. We even get a little lynx. Dad is happy. We go home. The basement is totally ripped apart.

Next day at school, I spend most of the time ducking from Eric and Mrs. Smythe before I finally get sick of the whole lot and go down to the Paradise. Tony is there with Billy, who asks me if I want to go to Vancouver with him until Eric cools off.

"Now?"

"No better time," he says.

I think about it. "When you leaving?"

"Tonight."

"I don't know. I don't have any money."

"Me neither," he says.

"Shit," I say. "How we going to get there? It's a zillion miles from here."

"Hitch to town, hitch to Smithers, then down to Prince George."

"Yeah, yeah, but what are we going to eat?"

He wiggles his hand. Five-finger special. I laugh.

"You change your mind," he says, "I'll be behind the RinkyDink around seven. Get some thick boots."

We're about to hitch home when I see Mrs. Smythe peer into the Paradise. It's too late to hide because she sees me. Her face stiffens. She walks over to us and the guys start to laugh. Mrs. Smythe looks at them, then at me.

"Will?" she says. "Can I talk to you outside?"

She glances around like the guys are going to jump her. I try to see what she's nervous about. Tony is grabbing his crotch. Billy is cleaning his nails. The other guys are snickering. I suddenly see them the way she does. They all have long, greasy hair, combed straight back. We're all wearing jeans, T-shirts, and sneakers. We don't look nice.

She's got on her school uniform, as she calls it. Dark skirt, white shirt, low black heels, glasses. She's watching me like she hasn't seen me before. I hope she never sees my house.

"Later?" I say. "I'm kind of busy."

She blushes, the guys laugh hard. I wish I could take the words back. "Are you sure?" she says.

Tony nudges my arm. "Why don't you introduce us to your girl-friend," he says. "Maybe she'd like—"

"Shut up," I say. Mrs. Smythe has no expression now.

"I'll talk to you later, then," she says, and turns around and walks out without looking back. If I could, I'd follow her.

Billy claps me on the shoulder. "Stay away from them," he says. "It's not worth it."

It doesn't matter. She practically said she didn't want to see me again. I don't blame her. I wouldn't want to see me again either.

She'll get into her car now and go home. She'll honk when she pulls into the driveway so Mr. Smythe will come out and help her with the groceries. She always gets groceries today. The basics and sardines. Peanut butter. I lick my lips. Diamante frozen pizzas. Oodles of Noodles. Waffles. Blueberry Mueslix.

Mr. Smythe will come out of the house, wave, come down the driveway. They'll take the groceries into the house after they kiss. They'll kick the snow off their shoes and throw something in the microwave. Watch *Cheers* reruns on Channel 8. Mr. Smythe will tell her what happened in his day. Maybe she will say what happened in hers.

We catch a ride home. Billy yabbers about Christmas in Vancouver, and how great it's going to be, the two of us, no one to boss us around, no one to bother us, going anywhere we want. I turn away from him. Watch the trees blur past. I guess anything'll be better than sitting around, listening to Tony and Craig gripe.

CAROL SHIELDS

Chemistry

If you were to write me a letter out of the blue, typewritten, hand-written, whatever, and remind me that you were once in the same advanced recorder class with me at the YMCA on the south side of Montreal and that you were the girl given to head colds and black knitted tights and whose *Sprightly Music for the Recorder* had shed its binding, then I would, feigning a little diffidence, try to shore up a coarsened image of the winter of 1972. Or was it 1973? Unforgivable to forget, but at a certain distance the memory buckles; those are the words I'd use.

But you will remind me of the stifling pink heat of the room. The cusped radiators under the windows. How Madam Bessant was always there early, dipping her shoulders in a kind of greeting, arranging sheets of music and making those little throat-clearing chirps of hers, getting things organized—for us, everything for us, for no one else.

The light that leaked out of those winter evenings filled the skirted laps of Lonnie Henry and Cecile Landreau, and you of course, as well as the hollows of your bent elbows and the seam of your upper lip brought down so intently on the little wooden mouthpiece and the bony intimacy of your instep circling in air. You kept time with that circling foot of yours, and also with the measured delay and snap of your chin. We sat in a circle—you will prod me into this remembrance. Our chairs drawn tight together. Those clumsy old-fashioned wooden folding chairs? Dusty slats pinned loosely with metal dowels? A cubist arrangement of stern angles and purposeful curves. Geometry and flesh. Eight of us, counting Madam Bessant.

At seven-thirty sharp we begin, mugs of coffee set to one side. The routines of those weekly lessons are so powerfully set after a few weeks that only the most exigent of emergencies can breach them. We play as one person, your flutey B minor is mine, my slim tonal accomplishment yours. Madam Bessant's blunt womanly elbows rise out sideways like a pair of duck wings and signal for attention. Her fretfulness gives way to authority. *Alors,* she announces, and we begin. Alpine reaches are what we try for. God marching in his ziggurat heaven. Oxygen mists that shiver the scalp. Music so cool and muffled it seems smoothed into place by a thumb. Between pieces we kid around, noodle for clarity, for what Madam Bessant calls roundness of tone, *rondure, rondure.* Music and hunger, accident and intention meet here as truly as they did in the ancient courts of Asia Minor. *"Pas mal,"* nods our dear Madam, taking in breath, not wanting to handicap us with praise; this a world we're making, after all, not just a jumble of noise.

We don't know what to do with all the amorous steam in the room. We're frightened of it, but committed to making more. We start off each lesson with our elementary Mozart bits and pieces from the early weeks, then the more lugubrious Haydn, then Bach, all texture and caution—our small repertoire slowly expanding—and always we end the evening with an intricate new exercise, something tricky to bridge the week, so many flagged, stepped notes crowded together that the page in front of us is black. We hesitate. Falter. Apologize by means of our nervy young laughter. "It will come," encourages Madam Bessant with the unlicensed patience of her métier. We read her true meaning: the pledge that in seven days we'll be back here again, reassembled, another Wednesday night arrived at, our unbroken circle. Foul-mouthed Lonnie H. with her starved-looking fingers ascends a steep scale, and you respond, solidly, distinctively, your head arcing back and forth, back and forth, a neat two-inch slice. The contraction of your throat forms a lovely knot of deliberation. (I loved you more than the others, but, like a monk, allowed myself no distinctions.) On and on, the timid fingerings repeat and repeat, picking up the tempo or slowing it down, putting a sonorous umbrella over our heads, itself made of rain, a translucent roof, temporary, provisional—we never thought otherwise, we never thought at all. Madam Bessant regards her watch. How quickly the time ...

In Montreal, in January, on a Wednesday evening. The linoleum-floored basement room is our salon, our conservatory. This is a space carved out of the nutty wood of foreverness. Windows, door, music stands and chairs, all of them battered, all of them worn slick and giving up a craved-for weight of classicism. The walls exude a secretive decaying scent, of human skin, of footwear, of dirty pink paint flaking from the pipes. Half the overhead lights are burned out, but it would shame us to complain. To notice. Madam Bessant—who tolerates the creaky chairs, the grudging spotted ceiling globes, our sprawling bodies, our patched jeans, our cigarette smoke, our outdoor boots leaking slush all over the floor, our long uncombed hair—insists that the door be kept shut during class, this despite the closeness of the overheated air, choking on its own interior odors of jointed ductwork and mice and dirt.

Her baton is a slim metal rod, like a knitting needle—perhaps it *is* a knitting needle—and with this she energetically beats and stirs and prods. At the start of the lessons there seems such an amplitude of time that we can afford to be careless, to chat away between pieces and make jokes about our blunders, always our own blunders, no one else's; our charity is perfect. The room, which by now seems a compaction of the whole gray, silent frozen city, fills up with the reticulation of musical notes, curved lines, spontaneous response, actions, and drawn breath. You have one of your head colds, and between pieces stop and shake cough drops, musically, out of a little blue tin.

Something else happens. It affects us all, even Mr. Mooney with his criminal lips and eyes, even Lonnie H. who boils and struts with dangerous female smells. We don't just play the music, we *find* it. What opens before us on our music stands, what we carry in with us on our snow-sodden parkas and fuzzed-up hair, we know for the first time, hearing the notes just as they came, unclothed out of another century when they were nothing but small ink splashes, as tentative and quick on their trim black shelves as the finger Madam Bessant raises to her lips—her signal that we are to begin again, at the beginning, again and again.

She is about forty. Old, in our eyes. Not a beauty, not at all, except when she smiles, which is hardly ever. Her face is a somatic oval with a look of having been handled, molded; a high oily worried forehead, but unlined. A pair of eye glasses, plastic framed, and an ardor for clear appraisal that tells you she wore those same glasses, or similar ones, through a long comfortless girlhood, through a muzzy, joyless adolescence, forever breathing on their lenses and attempting to polish them beyond their optical powers, rubbing them on the hems of dragging skirts or the tails of unbecoming blouses. She has short, straight hair, almost black, and wears silvery ear clips, always the same pair, little curly snails of blackened silver, and loose cheap sweaters that sit rawly at the neck. Her neck, surprisingly, is a stem of sumptuous flesh, pink with health, as are her wrists and the backs of her busy, rhythmically rotating hands. On one wrist is a man's gold watch that she checks every few minutes, for she must be home by ten o'clock, as she frequently reminds us, to relieve the baby sitter, a mere girl of fourteen. There are three children at home, all boys—that much we know. Her husband, *a* husband, is not in the picture. Not mentioned, not ever. We sense domestic peril, or even tragedy, the kind of tragedy that bears down without mercy.

Divorce, you think. (This is after class, across the street, drinking beer at Le Piston.) Or widowed. Too young to be a widow, Lonnie H. categorically says. Deserted maybe. Who says that? One of us— Rhonda? Deserted for a younger, more beautiful woman? This seems possible and fulfills an image of drama and pain we are prepared to embrace; we begin to believe it; soon we believe it unconditionally.

We never talk politics after class, not in this privileged love-drugged circle—we've had enough of politics, more than enough. Our talk is first about Madam Bessant, our tender concern for her circumstances, her children, her baby sitter just fourteen years old, her absent husband, her fretful attention to the hour, her sense of having always to hurry away, her coat not quite buttoned or her gloves pulled on. We also discuss endlessly, without a touch of darkness, the various ways each of us has found to circumvent our powerlessness. How to get cheap concert tickets, for instance. How to get on the pogey. Ways to ride the Métro free. How to break a lease, how to badger a landlady into repairing the water heater. Where to go for half-priced baked goods. Cecile Landreau is the one who tells us the name of the baked goods outlet. She has a large, clean ice-maiden face and comes from a little town out west, in Alberta, a town with a rollicking comical name. She gets a laugh every time she mentions it, and she mentions it often. A lively and obstinate girl—you remember—and highly adaptive. She moved to Montreal just one year before and already she knows where to get things cheap: discount shoes, winter coats direct from the manufacturer, art supplies marked down. She never pays full price. ("You think I'm nuts?") Her alto recorder, a soft pine-colored Yamaha, she bought in a pawn shop for ten dollars and keeps it in a pocketed leather case that she made herself in a leathercraft course, also offered at the Y.

The poverty we insinuate is part real and part desire. We see ourselves as accidental survivors crowded to the shores of a cynical economy. By evasion, by mockery, by a mutual nibbling away at substance, we manage to achieve a dry state of asceticism that feeds on itself. We live on air and water or nothing at all; you would think from the misty way we talk we had never heard of parents or cars or real estate or marital entanglements. The jobs we allude to are seasonal and casual, faintly amusing, mildly degrading. So are our living arrangements and our live-in companions. For the sake of each other, out of our own brimming imaginations, we impoverish ourselves, but this is not a burdensome poverty; we exalt in it, and with our empty pockets and eager charity, we're prepared to settle down after our recorder lesson at a corner table in Le Piston and nurse a single beer until midnight.

But Mr. Mooney is something else. Hungry for membership in our ranks, he insists loudly on buying everyone a second round, and a third. Robert is his first name, Robert Mooney. He speaks illiterate French and appalling English. Reaching into his back pocket for his wallet, a thick hand gripping thick leather, he's cramped by shadows, blurred of feature, older than the rest of us, older by far, maybe even in his fifties, one of those small, compact, sweet-eyed, supple-voiced men you used to see floating around certain quarters of Montreal, ducking behind tabloids or grabbing short ryes or making endless quick phone calls from public booths.

Here in Le Piston, after our recorder lesson, he drops a handful of coins on the table and some bills, each one a transparent, childish offer of himself. My round, he says, without a shred of logic. He has stubby blackened fingers and alien appetites, also built-up shoes to give himself height, brutal hair oil, gold slashes in his back teeth. We drink his beer down fast, without pleasure, ashamed. He watches us, beaming.

All he wants is a portion of our love, and this we refuse. Our reasons are discreditable. His generosity. His age. His burnished leather coat, the way it fits snugly across his round rump. His hair oil and puttied jowls. Stubble, pores, a short thick neck, history. The way the beer foam nudges up against his dark lip. Any minute he's likely to roister or weep or tell a joke about a Jew and a Chinaman or order a plate of *frites*. The joke, if he tells it, we'll absorb without blinking; the *frites* we'll consume down to the last crystal of salt. Dispassionate acts performed out of our need to absolve him. To absolve ourselves.

Robert Mooney is a spoiler, a pernicious interloper who doesn't even show up until the third Wednesday when we've already done two short Mozart pieces and are starting in on Haydn, but there he is in the doorway, his arms crossed over his boxer's chest. A shuffling awkward silence, then mumbled introductions, and bad grace all around except for Madam Bessant who doesn't even notice. Doesn't even *notice*. Our seven stretches to eight. An extra chair is found, clatteringly unfolded and squashed between yours and Pierre's. (Pierre of the cowboy boots and gold earring, as though you need reminding.) Into this chair Mr. Mooney collapses, huffing hard and scrambling with his thick fingers to find his place in the book Madam Bessant kindly lends him until he has an opportunity to buy one of his own.

Layers of incongruity radiate around him: the unsecured history that begs redemption, rough questions stored in silence. How has this man, for instance, this Robert Mooney, acquired a taste for medieval instruments in the first place? And by what manner has he risen to the advanced level? And through what mathematical improbability has he come into contact with Mozart and with the gentle Madam Bessant and the YMCA Winter Enrichment Program and with us, our glare of nonrecognition? When he chomps on his mouthpiece with his moist monkey mouth we think of cigars or worse. With dwindling inattention he caresses his instrument, which is old and beautifully formed. He fingers the openings clumsily, yet is able to march straight through the first exercise with a rhythm so vigorous and unhesitating you'd think he'd been preparing it for months. He has nothing of your delicacy, of course, nor Pierre's even, and he can't begin to sight read the way Rhonda can—remember Rhonda? Of course you remember Rhonda, who could forget her? Mr. Mooney rides roughshod over poor Rhonda, scrambles right past her with his loud marching notes blown sharply forward as if he were playing a solo. *"Bon,"* Madam Bessant says to him after he bursts through to the end of his second lesson. She addresses him in exactly the same tone she uses for us, employing the same little fruited nodes of attention. "Clearly you know how to phrase," she tells him, and her face cracks with a rare smile.

The corners of our mouths tuck in; withholding, despising. But what is intolerable in our eyes is our own intolerance, so shabby and sour beside Madam Bessant's spontaneously bestowed praise. We can't bear it another minute; we surrender in a cloudburst of sentiment. And so, by a feat of inversion, Robert Mooney wins our love and enters our circle, enters it raggedly but forever. His contradictions, his ruptured history, match our own—if the truth were known. Seated at the damp table at Le Piston he opens his wallet yet again and buys rounds of beer, and at the end of the evening, on a slicked white street, with the moon shrunk down to a chip, we embrace him.

We embrace each other, all of us, a rough huddle of wool outerwear and arms, our cold faces brushing together, our swiftly applied poultice of human flesh.

It was Rhonda of all people, timorous Rhonda, who initiated the ceremonial embrace after our first lesson and trip to Le Piston. Right there on the sidewalk, acting out of who knows what wild impulse, she simply threw open her arms and invited us in. We were shy the first time, not used to being so suddenly enfolded, not knowing where it would lead. We were also young and surprised to be let loose in the world so soon, trailing with us our differently colored branches of experience, terrified at presuming or pushing up too close. If it had been anyone other than Rhonda offering herself, we might have held back, but who could refuse her outspread arms and the particularity of her smooth camel coat? (Do you agree? Tell me yes or no.) The gravest possible pleasure was offered and seized, this hugging, this not-quite kiss.

Already after three weeks it's a rite, our end-of-evening embrace, rather solemn but with a suggestion of benediction, each of us taken in turn by the others and held for an instant, a moonlit choreographed spectacle. At this moment our ardor grows dangerous and threatens to overflow. This extemporaneous kind of street-love paralyzes the unsteady. (The youth of the eighties would snort to see it.) One step further and we'd be actors in a shabby old play, too loaded with passion to allow revision. For that reason we keep our embrace short and chaste, but the whole evening, the whole week in fact, bends toward this dark public commerce of arms and bodies and the freezing murmur that accompanies it. Until next week. Next Wednesday. (A passport, a guarantee of safe conduct.) *A la prochaine.*

One night in early March Rhonda appears in class with red eyes. The redness matches the long weepy birthmark that starts beneath her left ear and spills like rubbery fluid down the side of her neck.

You glance up at her and notice, then open your big woven bag for a Kleenex. "It's the wind," you say, to spare her. "There's nothing worse than a March wind." We're well into Bach by this time and, of all of us, Rhonda handles Bach with the greatest ease. This you remember, how she played with the unsupported facility that comes from years of private lessons, not that she ever mentions this, not a word of it, and not that we inquire. We've learned, even Mr. Mooney has learned, to fall back and allow Rhonda to lead us through the more difficult passages. But tonight her energy is frighteningly reduced. She falters and slides and, finally, halfway through the new piece, puts down her recorder, just places it quietly on the floor beneath her chair and runs, hobbling unevenly, out of the room.

Madam Bessant is bewildered—her eyes open wide behind her specs—but she directs us to carry on, and we do, limping along to an undistinguished conclusion. Then Lonnie H. goes off in search of Rhonda.

Lonnie H. is a riddle, a paradox. Her hair is as densely, dully orange as the plastic shopping bag in which she carries her portfolio of music and the beaded leather flip-flops she wears during class. That walk of hers—she walks with the savage assurance of the young and combative, but on Wednesday night at least she tries to keep her working-class spite in check; you can see her sucking in her breath and biting down on those orange lips.

Later, when we're doing our final exercise, the two of them, Rhonda and Lonnie H., reappear. A consultation has been held in the corridor or in the washroom. Rhonda is smiling fixedly. Lonnie H. is looking wise and sad. "An affair of the heart," she whispers to us later as we put on our coats and prepare to cross the street to Le Piston. An affair of the heart— the phrase enters my body like an injection of sucrose, its improbable sweetness. It's not what we've come to expect of the riddlesome Lonnie. But she says it knowingly—an affair of the heart—and the words soften her tarty tangle-haired look of anarchy, make her almost serene.

Some time later, weeks later or perhaps that very night, I see Pierre with his warpish charm reach under the table at Le Piston and take

Rhonda's hand in his. He strokes her fingers as though he possesses the fire of invention. He has a set of neglected teeth, a stammer, and there is something amiss with his scalp, a large roundness resembling, under the strands of his lank Jesus hair, a wreath of pink plastic. His chin is short and witty, his long elastic body ambiguous. The left ear, from which a gold hoop dangles, is permanently inflamed.

It is Pierre who tells us one evening the truth about Madam Bessant's husband. The story has reached him through a private and intricately convoluted family pipeline: the ex-husband of a cousin of Pierre's sister-in-law (or something of this order) once lived in the same apartment block as Monsieur and Madam Bessant, on the same floor in fact, and remembered that the nights were often disturbed by the noise of crying babies and the sound of Monsieur Bessant, who was a piano teacher, playing Chopin, often the same nocturne again and again, always the same. When the piano playing stopped abruptly one day, the neighbors assumed that someone had complained. There was also a rumor, because he was no longer seen coming or going, that Monsieur Bessant was sick. This rumor was verified one morning, suddenly and terribly, by the news of his death. He had, it seemed, collapsed in a downtown Métro station on a steamy summer day, just toppled off the platform into the path of an approaching train. And one more detail. Pierre swallows as he says it. The head was completely separated from the body.

What are we to do with this story? We sit for some time in silence. It is a story too filled with lesions and hearsay, yet it is also, coming from the artless, stammering Pierre, curiously intact. All its elements fit; its sequence is wholly convincing—Monsieur Bessant, swaying dizzily one minute and cut to ribbons the next, people screaming, the body collected and identified, the family informed, heat rising in waves and deforming the future. Everything altered, changed forever.

"Of course it might have been a heart attack," Pierre says, wanting now to cancel the whole account and go back to the other, simpler story of an unfeeling husband who abandons his wife for a younger woman.

"Or a stroke," Cecile Landreau suggests. "A stroke is not all that unusual, even for a quite young man. I could tell you stories."

Robert Mooney keeps his eyes on the chilly neck of his beer bottle. And he keeps his mouth clapped shut. All the while the rest of us offer theories for Monsieur Bessant's sudden collapse—heat stroke, low blood sugar—Robert keeps a hard silence. "A helluva shock" is all he says, and then mumbles, "for her."

A stranger entering Le Piston and overhearing us might think we were engaged in careless gossip. And, seeing Pierre reach for Rhonda's hand under the table, might suspect carnal pressure. Or infer something flirtatious about Cecile Landreau, toying with her charm bracelet in a way that solicits our protection. And calculating greed (or worse, condescension) in our blithe acceptance of Robert Mooney's rounds of beer. Lonnie H. in a knitted muffler, pungent with her own bodily scent, could easily be misunderstood and her cynical, slanging raptures misread. A stranger could never guess at the kind of necessity, innocent of the sensual, the manipulative, that binds us together, that has begun as early as that first lesson when we entered the room and saw Madam Bessant tensely handing out purple mimeographed sheets and offsetting the chaos of our arrival. We were ashamed in those first few minutes, ashamed to have come. We felt compromised, awkward, wanting badly to explain ourselves, why we were there. We came to learn, we might have said had anyone asked, to advance, to go forward, something of that order. Nothing crystallizes good impulses so much as the wish to improve one's self. This is one of the things that doesn't change.

After that first night, we relaxed. The tang of the schoolroom played to our affections and so did the heat of our closely drawn chairs, knees almost touching so that the folds of your skirt aligned with my thigh, though from all appearances you failed to notice. The fretfulness with which Madam Bessant regarded her watch put us on our honor, declared meanness and mischief out of bounds, demanded that we make the allotted time count—and so we brought our best selves and nothing else. Our youth, our awkwardness, our musical naiveté yoked good will to virtue, as sacredness attaches itself invisibly to certain rare moments.

I exaggerate, I romanticize—I can hear you say this, your smiling reproach. I have already, you claim, given poor Pierre an earring and a stammer, accorded Lonnie H. an orange plastic bag and a sluttish mouth, branded Rhonda with the humiliation of a port-wine birthmark when a small white scar was all she had or perhaps only its psychic equivalent, high up on her cheek, brushed now and then unconsciously with the back of her hand. But there's too much density in the basement room to stop for details.

Especially now with our time so short, five more weeks, four more weeks. Some nights we linger at Le Piston until well after midnight, often missing the last train home, preferring to walk rather than cut our time short. Three more weeks. Our final class is the fourteenth of May and we sense already the numbered particles of loss we will shortly be assigned. When we say good night—the air is milder, spring now—we're reminded of our rapidly narrowed perspective. We hang on tighter to each other, since all we know of consequence tells us that we may not be this lavishly favored again.

Lately we've been working hard, preparing for our concert. This is what Madam Bessant calls it—a concert. A little program to end the term. Her suggestion, the first time she utters it—"We will end the season with a concert"—dumfounds us. An absurdity, an embarrassment. We are being asked to give a recital, to perform. Like trained seals or small children. Called upon to demonstrate our progress. Cecile Landreau's eyebrows go up in protest; her chin puckers the way it does when she launches into one of her picaresque western anecdotes. But no one says a word—how can we? Enigmatic, inconsolable Madam Bessant has offered up the notion of a concert. She has no idea of what we know, that the tragic narrative of her life has been laid bare. She speaks calmly, expectantly; she is innocence itself, never guessing how charged we are by our guilty knowledge, how responsible. The hazards of the grown-up life are settled on her face. We know everything about the Chopin nocturne, repeated and repeated, and about the stumbling collapse on the hot tracks, the severed head and bloodied torso. When she speaks of a concert we can only nod and agree. Of course there must be a concert.

It is decided then. We will do nine short pieces. Nothing too onerous though, the program must be kept light, entertaining.

And who is to be entertained? Madam Bessant patiently explains: we are to invite our friends, our families, and these *invitées* will form an audience for our concert. A *soirée,* she calls it now. Extra chairs have already been requisitioned, also a buffet table, and she herself— she brings her fingers and thumbs together to make a little diamond—she herself will provide refreshments.

This we won't hear of. Lonnie H. immediately volunteers a chocolate cake, Robert Mooney says to leave the wine to him, he knows a dealer. You insist on taking responsibility for a cheese and cold-cuts tray. Cecile and Rhonda will bring coffee, paper plates, plastic forks and knives. And Pierre and I, what do we bring?—potato chips, pretzels, nuts? Someone writes all this down, a list. Our final celebratory evening is to be orderly, apt, joyous, memorable.

Everyone knows the fourteenth of May in Montreal is a joke. It can be anything. You can have a blizzard or a heat wave. But that year, our year, it is a warm rainy night. A border of purple collects along the tops of the warehouses across the street from the Y, and pools of oily violet shimmer on the rough pavement, tinted by the early night sky. Only Madam Bessant arrives with an umbrella; only Madam Bessant *owns* an umbrella. Spinning it vigorously, glancing around, setting it in a corner to dry. *Voilà,* she says, addressing it matter-of-factly, speaking also to the ceiling and partially opened windows.

We are all prompt except for Robert Mooney, who arrives a few minutes late with a carton of wine and with his wife on his arm— hooked there, hanging on tight. We see a thick girdled matron with square dentures and a shrub of bronze curls, dense as Brillo pads. Gravely, taking his time, he introduces her to us—"May I present Mrs. Mooney"—preserving the tender secret of her first name, and gently he leads her toward one of the folding chairs, arranging her cardigan around her shoulders as if she were an invalid. She settles in, handbag stowed on the floor, guarded on each side by powerful ankles. She has the hard compact head of a baby lion and a shy smile packed with teeth.

Only Robert Mooney has risked us to indifferent eyes. The rest of us bring no one. Madam Bessant's mouth goes into a worried circle and she casts an eye across the room where a quantity of food is already laid out on a trestle table. A cheerful paper tablecloth, bright red in color, has been spread. Also a surprise platter of baby shrimp and ham. Wedges of lemon straddle the shrimp. A hedge of parsley presses against the ham. About our absent guests, we're full of excuses, surprisingly similar—friends who canceled at the last minute, out-of-town emergencies, illness. Madam Bessant shrugs minutely, sighs, and looks at her watch. She is wearing a pink dress with large white dots. When eight o'clock comes she clears her throat and says, "I suppose we might as well go through our program anyway. It will be good practice for us, and perhaps Madam Mooney will bear with us."

Oh, we play beautifully, ingeniously, with a strict sense of ceremony, never more alert to our intersecting phrases and spelled out consonance. Lonnie H. plays with her eyes sealed shut, as though dreaming her way through a tranced lifetime, backward and also forward, extending outward, collapsing inward. Your foot does its circling journey, around and around, keeping order. Next to you is Robert Mooney whose face, as he puffs away, has grown rosy and tender, a little shy, embarrassed by his virtue, surprised by it too. Rhonda's forehead creases into that touching squint of hers. (You can be seduced by such intense looks of concentration; it's that rare.) Cecile's wrist darts forward, turning over the sheets, never missing a note, and Pierre's fingers move like water around his tricks of practiced tension and artful release.

And Mrs. Mooney, our audience of one, listens and nods, nods and listens, and then, after a few minutes, when we're well launched, leans down and pulls some darning from the brocade bag on the floor. A darkish tangle, a lapful of softness. She works away at it throughout our nine pieces. These must be Robert Mooney's socks she's mending, these long dark curls of wool wrapped around her left hand, so intimately stabbed by her darting needle. Her mouth is busy, wetting the thread, biting it off, full of knowledge. Between each of our pieces she looks up, surprised, opens her teeth and says in a good-natured, good-sport voice, "Perfectly lovely." At the end, after the conclusion has been signaled with an extra measure of silence, she stows the socks in the bag, pokes the needle resolutely away, smiles widely with her stretched mouth and begins to applaud.

Is there any sound so strange and brave and ungainly as a single person clapping in a room? All of us, even Madam Bessant, instinctively shrink from the rhythmic unevenness of it, and from the crucial difficulty of knowing when it will stop. If it ever does stop. The brocade bag slides off Mrs. Mooney's lap to the floor, but still she goes on applauding. The furious upward growth of her hair shimmers and so do the silver veins on the back of her hands. On and on she claps, powerless, it seems, to stop. We half rise, hover in mid-air, then resume our seats. At last Robert Mooney gets up, crosses the room to his wife and kisses her loudly on the lips. A smackeroo—the word comes to me on little jointed legs, an artifact from another era, out of a comic book. It breaks the spell. Mrs. Mooney looks up at her husband, her hard lion's head wrapped in surprise. "Lovely," she pronounces. "Absolutely lovely."

After that the evening winds down quickly. Rhonda gives a tearful rambling speech, reading from some notes she's got cupped in her hand, and presents Madam Bessant with a pair of earrings shaped, if I remember, like treble clefs. We have each put fifty cents or maybe a dollar toward these earrings, which Madam Bessant immediately puts on, dropping her old silver snails into her coin purse, closing it with a snap, her life beginning a sharp new chapter.

Of course there is too much food. We eat what we can, though hardly anyone touches the shrimp, and then divide between us the quantities of leftovers, a spoiling surfeit that subtly discolors what's left of the evening.

Robert and his wife take their leave. "Gotta get my beauty sleep," he says loudly. He shakes our hands, that little muscular fist, and wishes

us luck. What does he mean by luck? Luck with what? He says he's
worried about getting a parking ticket. He says his wife gets tired, that
her back acts up. "So long, gang," he says, backing out of the room and
tripping slightly on a music stand, his whole dark face screwed up into
what looks like an obscene wink of farewell.

Madam Bessant, however, doesn't notice. She turns to us smiling,
her odd abbreviated little teeth opening to deliver a surprise. She has
arranged for a different baby sitter tonight. For once there's no need for
her to rush home. She's free to join us for an hour at Le Piston. She
smiles shyly; she knows, it seems, about our after-class excursions,
though how we can't imagine.

But tonight Le Piston is closed temporarily for renovations. We find
the door locked. Brown wrapping paper has been taped across the
windows. In fact, when it opens some weeks later it has been transformed into a produce market, and today it's a second-hand bookshop
specializing in mysteries.

Someone mentions another bar a few blocks away, but Madam Bessant
sighs at the suggestion; the sigh comes spilling out of an inexpressible,
segmented exhaustion which none of us understands. She sighs a second
time, shifts her shopping bag loaded with leftover food. The treble clefs
seem to drag on her ear lobes. Perhaps, she says, she should go straight
home after all. Something may have gone wrong. You can never know
with children. Emergencies present themselves. She says good night to
each of us in turn. There is some confusion, as though she has just this
minute realized how many of us there are and what we are called. Then
she walks briskly away from us in the direction of the Métro station.

The moment comes when we should exchange addresses and phone
numbers or make plans to form a little practice group to meet on a
monthly basis perhaps, maybe in the undeclared territory of our own
homes, perhaps for the rest of our lives.

But it doesn't happen. The light does us in, the too-soft spring
light. There's too much ease in it, it's too much like ordinary
daylight. A drift of orange sun reaches us through a break in the build-
ings and lightly mocks our idea of finding another bar. It forbids

absolutely a final embrace, and something nearer shame than embarrassment makes us anxious to end the evening quickly and go off in our separate directions.

Not forever, of course; we never would have believed that. Our lives at that time were a tissue of suspense with surprise around every corner. We would surely meet again, bump into each other in a restaurant or maybe even in another evening class. A thousand spontaneous meetings could be imagined.

It may happen yet. The past has a way of putting its tentacles around the present. You might—you, my darling, with your black tights and cough drops—you might feel an urge to write me a little note, a few words for the sake of nostalgia and nothing more. I picture the envelope waiting in my mailbox, the astonishment after all these years, the wonder that you tracked me down. Your letter would set into motion a chain of events—since the links between us all are finely sprung and continuous—and the very next day I might run into Pierre on St. Catherine's. What a shout of joy we'd give out, the two of us, after our initial amazement. That very evening a young woman, or perhaps not so very young, might rush up to me in the lobby of a concert hall: Lonnie H., quieter now, but instantly recognizable, that bush of orange hair untouched by gray. The next day I imagine the telephone ringing: Cecile or Rhonda—why not?

We would burrow our way back quickly to those winter nights, saying it's been too long, it's been too bad, saying how the postures of love don't really change. We could take possession of each other once again, conjure our old undisturbed, unquestioning chemistry. The wonder is that it hasn't already happened. You would think we made a pact never to meet again. You would think we put an end to it, just like that—saying good-bye to each other, and meaning it.

MADELEINE THIEN

Four Days from Oregon

I

Once, in the middle of the night, our mother Irene sat on our bed and listed off the ways she was unhappy. She looked out the window and stroked our hair and sometimes she lapsed into silence, as if even she didn't know the full extent of it, where to finish, when to hold back. And all the things that made her unhappy were mixed in with things that made her happy, too, like this house. It was full to the brim. Sometimes, she said, she sat in the bathroom because it was the smallest room with a door that locked. But even then she could hear us, me and my sisters Helen and Joanne, and our father, all of us creaking the floorboards and talking over the television and filling the quiet. Hearing us pulled her out every time. She would come out of the bathroom and track us down. She said she wanted to tuck us under her arm like a rolled-up paper and run away.

We were just kids then—Helen was nine, Joanne was seven, and I was six—but we thought of our mother as a young girl. She cried so much and had a temper. She joked about running off on her thirtieth birthday. "Almost there," she told us, joking. "Better pack your bags."

When our mother was unhappy, she broke things. She slammed the kitchen door over and over until its window crumpled and shattered to the floor. In our bare feet, we tiptoed around the pieces. Our father ignored it. He said, "Tell your crazy mother there's a phone call for her." He said *crazy* with a funny look in his eye, like he didn't really believe it. But we saw it ourselves, the plates flying from her hands, her face empty. Our father turned away and left the house. He walked slowly down the alley.

Only once did Irene leave us. We waited for her tirelessly. In the middle of the night, in our bed wider than a boat, we listened for her car on the road. We fought sleep, but she didn't come that night or the next. While she was gone, our father sat at the kitchen table like an old man. Already his hair had tufts of grey and his skin hung loose around his mouth and eyes. "Like a dog," he said, running his hands over his head. "Don't I look just like a dog?"

My sisters and I rode our bikes up and down the alley. When we were winded, we played in the garage, climbing up onto the roof of our father's brown Malibu. He poked his head in, said, "What's this, now?"

"Tea party," Helen told him, though we weren't really doing anything.

He nodded, "You like it better in the garage than in the house. It's your mother. There's something wrong in her head."

One day after school, she was back on the couch, her fingers ragged from worry. "I missed you," she said, pulling us in. My sisters and I sat on top of her body. We held her arms and legs down while she laughed, struggling to sit up.

Sometimes Irene was well and she put on the *Nutcracker Suite,* twirling us around the room. At times like this, she would embrace our father. She would kiss his face, his eyebrows and mouth. They waltzed around the living room. She kept stepping on his feet. He shrugged. "It's not the end of the world," he said.

Our mother shook her head. "No," she told him, "it never is."

THE FIRST TIME Tom came by, he shook our hands. He said, "So you're the Terrible Threesome," winking at us. Irene told us he was someone she worked with in the department store. He worked in Sports and Leisure. The second time he came, he brought three badminton racquets and a container full of plastic birdies. He and Irene sat on the steps drinking pink-tinted coolers. We batted the racquets through the air, knocking the birdies from one side of the lawn to the other. Joanne, always moody, aimed one through the tire swing. Another cleared the fence and landed in the neighbour's yard.

"Can't you hit straight?" Helen said, impatient.

Tom stood up on the balcony, waving his arms in the air. "I can bring some more tomorrow!"

Joanne turned her back on him and whipped one into the hedge.

Afterwards, Helen pocketed the last remaining birdie and we went down to the storage area beneath the porch. We planted the birdie in a cinder block, covered it with mud, then left it to bake in the afternoon sun. Through the floorboards we could hear Irene's voice, shy and laughing, and the long silences that came and went all afternoon, interrupted by the creaky sound of the screen door swinging shut. We watched Tom drive away, his hand stretching out of the car window, waving back to us.

Our father came home at six o'clock. Helen told him the screen door needed oiling again and he took us out back, oil on his hands. He rubbed the oil along the metal spoke so that when he threw the door open again it closed slow as ever, but without a sound on the wind, just the quiet click of the latch closing.

My sisters and I sat outside with him, our bare legs dangling between the porch steps. Our father pulled a photograph from his pocket. He'd come across it at the office, he explained, a picture of Main Street from a hundred years ago. In the photograph, there were no cars, just wide streets but no concrete, dirt piled down, women in long dresses, their hems bringing up the dust. I told my father I couldn't imagine streets without cars, trolleys and everything, horses idling on the corners. He said, "It's progress, you see, and it comes whether you welcome it or not."

Our father laid the photograph down. He said he could stand on the back steps and stare out until the yard fell away. He could see the house where he grew up, plain as day. It was in another country, and he remembered fields layered into the hillside. A person could grow anything there—tea, rice, coffee beans. I would always remember this because he had never talked about these things before. When he was young, he wanted to be a priest. But he came to Canada and fell in love with our mother.

WE SPENT THAT SUMMER sunning in the backyard. Helen would grab the tire swing and hurl it loose. Joanne and I lay flat on the grass, fighting the urge to blink, watching it swoop towards us. The tire raced above us, rubber-smell fleeting and then blue sky.

We were there the day Irene came running out in her bare feet. She was wearing a white flowered dress, and her hair, wet from the shower, had soaked the back. My sisters and I stood up uncertainly when we saw her coming. She grabbed our wrists and dragged us into the house and upstairs to her bedroom. Through the window we saw our father turn into the alley, then drive straight onto the back lawn. He climbed out, forgetting to slam the car door behind him. We heard him running up the stairs. "Irene!" he yelled. "Irene!"

She looked at us. "Tom will be here soon."

"Irene!" Our father pounded the door with his fist. "Open this goddamned door!"

She shook her head at us. "He wasn't supposed to find out until later," she said. We stood beside the bed, next to her luggage, three plastic-shell suitcases, pale green, lined up all in a row. I went over to Irene and pulled at her arms, trying to get her attention. She looked past me, then stepped up to the door, unlocked it, and our father burst inside, his arms swinging. He was still in work clothes, suit pants and a white dress shirt. He was raging at Irene, saying, "I know, I knew it all along! You think I *didn't* know?" My father drove his fist into the closet door and the wood splintered. Then he turned around and grabbed the curtains and pulled them off the rod and the fabric balled up on the ground. We heard tires on gravel, turned to look through the window and saw Tom's car pulling up against the curb. Our father sank down, crying. "Do you know what I've put up with? Everything you do. All your crazy talk. Is this what I deserve?"

Irene folded her arms across her chest and stared at her feet. I wanted to go to my father but I could barely recognize him. His face was red and puffy, streaked with tears. We heard the front door open, Tom coming up the stairs. All of us listened to him and waited and then he was there. He held his back straight, looked right at Irene, and came into the room.

I thought my father would stand up, come at him, splinter his face the way he'd splintered the closet. He would tell Irene that enough was enough. But my father got to his feet, his face slick with sweat, and walked towards us. He crouched down to touch us but I backed away from him. My sister Helen said, "Dad, what's happening?"

He looked at her, his face old, suddenly. "You're going with them," he answered, his voice barely audible. "That's what your mother wants." He turned away from us and said to Irene, "Go wherever the hell you want." He never even looked at Tom.

Irene went to the window and watched him stagger down the back steps, walk across the lawn to the car. She screamed down at him to get out. She went over to the desk, picked up a stack of papers, old bills, letters, and flung them out the window. They showered the lawn. She kept screaming for him to get out, get out, even while he was reversing the car. Helen looked out the window and said, "He's left." Irene didn't hear. She pulled his clothes from the closet, shirts and pants tangled together, and threw them after him. Tom came and put his arms around her but she pushed him away. My sister Joanne ran out of the room, down the stairs, and out onto the back lawn, in the direction of our father's car. But Helen and I just stood there, watching in shocked silence. Helen turned to our mother and said, "What have you done?" Irene sat down on the bed, unmoving.

That night, we climbed into Tom's car. I was sitting up in the front seat, between Tom and Irene. Tom turned out of the driveway and I looked back at the house, all the lights left on.

Behind us, my sisters stared straight ahead, exhausted from the arguments and the yelling. They clutched their backpacks to their knees. "Mom?" Joanne said, when Tom pulled onto the highway and the city vanished behind a corridor of trees. "Mom?" Joanne said again.

"What is it?"

"Where are we going?"

Irene smiled, her face gentle. "Don't worry."

"I'm worried."

"Don't worry. We won't get there tonight."

"When?"

"Tomorrow night."

"How long are we going for?"

"Just a few days. I promise. Just a little while. I didn't think it would happen this way. But it's okay. I'm not angry."

Joanne leaned back rigidly in the seat. Beside her, Helen reached her arms out and held on to her.

Irene turned and watched them in the side mirror, her fingers tapping absently on the passenger-side window.

II

Irene was leaving our father because she was in love with Tom. In the car, she explained to us how she had married our father when she was nineteen. He was a good man, she said. He loved her very much and she had loved him. But now she was thirty, and he was thirty, and they had changed. She wanted to do what was best for us. "It's nobody's fault," she said, turning to look at me. "Everything will be okay." Tom drove straight ahead. On a winding road, he pulled over and Irene jammed her body out of the passenger door. She leaned over and threw up on the gravel.

My older sisters fidgeted in the back seat. Helen had a habit of biting her lips until they bled. She chewed her fingernails raw. She was forever picking at herself, pulling loose bits of skin from the corners of her mouth, her elbows and cuticles. Irene always said to let her be, she'd grow out of it one day. In the car, Helen nibbled angrily on her fingers. "Where are you *taking* us?" she said at one point, kicking the back of Irene's seat with her sneaker. Tom glanced at her in the mirror but no one answered. Joanne stared grimly out the window and I fell in and out of sleep, lying tipped over on top of Irene's legs. None of us spoke.

The clock on the dashboard read 1:00 by the time we got to Long Beach. Tom drove right up on the sand and parked the car. We couldn't see anything but the moon and the stars. Tom explained about the moon and gravity, how the tides were pulled in and out.

He turned to look at us. "Why the glum faces?" he asked. "You'll see. In the morning it will be beautiful." I had moved into the back seat by then, and my sisters and I were huddled together. Tom smiled. "Oh, I see," he said. "I can see what it's going to be like. You girls are a team, right? *Triple Trouble.*" He laughed out loud.

"Why don't you just shut up?" Helen said.

Irene stretched her arm out and touched him. "Not now. It's too late for jokes."

Tom lowered his chin. He got out of the car by himself, a gust of wind tearing through the open door, and began unloading the trunk. There was a big orange tent with metal poles that Tom assembled in the dark. Irene shone a flashlight out the car window, the beam tracing circles across the trees and the sky.

She spoke to the dashboard. "Don't tell anyone your names. Not for a little while yet, okay? Not until we sort things out."

Tom built a fire, tramping off into the night and returning with an armload of wood. We fell asleep in the car and Irene woke us, half dragging and half carrying us inside and tucking us into sleeping bags. We slept side-by-side all in a row: me between Irene and Tom, then Helen and Joanne. Tom had left the fire burning. Helen spoke up in the darkness. "That's a fire hazard. You better put it out."

"Enough," Irene said.

Tom turned over and faced the tent wall and all of us lay in silence.

WE HATED THEM so much it hurt. Helen kept a journal and she wrote: *Irene is not our real mother. Our real mother is living with our real father and we've been kidnapped by these hooligans. When the time is right, my sisters and I will run away.* We walked in single file along the beach, Joanne rushing ahead, Helen staying back to wait for me. Together, we poked at sand dollars and starfish, combed the sand for unbroken shells. Helen said to me, "Do you understand what's happening?"

I nodded.

"We're moving. Do you know why?"

"Yes." I knew all too well.

"Don't worry," Helen told me, shaking her head. "We'll stick together. I'm going to take care of us." In front of us, Joanne ran in circles then collapsed into an angry ball. We sat beside her, watching the tide move in.

That first night on the beach, Tom shook his head at us, said, "What have you been up to all day? I was going to take you swimming." He showed us how to crouch down on our hands and knees and blow the fire so smoke rose thick from the wood. After dinner, Irene washed our hair under the cold-water tap, her fingers rubbing circles. She told us to go and dry by the fire and we stumbled away. Tom poked at the embers with a tree branch.

"How long will we stay here?" Helen asked.

Tom shrugged, "Who knows?"

"You shouldn't have brought us, then."

Irene stood behind us with her hands on her hips. "No," she said. "But it was either that or leave you altogether." Tom looked at her and Irene looked away, embarrassed.

Our mother slipped off her sandals and sat cross-legged on the ground beside us. She held out her arms for us but we just stood there, watching. She took hold of us and crowded us into her lap. We resisted at first but the smell of her seeped into our noses and her hair swung around and wrapped us in a dark cave. We held on to her too, our six hands grasping her wrists, her arms, anything we could reach. "It's only temporary," she said, kissing our hair. "Just to see. We'll wait a few days and then go home."

Tom said, "Wait a second, Irene—"

"They're my kids," she snapped. "They're mine, okay? I just want to wait and see."

Tom leaned towards us and touched her face with his thumbs. Irene shook her head and held us tightly. I wanted to run at him, stop thinking and push him down, fill his mouth with sand, push it up his nose until he stopped breathing. My whole body could be angry, mad as when Irene pushed the television over and the screen cracked and broke.

Tom unzipped the tent and crawled inside, Irene staring after him. The wind blew smoke from the fire all around us. "Wait for me here," she said, gently removing our hands. She crawled after Tom into the tent.

We watched smoke from the fire drift above our campsite, no sounds from either them or us. Every so often Joanne scratched at the dirt with her feet to say that we were still there. By the time Irene came out again, the trees were indistinguishable from the night. She poked at the fire with a branch, sending a gust of embers into the air.

WE PACED THE BEACH. With the tide out, it seemed possible to walk forever. Other kids played with plastic shovels, dumped out bucket after bucket, ran ocean water through the moats of their castles. We wandered circles around them, taking stock of their clothes and their toys. I wanted to go home, even if it meant more of the same, Irene picking up the dishes one by one and throwing them out onto the back porch. Our father read the paper at the kitchen table. Sometimes when Irene screamed and screamed, he looked at her with complete incomprehension, not knowing why her face changed like that, why she scratched welts on her arms and then slid down against the wall like she was falling. Coming home from school, one of our friends cried when she saw the spoons and knives all over the floor, the bottles and the cracked dishes.

My sister Helen was the most pragmatic of us three. She said, "When we're sixteen, we can go home again."

Joanne stared morosely at her feet. That afternoon, she lay down in her shorts and T-shirt and we slowly buried her in sand.

During the days, my sisters and I avoided swimming in the ocean. Years ago, our father had taught us to swim. In a green lake, we floated on our backs, our bodies losing buoyancy. Our mother stood knee-deep keeping watch, pointing out to our father which one of us was going under, and he would pop us up as if we were weightless, keep us floating on the surface.

On our second night at the beach, we heard strange animal noises. Helen said it was a bear, pawing at our tent with his paws. Joanne tried to wake Irene but she just rolled over and sighed in her sleep. I dreamed Tom was sitting in the bathtub and I pushed the electric radio into the water. His body slapped against the bathtub. I watched in disbelieving silence until he died, his chest grey and shiny, sliding slowly underwater.

THE NEXT DAY, Irene forced us to go on a picnic. They took us to an outcrop of giant, black rocks where the tide came up in towering breakers. Tom said, "That's a whale," and pointed to where none of us could see. We sat at a nearby picnic table, chewing cold chicken and looking off into the distance.

Tom said, "Shall we go out a little farther?" Hand in hand, he and Irene walked up to the rocks, then climbed out on their hands and knees. At rest, they looked like seagulls, perched and waiting.

"Jerks," Helen said, her eyebrows tensed.

Behind us, Joanne walked silently through our picnic site. She was gathering things one by one—the glass bowl of potato salad, the two-litre bottle of orange pop, Irene's sunglasses.

"Are you making a run for it?" Helen asked.

Joanne ignored her. She climbed up onto the rocks above a shallow pool. Turning her back to us, she held the glass bowl out. Irene had just bought it, along with our groceries. It shimmered in the air. Joanne turned to look at us and her hands opened. The bowl tumbled down, cracking hard on a rock. She let go of the pop bottle. It fell upright, bouncing as it went. Then Irene's sunglasses.

I turned and saw Tom running towards the picnic site.

Joanne waved her empty hands. "Goodbye," she said. "Goodbye."

Tom was standing there, his mouth open. "What has gotten into you? For Christ's sake," he said, shaking his head. "For Christ's fucking sake." He picked up what was left and pushed past us to the gravel parking lot.

"For *Christ's fucking sake*," Joanne said.

Irene just stood and watched us, her expression calm. There were drops of water on her skin and the sun caught on them and made them glitter. She started to move closer but we stared her down. She stopped walking, brushed her foot in the dirt and drew a line. Her voice was low. "You don't believe me now, but it's better like this. I know you think it couldn't be. You think nothing is worse than this. But believe me, there are worse things."

She put her arms around our shoulders and took us with her, back to the car.

Off the rocks and onto the gravel, I tried not to hear anything, not Tom or Irene or my sister's shoes on the rocks or the wind on the ocean or the rain starting to fall. We got into the car and Tom pulled roughly away from the parking lot.

After the car hit the highway, we were going fast and smooth. Tom said, "This is what I think. I think we should leave tomorrow. You don't think he'll follow us, right? You said so yourself, he doesn't give a damn. Four days is long enough. If he doesn't care, let's just go."

Our bodies fell together as if the car were tipping, one body slumped to the next. Irene's voice was barely audible. "Yes," she said, nodding. "Let's leave tomorrow."

Joanne was crying in the back seat. "How do you know?" she said. "How do you know he doesn't care?"

Helen put her hand on Joanne's head and stroked it back and forth. "Mom left a note. I saw it. He could come if he wanted to."

Tom looked sideways at Irene then back at the road.

"You have to tell us where we're going," Helen said. "It isn't fair to keep us in the dark."

"To stay with my sister," Tom said. "She has a cottage, right beside the ocean, just like here."

Irene's voice was barely audible. "Tom and I will take care of everything. When it's warm you can swim in the ocean. I'm going to get a job. In a store maybe. You'll meet all new kids."

"We already have friends," Helen said.

"New kids," Irene said, smiling stubbornly. "You'll make new friends."

Joanne shook her head. "We don't want new friends or a new school. You said we'd go back. You promised. You said we'd stay here a few days and then go home."

Tom cut in, "Look, it isn't easy for any of us."

"I don't know," Irene said.

"How come you can't keep your promises?"

"Don't talk to me that way."

"You *lied* to us. You said we'd go home."

"I didn't say that. I said maybe. Maybe isn't the same thing. And anyway it's too late to go back now."

"Why is it too late?"

"Because I've decided, okay?"

"You never asked us," Joanne said. "Maybe we would have stayed with him. Maybe we wouldn't have missed you. Do you understand? I miss him, maybe we wouldn't have missed you."

Irene didn't move. "I'm sorry," she said. "This wasn't the way it was supposed to happen."

She leaned towards Tom and then she half turned and her face was against his sleeve. We were waiting for her to lash out, to bang her fist against the window or throw something, smash the cassette tapes on the floor. But she stayed where she was and Tom patted her shoulder steadily. My sisters and I held still, as if we could change things by refusing to move.

The car hit eighty, ninety, one-twenty, and Tom looked sideways at Irene. He was nothing like our father. Tom's face was handsome and strong, and his hair, light blond, curled in tufts. Our father's face was dark and sad. Our father combed his hair with Brylcreem until it shone. He smelled of eucalyptus and cooking and warmth. But he and Tom looked at Irene with the same expression, mixed-up sadness and love and strange devotion.

OUR LAST NIGHT on the beach, we listened to them breathing, the heaviness of it like their bodies were emptying out. We listened for animals, for a bear to come crashing through the trees. It could hear that breathing, we thought, and it would be drawn to us.

They said words aloud, mumbled like they were whispering secrets. She said, "Tom," and he started awake, put his arm around her.

Joanne complained that her stomach hurt. She pressed it with her fingers, wondered aloud if she had cancer, or if she were dying, slowly, in the middle of the woods and no one around. We heard other campers walking by, saw the finger-probe of their flashlights sliding across the tent, heard the trudge-trudge of their feet on gravel. I lay with my forehead pressed against Helen's neck. Every so often she would loop one arm across my shoulders, as if to reassure me.

Still Irene and Tom slept. Even when the ocean sounded so loud it seemed like it was coming right at us, all the land pushed under like a broken bowl, they slept, breathing heavily. We fell in and out of dreams, finally waking hours after they had risen. Tom slid the metal poles smoothly through the loops and the tent came down, the orange fabric floating like a parachute towards us.

III

On the fourth night, we arrived in North Bend. One by one, we climbed out of Tom's car. I remember Irene standing in the motel parking lot looking over us. Tom had gone into the office alone to sign for the keys. The wind fanned Irene's hair out around her face and she looked at us, then down at her shoes, then back at us again. Standing under the motel lights, I thought none of this was real. Even then, I thought Irene would change her mind, she would take us home again and all of this would end.

They were standing in the motel room, their coats still on, when Irene broke down. Tom was walking from room to room, testing the light switches. "What will I do?" she said suddenly, raising her voice in desperation. "What have I done?"

Tom's voice was muffled in the background. Irene screamed that he had tricked her, he had made her come with him.

"Irene," he said. "Irene."

My sisters and I crept out the motel door, into the concrete parking lot. We stood beside Tom's car. Truthfully, I can't say that we were angry with her. Only that everything she was no longer surprised us. From where we stood we could see the ocean. If we looked down, we could see where it met the sky in a thin white line. The air smelled salty and cold. Finally, our mother came outside. "We'll go home," she was saying. "Tomorrow morning. We'll pack everything up and go home." She was looking past us, as if directing her words to the lights across the courtyard, to other people in other motel rooms. We didn't even bother answering. Helen reached over and held our mother around the waist. The top of her head was level with Irene's elbow. Joanne and I kicked at the gravel with our sneakers, sending the little rocks pinging off the cars. We heard the far-away whistle of a kettle going off and when we looked back, we saw Tom standing there, an outdoor lamp lighting his face, drawing fireflies to the air above him.

In the morning we woke up and found Tom and Irene sprawled together on the motel couch, their arms and legs tangled, Irene's hair spread out against Tom's hands.

THIS IS MY MOST VIVID MEMORY of my father: he was leaning over the veranda, his white shirt brilliant in the sun. Something about seeing him standing there, the neighbourhood quiet in the background, made me want to confide in him. My father reached his hand down to rest on my shoulder. I held up the badminton birdie we had buried in mud. "Guess who gave this to me," I said.

My father raised his eyebrows.

"I got it from Tom."

"Tom who?" He took his handkerchief out and folded it once, then again.

"Tom from Sports and Leisure," I said. I explained that Tom came to visit all the time. And he brought us presents. Badminton racquets and bouncy balls. He and Irene sat up here in the afternoons, drinking and doing nothing. But I was sure that she liked him. The way she laughed all afternoon.

"Is that right?" my father said, after a moment. "And what do you think of Tom?"

I shrugged. "He's nice."

We stood quietly then, admiring the backyard. My father said he had always disliked the fence. It was made of cinder blocks stacked up one by one but he would much prefer a wooden gate. Then he turned and walked into the house. I stood looking at the yard. My sisters were playing on the tire swing, sitting spider, face-to-face, their arms and legs entwined. They swung back and forth and finally they looked up at me as if they knew what I had said, but they just kept swinging, the yellow rope extending out, my sisters hugging each other. I stood by myself, scared suddenly by what I had done.

When my father came home the next afternoon, and Irene forced us upstairs, I should have said then that I'd made a mistake, but I didn't. Irene started packing. She took the hot dogs from the freezer and threw them in with our T-shirts and sweaters. Tom had to do everything all over again. My sisters and I just sat and watched, nodding silently or shaking our heads, rejecting the extra sweater, accepting the crayons. Staring dumbly at Tom while he combed our hair and gave us grilled cheese sandwiches. I thought my father would return and everything would reverse itself. When Tom pushed the suitcase closed I started to cry. "I didn't mean it," I told Tom, hitting his chest with my fists. "I said I'm sorry. I didn't mean it." He picked me up and I kicked at him but it did no good. Irene kept bringing things out to the car, one box after another. Tom held on to me, though I was awkward, my arms and legs shooting out. I cried so hard his shirt was soaked. He whispered into my ear so that no one would hear, "I'm sorry. I'm sorry, too. I'm sorry," until I was finally quiet.

In the car, Tom took me with him into the front seat. When the car stopped at the intersections, he would look over at me without speaking. He would rest his hand on my knee, a moment of consolation, until the car began moving once more.

EVENTUALLY, it was Tom my sisters went to, instead of Irene. They told him about their boyfriends, the girls in school, the nights they crept out of the house and slept on the beach. They saw his sympathy, I think. When Irene had her breakdowns, they saw how he comforted her and didn't let go until she was well again.

My father had never been so patient with her, but even so, I yearned for him. I would try to get Irene to talk about him but she would shake her head, say, "Why do you ask me these things?" Once she asked me if I was trying, really trying to make her crazy, and another time, if I still had not forgiven her.

"This is the way things worked out," she said. "It does no good trying to imagine it differently."

From the time I was seven, I wrote to my father. His letters, though few and far between, were caring though restrained. After years of writing to him, I found it difficult to get past the first few sentences. *Dear Dad,* I'd write. *I hope you are keeping well.* I'd write about North Bend, or respond to the questions he asked about school. *Dear Dad,* I wrote once. *I am very sorry for everything that has happened,* but I never sent this letter. It was like writing a confession to someone from a dream. My father, himself, gave only the most general details of his life, and never asked for more from me. I can't blame him really. He probably still imagined me as a six-year-old child; he did not know me otherwise.

Not long ago, I said to Irene, "Did you ever know that I was the one who told? I was the one who gave everything away."

"If it wasn't you, it would have been one of the others." She shrugged. "It's over, in any case, and I'm not sorry."

I should have asked Irene why everyone else could pick up and go on, when that was the thing I found most difficult. Who left who, I often wondered. In the end, who walked away with the least resistance.

OVER TIME, it was easy to love North Bend. That first year, we spent countless afternoons on the boulevard, watching the tourists. They moved in great, wide groups, clutching ice-cream cones and cameras. At the tourist office, they posed beside the World's Largest Frying Pan—the town's main attraction. The frying pan is sixty feet high and stands upright, wooden handle pointing to the sky. Tom told us it was given to the town in 1919, as a tribute to the women who stayed behind during the First World War.

Irene laughed and nodded her head. "It's big," she said, peering up along the carved wood handle. "A great big pan."

Come winter, the tourists disappeared and half the shops boarded up for the off-season. One afternoon, Tom ushered my sisters and me up to the frying pan and sat us down on the lip. The chill wind blew our hair all messy and Tom snapped a picture, the three of us hugging each other, laughing into the cold. Then we all started off along the waterfront, Tom closing his eyes and walking blindly across the sand. He let a gust of wind push him forward, his feet stumbling through the foam and water. We laughed, holding our arms out too, tossing about like dizzy birds, the wind tripping us up. Tom pretended to lose his balance, falling sideways on the ground, the freezing tide pouring over him. He sat up, laughing and spitting while we stood over his body, pretending to stomp him.

"No, no," Irene said. "You'll catch your death of cold."

We pretended to kick Tom in the stomach. "Enough!" he roared, leaping up, shaking foam and water from his head. My sisters and I scattered along the beach while he ran after us, Irene's voice barely audible in the background. "No! Stop it! Jesus Christ, be careful!"

That afternoon, he snapped close-ups of us, the lens of his camera inches from our faces, our hair tangling in front. Days later, he put a picture of Irene and the three of us up on the wall, my sisters and

I transformed into bold sea creatures, the clouds and the sky brimming behind us. "What about you?" Helen asked, when we stood admiring the photograph. "Why didn't you put up one of you?"

"Me?" he said, laughing. "I'm just the photographer, nothing more."

Irene stared hard at the picture, her expression sad all of a sudden. She looked from Tom to us, as if from a great distance, then she turned and left the room. Tom did what my father had never done—he followed her, down the front steps, into the street. From inside, we could see the two of them standing together, heads touching, a moment of stillness, before they started back to the house.

ONE NIGHT, when Joanne was seventeen, she came home drunk and sick. She and Tom sat on the front steps all night. Her boyfriend, she wept, was sleeping with someone named Elsa, and had been for months. Joanne stomped up and down the stairs in frustration, then collapsed on the bottom step. "I don't even like him anyway," she sobbed, "so why does it hurt so much?"

Irene and I sat at the kitchen table, eavesdropping. There was no response from Tom.

Joanne told him she was sick of North Bend, sick of living by the water, the floods in winter. Listening to her, I thought of the groups of old men leaning their fishing lines out the back of their pickups, reeling fish in from the highway, how Joanne and I used to drive by and watch them. She told Tom she didn't know what to do next, thought alternately of running away, of drowning herself. There was no way she was going back to school.

"Why don't you run away, then?"

She started crying again. "Why do you want me to leave?"

Tom's voice was tired. "It's not a lack of love. I don't want you drowning. That's all." He gave her five hundred dollars right there. Irene didn't interfere. She sat at the kitchen table, letting Tom do what he thought was right. In the morning Joanne packed her things and left, caught a bus straight out of Oregon and headed north. My sister Helen moved out not long after. She'd met a bio-technologist from

Vancouver and married him. We threw a big party for her at the house, then they drove away to Canada.

THESE DAYS, our town is visited by many tourists. They come from far and wide. On a Saturday during the busy season, the cars hail from every state, from Alaska to New Jersey, and from all across Canada.

I am in charge of the walking tours, the 9:30, 12:15, and 3:00 groups. We start at the town hall and head east along the boulevard, past Flotsam & Jetsam, the Whale's Tail, and Circus World, with its natural and unnatural artifacts—fish dishes, glass buoys, bone fossils. Circus World boasts the skeleton of a half-goat, half-human boy, mounted in a glass case. For one dollar, you can buy a snapshot of him and send it, postage paid, anywhere in the country. The tour ends at the big frying pan.

It's the *why* of it that nobody understands. I tell my father's version of the story, the frying pan as war memorial, erected as a tribute to the women who stayed behind. Then I tell my mother's version, the frying pan for the sake of the frying pan, one monumental gesture. North Bend's Eiffel Tower, the wooden handle visible for miles.

The Japanese tourists giggle, cupping their hands to their mouths. But the big East Coast men with Hawaiian shirts and baseball caps tell me, "You can never have a thing too big. We've got the skyscrapers, you know. Sky*scrapers*. Unbelievable." They tilt their heads back then, and focus on the air above.

Tom and Irene own a sporting-goods store in North Bend, selling things like scuba gear, flippers and surfboards. In the mornings, Tom takes a walk inland, just for the pleasure of turning around again and walking downhill to the ocean. Irene stands on the front steps looking out for him. She has a longing for him. I could be standing right beside her and she wouldn't even know me.

I am thirty years old and I don't know if I will ever leave this town. I should, of course, just to see the world. But I would want to come back here. Some changes happen so slowly, you can't know until it's done—my parents aging, the beach washing back from the water.

Maybe when I am sixty, the town itself will have receded. All of us who stay here will creep backwards too, watching and watching for change, then being surprised when it strikes us, out of the blue. No reason but the fact that it is all different. In our house uphill from the ocean, Irene and Tom and I sit in the kitchen reading books and magazines. From morning until night we can hear the water and the wind and the two mixing together. At night, I can hear their voices through the walls, and the past finally seems right in its place. Not everything, not large, but still present.

JANE URQUHART

Italian Postcards

Whenever she is sick, home from school, Clara the child is allowed to examine her mother's Italian postcards, a large pile of them, which are normally bound with a thick leather band and kept in a bureau drawer. Years later when she touches postcards she will be amazed that her hands are so large. Perhaps she feels that the hands of a child are proportionally correct to rest like book ends on either side of landscapes. Or maybe it's not that complicated; maybe she just feels that, as an adult, she can't really see these colours, those vistas, and so, in the odd moments when she does, she must necessarily be a child again.

The room she lies in on weekdays, when she has managed to stay home from school, is all hers. She'll probably carry it around with her for the rest of her life. Soft grey wallpaper with sprays of pink apple blossom. Pink dressing table (under the skirts of which her dolls hide, resting on their little toy beds), cretonne curtains swathed over a window at the foot of the bed she occupies, two or three pink pillows propping her up. Outside the window a small back garden and some winter city or another. It doesn't really matter which.

And then the postcards; turquoise, fuchsia, lime green—improbable colours placed all over the white spread and her little hands picking up one, then another, as she tries to imagine her mother walking through such passionate surroundings.

In time, her mother appears at the side of the bed. Earlier in the morning she brought the collection of postcards. Now she holds a concoction of mustard and water wrapped in white flannel and starts to undo the little buttons on the little pyjama top.

WHILE THE MUSTARD PLASTER BURNS into her breastbone Clara continues to look at the postcards. Such flowers, such skies, such suns burning down on such perfect seas. Her mother speaks the names of foreign towns; *Sorrento,* she says, *Capri, Fiesole, Garda, Como,* and then after a thoughtful pause, *You should see Como. But most of all you should see Pompeii.*

Clara always saves Pompeii, however, until the end, until after her mother has removed the agonizing poultice and has left the room— until after she has gone down the stairs and has resumed her orderly activities in the kitchen. Then the child allows the volcano to erupt, to spill molten lava all over the suburban villas, the naughty frescos, the religious mosaics. And all over the inhabitants of the unsuspecting ancient town.

IN THE POSTCARDS Pompeii is represented, horrifyingly, fascinatingly, by the inhabitants themselves, frozen in such attitudes of absolute terror or complete despair that they teach the child everything she needs to know about heartbreak and disaster: how some will put their arms up in front of their faces to try to ward it off, how others will resign themselves, sadly, to its strength. What she doesn't understand is how such heat can freeze, make permanent, the moment of intensest pain. A scream in stone that once was liquid. What would happen, she wonders, to these figures if the volcano were to erupt again? How permanent are they?

And she wonders about the archaeologists who have removed the stone bodies from the earth and, without disturbing a single gesture, have placed them in glass display cases inside the museum where they seem to float in the air of their own misfortune ... clear now, the atmosphere empty of volcanic ash, the glass polished.

These are the only postcards of Pompeii that Clara's mother has. No bright frescos, no recently excavated villas, no mosaics; only these clear cases full of grey statues made from what was once burning flesh.

TWENTY-FIVE YEARS LATER when Clara stands with her husband at the entrance to Hotel Oasie in Assisi she has seen Sorrento, Como, Capri and has avoided Pompeii altogether.

"Why not?" her husband asks.

"Nobody lives there," she replies.

But people live here, in this Tuscan hill town; the sun has burned life into their faces. And the colours in the postcards were real after all— they spill out from red walls into the vegetable displays on the street, they flash by on the backs of overdressed children. Near the desk of the hotel they shout out from travel posters. But in this space there is no sun; halls of cool remote marble, sparse furnishings, and, it would seem, no guests but themselves.

"Dinner," the man behind the desk informs them, "between seven and nine in the big salon."

Then he leads them, through arched halls, to their room.

Clara watches the thick short back of the Italian as she walks behind him, realizing as she does that it is impossible to imagine muscle tone when it is covered by smooth black cloth. She looks at the back of his squarish head. Cumbersome words such as *basilica, portcullis, Etruscan* and *Vesuvius* rumble disturbingly, and for no apparent reason, through her mind.

Once the door has clicked behind them and the echoing footsteps of the desk clerk have disappeared from the outside hall, her husband examines the two narrow beds with displeasure and shrugs.

"Perhaps we'll find a way," he says, "marble floors are cold." Then looking down, "Don't think these small rugs will help much."

Then, before she can reply, they are both distracted by the view outside the windows. Endless olive groves and vineyards and a small cemetery perched halfway up the hill. Later in the evening, after they have eaten pasta and drunk rough, red wine in the enormous empty dining room, they will see little twinkling lights shine up from this spot, like a handful of stars on the hillside. Until that moment it will never have occurred to either of them that anyone would want to light a tomb at night.

> *Go and light a tomb at night*
> *Get with child a mandrake root.*

Clara is thinking Blake ... in Italy of all places, wandering through the empty halls of Hotel Oasie, secretly inspecting rooms. All the same so far; narrow cots, tiny rugs, views of vineyards and the graveyard, olive trees. Plain green walls. These rooms, she thinks, as Blake evaporates from her mind, these rooms could use the services of Mr. Domado's Wallpaper Company, a company with one employee—the very unhappy Mr. Domado himself. He papered her room once when she was a sick child and he was sick with longing for his native land. When Italian postcards coincidentally littered her bedspread like fallen leaves. *Ah, yes,* said Mr. Domado, sadly picking up one village and then another. *Ah, yes.*

And he could sing ... Italian songs. Arias that sounded as mournful as some of the lonelier villages looked. Long, long sobbing notes trembling in the winter sunshine, while she lay propped on pink pillows and her mother crept around in the kitchen below silently preparing mustard plasters. Mr. Domado, with tears in his voice, eliminating spray after spray of pink apple blossoms, replacing them with rigid geometric designs, while Clara studied the open mouths of the stone Pompeii figures and wondered whether, at the moment of their death, they were praying out loud. Or whether they were simply screaming.

Screaming, she thinks now, as she opens door after door of Hotel Oasie, would be practically a catastrophe in these echoing marble halls. One scream might go on for hours, as her footsteps seem to every time she moves twenty feet or so down to the next door, as the click of the latch seems to every time she has closed whatever door she has been opening. The doors are definitely an addition to the old, old building and appear to be pulled by some new longitudinal force back into the closed position after her fingers release their cold, steel knobs. Until she opens the door labelled *Sala Beatico Angelico* after which no hotel room will ever be the same.

NEITHER CLARA nor her husband speaks Italian, so to ask for a complete explanation would be impossible.

"A Baroque church!" she tells him later. "Not a chapel but a complete church. All the doors are the same, *this* door is the same except for the words on it, and you open it and there, instead of a hotel room, is a complete church."

"It appears," he says after several moments of reflection, "that we have somehow checked into a monastery."

SURE ENOUGH, when she takes herself out to the rose garden later in the afternoon to sit in the sun and to read *The Little Flowers of Santa Chiara* in preparation for the next day's trip to the basilica, the hotel clerk greets her, dressed now in a clerical collar. Clara shows no surprise, as if she had known all along that hers was not to be a secular vacation; as if the idea of a retreat had been in her mind when she planned the trip. She shifts the book a little so that the monastic gardener will notice that she is reading about St. Francis's holy female friend. He, however, is busy with roses, his own little flowers, and though he faces her while he works his glance never once meets hers. She is able, therefore, to observe him quite closely ... the dark tan of his face over the white of his collar, his hands, which move carefully but easily through the roses, avoiding thorns. Clara tries, but utterly fails, to imagine the thoughts of a priest working in a rose garden. Are they concerned, as they should be, with *God* ... the thorns, perhaps, signi-fying a crown, the dark red stain of the flower turning in his mind to the blood of Christ? Or does he think only of roses and their health ... methods of removing the insect from the leaf ... the worm from the centre of the scarlet bud? His face gives her no clue; neither that nor the curve of his back as he stoops to remove yet another vagrant weed from the soft brown earth surrounding the bushes.

Clara turns again to her book, examining the table of contents; "The Circle of Ashes," "The Face in the Well," "The Hostage of Heaven," "The Bread of Angels," "The Meal in the Woods," and finally, at the bottom of the list, "The Retinue of Virgins." St. Francis, she discovers, had never wanted to see Chiara. The little stories made this perfectly clear. Sentence after sentence described his aversion. After he had clothed her in sackcloth and cut off all her hair in the dark of the Italian night, after he had set her on the path of poverty and had left her with her sisters at St. Damien's, after she had turned into a *hostage of heaven* and had given up eating all together, Francis withdrew. *Beware of the poison of familiarity with women,* he had told his fellow friars. In a chapter entitled "The Roses," the book stated that Francis had wanted to place an entire season between himself and Chiara. *We will meet again when the roses bloom,* he had said, standing with his bare feet in the snow. Then God had decided to make the roses bloom spontaneously, right there, right then, in the middle of winter.

Clara cannot decide, now, what possible difference that would make. As a matter of fact, it looks to her as if God were merely playing a trick on Chiara and Francis. If Francis said they would meet again when the roses bloom, why not have the roses bloom right now? Perhaps then there would be no subsequent meeting since the roses had already bloomed. This would have certainly been a puzzle for Chiara to work on during the dreary winter days that stretched ahead of her in the unheated convent. She could have worked it over and over in her mind like a rosary. It might have kept her, in some ways, very busy.

Francis, on the other hand, was always very busy. As the book said: *Francis came and went freely from St. Mary of the Angels but Chiara found herself like a prisoner at St. Damien's.* Francis might have dropped by to see Chiara while he was out rushing around, but he didn't. *On the other hand, Francis stayed well away from St. Damien's,* the book continued, *for he did not wish the common people should take scandal from seeing him going in and out.* So basically, it would appear that poor

Chiara, poison that she was, rarely spoke to her mentor; the man whose principles she built her life around. At least not until "The Meal in the Woods."

After she had asked him repeatedly to share a meal with her, Francis finally relented. Speaking, once again to his fellow friars (he seemed never to have spoken to Chiara), he argued, *She has been a long time at St. Damien's. She will be happy to come out for a little while and to see in the daytime that place to which she first came at night, where her hair was cut from her, and where she was received among us. In the name of Jesus Christ we will picnic in the woods.* Somehow, during the course of this unusual picnic, the woods began to glow as if they were on fire. It is not clear to Clara whether God or Francis was responsible for this miracle. It may have been a collaboration. It is perfectly clear, however, that Chiara had nothing to do with it. Her role was that of appreciator—one that she, no doubt, played very well. And, as usual, she wasn't eating. The chapter ends with this statement: *Finally Chiara and Francis rose from the ground, overjoyed and filled with spiritual nourishment, not having touched as much as a crumb of the food.*

Clara is beginning to feel hungry. Delicious smells are coming from what she now knows is the refectory. The gardener is placing his tools, one by one, in the wheelbarrow. Then, without looking in her direction, he pushes the little vehicle away from her, towards the potting shed.

"OUR HOTEL CLERK," she informs her husband at dinner, "is a gardener as well as a priest. I was reading up on my namesake out on the terrace and I saw him in the garden, working away."

"I discovered the other part of the building," her husband replies. "There is a glass door with *Keep Out* written on it in four languages, and then an entire wing where the priests must stay when they open the place to tourists."

"You didn't peek?" asks Clara, fully aware that, had she discovered it, she might have opened the door.

"No ... written rules you know," and then, "Have you decided to like your namesake? Do you think you take after her?"

Clara reflects for a while. "I think she was a very unhappy woman. She kept on wanting to see Francis and he kept not wanting to see her."

"Probably just propriety, don't you think? You can't have Saint Francis spending a lot of time hanging around the convent you know, wouldn't look good."

"Possibly ... but maybe it was just an excuse. Maybe he really *didn't* want to see her. The poor girl ... she was in love with him, I expect. He was probably God to her."

"Maybe *he* was in love with *her* ... did that ever occur to you? Maybe that's why he stayed away." Her husband glances to the end of the room. "Look who's coming," he says. "Our desk clerk is not only a gardener and a priest, he is also a waiter."

THE NEXT AFTERNOON Clara decides she will not visit the basilica after all. She would rather read in the rose garden than gaze at frescos.

"Later," she tells her husband. "You check it out, tell me about it."

Postcard views and skies are outside the walls of the hotel as usual, and now the closer, more exaggerated colours of the roses. It is hotter than the previous day so the priest has abandoned his collar. Clara notices that he has a perfect mole situated right in the centre of his throat. A sort of natural stigmata, she decides.

The chapter entitled "The Door of the Dead" fascinates her. She is reading it for the fourth time. It seems that the ancient houses in Assisi often had two doors; a large one through which the family normally came and went, and a smaller one, elevated above the ground, through which the dead were passed, feet first in their coffins. Chiara, on the night she went to meet Francis in the woods, decided to leave the house through the second door. *She wanted to get away secretly,* the book states, *and she was absolutely sure she would meet no one on the threshold of that door.* With the help of a minor miracle on God's part she was able to slide bolts and move hinges that had been rusted in position for fifteen years. Then she jumped lightly to the ground and ran out of the village. *Never again would she be able to return to her family,* the chapter concludes, *Chiara was dead. Chiara was lost. Chiara had passed over into another life.*

Clara wonders if the priest, who is working directly in front of her, has also passed over into another life, and whether, if this is so, the roses look redder to him than they do to her. Whether he lives a sort of *Through the Looking Glass* existence.

She adjusts the angle of her chair. He is working close enough now that their shadows almost touch. A vague sadness stirs near Clara's heart, stops, then moves again. Restless lava shifting somewhere in the centre of a mountain.

HER HUSBAND has decided that they will stay at Hotel Oasie for the remainder of their vacation. He likes it there. He likes Assisi. He is moved by all of it; as much, he says, by the electrified confessionals in the basilica as by the Giottos. He claims that the former are like the washrooms on a jumbo jet in that they have automatic *occupied* and *vacant* signs that are lighted from behind. He is amazed, he continues, at how easily the Italians have adapted their highly super-stitious religion to modern technology ... the lighted tombs, the electric candles in front of religious statues, the *occupied* signs. This amuses and pleases him. He will write a sociological paper on it when they return to North America.

She isn't listening to him very carefully because she has fallen in love, just like that, bang, with the gardener, waiter, desk clerk, priest. She has, by now, spent four long afternoons with him in the rose garden and he has never once looked her way. Unless, she speculates, he looks her way when she is absorbed in *The Little Flowers of Santa Chiara,* which is possible. On the third afternoon she made up a little rule for herself that she would not lift her eyes from the book until a chapter was completely finished. In that way she has balanced her activities. Ten minutes of reading followed by ten minutes of studying the priest. This means, of course, that he is never in the same location after she finishes reading "The Door of the Dead" as he was after she finished reading, say, "A Kiss for the Servant." She is then forced to look around for him which makes the activity more intriguing. One afternoon, after finishing the chapter called "Infirmity and Suffering," she looked up and around and discovered that he had disappeared completely, simply slipped away while she was reading. Almost every other time, though, she is able to watch him collect his tools, place them in the wheelbarrow and walk towards the potting shed. And this makes her grieve a little, as one often does when a lengthy ritual has been appropriately completed.

"DID YOU KNOW," she asks her husband angrily at dinner, "Did you know that he wouldn't even let her come to see him when he was *dying*? I mean, isn't that taking it a bit too far? The man was dying and she asked if she could see him and he said no … not until I'm *dead*."

The priestly waiter serves the pasta. Clara watches his brown left hand approach the table and withdraw. *"Scusi,"* he says as he places the dish in front of her. She cannot accuse him of never speaking to her. He has said *Scusi* in her presence now a total of seventeen times and once, when a meal was over, he looked directly into her eyes and had asked, "You feeneesh?"

Now she stabs her fork deliberately into the flesh of the ravioli. "Moreover," she continues, "that little book I am reading has next to nothing to do with Chiara … mostly it's about Francis … until he dies, of course … then it's about her dying." Forgetting to chew, Clara swallows the piece of pasta whole.

"Well," says her husband, "at least Giotto included her in some of the frescos."

"Hmm," she replies, unimpressed.

Clara gazes at the priest and her heart turns soft. He is staring absently into space. Imagining miracles, she decides, waiting out the dinner hour so that he can return to his quiet activities. Evening mass, midnight mass. Lighting candles, saying prayers. Does he make them up or follow rituals? Are there beads involved? Does he kneel before male or female saints? Any of this information would be important to her. Still, she would never dare enter the church she has discovered at the end of the hall. In fact, with the exception of the basilica with its electrified confessionals and famous frescos, she has not dared to open the door of any church in town. They are spaces that are closed to her and she knows it.

"Have you ever felt that a church was closed to you?" she asks her husband.

"Of course not," he answers. "After all, they are not only religious institutions ... they are great public monuments, great works of art. They are open to all of us."

Clara sighs and turns her eyes, once again, to the priest. The way he is carrying the crockery back to the kitchen, as if it were a collection of religious artifacts he has recently blessed, almost breaks her heart.

IT IS HER fifth afternoon in the rose garden. He is there too, of course, pinning roses onto stakes. "Crucifying them perhaps," she thinks vaguely, lovingly.

By now she knows that this man will never *ever* respond to her, never *ever* speak to her; not in his language or hers—except at meal time when it is absolutely necessary. Because of this, the sadness of this, she loves him even harder. It is this continuous rejection that sets him apart. Rejection without object, without malice, a kind of healing rejection; one that causes a cleansing ache.

The ache washes over her now as she watches him stand back to survey his labours. She loves the way he just stands there looking, completely ignoring her. She is of absolutely no consequence in the story of his life, none whatsoever, and she loves him for this. She has no desire for change; no mediaeval fantasies about being the rose that he fumbles with, the saint that he prays to. She wants him just as he is, oblivious to her, causing her to ache, causing her to understand the true dimensions of hopelessness, how they are infinite.

She turns to the chapter in the book called "The Papal Bull." This is an oddly political section and her least favourite. It concerns the legitimization of the various Franciscan orders including Santa Chiara's Poor Sisters; the legitimization of lives of chosen self-denial. At this point Clara is finding it difficult to concentrate on what the Pope had to say, finds it difficult to care whether it was legitimate or not.

She is surprised, when she allows herself to look up, to find the priest's gaze aimed in her direction. She prepares to be embarrassed until she realizes that he is, at last, reading the title of her book.

"SHE WANTED WORDS from him," Clara tells her husband later. "Words, you know, spiritual advice. You know what she got instead?"

"What?"

"She got a circle of ashes … a circle of goddamn ashes! The book tries to make this seem profound … the usual, he put a circle of ashes on the convent floor to demonstrate that all humans were merely dust or some such nonsense. You know what I think it meant? I think it meant that regardless of what Chiara wanted from him, regardless of how bad she might have wanted it, regardless of whether or not she ever swallowed a single morsel of food, or wore hair shirts, or humiliated herself in any number of ways, regardless of what she did, all she was *ever* going to get from him was a circle of ashes. I think it meant that she was entirely powerless and he was going to make damn certain that she stayed that way."

"Quite a theory. I doubt the church would approve."

"God, how she must have suffered!"

"Well," he replies, "wasn't that what she was supposed to do?"

IN THE MIDDLE of her seventh afternoon in the rose garden, after she has finished reading a chapter entitled "The Canticle of the Creatures" (which she practically knows now by heart), and while she is studying the gestures of the priest who has moved from roses to vegetables, Clara decides that her heart is permanently broken. How long, she wonders, has it been this way? And why did it take this priest, this silent man who thinks and prays in a foreign language, to point it out to her? This is not a new disease, she knows suddenly. It's been there for a long, long time; a handicap she had managed to live with somehow, by completely ignoring it. How strange. Not to feel that pain that is always there, by never identifying it, never naming it. Now she examines the wound and it burns in the centre of her chest the way her mother's mustard plasters used to, the way molten lava must have in the middle of Vesuvius. Her broken heart has burned inside her for so long she assumed it was normal. Now the pain of it moves into her whole body; past the pulse at her wrists, down the fronts of her thighs, up into her throat. Then it moves from there out into the landscape she can see from the garden, covering all of it, every detail; each grey, green olive leaf, each electric candle in front of each small pathetic tomb, every bird, all of the churches she can never enter, poppies shouting in a distant field, this terrible swath of blue sky overhead, the few pebbles that cover the small area of terrace at her feet. And all the air that moves up and down her throat until she is literally gasping in pain.

Pure eruption. Shards of her broken heart are everywhere, moving through her bloodstream, lacerating her internally on their voyage from the inside out into the landscape, until every sense is raw. She can actually see the sound waves that are moving in front of her. She wonders if she has begun to shout but then gradually, gradually isolated sound dissolves into meaning as her brain begins its voyage back into the inside of her skull.

"Meesus," the priest is saying, pointing to her book. "She is still here, Santa Chiara. You go see her ... you go to Chiesa Santa Chiara ... you go there and you see her."

Then he collects his gardening tools, places them in his wheel-barrow, and walks purposefully away.

SHE GOES ALONE, of course, two days later when she feels better and when she knows for sure they will be leaving Assisi the following morning. She is no longer in love with the priest; he has become what he always was, a small brown Italian busy with kitchen, clerical and gardening tools. The heartbreak, however, which preceded and will follow him is still with her, recognized now and accepted as she stands across the road from the Church of Santa Chiara watching a small cat walk on top of its shadow in the noonday sun.

Inside the door total darkness for a while, followed by a gradual adjustment of the eyes to dark inscrutable paintings and draped altars and the slow movements of two nuns who are walking towards the front of the church. She follows them, unsure now how to make her request and then, suddenly, the request is unnecessary. There, boom, illuminated by the ever present electricity, is the saint, laid out for all to see in her glass coffin. "She is, you see," one of the nuns explains, "incorruptible. She is here seven hundred years and she does not decay because she is holy."

Clara moves closer to see the dead woman's face, now glowing under the harsh twentieth-century light, and there, as she expects, is the pain. Frozen on Chiara's face the terrifying, wonderful pain; permanent, incorruptible, unable to decay. The dead mouth is open, shouting pain silently up to the electricity, past the glass, into the empty cave of the church, out into the landscape, up the street to the basilica where images of the live Chiara appear, deceitfully serene, in the frescos. It is the heartbreak that is durable, Clara thinks to herself, experiencing the shock of total recognition. Everything else will fade away. No wonder the saint didn't decay. A flutter of something sharp and cutting in Clara's own bloodstream and then she turns away.

Before she steps out into the street again she buys a postcard from one of the nuns. Santa Chiara in her glass coffin, as permanent as a figure from Pompeii in her unending, incorruptible anguish.

Clara places the card in an inside pocket of her handbag. There it will stay through the long plane ride home while her husband makes jokes about the washrooms resembling Italian confessionals. It will stay there and she will clutch the leather close to her broken heart; clutch the image of the dead woman's mouth. The permanent pain that moves past the postcard booth into the colours of the Italian landscape.

ALISSA YORK

The Back of
the Bear's Mouth

G od knows how long Carson was watching me before I caught
on—it was dark where he was sitting, like he'd brought some of
the night in with him. I matched his look for a second, and a second
was all it took. He stood up out of his corner and made for the bar.

I saw this show on the North one time. About the only part I
remember was these bighorn sheep all meeting up at the salt-lick. They
were so peaceful, side by side with their heads bent low, and no rutting
or fighting, no matter if they were old or up-and-coming, no matter if
they were male or female, injured or strong. That's the way it was with
me and Carson. Neither one of us said much. We just sat there, side by
side, and it felt like the natural thing.

When the time came, Carson just stood and made for the doorway,
the same slow bee-line stride he'd taken to the bar. Beside me, the
bartender cleared our glasses and talked low into his beard, "Think
twice little girl, the Northern bushman's a different breed."

But then Carson looked back at me over his shoulder, and just like
a rockslide, I felt myself slip off the barstool and follow.

THE TRUCK took its time warming up, so we sat together in the
dark, both of us staring at the windshield like we were waiting for

some movie to start.

"Robin," he said finally, "I figure you got no place to go."

I turned my head his way a little. I was just eighteen and he must've been forty, but none of that mattered a damn.

"No, Carson, I don't."

"Well." He handed me a cigarette and put one to his own lips, leaving it hanging there, not lighted. I brought the lighter out of my coat pocket and held the flame up in front of his face, the flicker of it making him seem younger somehow, a little scared. After a minute I sat back and lit my own.

I MUST'VE FALLEN ASLEEP on the drive. It was no wonder with the kind of hours I'd been keeping—hitching clear across the country in just under three weeks. God knows how I landed in Whitehorse, except I remember hearing some old guy in a truck-stop talking about it, calling it the stop before the end of the line.

I OPENED MY EYES just as Carson was laying me out on the bed. The place was dark and cold as a meat locker. It stunk of tobacco and bacon, oiled metal and mould and mouse shit, but somewhere underneath all that was Carson's smell, a gentle, low-lying musk. I know it sounds crazy, but I'll bet that smell was half the reason I went with him in the first place.

I pulled the blanket around me and sat up, watching the shadow that was him pile wood into the stove. He lit the fire, then settled back into the armchair, watching me where I sat. I'd always hated people staring at me. I guess that's why I left school in the end—the teachers and everyone staring at your clothes, your hair, staring into your skull. But Carson was different. His eyes just rested on me, not hunting or digging, just looking because I was there, and more interesting than the rug or the table leg.

Who knows how long we sat like that. I remember him pulling a couple more blankets down from a cupboard, laying one around my shoulders and leaving the other at the foot of the bed.

IN THE MORNING, sun was all through the place. The bed was an old wrought-iron double, with only my side slept in. Coals burnt low in the stove. A grizzly head hung over the bed, mounted with its mouth wide open and the teeth drawn back like a trap.

Carson was nowhere, so I stepped outside and lit a smoke. It was warm, the sun already burning holes in the last patches of snow. We were in the bush all right, the clearing was just big enough for the cabin, the outhouse, and the truck. The dirt road that led in to the place closed up dark in the distance, like looking down somebody's throat. A skinny tomcat squeezed out the door of the outhouse and sat washing what was left of one of its ears. The trees grew thick and dark and the sound of jays and ravens came falling.

I found Carson round back of the cabin, bent over the carcass of a deer. There was another one in the dust nearby, a buck with small, velvety antlers. Carson looked up at the sound of my footsteps, his eyes all quick and violent.

"Morning," I said.

"Morning."

"You get those this morning?"

"—No."

Something told me to shut up. I walked back round to the door and went inside. The place looked like it hadn't ever been cleaned, so I threw a log in the stove, put the kettle on top, and set about finding some rags and soap.

HE NEVER TOUCHED ME for the whole first week. A couple of times he walked up close behind me and stood there, smelling my hair or something, and I waited for his hand on me, but it didn't come.

The days passed easily. I got the place clean, beat the rugs and blankets, swept out the mouse shit, oiled the table, and washed the two windows with hot water and vinegar. I even stood up on the bed and brushed the dust out of the grizzly's fur. There were gold hairs all through the brown, lit up and dancing where the sunlight lay on its neck.

Carson never thanked me for cleaning up, and I never thanked him for letting me stay. On my eighth night there he turned in the bed and I felt him pressing long and hard into the back of my thigh. He held me tight, but it didn't hurt. He fit into me like something I'd been missing, like something finally come home.

CARSON WAS SOMETIMES GONE for part of the night, or all of it. He either went out empty and brought a carcass back, or went out with a carcass or two and came back empty. Usually it was caribou or deer, but one time there was a lynx. He let me touch the fur. It felt just the same as a regular cat—a few hairs came away in my hand.

Time went by like this, me cooking and cleaning and watching, sometimes reading the *Reader's Digest* or some other magazine from a box in the cupboard, sometimes just sitting and smoking on the doorstep, watching the forest fill up with spring. Carson got more comfortable when I'd been there for a while, started teaching me how to shoot the rifle—first at empty bean tins, then at crows and rabbits that came into the clearing. When I finally hit a rabbit, Carson let out a whoop and ran to get it. Then he took the gun from my hands and held the rabbit up in front of my face. Its hindlegs were blown clear off. I felt my fingers go shaky when I reached for its ears, felt tears come up the back of my throat when I took it from him, the soft, dead weight of it in my hand.

ONE NIGHT I got Carson to let me go along. That sounds like I had to talk him into it, but really all I said was,

"Can I come?"

"You can't talk if you do."

"You heard me talk much?"

"—All right."

IT WAS LIKE DRIVING through black paint—the headlights cut a path in front of the truck, and the dark closed up behind us. I had to wonder how Carson found his way around, how he ever managed to get back home. When we got a ways off the main road, he slowed right down and started zigzagging, the headlights swishing over the road and into the bush, then back over the road to the other side.

I was just nodding off when Carson cut the engine, grabbed the gun, and jumped out into the dark. I caught a yellow flash of eyes in the bush, then came the shots, the gun blazing once, twice, and the moose staggered into the lights, forelegs buckling, head slamming into the dirt. Carson pulled a winch out from under the seat and rigged it up to some bolts in the bed of the truck. We got the moose trussed up, but it took us forever to get it in the back.

"This is a big one," I said, not sure if it was true. I'd only ever seen one from far away, standing stock-still in a muskeg, the way they do.

"Not one," he said, "two. Springtime, Robin."

THE NEXT NIGHT Carson headed off on his own and I was just as glad. I was still trying to lose the picture of that moose's head hitting the ground.

IT SEEMS LIKE it would be creepy being out there in the middle of God-knows-where, Yukon Territory, but I got used to it pretty fast. Even when I was alone it felt safer than any city I'd been through—all those junkies and college kids and cars.

One night, though, I woke up slow and foggy, feeling like I couldn't breathe. It took a while for me to realize the tomcat was sitting on me, right on my chest, and when my eyes got used to the dark I could make out the shape of a mouse in its jaws.

I'm no chicken, but that dead mouse in my face scared the shit out of me. I threw the cat clear across the room and the mouse flew out of its mouth and landed somewhere near the foot of the bed. The tom yowled for a minute, then found the mouse and settled down. I swear I didn't close my eyes until dawn. I just lay there, listening to that cat gnawing and tearing at the mouse, snapping the bones in its teeth.

I'd been out there for about three months as close as I could guess, and I had no ideas about leaving. It wasn't that Carson was such great company—half the time he wasn't there, and the other half he was busy skinning something, or cleaning his guns, or doing God knows what round back of the cabin. At night was mostly when we met up. He'd climb into the bed after me, and hold me hard and gentle, always the same way, from the back with me lying on my side. I didn't mind— it felt good, and I figured he was shy about doing it face to face. It made sense, a man who lives out in the bush on his own for so long.

By that time I was sure I was pregnant. I hadn't bled since I'd been there, my breasts were sore, and my belly had a warm, hard rise in it. One night when Carson was lying behind me, I took his hand and put it there. I turned my face around to him, and even though it was dark as the Devil, I could tell he was smiling. I don't know that I've felt that good before or since.

I ONLY ASKED Carson about the hunting once.

"Carson, all these animals …"

The way he looked at me made me think of that first day, when he looked up from that deer like he was a dog and I was some other dog trying to nose in on the kill. His eyes were really pale blue, sometimes almost clear. They didn't usually bug me, but times like that I always thought of that riddle—the man gets stabbed with an icicle, and it melts, and then where's the murder weapon?

IT WAS MAYBE a week or two later when I woke up to the sound of Carson coming home in the truck. That alone told me there was something wrong—he usually coasted up to the cabin and came in without waking me up. I was lighting the lamp when he threw open the door.

"Can you drive?"

"What's wrong?"

"Can you drive!"

"Yes!"

"Get dressed."

"What's wrong, Carson?"

"Goddammit, Robin!"

I crawled out from under the covers and grabbed for my clothes. He jumped up on the bed and stood where my head had been, reaching one hand deep into the grizzly's mouth. I thought he'd lost it for sure, but a second later he jumped back down and stuck a fistful of money in my face, twenties and fifties, a fat wad of them.

"There's more up there," he said, "if I don't come back you come and get it, just reach past the teeth and push the panel. And watch you don't cut your hand."

He shoved the truck keys into the pocket of my red mac.

"Carson," I said, and my voice came out funny. I was thinking about what he said, about him maybe not coming back.

"Get going. Lay low in Whitehorse. I'll find you."

"But where will you go?"

"Out in the bush. Get going."

He touched my hair for a second, then held the door open and pushed me outside.

I GOT A ROOM at the Fourth Avenue Residence. I didn't check in until morning, after spending the whole night driving around in the dark, scared shitless. When dawn came and I finally saw the road sign I'd been hoping for, I felt about two steps from crazy.

Whitehorse was waking up when I pulled into town. I bought a bottle of peroxide at the Pharmasave, and a big bag of Doritos, then I found the Fourth Ave. and parked around back.

First thing I did in my room was eat that whole bag of Doritos, fast, like I hadn't had anything for weeks. Then I took the scissors from the kitchen drawer and cut off all my hair. It fell onto the linoleum and curled around my feet, shiny black as a nest of crows. I left the peroxide on until it burned, and when I rinsed it out and looked at myself in the mirror I had to laugh. And then I had to cry.

I SLEPT THE WHOLE DAY and through the night, and the next morning I went down to the front desk and bought a pack of smokes, two Mars Bars, and a paper. I folded the paper under my arm and didn't look at the front page until I was back in my room. I ate the Mars Bars while I read, and my hunger made me remember the baby. Our baby—mine and Carson's.

PITLAMPER GOES TOO FAR

Conservation Officer Harvey Jacobs was shot and badly wounded late last night when he surprised a lone man pitlamping on a back road off the Dempster Highway. The man who fired at Jacobs is believed to be one Ray Carson, who has a cabin in the area. RCMP have issued a warrant for Carson's arrest and ask that anyone with information pertaining to his whereabouts come forward. Jacobs took a single .38 bullet in his right side. He is currently in intensive care ...

I LAY ON MY BACK on the bed, until it felt like the baby was screaming for something to eat. I thought about going out, but I ended up calling for pizza.

I WAS IN THE CORNER STORE when I heard. The old bitch behind the counter leaned across to me and said, "Did you hear? They got that nut case, Carson."

I looked down at the lottery tickets, all neat and shiny under a slab of Plexiglas.

"They had to take the dogs in after him. Got him cornered up in the rocks of a waterfall, but he turned a gun on them. Well, they had to shoot him, the stupid bugger ..."

She kept on talking, but that was the last I heard. I closed the door on her voice, walked up the road a ways, and sat down in the weeds. I thought about staying there forever, thought about the grass growing up around my shoulders, turning gold and seedy, then black and broken under the snow.

Then I thought about the baby and figured I better get up.

THE AUTHORS

MARGARET ATWOOD (1939–) is the author of many novels, including *The Handmaid's Tale* (1985), *Cat's Eye* (1988), *The Robber Bride* (1993), *Alias Grace* (1996), *The Blind Assassin* (2000), and *Oryx and Crake* (2003). Her short story collections include *Dancing Girls* (1977), *Murder in the Dark* (1983), *Bluebeard's Egg* (1983), *Wilderness Tips* (1991), and *Good Bones* (1992). Atwood has written numerous books of poetry and non-fiction, as well as children's literature. She has won many awards and honours, including the Booker Prize, the Giller Prize, the Trillium Award, the Commonwealth Writers' Prize Best Book Award, Caribbean and Canada Region, and the Governor General's Literary Award. Margaret Atwood lives in Ontario.

JACQUELINE BAKER (1967–) studied creative writing at the University of Victoria and is a recent M.A. graduate of the University of Alberta. Her work has appeared in literary magazines across the country. Her first collection of stories, *A Hard Witching and Other Stories*, was published in 2003. Baker was raised in Saskatchewan.

BONNIE BURNARD's (1945–) books of fiction include *The Old Dance* (1986), *Women of Influence* (1988), *Casino and Other Stories* (1994), *Stag Line* (1995), and *A Good House* (1999). She has won the Giller Prize, the Marian Engel Award, Periodical Publishers Award, Saskatchewan Book of the Year, and the Commonwealth Writers' Prize Best First Book Award. Burnard was born in southwestern Ontario.

LYNN COADY (1970–) is the author of three novels, *Strange Heaven* (1998), *Saints of Big Harbour* (2002), and *Mean Boy* (2006). Her short story collection is called *Play the Monster Blind* (2000). Coady has been the recipient of the Dartmouth Book Award, the Atlantic Independent

Booksellers' Choice Award, the Canadian Authors Association Air Canada Award for Most Promising Writer Under Thirty, and the Canadian Authors Association Jubilee Award for Short Stories. She was born in Cape Breton.

LIBBY CREELMAN (1957–) is originally from Massachusetts but now lives in St. John's, Newfoundland. Her stories have been selected for *99: Best Canadian Stories* and *The Journey Prize Anthology*, numbers 10 and 11. Creelman has published in many Canadian literary magazines. She is a six-time winner in the Short Fiction category of the Government of Newfoundland and Labrador Arts and Letters Awards. Her first collection of stories, *Walking in Paradise,* was published in 2000.

RAMONA DEARING (1965–) lives in St. John's, Newfoundland. Her poems and stories have appeared in Oberon's *Best Canadian Stories* (1997, 1998, and 2001) and *Coming Attractions 01,* as well as many other Canadian literary journals. Her debut short story collection, *So Beautiful,* was nominated for the Winterset Award and was a runner-up for the Danuta Gleed Literary Award. Dearing works for CBC Radio as a producer.

MAVIS GALLANT (1922–) has published over one hundred stories in *The New Yorker.* She was born in Montreal, where she earned a reputation as an excellent journalist, and moved to Paris in 1950 to write fiction. She is the author of *Home Truths: Selected Canadian Stories* (1981), which won the Governor General's Literary Award. Other collections include *From the Fifteenth District* (1979), *Across the Bridge* (1993), *The Selected Stories of Mavis Gallant* (1996), *Paris Stories* (2002), and *Montreal Stories* (2004). She was made an Officer of the Order of Canada in 1981 and raised to Companion, the highest level, in 1993. She has also received many honorary doctorates from Canadian universities and won numerous awards, including the Canada Council for the Arts Molson Prize, the Matt Cohen Prize, The Blue Metropolis International Literary Grand Prix, and the Rea Award for the Short Story. Gallant lives in Paris.

ZSUZSI GARTNER (1960–) was born in Winnipeg and lives in Vancouver, where she writes fiction and works as a journalist. She has written for *The Vancouver Sun, The Globe and Mail, Saturday Night,* and *Canada AM.* Her first short story collection, *All the Anxious Girls on Earth,* was published in 1999.

CAMILLA GIBB (1968–) was born in London, England, but grew up in Toronto. Gibb's novel *Mouthing the Words* (1999) won the Toronto Book Award in 2000 and, along with *The Petty Details of So-and-so's Life* (2002), has been published in eighteen countries. Gibb's third novel, *Sweetness in the Belly* (2005), was nominated for the Scotiabank Giller Prize and won the Trillium Award in 2005.

JESSICA GRANT (1972–) was born in St. John's, Newfoundland, and lives in Calgary. Her short story "My Husband's Jump" won the Writers' Trust of Canada/McClelland & Stewart Journey Prize in 2003. She has published in many literary journals and was also featured in *Coming Attractions 03*. She is currently completing a Ph.D. in creative writing at the University of Calgary. Her first collection of stories, *Making Light of Tragedy*, was published in 2004.

ELISABETH HARVOR's (1936–) first novel, *Excessive Joy Injures the Heart* (2000), was named one of the ten best books of the year by the *Toronto Star* in 2000. Her first poetry collection, *Fortress of Chairs* (1992), won the Gerald Lampert Memorial Award for the best first book of poetry written by a Canadian writer, and *Let Me Be the One*, her most recent story collection, was a finalist for the Governor General's Literary Award. Harvor's fiction and poetry have appeared in many periodicals, including *The New Yorker*. She won the Alden Nowlan Award in 2000 and the Marian Engel Award in 2003.

FRANCES ITANI (1942–) is the author of the novel *Deafening* (2003), winner of the 2004 Commonwealth Writers' Prize Best Book Award, Caribbean and Canada Region, and the Drummer General's Award for Fiction. Itani was a finalist for the International IMPAC Dublin Literary Award. She has won three CBC Literary Awards and has published five acclaimed story collections, three books of poetry, and a children's novel. *Poached Egg on Toast*, her most recent story collection, was published in 2004. Itani lives in Ottawa.

NANCY LEE (1970–) was born in Cardiff, Wales, and now lives in Vancouver. She is a fiction writer and poet, and she teaches creative writing at Simon Fraser University's Writing and Publishing Program. Her first story collection, *Dead Girls* (2003), was picked as the number-one book of the year by *NOW* magazine. It was also chosen as a book of the year by *The Vancouver Sun, The Globe and Mail,* and the *Toronto Star* and shortlisted for the Danuta Gleed Literary Award.

LINDA LITTLE (1959–) grew up in the Ottawa Valley. Her short fiction has appeared in numerous literary journals, including the *Journey Prize Anthology* (1999). *Strong Hollow* (2001) is Little's first novel, followed by *Scotch River* (2006). Little won the 2002 Cunard First Book Award and has been shortlisted for the Dartmouth Book Award, the Thomas Head Raddall Atlantic Fiction Award, and the Books in Canada/Amazon First Novel Award.

ANNABEL LYON (1971–) published her first collection of short fiction, *Oxygen,* in 2000 with great critical success. Her short fiction has appeared in *Toronto Life, The Journey Prize Anthology,* and *Write Turns: New Directions in Canadian Fiction,* and she is the author of a collection of three novelas titled *The Best Thing for You* (2004). As well, Lyon is a frequent contributor to *The Globe and Mail* and *The Vancouver Sun.* In addition to creative writing, she has studied music, philosophy, and law. She lives in Vancouver.

ALICE MUNRO (1931–) grew up in Wingham, Ontario. She has published many collections of stories, the most recent being *The Progress of Love* (1986), *Friend of My Youth* (1990), *Open Secrets* (1994), *The Love of a Good Woman* (1998), *Hateship, Friendship, Courtship, Loveship, Marriage* (2001), and *Runaway* (2004). Munro has won many awards and prizes, including the Governor General's Literary Award, the Giller Prize, the Rea Award for the Short Story, the Lannan Literary Award, the W.H. Smith Literary Award, and the National Book Critics Circle Award. Munro divides her time between Ontario and British Columbia.

EMMA RICHLER (1961–) was born in England and grew up both in London and Montreal. She studied acting in New York and has worked as an actor in both Canada and the United Kingdom. *Sister Crazy,* her first story collection, was published in 2002, and her first novel, *Feed My Dear Dogs,* was published in 2005. Richler won the 2002 Canadian Jewish Book Award for Fiction and was nominated for the Orange Prize.

EDEN ROBINSON (1966–) grew up in Kitamaat, British Columbia. Her first collection of stories, *Traplines* (1996), won the Winifred Holtby Memorial Prize for best work of fiction in the Commonwealth and was a *New York Times* Editors' Choice and Notable Book of the Year. Robinson's novel *Monkey Beach* (2000) was nominated for the Giller Prize and the Governor General's Literary Award. Her latest novel is called *Blood Sports* (2006).

CAROL SHIELDS's (1935–2003) novel *The Stone Diaries* (1993) won the Governor General's Literary Award in Canada, the Pulitzer Prize and the National Book Critics Circle Award in the United States, and the Prix de Lire in France. Her novel *Larry's Party* (1997) won the Orange Prize for Fiction and was a finalist for the Giller Prize. Shields also won the Charles Taylor Prize for Literary Non-Fiction for her biography of Jane Austen (2001). Her novel *Unless* was published in 2002 and was a finalist for the Man Booker Prize, the Giller Prize, and the Governor General's Literary Award. Shields's numerous stories have recently been published together in *Collected Stories* (2005).

MADELEINE THIEN (1974–) received the Canadian Authors Association Air Canada Award and the Asian Canadian Writers' Workshop Emerging Writer Award for Fiction for her collection of stories, *Simple Recipes* (2001). Thien's *Simple Recipes* was also named a notable book by the Kiriyama Pacific Rim Book Prize. Her first novel, *Certainty,* was published in 2006. Thien lives in Vancouver.

JANE URQUHART's (1949–) novel *The Stone Carvers* (2001) was a finalist for the Giller Prize and the Governor General's Literary Award and was nominated for the Man Booker Prize. *The Whirlpool* (1986) received Le prix du meilleur livre étranger (Best Foreign Book Award) in France. Urquhart's novel *Away* (1993) was the winner of the Trillium Award and a finalist for the International IMPAC Dublin Literary Award. Her novel *The Underpainter* (1997) won the Governor General's Literary Award. Urquhart is also the author of a collection of short fiction, *Storm Glass* (1987), and three books of poetry.

ALISSA YORK (1970–) has lived all over Canada and makes her home in Winnipeg. She is the author of the short story collection *Any Given Power* (1999) and the novel *Mercy* (2003). York received the John Hirsch Award for Most Promising Manitoba Writer and the Mary Scorer Award for Best Book by a Manitoba Publisher, and she was shortlisted for the Danuta Gleed Literary Award. York won the Journey Prize for her story "The Back of the Bear's Mouth" (1999).

ACKNOWLEDGMENTS

I would like to offer a very big thank you to all the writers in this anthology. It was an intense joy and a privilege to read and re-read these stories. I am extremely grateful to Andrea Crozier for her vision, imagination, and editorial support. Thank you to Marcia Gallego and Eliza Marciniak. Thank you, finally, to Penguin Group (Canada) for supporting short stories.